THE OLD WEST COMES ALIVE . . . OR UNDEAD!

Then I did hear something, the distinct clatter on hard earth of galloping hooves. It intensified curiously to a din, to a cacophonous pounding, flying anvils beating a recalcitrant surface. A shape came into view from the right, moving rapidly. I craned my head out the window to observe more closely, drew in hastily, for there was that in the vague form which did not appeal. Closer it came, and clearer. I knew now: a man on a buckboard, furiously lashing a horse. The driver, with his tall hat and tight-fitting attire, seemed the archetypal cowboy. He shouted and bellowed harshly, only the words were gibberish, and as he began to pass in front of my vantage point I developed grave doubts about that horse.

For it was not a horse, you see. I suffer from difficulty in describing what I saw, for when the wagon raced across my line of sight the image receded weirdly, as if I viewed it through the wrong end of a telescope. What pulled the conveyance at such alarming speed was no horse, but rather a different sort of beast. I struggled to picture it as a giant rooster—there were feathers, and three-toed feet, and a semblance of tail—but I descried an over-abundance of flailing legs, a flash of jagged teeth, a repulsively large and reptilian eye, a single black globe like the eye of a spider. All at once the procession of the image shifted violently, appeared to lurch impossibly toward me, expanding like a photograph under extreme magnification. I started, slammed shut the window, yanked closed the drapes. I sat there on the bed, perturbed, bathed in the glow of an oil lamp which I had not lighted. I had gotten at the last a good look at the cowboy's face, and the single glimpse sufficed to sate my curiosity. There was not much left of that visage, and what there was appalled me with its expression of loathsome evil.

From "At the End of a Dusty Road"

Eerie Arizona: Sixteen uncanny stories of the weird set amidst the awesome landscapes of wild and exotic Arizona.

EERIE ARIZONA
Strange Tales of the Wild and Wonderful West

by Jeffery Scott Sims

Published by the Press of Dyrezan

CONTENTS

ARIZONA, FILTERED THROUGH STRANGE IMAGINATION

Having lived long and happily in the beautiful, varied, and historic state of Arizona, it can not surprise that I, a teller of spooky and fantastic tales, should choose to set some of my bizarre productions in this territory. After all, there's plenty of room in these gloomy canyons and under those lowering buttes for lurking horrors, and terrors may be readily tucked into many a crumbling old house among the cacti atop rocky, windswept hills. Along the way, without any great planning involved, I find that I have developed in these stories of eerie Arizona a major sub-set of my literary work. I've turned out a lot of them, so much so that, I deem, the time has come to collect in book form a sampling of the better published tales in that vein.

To business then. All of the stories herein share two attributes: they possess crucial elements of the weird, and all occur in genuine Arizona landscapes trodden and explored by me. The first requirement should be obvious; the second I would amplify. In general, the locales really do matter to the tales. They wouldn't carry the same weight if based in Connecticut or Kansas. Also (that there be no misunderstanding), these backgrounds are employed imaginatively, twisted and bent within the writer's mind to serve the particular story's needs. Don't treat them as pages torn from a guidebook to the state. The play's the thing, and Arizona serves as a means—a beloved means—to an end.

That stated, where do I intend to send you, and what mischief will you get up to when you arrive? Sixteen uncanny destinations lie before you, presented with an attempt at rough categorization.

If it be truly Arizona, then there must be ghost towns, and I ease you gently into strangeness with (what else?) "The Ghost Town," which in this story at least isn't such a bad place.   Located in the pretty San Pedro River valley, it derives loosely from the pioneer mining center of Millville.   Then, cranking up the dread a notch or three, move on to what lies "At the End of a Dusty Road," a wild blast from the Wild West suggested by the southern border town of Lochiel.   If you escape intact from there, proceed via "A Detour to Skull Valley" to the unexplainable morbidity focusing on that real and rather charming village.

Of course the Arizona back-ways are full of hauntings, as you will learn when venturing into the picturesque highland wilderness to "The Shack on Escudilla Mountain."   The shack with its horrid history is my own invention, while I attest to the rest of that glorious terrain. "The Witch's Cave" and its menacing inhabitant hail from broad transformations of the village of Cherry and the reviving old mining town of Jerome in the Black Hills overlooking the Verde Valley.   On the other edge of that spacious valley visit the justly world famous "Sedona," only come for its unmatchable scenic beauty rather than in search of cosmic powers; despite the Chamber of Commerce bulletins, those unfathomable forces can be mighty dangerous.   This tale utilizes an unusual mix of prose and poetry to generate its warped atmosphere.

Tarrying in the Verde Valley, take a turn into the world of macabre science fiction with "My War Against the Invisibles," in which especially hateful alien invaders plot evil doings.   The Sci-Fi theme continues in the avowedly dreamy (and dreadful) offering, "The Diary of Philip Wyler."   This dash of paranoid lunacy leads back to the valley of the San Pedro, where lies the ghost town of Fairbank, here the setting for nefarious weirdness.

The previous story is narrated by Professor Anton Vorchek, noted investigator of esoteric mysteries and my most popular serial character, who stars in the remainder of the tales in this collection. Often accompanied by his lovely if querulous assistant Theresa Delaney, he gets to exhibit his full range of impressive scholarship and provocative personality.   He commences "Among the Hoodoos" in the geological wonderland of the Chiricahua Mountains, where he runs afoul of a crazed cultist seeking to wake horrors that should forever sleep.   In "A Chance Result" he crosses swords with a snooty archeologist who won't accept that what he's digging up in Sedona's majestic Red Rock Country is an age-old nightmare.   "The Mystery of the Inner Basin Lodge" lures him into the lonely volcanic fastness of the San Francisco Peaks, where among the snowy pine forests he faces an irruption of prehistoric peril.

After this the stories increasingly reveal the darker side of Vorchek himself, the callousness of his obsessive quest for weird knowledge. Researching "The Legend of the Vulture Mine," a famous historic site in the desert near Wickenburg, sees him delving into subterranean creepiness and, in the crudest fashion, looking out for No. 1. "The Revenge of the Past" brutalizes the poor folk moving into their upscale dwellings hard by the White Tank Mountains outside of Phoenix—the theme of urban sprawl a big deal in Arizona—while merely providing Vorchek with enrichment of his data. Events in and about "The House on Anderson Mesa" in the wooded wilds near Flagstaff torment and terrify his unprepared student, all of which pleasantly intrigues the professor.

The two big stories rounding out the collection show Vorchek pushing the boundaries of tolerable behavior toward his hapless students as he again investigates the strangeness fulminating in the Sedona area. Blackest evil wells up from "The House on the Hill of Stars," but where lies the true menace? The locale description fairly accurately depicts the impressive Frye House, known as the House of Apache Fire, in the territory now protected by Red Rock State Park. Vorchek's goals and motivations must be scrutinized and questioned in the grand finale, "Into the Vortex," as he leads an expedition seeking arcane lore into the highlands beyond Oak Creek Canyon. Vorchek certainly crosses the line in this one; the reader may determine what that has meant to his subsequent exploits.

I trust you will enjoy plumbing these imaginative constructs of the state of Arizona. Read them with pleasure, and a modicum of spine-tingling disquiet. Give thought also, if opportunity allows, to visiting the delightful places mentioned in the tales. I guarantee that they, among many others, shall prove most rewarding.

Jeffery Scott Sims
February 3, 2016, at Dead Horse Ranch, near Cottonwood, Arizona

THE GHOST TOWN

So came to pass this phase of my life. I'd worked for the company twenty-four years, building up a solid record as I saw it, always steady, always dependable, ever on time, clocking in regularly, never missing a day. I had no use for my latest boss, and I suspected he returned the favor, but that wasn't a fresh experience. Then my mother fell ill—my last close relative, or close anything—and I lost a lot of hours dealing with her encroaching infirmities. After she went I imagined life would get back on something resembling a strong foundation, but my employer had other designs for me. Brusquely informed that the company must "engage in necessary down-sizing," my position was scheduled for elimination. The post of personnel manager had opened at another—far—location, and would I accept that or starve? Thus I went to Otwich.

Otwich was a little, nondescript town on a big, dry, scrubby plain. On the drive in I spied among the scattered fields a few small herds of horses, a few head of cattle, the paltry remnants of the ranches that once dominated the area. On the way, just short of town, I passed over a weakly flowing river, the San Pedro, thickly lined with leafless cottonwoods, the only running water for a hundred miles. Where I came from we'd call that river a creek. Brown, rolling hills rose at a moderate distance up the stream, otherwise all was flat and barren until the hazy ragged mountains way off to the east and west.

Otwich neither pleased nor surprised. The community itself, wholly modern, was a product of land booms in the past twenty years, a suburb without the urb, growing where it did for no reasons other than that a lot more people needed a place to live, and land could be

1

had cheaply compared to the city. The people there were like those everywhere, in this age of connection via television, video, and Internet. I wouldn't have sought it of my own volition, but the firm had a new office there, so I went. Welcome to Otwich, I said to myself.

I didn't have much money (I'd eliminated my mother's bills along with my own before I pulled out, nor did a raise accompany the move), so I settled for a room in a boarding house. It wasn't the real thing, of course—no meals served, no laundry or cleaning service, like once upon a time—but the old widowed lady, Mrs. Murphy, had a big house and needed money, so she let rooms. Call it a cramped, inexpensive apartment. That did for me, as the large complexes on the edge of town charged an arm and a leg.

My room was okay, but I didn't kid myself about coming down in the world. In fact, I felt as if I'd lost everything of value to me. Some of my stuff went into storage, but most I'd sold off for a pittance. I arrived with not much, and with no one. There was a girl back home, a woman I'd met at the office, we'd amused ourselves on occasion and, who knows, maybe something would have come of it. We said we'd write, but we didn't. The new office was as bad as I'd feared, a staff of faceless entities governed by a general manager considerably younger than myself, a coarse, boisterous fellow with a cutting manner and execrable taste in the trash music he played loudly at all times from the intercom he controlled inside his cubbyhole. I knew immediately that I'd never fit in, but that accorded with prediction. Much of this had been foreseen; only the degree of cultural and personal squalor had remained in doubt.

So did I spend my new life sitting around bemoaning fate? Well, no (though that sounded attractive at times), for what's the point? Five days out of the week I was nailed to that ghastly job. The other two I was on my own, and I made the most of my opportunities, lonely perhaps, yet free to do as I pleased. I got to know the area. I sometimes drove, more often walked, the streets of Otwich, exploring the little of interest it had to offer, acquainting myself with the uninviting shops on various corners, or the patch of artificially watered elms in the municipal park, or the generic dwellings in an upscale lane. My second weekend there I drove out into the countryside, absorbing the lie of the land, parking by the state highway bridge to stroll along the San Pedro. That kept me occupied.

It was the third weekend when I drove up into the hills. They had

2

begun to interest me, among other reasons because they constituted the major break in an otherwise bland landscape. Also, on my previous wanderings I'd noticed something out that way a bit different from the aggressively growing pre-fabricated, archetypal modernity within which I was confined. Over on the north side of town, toward the hills, I came across a few stray outcroppings of ruined stone structures, not much more than big piles of rock, apparently quite old, about which I'd heard nothing. My curiosity piqued, I asked around about them, at first with meager results. Several of the longer term residents (they called themselves natives after ten years) were aware of them, but only so far spanned their knowledge or their interest. Teenagers, I was told, sometimes headed out that way in order to revel in unsupervised drinking parties.

Old Joe, an electrical technician and one of my fellow lodgers at the house, told me more. He said, "You're referring to that little place in the Oton Hills, I guess, those heaps of cut stone at the city limits. As I heard it once, Oton is the remains of an old mining town. There used to be plenty of those up and down the river. Wherever the gold and silver ore was dug up, they'd send it to these ore processing mills that used river water to sort and separate the stuff. It was big business for a while. Of course when the mines played out the processing towns went too. They disappeared, or withered into ghost towns. All that's left, as I hear it, is the rubble of the mill." That fit, I supposed. About thirty miles south-east of Otwich stood Tombstone, icon of the wild west, a place with a colorful, popular history that had converted itself into a gigantic tourist trap. I'd been meaning to pay it a visit, but somehow this Oton mill thrilled me more. The latter, despite its ruinous state, seemed more the real thing, the other, for all its fancy restoration, merely an overgrown stage prop.

So one Sunday afternoon I drove out to take in the lingering bits and pieces of Oton. Getting to the edge of the area was easy; I chugged out of Otwich and I was there, on the outskirts of the forlorn and forgotten. I didn't know what to expect for certain, for the term "ghost town" can mean anything, from heaps of rubble by the road to a dying, ratty village populated by social rejects, and Joe's account was largely hearsay. At the limits of contemporary civilization the paved road ran out to gravel, and before the first bend around a hill became rutted dirt. That bugged me, but my vehicle boasted decent clearance so I kept going. I reached the mill, briefly touring the site, which did offer nothing else but rock piles. Here and there, in that area close to recent development, signs of campfires and shattered beer bottles indicated callous intrusion. Scattered debris despoiled the roadside as well. I noticed that the dirt road kept climbing past the mill, so I hopped back into my car and trundled on, to see what else might lie out that way. This decision bore fruit, for as I wound up into the hills I observed evidence of foundations obscured by thorn bushes and lower portions of standing walls rising among the stunted mesquite trees.

I stopped below the highest rise, where the ruins survived most densely, parked by a bush (on rocky soil, avoiding treacherous sand which might trap my tires), got out and surveyed the scene. So this was the ghost town of Oton, horribly decrepit, but more to it than I'd been led to expect. The unusual vista gave me a curious feel for history, but I experienced difficulty in adequately judging or analyzing what I saw. Here were tottering walls and collapsed roofs, weedy angular outlines and old refuse, stones and scraps of rusty iron. Here men had lived and died once upon a time, but the time scale threw me. The site looked a million years old, yet elements of this abandoned wreckage suggested what, to my mind, could have been far more recent than the heyday of the pioneer settlers. Some of those foundations were poured and pressed concrete, certain of the walls red brick and nicely faced stone to which grimy patches of stucco clung. My parents had grown up in houses like that. I must admit that I knew next to nothing about such things, so the significance of it all was lost on me. I strolled around the area, kicked over a stone here and there, wished I owned a camera, then walked back to the car and drove back to the real world.

Later that week, during a lunch break at work while my compatriots, inanely chatting, drank endless cups of coffee, I called the regional headquarters of the Forest Service which administered much of the local territory in the vicinity of the San Pedro and asked a ranger many questions concerning Oton. He knew vaguely of that specific locale, didn't recall much being there other than the stone foundations of the old mill, dating to the 1880s, but he was familiar with others like it, and could speak to the generalities of what people called ghost towns. "Everything you see," he pointed out, "doesn't have to be a hundred years old or more. Some of these towns, like the copper mining centers farther north, slowly faded away as the ore gave out or prices fell. The inhabitants continued to work and build, only there weren't as many of them as there once were. Some of those sites

4

were going concerns into the Forties. I've got a newspaper clipping on my office wall dating to 1947; yes, May third it is, when the Piedmont hospital finally shut down. There were still a few hundred folks living there then, although they didn't last much longer. From what you say, Oton sounds much the same."

That was a good enough explanation for me. In that respect Oton, in its later years, constituted a survival from an earlier time, a link to a very different past which had eventually snapped, perhaps, not long before I came into the world. I was pleased that it might have contrived to approach my own day, for my fancy whirled at the notion of a genuine ghost town arising in my lifetime; displeased, for I sensed that I had just missed something of importance, although I couldn't have said what that was. Maybe the appeal lay in its difference from my tepid norm. The people of Oton had known, in their prime at least, a different world from mine, one I imagined had to be better or more charming than the hand I'd been dealt.

After that day of work, as tiresome as any, I spent a quiet evening at the library trying to collect information on Oton. I found plenty of fulsome data relating to the regional tourist spots, quite a bit about the frontier heritage of Oton, nothing specific about the later history of my ghost town. The fragments still lay out there in those hills, tangible remnants of those times, only they mysteriously failed to impinge upon modern consciousness. I supposed that must be, for somebody had to care in order to keep a dream alive. Strange it was, however, that Oton should vanish so entirely from memory, for despite what Joe, and even the knowledgeable ranger, had indicated, Oton looked to have been a big place back then. Those ruins sprawled all over the hills, encompassing an area as large or larger than Otwich itself. Thousands of people must have lived there, if my reckoning meant anything. How was it forgotten?

Early the next Saturday morning I returned to Oton, now bearing a new digital camera. I bought one of those cheapies, without a real zoom lens or any fancy features, but it would serve my purpose. Skipping the really messy area just beyond the pavement, I headed back into the depths of the hills where the good stuff was. The fresher, more recent ruins up there drew me more, perhaps because they were more indicative of a once thriving world into which I could imaginatively enter. I went back to the same spot, where I could truly discern the outlines of a town, strolling about and cheerfully snapping away. Beneath the crushed litter of a fallen wall I found a mass of

5

barely corroded piping, elements of a reasonably complex plumbing system. I couldn't deduce the time period, but I had to admit those folks had been doing all right for themselves. In a depression between two massive horizontal slabs of concrete, a kind of hole filled with apparently ancient garbage, I observed weathered aluminum cans bearing traces of their paper wrappings. Those were, among other items, cans of soup, suspiciously similar to those I routinely purchased. Either the march of years didn't produce as much change as I thought, or somebody of a later age had dumped their trash there. The cans appeared to belong, though, not suggesting an addition to the milieu the way those smashed beer bottles had farther below. Indeed, I couldn't convince myself that anyone had visited Oton proper before me, not since it had been an inhabited place. That was fine, for I believed I had it all to myself, a truly satisfying thought. I even climbed the last mound beyond the ruins and stood atop the peak, gazing out upon the wide, flat valley with the tiny forested river trickling through it, struggling to imagine what I would have seen from there in the old days, trying to blank the discordant blot of Otwich from the picture. I stayed up there for hours.

That Monday, at the office, I initiated a conversation with a co-worker named Dora, a hefty, loud-talking middle-aged woman who perpetually wore mammoth blue jeans and the same bloated shirt advertising a brand of motorcycle. I spoke to her because she sat nearby, and I wanted to say something about my latest experience exploring the wonders of the Oton Hills. This was a strange conversation. I bragged of all I had seen and done, at which she expressed scant interest and somewhat more puzzlement. "I used to go out there drinking," she said, "but I don't remember anything like that, just a lot of rocks. Guess I had too much," and she giggled stupidly. I pointed out, rather sharply, that her purpose hadn't been mine, that perhaps I had gone farther, seen more. "Maybe," she granted, "but I'd think we'd all have heard something about it, if there was much out there. How do you keep that a secret?" I had no answer, although her views meant nothing to me. She could miss the drip hanging from her nose.

I did come to believe that I had Oton—the real Oton—as my private preserve. I felt joyous, and a sort of pleasurable mania gripped me. I wanted to indulge myself in that place, master what remained for my own edification. I eagerly awaited the development of my photographs. Since I didn't own a computer, I had to turn them in to a store which handled such things. When I got them back I was confused and angry. Presumably the developers had screwed up, for virtually none of my pictures came out. I received the landscape shots and the vista images from the peak, and there was that single snap of baleful Otwich looking like a cancer on the plain, but where my numerous photos of the higher, more impressive ruins? Not a single one made it through processing. I wasn't charged for them either, yet still the snafu rankled. This result merely signified ineptness at the time. I didn't think then in terms of mystery. That conception began to grip me forcibly a little later, the following weekend, when I returned to Oton prepared for action.

I brought my camera again, and this time a spade. I planned on doing a bit of digging among those foundations. I knew that wasn't entirely ethical, but no one else seemed to care, so why shouldn't I, who did care, satisfy my avid curiosity? I drove out to the farthest ruins, a journey which now came easily to me, and got to work. I retook all of my ghost town pictures, then settled myself in the bottom of a sunken pit beneath a standing concrete slab faced with crumbling brick, where sitting on an exposed pipe I began to dig. Stuff turned up right away. I may have been excavating the wreckage of an old basement, but the broken items uncovered spoke of a kitchen. I found shards of china dishes, splinters of glass cups, fragments of gleaming white enamel from a stove top, and a crushed electric toaster. The latter find gave me pause, but really everything I dug up appeared to tell the same story. None of it, despite damage and wear, looked all that old. I found something more that clinched the matter. A dry, cracked leather case contained papers, mostly illegible, but one sheet could be read through its water stains. I'd found a perfectly normal gas bill, sure enough, like many I'd paid where I used to live. It was dated September 22, 1957.

I couldn't figure that at all. I knew sufficient local history by now to know that Oton had dropped off the radar screen by then, and Otwich wasn't even an evil dream back in the Fifties. At least one household had survived, apparently, to that date, its folks getting along cozily. These hadn't been hermits holding out in the wild. They had to pay their gas bill, and I'd been sitting on top of their modern plumbing. There were ways to rationalize the discovery; I just hadn't expected to need doing so.

I went again the next day, dug at the same spot, brought up from the rubble more smashed crockery and the furry stub of what I concluded was a child's toy. It was my general intention to leave everything in place, but the previous day I'd carried off the leather case and its contents, which would only rot out there, as souvenirs. Monday morning I turned in my new batch of pictures, made a point of telling my co-workers how I'd shortly have something to show them. I didn't. That night I dropped by the store to collection my visual treasures, learned to my chagrin that not one had developed. The dopey girl assured me that the trouble lay in my camera, a statement which, from testing on casual scenery, I knew to be false. At work I subsequently explained about my photographic difficulties. Chris, the supposed office wit, openly averred that I didn't provide pictures because there wasn't anything to photograph up in those hills that they didn't already know about, more than hinting that I was pulling their legs or being foolishly boastful. That infuriated me (especially when everyone present appeared to tacitly agree with him), but I bit my tongue, shrugged with a feigned laugh and silently swore that I'd deliver the goods. Before the end of the week I'd splurged on a rock-bottom desktop computer, a used model, and a cheap printer which I hustled home to set up in my room. There I experimented, teaching myself how to feed photographs from one machine to another, establishing that everything worked, however slowly, as promised.

So back to Oton for me, inching past the defaced mill along that wretched dirt road into the marvelous region where the copious ruins lingered to show that my fellow human beings had once taken their stand up there and made a go of it for longer than anyone today realized or was willing to admit. This time I stopped at a different location, one I hadn't noticed before, which bugged me not a little, for I'd driven through enough times by now to know the territory, or so I thought. This site was the most impressive yet, a tight complex of rectangular foundations and some few brick walls, even one house with a partly intact shingle roof, grouped in a circle around what I presumed had been a dead end lane. The circle, to my mounting mystification, retained traces of asphalt. I photographed everything, clicking away sixty-three times, freezing for posterity anything that looked barely more than natural. Then with my spade I tore into a mound heaped above an intact foundation. Through much silt and crumbled brick I dug, uncovering shortly a wealth of lively wreckage. This stuff, if anything, seemed more modern yet than what I had earlier found. It was better preserved, for one thing, and the styles of artifacts recalled to mind objects I remembered from my youth. I found, among other things, a fair specimen of electric blender. When I'd moved to Otwich I discarded an old one much like it. I wouldn't have dated the thing farther back than twenty years, thirty tops.

Of course the relatively intact building fascinated me. It had to be a typical stucco-faced home, of the sort common to the region, common even (or as I thought, especially) in the present day. I gingerly entered it, exploring its dusty caverns of halls and rooms. It was a wreck inside, but I could identify the basic attributes of living room, den, kitchen, three bedrooms, two baths. The back wall, where myriad sparkling shards and warped steel rails indicated a sliding glass door, had fallen down. Most of the contents had been cleaned out, but in a bedroom closet I discovered a treasure trove, a heap of old magazines mixed with a few newspapers. All of these I confiscated.

Back home, that night and the next day, I studied the spoils of this expedition. I forget the order in which I approached my materials, so I'll just describe the revelations as they strike me. All of my pictures showed perfectly on the computer screen. I could peruse them as I liked, and everything I saw was as I remembered. I couldn't, however, print anything of consequence, meaning any image of my ruins or archeological items. The photographs came out black. By this time I wasn't fooling myself; this business had gotten simply too weird. Other pictures developed properly, all did save those of unremembered Oton. I paged through the glowing images on the screen, backwards and forwards, for a good hour, without ever convincing myself that they were imaginary or that I was losing my mind.

If that sounds peculiar, get a load of what I picked up from those documents. The handful of newspapers were all publications of *The Oton Gazette*, bannered with the phrase "Continuously In Print Since 1882!" The editions at hand dated from the period 1977 to 1981. They contained a wealth of local news items, basic stuff—PTA meetings, car crashes, minor arrests, club gatherings—all indicating a thriving community at the time. There was no reference to the kinds of casual horrors that had become so common since the '60s, and photographs showed smiling, decently attired folks, men in suits and ties and hats, women in becoming dresses and sporting unusual hairdos. It was inconceivable, but there it was, the evidence lying before me. It was a complicated and pointless gag, if such be the answer, yet already I rejected that idea. Too much was piling up on me.

EERIE ARIZONA

It was those magazines, dating to roughly the same period, that did the trick. They were full color glossies, the quality popular stuff that anybody might buy, with titles like *Live* and *Views*, not entirely familiar but considerably resembling magazines I had known in those days in name and appearance. They contained a wealth of national, international, and pop social news. What was really strange was that nothing in those magazines clearly connected with the known events of those times. I detected a crude correspondence in styles and personages, but never anything exact. The movie stars of the day were a cleaner, more cultured lot than they ought to be, the advertised films more wholesome. The foreign statesmen alluded to in the news accounts were a less menacing lot than the period could allow, with some mentions of places like Russia or China, for instance, only without any tags of "Soviet" or "Red" whatsoever. These quandaries I might have overcome, writing them off to unexpected ignorance on my part (I didn't keep up with everything that went on), but the recorded facts derived from the national stories stumped me. Who was this President Branigan whose name cropped up several times in different periodicals? In every case allusions to this apparently respected fellow suggested President of the United States of America. Now, really, was that somebody I'd blinked and missed along the way?

At work that Monday I presented no reports to my colleagues, though I was figuratively bursting with happy wonder, nor did I say anything to them on subsequent days of my adventure. I knew it was no use. I had uncovered a marvel, one that could not be genuinely explained, only experienced. Throughout those weeks of investigation I had not been exploring relics of the past, but rather aspects of another world; sorting debris not of a dead age, but sifting through elements of alternative time, a history in which Oton had not died but lived on, existing—as real a place as any other—only separated in some crazy fashion from the world I'd known. My glimpses of fabulous impossibility came as images of ruin, but it had not been so while I'd walked this planet, had not been so until quite recently, though no one I could talk to even guessed at its presence. Naturally I should have been spooked by what was happening, yet it didn't take me that way. I rather liked the other world I learned about, began to appreciate it more than the one in which fate stuck me. I started to dream of peeling back the murky barrier that divided me from the living Oton, if such a place could still be.

I can discuss a dream I had, without feigning expertise as to what it meant. One night that last week I dreamed of Oton, not the old mining town but the later one, the fake, the lunatic one that wasn't there. In the dream I walked the pleasant, paved streets of Oton, strolled among the clean, inhabited brick and stucco homes in the hills, chatted with folks lounging on porches or walking their dogs, folks who greeted me as their neighbor. We enjoyed plenty of conversation, most of which went out of my head so soon as I awoke, but one simple question from a nice old woman remained to reverberate in my thoughts: "Why don't you stay a while?"

Now I'll tell about my last venture but one into the strangely private zone of Oton. The next Saturday I drove up there as usual, keen to imbibe more of the lingering fragments of that realm. Instead I found evidence, definite evidence this time, of what I call a developing. There, off to the right of the dusty road, stood another batch of ruins, where I never could have overlooked them for a minute, in a better preserved state than anything I'd seen yet. I won't claim surprise. I don't think I was especially, but even if I was that no longer signified in my mind. One dwelling in particular, the one right down a rugged lane from what I presumed used to be the fire house, attracted me, perhaps merely due to its impressively intact condition. The mail box lay by the cracked sidewalk. I propped it up with stones, crossed the weedy yard and entered the place. This one hadn't been emptied. There were old rags of rotten furniture within, a sagging, stained bed, scattered implements of life. There was no indication of great age in these artifacts; I would have blamed disuse or abandonment for what I saw. Kitchen drawers contained utensils, dusty but otherwise ready for use. There were packaged goods in the pantry, except for their corroded labels identical to those I bought regularly. Even their blurbs were similar. From a busted cabinet in the den, where a personal office might once have been set up, I extracted a mass of papers, each one unimportant in itself, shreds of an unknown life, and in addition a discarded driver's license, in its worn plastic sheath, which had expired in 2004. That license bore my name and my photograph.

I didn't quit my job. I walked away from it, without a second thought, and from my room at the boarding house, from all of that world, without hesitation, never looking back at a fading existence which meant little before and nothing now. I collected the few necessaries to tide me over and made a beeline for Oton, where I presently squat merrily among the ruins, eating my crackers and potted meat, sipping idly from my water canisters and my stack of canned ginger ale. Here I am in the ever more inviting home near the fire house, and here I wait—not long, I trust—for the change. I'm alone here, forgotten and unmolested, but I know I won't be alone much more. One morning I'm going to wake to my Oton, the whole, wonderful, living, peaceful Oton, the town that never died in a world that never was, and there I shall dwell all of my days in contentment and bliss.

AT THE END OF A DUSTY ROAD

Deep in southern Arizona, traveling alone on holiday, I found myself in the quaint little town of Patagonia, in the vicinity of which I had enjoyed the natural pleasures of scenic Sonoita Creek; but now time pressed, and I had to get going. My carefully wrought reservation scheme required that I reach my hotel in Deming by that evening, prior to driving on in the next day to Albuquerque and home. It sounded a simple plan, yet I was way south of the interstate, so the drive would require passage along two lengthy sides of a triangle, a time consuming journey, and while pondering my route over a late breakfast of chicken fried steak and potatoes at the Stage Stop Inn, with my Arizona atlas spread at my elbow, I wondered if there might not be a better way. The old fellow across the aisle, eating ham and scrambled eggs with green chilies mixed into them, took an interest in my studies. Apparently a local, he offered a suggestion when I explained my plight.

"You might take the back road," he wheezed, "the old road to Harshaw, that connects you to Washington Camp, and then heads down to Dusquene, and from there to Lochiel, and via the border road leads you all the way past the southern edge of the Huachuca Mountains, and if you got that far it's just a skip and a jump to Sierra Vista, from where you roll in to Willcox and you're on your way. It's a straighter path than you intended, if you can make it." I asked him why I might have trouble making it. "It's a dirt road," he replied, "and a dead one. The government men pass through once a year grading the surface, so you have to time your travel just right. Nobody lives out there anymore. From here to Sierra Vista it's only ghost towns, nor much left of them. They were mining locales once, a long time ago. All the people are gone now, leaving only ruins and the ghosts.

13

I've heard lots of stories about those, from folks who aren't given to telling tales. Too much wild history, I reckon, not enough peace. If you're going for it, don't be caught out there after dark."

I thanked him for his information. In the truck I studied my larger topographical map, which did bear a series of dashed lines running across that forsaken territory. Not so long a drive, apparently, would get me to pavement near Sierra Vista, and from there I would have it easy. But did I want to do it? Still debating, I drove up to the Harshaw turn-off, hesitated, turned in and proceeded until asphalt gave way to smooth, hard-packed dirt with a minimum of pesky gravel. It looked safe enough. I pushed on, telling myself I could back out with little loss of time if the road shortly deteriorated.

It did not, and within the hour, after a fine drive through pretty hills and forested valleys I reached the site of Harshaw, which dated to the 1880s or thereabouts. Not much remained of its former glory, if it ever boasted any. I found one toppling wooden dwelling, a forlorn adobe wall, and a fairly large cemetery stretching up a hillside. I did not run across any ghosts there. Maybe too little was left to hold them. I poked around there a few minutes, snapping pictures for posterity, then went on. One leg down, next stop Washington Camp; call it another hour, and I rolled past bleak foundations and scattered stone rubble. The road held good, and I was making reasonable progress for the time spent. The next item on the tour, Dusquene, came and flashed by, offering no more than the previous site. Okay, having gone that far I was in for it; I meant to go all the way. Backtracking from this point would mean enormous lost time and mileage.

Then, naturally, the road went to pieces. Suddenly it grew rough and steep, climbing and dipping unexpectedly through scrubby gorges and washes. The powdery surface sprang ruts and big rocks, the kind with an affinity for oil pans. The road narrowed dramatically as well, limiting my half-hearted considerations for turning around. After all this time I really did not want to, yet it bugged me that I did not have the clear option. So morning gave way to afternoon, which seemed to wear on glacially, yet—according to my dashboard clock—actually with aggravating speed. Is not that always the way with shortcuts?

I mounted a rise in the ground which afforded something of a view, killed the engine and took stock: semi-arid hills round about with thorny bushes and infrequent cacti, while in the distance before me I could discern a featureless white plain. Once down there, I

14

supposed, I would be all right. Within the last few minutes a funny feeling had crept over me, as if I were taking sick. I felt hot and cold, and my vision seemed to obscure, with images appearing alternately too bright or too dim, like staring too long into a mirage on a hot, heat-shimmering day. For one moment, glancing into my rear-view mirror, I saw merely darkness. It was this that made me stop, rub my eyes which were fouled by grime kicked up by the truck's tires, eat a handful of trail mix from the convenient open bag on the cluttered passenger seat. I guessed I was concentrating too hard.

If the indications of the map meant anything, then Lochiel should not be far ahead. I sighed, cranked the engine, rumbled down into the latest declivity and onward through clouds of silty brown dust into the unknown lands far from human habitation. To my joy the rugged terrain soon receded, leaving me on that inviting plain, flat and grassy, with the road stretching before me straight and true, just as it was supposed to do. The surface improved somewhat, and I made pretty good time, until I came over a low mound and reached Lochiel.

Speaking of mirages, my first glimpse of the town from a modest distance presented me with a wholly impossible image, the pristine outlines and features of a beautifully alive Old West town, like something on a movie studio's back lot. The illusion passed with one watery blink, reducing itself to a huddle of collapsing hovels grouped about a couple of forlorn dirt streets. I entered Lochiel.

Something survived there, far more so than in any other place I had seen. This was, more or less, what I thought of as a ghost town. I ground to a dusty halt at the intersection before the largest remaining building, a two-story structure with partially intact roof and solid walls, though the windows and large front door were long gone. It could have been a saloon in ye olde days, or perhaps a hotel, with comfortable rooms and a bath at the end of the hall. I liked it, liked the whole place. I took a long swig from a can of soda, ice cold from my cooler, then scampered out to photograph the historical treasures. Timetable be damned! I could make up any lost time once back on the interstate.

It took no time at all to prowl the streets, clicking away, an area of four or five acres providing the bulk of what materially lingered there. Shortly I had circled back to the big building, the only one not locked up, and promising an interior of architectural complexity. So, I went inside. I intruded into a cavernous hall of bare, weathered boarding along the walls, a groaning wooden floor heaped with wind-blown grit, with a long counter on the left, a short one to the right. Obviously this was a saloon, currently closed due to lack of clientele. Once upon a time the long counter had been crowded with hard-bitten men and whisky glasses, the sagging shelves behind bedecked with their burden of colored bottles hauled in by train from the east. I could picture all of that. There would have been laughter and cursing, murmuring and song. Now, that short counter: there was that upper story, reached now by a hideously creaky looking staircase; of course, this was the hotel as well. Sure, that was probably typical then, a little something for everyone, all in one spot. I chuckled to myself, thinking they might have provided girls with those feather beds. Well, the whiskey and the cowboys and the girls were blown away with the years, replaced by dust and rot and furtive insects. A mournful wind whistled through a window's gaping socket.

Just for fun I marched up to the little counter, jocosely demanding a room for the night. The frowzy, over-painted woman resting with her elbow on the counter top said, "That'll be a dollar, two if ya want a bath," and she reached back for a key hanging from a rack. Let me be plain (I had better be from this point on): she did and she did not. All of a sudden it was as if I were viewing two related but different worlds, one through my left eye, the other through my right. Through the left I beheld the corroded squalor of discarded years, the rough, chipped counter, the empty, dusty wall of featureless slats beyond; through the right I saw a lacquered surface, shiny with new polish, and the papered wall with its rack of many bright keys, and hand-lettered signage, and that woman, extending a hand for my dollar. I took out my billfold, removed a dollar, handed it to her. She was not there, but the dollar vanished. I might have dropped it, searched idly, did not see it in the floor's dirt, though in a manner of seeing there was no dirt, only well-swept and waxed wood. She said, "Upstairs, make a turn, second on your right."

I mounted the stairs, ignoring the swelling, raucous sounds from the direction of the bar, eyeing dubiously each groaning, sagging step, but I need not have done so, for in a sense they did not groan or sag. The stairs, in fact, bore lush carpet, an historical feature with which I was entirely unfamiliar. I made my turn and came to the requisite door, turned the key in the oiled brass lock, pushed and walked in. A scene of frightful decay met my gaze . . . and I found myself in a pleasantly furnished if, to my tastes, very small room, with a double bed, a Spartan chair and a little table bearing a pitcher and glass, and a modest chest of drawers. Two quaint paintings of sylvan scenes adorned the walls. It was a fine room, one redolent of lost charm, an abode in which I could relish a stay. That bed really looked inviting. I entertained a desire to throw off my clothes, to toss myself under those silky sheets and carefully arranged hand-made quilt. Soon, perhaps, I would rest. I removed the camera from around my neck, set it on the table, made for the single good-sized window. The curtains were drawn, the pane opened to allow a refreshing breeze. I sat on the bed, looking out.

I stared down on a pretty town, quiet, relaxed, yet undeniably living. A man on horseback sauntered up one street, while a young couple strolled down the other. The woman was remarkably well dressed by any standard to which I was accustomed. I detected muted drifts of conversation, a sound of laughter farther away, still farther the occasional ring of metal on metal. Things were going on down there, lazily, easily. It was an attractive tableau. I could imagine it as being my kind of place. Something, I realized, actually did survive in these old towns: ghosts, I called them, ghosts of lives and life ways. I took up my camera and snapped a few shots.

Even as I endeavored to record the wonderful images, however, the scene shimmered, darkened. I thought that time passed, or a sea change occurred of a sudden; regardless, gloom now reigned, the gloom of darkest night, with an oppressive, starless sky, and only one isolated street lamp flickering to relieve the murk. Nothing stirred in the lanes below, no sound wafted up to my window. I felt a radiating pressure of disquieting stillness beating against me. Then I did hear something, the distinct clatter on hard earth of galloping hooves. It intensified curiously to a din, to a cacophonous pounding, flying anvils beating a recalcitrant surface. A shape came into view from the right, moving rapidly. I craned my head out the window to observe more closely, drew in hastily, for there was that in the vague form which did not appeal. Closer it came, and clearer. I knew now: a man on a buckboard, furiously lashing a horse. The driver, with his tall hat and tight-fitting attire, seemed the archetypal cowboy. He shouted and bellowed harshly, only the words were gibberish, and as he began to pass in front of my vantage point I developed grave doubts about that horse.

For it was not a horse, you see. I suffer from difficulty in describing what I saw, for when the wagon raced across my line of sight the image receded weirdly, as if I viewed it through the wrong end of a telescope. What pulled the conveyance at such alarming speed was no horse, but rather a different sort of beast. I struggled to picture it as a giant rooster—there were feathers, and three-toed feet, and a semblance of tail—but I descried an over-abundance of flailing legs, a flash of jagged teeth, a repulsively large and reptilian eye, a single black globe like the eye of a spider. All at once the procession of the image shifted violently, appeared to lurch impossibly toward me, expanding like a photograph under extreme magnification. I started, slammed shut the window, yanked closed the drapes. I sat there on the bed, perturbed, bathed in the glow of an oil lamp which I had not lighted. I had gotten at the last a good look at the cowboy's face, and the single glimpse sufficed to sate my curiosity. There was not much left of that visage, and what there was appalled me with its expression of loathsome evil.

Too much survives, I thought to myself, the bad with the good, and (so I deduced, then or later) while the good lingers complacently, the evil, perhaps, feeds and festers and takes root, breaking out in an insidious growth of cancerous forms. Not for that had I come to Lochiel. Why had I come? A twinkling of normality illuminated my mind. I remembered, as from an old story read in childhood, my purpose, my plans. Surely I must be on my way.

Retrieving my camera, slipping its strap around my neck, I departed from the room, made for the stairs. As I did so the building shuddered, a slight sensation as of earthquake. Commencing the descent, I overheard a snatch of laughter and cracked song, which even as I listened gave way to an ominous growling murmur. I wished there were another way out. I wished more fervently when I reached the bottom and beheld the changes that had occurred, just then or since my previous passage. The lobby, as I styled it, had gone to seed, along with its denizens. It was not yet a century's worth or more of falling down, but a creeping disintegration, as of a disused stage set left to rot. The varnish on the walls had clouded and oozed, the paintings hung askew and mildewed, the furniture crawled with lice. I meant to give the hag woman my key, but she looked half dead—quite a bit more than half, I am afraid—and her strangely disjointed, jerky motions at me fostered a delirious terror in my benumbed brain. I stepped away in avoidance, stumbling against an empty table, drawing the attention of the men at the bar. They rose to a man, turned to face me. I screamed. Those guys were long gone, every one of them, far past hope, nothing but bones tied together by desiccated sinews. Such shades should not move or react, only they did, staggering forward with sudden, spasmodic motions. They came right for me, knocking aside chairs in their path, and with a shriek I scrambled through the narrowing avenue leading to the door. I crashed into the swinging panels, ripping one with a squeak from a rusted hinge, dove into the street. It was black as midnight out there, a midnight in hell, like the view from the upper window. The world as I knew it had vanished.

I ran down the dusty lane seeking something, anything that could recall me to the land of the living. Desolate storefronts loomed darkly to both sides, crouching in attitudes of menace. A sound of approaching galloping assailed, urged me on. Was it that terrible rider, hunting for me? Black figures swayed into the street, dreadfully thin, shambling approximations of human form. Each and every turned at my appearance, halted, came toward me. I yelled again and fled. Once I dashed onto the bouncy, vibrating porch of a shop and, at that moment, a husk of humanity lunged from the doorway. Its skinny, fleshless hand touched me, grazing my cheek, and the feeling, and the accompanying moldy stench, made me want to vomit. I backed away, whirled, charged on into darkness.

And I ran into my truck! How can it be that I found it? Had I not run for miles and years through that nightmare ghost of a town? There it was, the only modern item within that grim, monstrously dark vision of the past. I circled to the driver's door, yanked savagely and fruitlessly, realized I had, according to habit, locked it. I fumbled with my keys. At the corner of vision nasty shapes inched closer. The single key in my hand did not work—the wrong one, what was I doing?—ah, there my key chain, there the familiar feel of the proper one, and the door opened, I toppled inside, fired the engine, and in a screaming gust of   exhaust and with a squealing of tires barreled away into the unholy night.

Scarcely had I passed the last building than I drove into a pale dawning. The terrain before me lightened, brightened, the long line of dirt road and the scrub and cacti of the forgotten land. Presently I attained a rise where I parked in the road, gasping, surrounded by broad daylight. According to the vehicle clock the time was mid-afternoon, very little later than when I had last checked it. In my rearview mirror I could see the dead pile of Lochiel behind me, knew this for the point at which I had first seen it. I was heading back the way I had come.

19

EERIE ARIZONA

That was good enough. I drove, eventually returning to civilization. Of course my precious schedule was shot to pieces. I never made it to Deming, having to spend the night in Benson, and naturally gave up the pre-paid reservation. I took that snafu with, for me, remarkably good grace.

I have in my files photographs taken from my initial wanderings in Lochiel. They show that which is to be expected. I ended up with a series, also, of blank black shots, all that could be derived, I must assume, from the pictures taken at the second story window. I retain an unusual, unplaceable key, the one with which I first tried to open the door to my truck, the sole key not on the ring. I am convinced that it is the key to my room in the Lochiel hotel. I will rest satisfied with the assumption, for I have no plans to return in order to test that theory.

A DETOUR TO SKULL VALLEY

Carmichael pulled into Wickenburg late that afternoon. Entering, he beheld a quaint collection of refurbished 19th Century buildings, surrounded by, and in the process of being overwhelmed by, typical modern claptrap. The uneasy borderland between the old and the new in Arizona, he thought with a glum burst of poesy that surprised him. Obviously a town catering to tourists, he decided that he might as well break for the night. The too-familiar tedium of the road, he felt, had unusually ground him down. His destination, Prescott, wasn't so very far ahead, but he wasn't expected there until after noon the next day, and he was in no hurry to arrive anyway.

A couple minutes of automotive research led Carmichael to the exotically named Hassayampa Motel, an affordable haven which appeared decently clean. Checking in, he carried his single bag into the room, sat down and, curiously unmotivated, did nothing for a spell. A fell, unsourced mood bugged him. It briefly occurred to him to look over his business papers once more, but the mere thought induced revulsion right now. Going out for a walk, he discovered the local hang-out where he ate a very good hamburger, then returned to the room and attempted to place a call back home, without success. He could only hear an electric whine, starting off low, then mounting in intensity. Never mind, it could wait. No question, he felt oddly out of sorts just at the moment. A darkness seemed to close over the tiny room and his soul, a darkness superseding the gathering dusk. There was a sense (of which he really couldn't make sense) of a threshold having been crossed. Somehow everything was different, and not pleasantly so. Carmichael idly wished he hadn't stopped for the night, then idly wondered why that should matter.

21

EERIE ARIZONA

Eventually night settled in. He turned on the television, which promised a plethora of cable channels, but couldn't get much out of it. The reception, or the cables, or something, must be bad. Most of what he could see was thoroughly inane. He found what could be marginally superior, a very old movie, some kind of soapish melodrama, of a kind common way back when. Early thirties, mid-thirties at most, he reckoned. With quite a poor image, it looked like a copy picked up from the film vault floor by a low budget local outfit. Typical for its time, it consisted mainly of conversation presented before a frozen camera. He'd missed the first part, nor had he any idea what movie he watched. In the current scene a well-dressed man and woman, both striking brunettes, neither of whom he recognized, earnestly talked. Their subject apparently dwelt on romantic matters; an emotional conflict had arisen, with a third party was involved; this much Carmichael quickly grasped, but little more, for his attention was distracted from the sluggishly unfolding plot by a curious realization. Hard to tell at first, so fuzzy was the picture, but peering closely he could see that there was something definitely wrong with the actress. Her posture, the way she held herself, wasn't right. She turned slightly, and he saw clearly. Underneath the expensive gown she bore a prominent hump on her back. The sight so astounded him that he couldn't take his eyes off of it, and from that point he lost even the gist of what they were saying.

It crossed his mind that there might be a medical component to the story—doomed heiress, say, suffering from rare disease—but Carmichael shortly disabused himself of that notion. When the hero rose from the elegant lounge, it transpired that one of his legs was crippled, twisted and unduly short. The scene changed abruptly, due to a bad edit, and now the heroine could be seen theatrically chattering with two of her fashionable, less pretty girlfriends. What they discussed he would never know. One girl had a bad eye, swollen and fishy, which shocked him, so disgusting was her appearance. The other girl initially seemed healthy and normal enough. She kept one profile rigidly before the audience at all times, until she turned at the end of the scene, as the image darkened revealing her farther arm, which was missing below the elbow.

Carmichael watched the show until the end, but all he could subsequently recall was that every major character in the film possessed an egregious physical defect, and yet these tragic flaws never had any bearing on the plot. How such a movie ever got produced defied imagination. He wasn't a buff by any means, but he thought it unlikely that he should be unaware of such a freakish bit of film lore. A television guide was available, but it contained no reference to anything remotely like this. When the show concluded he turned off the set, determined to take no more chances with his already troubled mood.

Sleep came late, proved sporadic. When he finally rose, very early in the morning, he remembered waking several times in darkness to absolute silence. Of course he hadn't derived refreshment. He suspected that a long day lay ahead of him. After leisurely performing the morning necessities, he found that it was still scarcely dawn, just a hint of brightening murkiness. Despite the awkward hour he tried calling home again. Dial, ring, ring, then the snap of connection, yet he had no more success this time than before. There was an indication of somebody answering, followed by sounds vaguely imitative of speech, but Carmichael could make nothing of them. The rush of muddled tones irritated, then disturbed him. Perhaps those were distorted words; if so, somebody, he didn't know who, was intently endeavoring to communicate; or they might be more line noise. He gave up, rang off, would take another stab at it later in the morning. He didn't care to remain here any longer, though; might as well get going, and catch breakfast in Prescott.

The streets of Wickenburg stretched empty. Once on the road and out of town heading north, the red sun cracked the horizon, but even after it yellowed and fully rose, Carmichael saw no one else driving this morning. They weren't quick to wake in these parts. He flashed through a sleepy, quiet town or two, otherwise rolling past endless vistas of rock, gray scrub, tall cacti poking up like fat spiky fingers, occasional swarms of large, wheeling black birds. At one point the state highway wound dangerously up the steep incline of a sheer cliff, leading to the top of a rugged plateau from which he fleetingly received a dizzying view of the stark, monotonous countryside through which he'd driven. Up here the rock and cacti continued, joined at these heights by patches of farm and ranch land, all of which had seen better days.

An incredibly lonely territory, this, and unaccountably distressing. Everything about this journey now rubbed him the wrong way. The lighting bothered him. Now broad daylight, without a cloud in the sky, yet he seemed to be traveling under haze; at least, there was distinct gloom, for no explicable reason. Also, either the car radio was on the blink, or this region was so situated geographically that no station could get through properly. At any rate, he had little luck tuning in to anything. The radio, often his defense against encroaching boredom, failed him this day. What he did pick up could more adequately be described as sound effects; no music of any kind, and only meaningless grunts and moans that might be garbled speech. After switching channels right through the spectrum, Carmichael turned it off, and left it off. He was alone.

He hadn't seen a road sign in a while, but estimated that Prescott couldn't be more than forty miles away, somewhere beyond those blue-green mountains looming ahead. Sure enough, a sign approached; an old one, not very official looking, an arrow pointing to a narrow paved road stretching out to the left. *Skull Valley* it read. What a dreadful name for a town, if such it was, in a place like this. Carmichael stopped, stared in that direction, seeing nothing. Skull Valley. It sounded picturesque and old-timey, redolent of vanishing history. Wickenburg hadn't impressed, but this could be different. He still had hours to kill, and wasn't really hungry yet. The sign gave no mileage, but it shouldn't be far. He hesitated, doubting his judgement, then on impulse maneuvered onto the little road and proceeded west.

At first the lie of the land rose slightly, evened out in an area of farming country, then began a gradual descent. Some distance away he saw scrubby bluffs and ridges which probably marked the boundaries of a valley. The road began curving to the north about the same time that the quality of the pavement diminished. Possibly this route eventually swung round over the mountains to Prescott. If so, this little diversion wouldn't take up much time.

Something moved on the road ahead, the first vehicle or evidence of human life that he'd seen since the previous evening. The thought startled him; could that really be true? It was going so slowly that, despite his reduced speed on the crumbling asphalt, Carmichael caught up with it in no time. It was a school bus, lumbering along at a rate not significantly faster than that of a man walking. He could tell that it was occupied. The condition of the road, really scandalous now, and the rugged up and down terrain through which it was winding made him leery of passing. Suddenly a little red stop sign swung out on the driver's side, and the bus halted. Carmichael did likewise, drumming his fingers on the wheel while he waited. He hadn't noticed any kids standing there, nor was there an obvious bus stop.

He hadn't been paying attention, however. He did notice how old and weather worn the big beast appeared. Shortly it grumbled forward again, creeping at the same snail's pace.

Fair enough, but he wasn't going to sit behind it all day. It might be going all the way to Prescott. Choosing to pass, he gritted his teeth and sped up, just as the lane unexpectedly plunged into a road cut on a turn. Hopefully nobody raced up from the opposite direction! Not likely out here, but he fretted for a moment. Overtaking the bus and inching ahead, he gained random impressions. An antique conveyance, the yellow finish dulled, cracked, and scarred. Words in black running along its length: the something Independent School District, and a number, 249. Shadowy images of children inside, not too many, followed by the face of the driver, which in that instant before it was lost to view didn't quite register, except for the leering grin. Then Carmichael swung back to the right, quickly leaving the bus far behind.

Down he drove a considerable way, as the bluffs reached higher and crept closer. Rock spires dominated the scene; huge, jagged formations barren of vegetation, white as bone. An aura of eternal desolation clung thickly to this austere topography. It astonished him that a town could be located in these parts.

Another broad loop carried him to the bottom of the shallow valley, where he actually saw real trees and occasional dilapidated homesteads. So, there must be water in the vicinity. In this state, that alone would justify habitation. Something in the configuration of the highest ridge caught his eye. The shape of the rocks up there, the illusion of depth was suggestive. Rather like reading clouds, it brought a picture to mind. Those might be eye sockets, and that could, from the proper angle, resemble a skull. Skull Valley, indeed. Within a minute he had bounced over weed grown railroad tracks, then crossed a one lane wooden bridge spanning a turgid creek, and arrived.

Carmichael could tell at a glance that there wasn't much to Skull Valley. As he closed in he saw a drab cluster of buildings, mainly wooden with graying whitewash, surrounded by a dense ring of bushy trees. Dirt roads lined with trees ran left and right by the stream, and beyond them he could discern a handful of houses, mostly peaked two-story affairs. Nothing else was evident. He assumed that he saw all there was.

The first and largest structure, to the left of what he might term the intersection, bore a steeply sloping roof on which was painted in large letters the words "Skull Valley General Store," and below that, by the window, in smaller lettering, the word "Feed." Two pickup trucks, which looked like they ought to belong in a museum, were parked in front. He casually noted the presence of three men, the standard roughhewn, small town western types, he supposed, leaning against one of the trucks, engaged in conversation. Shooting the breeze, as they would say. Across the road on the right stood a long, low building labeled "Café," where more cars and pickups were parked, and up the paved street from that he spotted an enclosed stand with gasoline pumps sprouting before it.

Carmichael ground into the gravel parking lot of the general store and cut the motor. Wind howled, dust twirled, unseen things rustled. Dimly, through the window, he could make out the hunched shape of a man by the counter. The proprietor was in. Maybe he could buy something to snack on here. If not, the restaurant across the street obviously served breakfast. He got out, expecting to be hailed by the loungers, but they were gone. Funny that, because he hadn't looked away for more than a second. They must have darted into the store as soon as he stopped. Perhaps they were wary of strangers here. He examined their trucks with modest fascination. Old models, no later than the forties, not well maintained to look at them. Surely they still ran, even if close up they resembled candidates for the junk heap more than museum pieces. There were lots of rust spots, and an unbroken film, or blanket, of desert dust lay thickly on the metal and glass. Off the beaten track folks didn't live fancy.

He creaked open the screen door of the store and entered. If Carmichael expected service in this establishment, he was sadly mistaken. No one was inside, not the three men, not the clerk. Really, judging from appearances, he couldn't be certain that the shop was open. There were items on the shelves, not well stocked, mainly canned goods, and several big burlap bags of farm animal feed dumped on the floor in a corner. From what he observed, however, he didn't derive the impression of a business in operation. The interior was in a fearsome state of disorder. Dust and dirt lay everywhere, covering all exposed surfaces, mounding against fissures in the floorboards. He didn't know to what county the village belonged, but even the worst hick health inspector shouldn't allow this to get by. All things considered, it seemed as if the owner had recently shut the place down. No wonder; trade had to be lousy out here. The explanation made sense, although such squalor might be the product of years. The shape by the counter turned out to be a moth-eaten jacket draped over a stand.

He departed the store. Yonder the cafe drew his attention. Now that he examined it, it looked pretty run down as well. On the other hand, it was clearly open. Through the oblong shop window he could barely discern numerous shadowy figures moving about, and the front door yawned invitingly. Above the wind he thought he heard the mumble of conversation and the clacking of dishes. Okay, so this was where the elite meet to eat. Carmichael might as well join them, if nothing else for the experience.

Crossing over, he noted, with unwelcome curiosity, that all the vehicles in front of the restaurant were also tired, ramshackle antiques. Grime darkened the windows of the eatery, so that he still couldn't resolve inner details. He questioned the advisability of breakfasting here. Perhaps he could just pop in, as if to ask directions, and in the meantime look around.

Within he found no one. No one inside, nor had they been for a very long time. This wasn't a restaurant; rather the shell of one abandoned years, even decades ago. The front door hung open because it was broken. The dirt on the big window didn't quite hide an extended hairline crack. Most of the furnishings and appliances had been ripped out in ages past, with the dense coating of dust on the floor retaining no marks of footsteps at all. The joint stank with the stale smell of long rotten food. Not quite believing what was happening to him, Carmichael backed out in a hurry.

He paused outside, oblivious to his surroundings, his thoughts turned within. He didn't understand how he could have made such a mistake. What of the people, the sounds? Of course he couldn't swear to anything; he hadn't paid that much attention, only brief glimpses, and wind plays tricks with the ears. He could have been wrong. Frankly, under the circumstances there wasn't much doubt about that. Reflections on the window had fooled him. Only, the impression of occupancy had been so strong.

This concern belied the main question, he thought, as once more he focused on the nearby scenery. What kind of town was Skull Valley, anyway? If the citizens didn't gather in public places like these, where were they? Possibly he assumed too much. Carmichael entertained the notion that this might be more than a crossroads village, that there was a more modern section close by, and he was in what the locals referred to as the old town. That's it. This section, once thriving on outsiders, had gone downhill when hard times came. He was familiar with populated centers where that pattern had developed. People lived in those houses, after all, and they required basic services. There was the gas station, just up the way. There would be no excuse for it to shut down.

He could check on that right away, and might as well fill up while satisfying curiosity. Back to the car, crank, then just down the road on the right. As he drew nearer, Carmichael cared less for what he saw. The station looked dingy, unkempt, like everything else around. From a distance he'd surely detected the indistinct presence of a personage in the booth; only that turned out once again not to be the case. He got out to take a good look. The station was hopelessly vacant. Those pumps hadn't dispensed gasoline since the days of the big war, if their rusty corrosion meant anything. One didn't even have a hose. There was a truck parked there, but it was as decrepit as the others.

If that didn't beat all. This was a ghost town, all right. From this vantage point he had a wider view, and could see nothing else but scattered houses. There was no new center, not in the vicinity. If he hadn't seen those three men earlier (of course he had seen them) he'd wonder if anyone still lived here. The aspect of those houses wasn't agreeable. There was still some kind of haze or gloom in the air playing tricks on his eyes, but from what he could tell all the visible structures had known better days.

A sound, quite close, as of murmured words, spun him around. Nothing there, yet he spied motion farther away. On the dirt road, the one leading behind the general store by the creek, someone was walking. He saw a suggestion of a human figure, just for a moment, before it disappeared behind the building. For no reason that he could explain to himself, Carmichael felt vastly relieved.

He walked back that way, for no ostensible purpose. On the contrary, it did occur to him that he was wasting valuable time. He consulted his watch, which did him no good whatever. The mechanism hadn't stopped, but what it told him made no sense. Apparently it needed work, or he needed a new one. It wasn't a cheap piece, either.

What bothered him most, now that he tried to puzzle out the situation, were these vehicles parked all over the place. They had to belong to somebody; they couldn't just be dumped here. Were it not for their uniformly wretched appearance, he wouldn't have given them any thought. He imagined himself a tourist ambling through a bizarre open air museum devoted to vanished rural Americana. But where was the ticket-taker?

On the other side of the general store he saw no one. Predictable, really, but then he'd refused to hurry after the man. That fellow might have taken off running just as soon as he was out of sight. Carmichael chose not to wonder why he should have done such a thing. Or he could be hiding, under the banks of the creek, or behind those trees. No, Carmichael wouldn't dwell on that possibility, either.

Human sounds wafted to him on a gust of wind. Just a snatch, which momentarily dispelled his darkening mood. Beyond doubt the voices of children at play, a multitude of children laughing, not far away, right ahead. It was such a happy, healthful sound that he immediately made for it. He walked down the dirt road paralleling the creek. The muddy waters quavered as the breeze moved over them, but scarcely flowed. Bits of rusty metal littered the banks or protruded from the sandy soil. A depressing sewer smell crept to his nose. He heard a burst of giggling, quite close now.

Carmichael presently came upon a modest white building to the right of the road, opposite the stream, surrounded by a chain-link fence. The metal barrier was corroded, overgrown at its base by weeds, and to his intense dismay he saw that the building wasn't in much better shape. On the remnants of a sign still fastened to a wall he could read the word "Kindergarten." He found the gate in the fence, hanging loosely. He entered the grounds, which more resembled a disused vacant lot than a play area.

The door didn't respond to pressure but, peeping through the front windows, he saw no children, no teachers. Two rooms contained dusty desks and little else. Straight ahead of him, across the larger compartment, hung a blackboard. He spied pictures scrawled on it in chalk, artistically childish pictures. It was dark in there, darker than it ought to be, as it was out here; also, dust lay thick on the board, obscuring the scrawls, but he could make out something, and . . . well, really, he didn't know what to think. He simply could not believe that he was seeing such drawings, in this kind of setting. He turned from the window, shaking from revulsion. Carmichael already knew how this situation would play out, yet he nevertheless forced himself to investigate the back yard. There, in a space dominated on three sides by a dense stand of trees, he found the framework of a swing set, minus swings, and the ruins of another contraption too far gone to precisely identify. There were no laughing children in sight. There might have been, but not just now, perhaps once upon a time, long before he was born. This place was frighteningly dead.

He chose not to give thought to the matter until he'd left the kindergarten and regained the dirt road. Houses lay to the west, but he went the other way, towards the car. There was no getting around it: this town terrified him. Try as he might, Carmichael could no longer rationalize anything that was happening here. Skull Valley wasn't a normal village fallen on hard times, nor a picturesque relic of bygone days. He grappled with the stunning conclusion: this was indeed a ghost town, in the worst sense of that term. Evil lurked here, furtively creeping, yet demanding to be noticed. He had stumbled into the kind of situation which wasn't supposed to happen—wasn't supposed to be possible—and he could only wonder why it had happened to him. There were people, he surmised, who deserved this kind of treatment, but surely he didn't qualify. Whatever the case, he wanted no part of it.

A short walk, utterly alone, and yet throughout he sensed someone behind him, unseen, waiting to be glimpsed if he turned. He didn't. The car—the door—the key; he gunned the engine. The harsh noise reassured him. As expected, nothing had changed around the shops. Backing into the street, he advanced slowly past the general store, the cafe, the filling station, continuing north on the road which he trusted would lead him to his destination. Here a few more trees, then several homes, mostly scattered some distance from the road, surrounded by empty pasture. The houses stood bigger on this side, older too, their architecture classic late Victorian, as it was once known in this part of the world. All were bleak and forbidding, obviously abandoned except for one, that impressive three-story structure at the top of the sloping, grassy hill. Although he should have been able to see them more clearly in the direct sunlight, Carmichael did spy that line of shadowy figures inching up the hill in the direction of the house.

He brought the car to an abrupt halt, this time never taking his eyes off those moving shapes. They didn't disappear. All entered the house, just like real people might. Could it be? Had he broken the spell? He wanted to know, to convince himself. Only that could explain his next ridiculous action. He jumped out and raced up the hill after them.

At close quarters the house looked as alarming as any other place he'd visited this day. The window panes were cracked or missing. The front door wasn't just open; it lay in splinters on the creaking porch, as if hacked to pieces with an ax. On the other hand, he distinctly heard voices emanating from within. Maybe he'd hit the jackpot this time.

So Carmichael told himself, until he entered the hall. No more voices, naturally (naturally!), and the interior resembled the aftermath of a tornado. This house was more of the same. Some furnishings remained, rotten and stinking like everything here. The odor made him feel sick. No one else had entered; that was a ghastly joke conjured by the weird force enveloping him. He truly felt like laughing.

The upper floors proved unapproachable—no way he would risk that disintegrating staircase—but the main level lay open for inspection. He examined each room, gingerly guiding his feet through the squalid mess, groping over stylish wreckage. It must have been a grand life in those days, for somebody. He hesitated at the door to the cellar. Those steps appeared sturdy, but why would he want to go down there? He did so, a short distance, as long as the light lasted. Very little to be seen, dark masses composed of shadows and dust rising from the gloom or heaped on the littered floor below. Nobody there.

Faintly though the illumination reached to the bottom of the stairs, his eyes adjusted, and Carmichael began to pick out detail. Those objects piled on the floor drew his attention. An idea suggested itself to his unwilling brain. At first it was a matter of outlines, textures, perceived subtleties, then something more. The objects didn't change; awareness grew, doubts arose and faded, certainty crystallized. Yes, yes, he got it, took it all in, then staggered up the stairs, out of the cellar. The powers in force here, it seemed, wanted him to see all. Yes, those were bodies, horribly mutilated and decayed, on the floor below.

Carmichael returned to the auto very slowly, attempting to present an illusion of normality to the watching landscape about him. Panic urged him to flee, but he refrained from doing so lest the revelation of fear be the signal for an all-out attack. He definitely sensed something near at hand, crouching tensely, awaiting a chance to spring. In the event, nothing happened. He got into his car and drove away from the house. Soon the last images of Skull Valley receded from view behind him.

EERIE ARIZONA

Ahead towered the mountains, and beyond them, he prayed, Prescott and the sane world free of morbid phantoms. The feeling of entrapment persisted. He counted on leaving the horror behind at its source, but the more he dwelt on the subject, the less sure he felt about that source. Something awful had that town in its grip, but was that power *of* the town, or had it intruded from outside? Had he brought it with him? He recalled the strangeness which had begun to settle over him the previous night in Wickenburg, the odd happenings. Remembering that nasty film he'd sat through, the implication jolted him. It would be possible to argue that his world had shifted out of kilter before he ever heard of Skull Valley.

It wasn't, couldn't be the place, a matter of geography grown old and psychotic. That was crazy. Every motorist didn't confront these horrors! It was him; something inside him; something that had infiltrated and invaded his life, choking him in musty shadow. Carmichael didn't pretend to mastery of philosophy, but he realized these were solitary terrors manufactured for him alone, a unique presentation conceived within a fearful realm not found on any map. He had entered its jurisdiction, maybe, by chance or mistake. Could he willingly depart? All of this—please—must be a passing phase.

The pavement gradually improved, the highway curving upward into the highlands, the elements of desert terrain rapidly dwindling. The fringes of cool pine forests approached. A great ravine opened below to his left. Something large at the bottom diverted his attention from the road. Carmichael stopped and stared. It was an overturned school bus which had tumbled into the chasm. Bent, broken, smashed, discolored and scattered, it might have lain there since the beginning of recorded time. Most of the black lettering on the side was illegible, yet he could easily make out the number of the bus: 249.

What signified this evidence? There was only one way to find out. Carmichael drove on.

THE SHACK ON ESCUDILLA MOUNTAIN

I would hike Escudilla Mountain. Having heard the trail to the top was a good one, I'd arrived late the previous afternoon under oppressive skies, finding a level spot near the trail head. I got my truck unloaded and the tent up just before the rain came, accompanied by bright flashes and quick booms of thunder. It was a wet night, and dawn didn't break, it bent ever so slightly, leaving my forested camp site still shrouded in gloom. I didn't care for the look of that sky. It offered more of the same. I considered pulling out, heading elsewhere for dryer prospects. The thought rankled. I was here, ready for action, and I'd been looking forward to this. So be it: I was hitting the trail.

And I made it to the top without incident. It's an interesting trail, that to the summit of Escudilla Mountain, third highest in Arizona. First it's up, ever up, through the biggest aspen grove in the world, before the path evens out on a gentle slope providing a sweeping view of the higher, grassy ridges crowned with conifers. Then it passes into dense woods, shoots up again, then down, way down to a beautiful meadow, at that time of year painted with flowers and humming with insects. A fine scene, though I had trouble with biting flies. My spray protected against the nonexistent mosquitos. Back into the forest, steeply upward, nothing but trees, until a little patch of blue peeked through the needles. Yes, the clouds had momentarily cleared, and I saw framed against the morning sky the fire lookout tower which marked the third highest point in Arizona. In another minute I stood at the base of the tower. The ranger kindly called me up, allowed me to photograph as I pleased the astounding vistas of lesser mountains and endless seas of alternating dark and light green. I tarried in the tower or about its clearing for an hour, until the return of billowing darkness urged me back down the trail to the relative security of camp so many miles away.

I was deep within the descending spruce forest when the storm struck. I came prepared, as I thought, with plastic poncho and collapsible umbrella, sufficient to carry me through normal rain with a minimum of discomfort. I didn't count on what I got. This late morning grew black as night. Lightning flared directly overhead, the earthquakes of thunder simultaneous. That was a bad sign, with me still so high up. And the rain; how do I describe the rain? One speaks of rain falling. After the introductory sprinkles this one crashed upon me like an avalanche. It crushed me with its weight. I might have been marching under a waterfall. It wearied me, stooped my shoulders. It soaked me, too. The spray splashed in my face, steamed my glasses, trickled down my neck into my clothing. The poncho couldn't prevent that, nor did the pathetic umbrella serve other than to keep the incessant drumbeat off my skull. The pants of my lower legs, exposed to the elements, were quickly drenched, fouled with mud to the knees. My high-topped hiking shoes sank into quagmire.

I couldn't see well, necessarily advanced slowly. I saw only the misty shapes of trees looming in murk. That, I guess, is how it happened. Directionless, unable to measure my progress (I kept expecting, in vain, to hit the meadow), the horrible realization stole upon me that I was lost. There was no trail beneath my feet.

I didn't panic. I had plenty of water, food to snack, and I knew the basic rules of the wild. Keep heading downhill, for the slope couldn't go on forever. I'd reach the meadow or, missing that, plunge straight through the next piney barrier to the grassy ridges, where I could take bearings. Off trail, in those conditions, it would be a slow trek, but I had time. Besides, the storm might slack, and if I could see, I could recover my way.

Before I knew it was there I stood well into an open space choked with soggy grass, a single misplaced oak spreading tall and fat before me. Beyond that I spied the shack. I swirled the moisture on my glasses with my thumbs, peered through a particularly energetic squall. It was a sorry, decrepit place, a hundred years old if a day, composed of rotten, uncured boards. The doorway seemed empty, the window a vacant socket, the roof entirely gone, only the sagging lattice of support beams showing. Precious little shelter to be had there, but I might huddle against a wall until I pulled myself together and took stock.

Glare of lightning, a reverberating crash, freakish darkness, and then the rain tapered a bit, and I raced for the shack, struggling against the suction of mud. I approached the door. Initial appearances had deceived me. Something having to do, I guessed, with shadow and perspective; at any rate, the structure was considerably more intact than I first imagined. Indeed, despite its quaint, rustic air, I felt unable to rule out the possibility of habitation. I detected the odor of a fire. Of course that was grossly unlikely, in such a setting, miles from the worst dirt road, deep in a wilderness preserve. I hesitantly knocked at that solid door. The storm swirled up around me. I tried to peer past the heavy burlap curtain in the window. I was about to try the brass knob when the door swung open.

There stood a man. An old guy, I thought, although maybe not so old as he looked; seamed and lined, like the house, rather than truly aged. He wore a long graying beard and patched together, unfashionable clothes. He glared at me for a moment, with the meanest expression, then his eyes relaxed and he asked, "You ain't with them, are you?"

I launched into my story, didn't get far. He said, "Git in, git in," so I git. Within a fire crackled in its stone hearth. The furnishings were simple, crude, suggestive of the home-made. The shack boasted two rooms, this main one and another quite small, containing three horribly primitive beds, seen past a rough half wall. Everything I saw indicated a revival or restoration of what I call the Early American Provincial. I asked the fellow if this were a cabin maintained for hikers.

He said, "This is my place. Ain't fancy, but it's stout enough to keep out the grizzlies." I laughed politely at what I deemed his outdated joke, the notion that the fierce bears still haunted this mountain. Those days were dead long before our time.

He told me to sit down. I settled on an unbalanced stool, shed my gear. The fire warmed. I expressed surprise at anyone living out here. He replied, "I'm William Powers. I live here with my sons, Billy and Luke. We're decent folks, don't want any trouble. My boys are out running an errand for me. They bear most of the work now, since I hurt myself in that fracas by the Black River. They ought to be back before long; should have been by now. Can't think what's keeping them."

His English was appallingly uncouth, but I'm not attempting to

35

reproduce it accurately, just translating the gist. Really, at odd moments his voice came to me as gusts of wind which I interpreted as speech. Mr. Powers limped to the window, fingered aside its thick covering, glanced beyond. "They're on the way, or somebody else is coming. This might be the day. Say, that's a peculiar rig you got."

He marveled at my stuff. In fact his behavior irked me, for he made too freely with my belongings, as if he were claiming them for his own, with too many comments pertaining to their utility to himself. I had to explain the camera, but he was equally impressed by my rucksack and my plastic poncho, which I'd slung off and wadded into a pocket. I figured he didn't get around much. When I tactfully suggested this, he "reckoned" it was so, adding, "My boys took the horses, so there's no way out presently. I've got to stick a spell."

He casually offered me food. I gratefully accepted, yet nothing came of the transaction. He busied himself about the fire, tinkered with a big pot, stirred its contents and clattered stray dishes, yet in the end I do not recall eating. That period passed vaguely. Then he was saying:

"You know, a man has to live, has to provide for his sons. It ain't like we take much. The townsfolk, them ranchers make big of every little thing. We're just making our way. Been at it for years, teaching the boys, no one hurt up to now, except those that deserved it, that wouldn't see reason. It ain't right they should fuss so. All I've got for my trouble is this here place, and for that it has to end on that oak tree out there in the yard. It ain't right."

I sympathized, as I could, without understanding. He replied, "You git me, then? That's good. Something is coming—there's been shooting down on the Nelson spread—I hear they bagged a couple of quail. That's how it happened before, or is happening—funny how it's all mixed up—and now they're coming, only it ain't Billy and Luke. No sir, it's them others, and they're gunning for me. It's all supposed to end on that tree."

This talk of "gunning" alarmed me. I expressed concern, rose to my feet. Mr. Powers produced an antique rifle, shiny new, from a corner. He said, "I can make a fight of it, unless they creep up and take me unawares. I recollect that's how they did it that last time, or this time. Couldn't git off a shot, and then there was the tree. There ought to be another way.

"Maybe there is." He studied me with an ostentatiously shrewd gaze. "You weren't here then, sonny. You just dropped out of a dream, like. Shoot, there's got to be a reason for that. Maybe it would suit who ever runs things if you took my place. It's been done before. I know how to swing it. I always was the clever one. That won't help Luke and Billy much—it's already too late for them—but it would do me a powerful good. I don't aim to git stretched if I can avoid it."

I began to let on that I needed to be on my way. I noted aloud that the storm had lessened (it hadn't), that I feared for my unattended camp. I certainly did not tell him I desired no more time in the company of a reclusive lunatic, and presumably an illegal squatter. He chuckled at what I did say, grinned. He said, "You ain't going nowhere. You've got to stand in for me this day. That's how it's set up."

He chuckled again, gestured with the rifle. "It makes sense," he mused, "that's why I keep showing up here, like it was that day over again. I've been waiting for somebody. Sooner or later you'd turn up, all part of the plan, and the story would be written different this time. It doesn't have to be me; you'll do just as well, and you can't count for much, so it ain't no bother. Yes, I reckon that's the way it'd better be."

He stiffened, the smug grin frozen within his dense beard. He turned, in an attitude of listening, hefted the rifle, strode warily into the bedroom, pressed himself against the window there. I grabbed my things and bolted for the door. It flew open. Driving rain and hail pummeled my face. Wet through on the instant, I dashed past the great oak tree and plunged into the woods. In the split second before I fled out of the clearing I thought I had company: fleeting images of forms, rough-hewn men, a number of them. I didn't pause to analyze, nor do I recall particular actions on their parts. They were there, I was past, distinctly heard the reverberations of gunshots. No, it was thunder. The tempest raged on, crash after crash.

Along the line I donned my poncho, which kept a bad situation from compounding, but the gusting rain and rattling hail maintained their battering until I reached the edge of the forest and stepped into meadow. I didn't recognize the locale yet, nor did I strike the trail until bright slivers of blue showed between scurrying gray cloud. Then I knew where I was, and two miserable, mentally tumultuous hours saw me back at camp. The rains came again, and there I spent a wretchedly wet, sleepless night until dawn offered escape and I could hit the road. I didn't feel safe until I was off Escudilla Mountain and olden muddy lanes and back on pavement.

Inquiries at the ranger station in Alpine confirmed for me that an historic shack existed on the mountain, abandoned lo these hundred years, and so far from the beaten trail that no one could conceivably stumble upon it by accident. Further questioning of the gracious hosts of the Springerville Historical Society yielded other answers, several of them oddly pertinent. I learned there of Old Man Powers, as history remembers him, and his two sons—those names provided—the worst gang of cut-throats to haunt that region after the turn of the last century. Cattle rustling and stage robbing were their specialties, and woe to the man who stood in their way. They left a bloody trail, nor were even their associates immune. History recorded that the elder Powers, when implicated in an unethical round-up early in his reign of criminality, had conspired to implicate in his stead one of his few neighbors. The ruse worked that time. That man paid the ultimate price in place of Powers.

Their cruel careers came to an end in '07, when the Powers boys raided the Nelson Ranch and marched smartly into an ambush. When the gunsmoke had wafted from their dead bodies a posse set out for the Powers hideout on Escudilla Mountain. The elder Powers expected family to come calling with their loot. Instead his enemies surprised him, and his life ended on a rope dangling from his own tree.

So ended that trivial footnote to the history of Arizona and Escudilla Mountain. In the natural order of things it should have meant little to me. The hostess pointed out a print hanging on the wall, of an ancient sepia glass-plate photograph, portraying a rugged gentleman in the garb of a cowpoke, reputed to be none other than William Powers, Sr. The heavy aspect of age was missing from that face, and much of the beard as well; but you know, I can vouch that it was a tolerable likeness.

THE WITCH'S CAVE

Gerald Sloane came to the little Arizona town in the lee of the big mountain because he was a freshly degreed, newly employed anthropologist, and he had been delegated to investigate the folkways of the simple people who dwelt there. "This constitutes a fruitful new avenue," the head of the department had said, "the analysis of local, enclosed societies in our midst, passed up by modern ideas, retaining much that is old. Here, for example, is a likely candidate." So, with the locale virtually drawn from a hat, Sloane ventured askance to Copper Hill, on the rim of the Verde Valley, there to sojourn for a month among the locals, record their views, catalogue their manners, and then publish in a specialized journal which even his colleagues were unlikely to read. He cheered himself by thinking of the expedition as a vacation, a break from routine, from which little need be expected of him.

Sloane took lodgings with a Mrs. Gaumont, a dour, middle-aged woman who let out hired rooms in her old house to self-supporting transients. She did not run an old-fashioned boarding house, as Sloane had postulated; not here the communal meals of old (one ate at the diner down the street) nor the sense of faux family. She needed the money, so she let rooms. There was much about the place which was old, however, and about the town, which hailed from the days of the pioneers, when great cattlemen owned the plains, subsistence farmers the watered valleys. Copper Hill lay by the banks of a turgid riparian creek (save for summer, when the creek ran dry until the monsoons), in the shadow of Fosters Mountain, which had drawn early settlement. Many more had come for the copper mines in the parched hills, a few folk remaining when the mines petered, dwelling in their tottering houses passed through generations, racing their pickup trucks on the dusty roads. Such was the history of Copper Hill as Sloane knew it. He didn't think it promising.

What lore could these people teach? Two other lodgers shared the house with him: a Mr. Graham, a weathered fellow of indeterminate age who worked at a sewage treatment plant in the valley outside of Cottonwood, and a Mr. Harris ("Call me Doug"), a young man involved in construction. They were local enough to suit Sloane, but they hadn't much to say. Mrs. Gaumont knew a thing or two, but the bulk of her wisdom could best be dismissed as gossip. Sloane went out and about, exploring the few streets and the sole paved lane, wandering amidst the creaky habitations, accosting and seeking insights from the dwellers therein. He learned, from the older folk, about the storm of '57, the mine closure of '46, the sickness of '19, and more besides, all of the same caliber. From the young, here too as elsewhere surviving on television, the Internet, and cell phones, he learned nothing at all.

There was, however, the story of the Witch's Cave, a tale which came to him from quite close to home, so to speak. It wasn't the sort of intellectual meat he'd expected, but it added spice to his deadly dull notes. There was another occupant of the house, a twelve year old girl named Laura Whitley, the ward of Mrs. Gaumont. That lady, intrigued by Sloane's profession, had asked him to breakfast on the third morning, where they discoursed. This was the morning when he'd first seen Laura, who seemed to be throwing a fit. Sloane, who hadn't spent much time so far at the domicile, had previously overheard what he imagined to be youthful tantrums, without knowing the source.

"My brother's child," explained Mrs. Gaumont as she passed the jam. "He got himself killed in a fight, and that tramp he married took off (I'm sure the fight was over her), so I got stuck with the girl. She's a handful, but I know my duty." "It must be difficult raising her by yourself," Sloane replied diplomatically, while choking on an over-baked biscuit; "I take it she has problems?" From what little he had seen of her he thought Laura looked pretty wild, unkempt, hysterical and withdrawn by turns. There was a lot of that these days, of course. Mrs. Gaumont shook her head, said sourly, "She was always a handful, that's for certain—crying as a baby, getting into scrapes before I pulled her out of regular classes at school down in Clarkdale—but it's a deal more now. Eldorada Martin has gotten hold of her."

40

THE WITCH'S CAVE

Sloane, clucking his tongue, asked knowingly, "Bad associations?" only to discover that his hostess meant nothing of the sort. "Eldorada the witch," she cried. "She's fastened on the girl, and will take her soon enough, just like she's done the others all these years." Sloane sputtered, said something perhaps not wholly appropriate, recovered himself and pressed for particulars. Thus he received the story.

As it was told to him at table, there had lived, over a hundred years before, a young, lovely, evil woman named Eldorada Martin, sprung from a family of foreign immigrants who had trekked to Copper Hill from far parts unknown at the turn of the last century, when the mines ran at top speed and the little settlement briefly boomed. Eldorada had been an awful person, of low character, stirring up trouble among the men, dressing distastefully (Mrs. Gaumont harped on that point), but her chief claim to fame stemmed from the fact that folks widely regarded her as a witch, one of those disreputable types presumably common in her old country who trafficked with spirits, knew more than she ought about things no one should know anything about, and refused to tolerate those who crossed her in any way. There were tales of her spells, her potions, her nocturnal wanderings—stories, from later in her life after her people were deceased, of mysterious guests she entertained in her house by the midnight moon—and of the terrible vengeance she wrought against those who fell afoul of her. What happened to those unfortunates could never be laid officially at her doorstep, but the good people knew and shunned her, so that she spent her final decades in solitary rage, outliving her own time, fuming at or threatening any who came near enough to annoy her. Some of the tales from those days, assured Mrs. Gaumont, were unbearably ugly, but nothing like what was told since the death of the witch.

It seemed that Eldorada had ever craved to pass on her devilish knowledge to the coming generation, yet failed to do so in life, never having married or produced offspring. In her last years she strove to lure to her young girls who would receive sinful training at her hands, but their families scotched that, even calling in the law when her offers became too aggressive. So she died in the end, alone and feared, with the fine folk dumping her into an unmarked hole and praising God that she was gone.

That should have been the end of her story, but it wasn't. In the years to come the legend of Eldorada garnered new accretions, added to the tale by those who remembered the old days and drew furtive connections between past and present. A terrible, if irregular, curse seemed to fasten itself upon the town, always following the same pattern. At long intervals adolescent girls of a certain character ("hectic", Mrs. Gaumont called it, by which Sloane guessed she meant disturbed)) would fall prey to what could only be deemed a form of possession from beyond the grave. They would behave badly, speak of things no one their age should know and, most frightful of all, invoke the dreaded name of Eldorada. Once afflicted by the supernatural malady—surely sent them by the unrestful spirit of the witch—the girls rapidly succumbed, and in time would make their way to the Witch's Cave, never to be seen again by mortal eyes.

At this point Sloane learned of the cave, only to realize that it was not entirely new to him. Atop Fosters Mountain, the long, high hogback ridge overlooking the town, there loomed a striking granite formation known for its unique shape as the Frying Pan, and beneath this, observed from the considerable distance as a sliver of darkness, lay the fabled cave. He had thought nothing of it before, except as a potential hiking destination, only to find that no formal trail to the top existed. He heard plenty now, however. Mrs. Gaumont earnestly related the unusual anecdotes concerning the site. In the ancient days, before the white man came to live in Verde Valley, the Yotapai Indians had dwelt in the cave, performing cruel ceremonies upon their captives, rites that involved morbid gastronomic practices. Much later Eldorada adopted the site for her own rituals, those which could not be carried out too close to decent folk. At specific times of the year, such as May Eve, All Hallows, perhaps the solstices (Mrs. Gaumont was hazy on these points, but Sloane gleaned the dates from her descriptions), the witch would repair to the cave, despite the inordinate difficulty in reaching it, there to conjure her nastiest magic. Whenever she did, somebody she disliked would sicken or die. With Eldorada's death that phase had thankfully ended, but the old people claimed her spirit still lurked up there, and when the mood was on her she called to selected girls, enticing them to her, craving to make them her own. They went there if they could, to vanish from the earth because, as Mrs. Gaumont surmised, none of them were evil enough to satisfy the witch's needs. Regardless, no one else ever went there.

Such the story from his voluble landlady, which Sloane thought might deserve a write-up, if only for amusement's sake. Certainly, however, that little girl was in a bad way. He attempted to pay her benevolent attention, with poor results. A secretive, sullen sort, she rarely played with those her own age, and with adults she apparently had nothing to do whatever. Sloane's stabs at conversation elicited indifferent monosyllables by way of reply. Only once did she truly speak to him. That day, in an idle moment, he studied the distant Witch's Cave with binoculars from his second floor window. He could tell that it should properly be deemed a rock shelter instead of a cave; the opening was long and narrow rather than deep, and he could clearly discern the wall of the cliff within the shallow depth. He also noted that Mrs. Gaumont was wrong about people visiting the cave. He could barely make out a minute human figure standing on the lip of the ledge: a tall adult form, probably a woman, dressed in black. As he watched she moved, seeming to wave her arms above her head.

Immediately his attention was diverted by a piercing scream from within the house. Sloane dashed downstairs to the parlor to find Laura crouching piteously on the carpeted wooden floor, shrieking and thrashing. When he gingerly laid hands on her she shrank back, crying, "She's going to get me. I know she will. She's calling now. She wants me to come to her." "Your aunt wants you?" asked Sloane, to which the girl sobbed, "The bad woman, she wants me, Eldorada wants me to be like her." Then Mrs. Gaumont rushed in, saying, "I'll deal with this, Mr. Sloane. Please don't trouble yourself," adding after her stern ministrations to the child, "It's always the same, only worse these days."

Sloane thought the pathetic girl required vigilant medical care, but it was none of his business, and the whole matter frankly repelled him. He doubted that his landlady would appreciate forceful or demanding recommendations from him; she didn't seem the sort to gladly accept advice. Furthermore, he had his own concerns, which were at best tangentially related to the sorrows playing about him. Sloane had a job to do. He pondered a paper on "Folk Beliefs and Their Impact on Psychological States," or vice versa, but the material at hand seemed a little thin. What about "Survival of Primitive Thought Systems?" That had a ring to it, although the touchy department might judge it as overly condemnatory. Regardless, one line of endeavor did begin to stir his interest. It occurred to Sloane that a trip to the Witch's Cave might prove profitable. The fable of Eldorada aside, it struck him as possible that, given what he'd been told, there might be traces of prehistoric Indian occupation up there. Analysis of ancient ruins, however decrepit or meager, would at least provide hard, tangible results.

He did go there, and sooner than he expected, but for a very different reason. A few mornings later, while Sloane listlessly pecked at his portable computer, Mrs. Gaumont came to him, wringing her hands and crying, "She's gone. Laura has run off to the Witch's Cave." When he asked how she knew that, she glared at him disdainfully and sniffed, "Because she said she would. She told me last night what Eldorada wanted. Naturally I called the sheriff when I saw she'd disappeared, because I knew what kind of nastiness it meant. He says he'll keep an eye out for her. What kind of talk is that? Nobody will do anything, they never do. She'll be taken away like the others." She raced away, perhaps to spread her tale of woe.

Sloane broached the matter to his fellow lodgers, who were both still in, but found them unresponsive. "She already told me about it," said Mr. Graham. "She's a bit of a kook, you know. It's best to keep out of these family squabbles. The girl will come back when she's hungry." Mr. Harris opined cheerfully, "I'll bet it's boyfriend trouble. Some of these girls start early, you know. The generations never see eye to eye." Sloane supposed that both were likely right, but the affair distressed him. He believed that the superstitious Mrs. Gaumont had filled the girl's head full of wild tales, and a moody child might be inclined to take seriously such rubbish. An idea occurred to him, one which he found appealing on the instant. He would undertake his journey to the cave right away. He could carry out his research, whatever that would entail, and if (a minimal if, surely) Laura were making for that place, he could round her up and bring her back safely, which would be something in the nature of a good deed.

Sloane set out, with his notebook, a bottle of water and a candy bar in his backpack. Presently he mounted the steep, scrubby slope of Fosters Mountain. In the absence of a trail his progress required bushwhacking and rock climbing, tedious activities at which he was experienced, yet which consumed much time. He judged that he climbed five or six hundred feet over a couple miles of ground, with the latter half considerably more vertical. Toward the end, around mid-morning, he negotiated a sixty degree sandstone slope before he reached out and, under the shadow of the immense Frying Pan, pulled himself up onto the ledge of the rock shelter. As he had already surmised, given the difficulty of the ascent, he was alone. If, perchance, the girl had made for this place, she must have long ago given up.

He did find evidence of human habitation or ancient presence, however. Charred circles outlined by jagged pebbles marred the dusty, weedy rock floor. The back wall of the opening was decorated with images, some of which, to his practiced eye, appeared to be weathered or effaced petroglyphs of Yotipai provenience. Most, though, obviously dated from the historic period, though still quite old. There were odd, abstract dabbings of paint forming spirals, starbursts and pentagrams, with scribbled notations in the familiar alphabet spelling gibberish. There was more to see: a series of disheveled or broken appliances which might once have been pioneer implements or machines, some possessing adaptations unfamiliar to him. Sloane didn't specialize in such contraptions, but he theorized that they had, in certain cases, been modified from their original forms and intentions. Examining them as they now appeared, he thought inanely of medieval instruments of torture.

Sloane detected the faint sound of a gasp, turned to spy two little hands protruding above the lip of the shelf. Laura emerged over the edge, scrambling heroically for purchase. He would have made for her, but at that moment a shadow distracted him, a sense of aerial darkening, no doubt caused by a stray cloud obscuring the sun. He glanced skyward, saw no cloud. A louder cry from the girl drew him. Facing her again, he observed something strange. Laura was up now, poised precariously on the ledge, apparently confronting someone. Sloane could not be sure, for this one aspect of his vision failed him, rendering the sight problematical. He did or didn't see a dark, hazy human figure standing before the girl with arms outstretched; he thought he did. It looked the image of a woman, very old, with long, straggly gray hair and sharp, wizened features. The hard, thin mouth of that cold face worked, seemed to form words, though Sloane heard nothing. Laura quailed and sank to her knees, crying. Indistinct arms seized her, began dragging her under the low ceiling of the shelter.

Sloane called out to Laura, who didn't respond. He stepped forward, shouting something incomprehensible even to himself, charged in. The girl fell limply to the earth, the woman turned, so he thought, to face him. She glared, with a look of puzzlement on her hideous face, as if noticing him for the first time. Then she seemed to rush at him, or around and about him—this wasn't easy to describe to himself afterward—and he no longer saw a weird old woman, but a dark, cloudy black mass swirling across his vision. Fright gripped his mind as he felt an awful sickness assail his being, and a clamminess like the hand of death. He shook off the baleful impression of a hostile will beating down his own, struggled through the miasma to the prostrate girl and lifted her to his chest. Then he slid down from the edge, leaving behind him the Witch's Cave and its feeling of lethal dread.

Sloane endured great trials descending with an unconscious child in his arms, yet he did so, returned to Copper Hill and delivered his charge. He strongly advised relocation to Mrs. Gaumont, removal to a healthier environment for her and her niece, along with competent professional intervention. He never learned whether she accepted his strictures. Sloane presently contrived to cut short his stay in that town, returning to what he called civilization with little to show for his efforts. The head of the department wasn't pleased, finding numerous occasions to criticize the weakness of the collected information, which eventually made its way into a more general, regional report written by diverse hands. Actually Sloane had no one to blame but himself for his chilly reception, since he had suppressed his most interesting data, an act most unusual for an aspiring anthropologist. Nor did he ever choose to raise the subject again.

SEDONA

Sedona, city of possible dreams
   Calling to vibrant imagination
   Affording to life, regeneration
The stuff of which the sensitive mind teems.
Behold the land where the dusk-red rocks grow
Towers of stony crimson rising high
Framed against the backdrop of bright blue sky
Sweet nature's ultimate artistic show.
There at the foot of the gorge of Oak Creek
Sedona resides, a jewel man-made
Where beauty marches in endless parade
Before those who come, eagerly, to seek.
Enter these gates, O dreamer, and dream well
At the focus of hope celestial.

Above, below, and beyond, Mind awakens like the blinding crack of the red sun at the infinitesimal moment of dawn. Something, every place and no place, stirs. From very nearby, and from the outer chambers of the universe, that which is, was, and will be grumbles, blinks, querulously frowns. As it does so, stars explode, planets crumble, distant galaxies reel. It knows nothing of these happenings, nor does It care. It is interested only in the source of the disturbance, where ever that may lie in the cosmos, which has troubled Its eternal reverie. Tentatively, randomly, It reaches out in all directions, feeling Its way, questing, seeking. It senses that something is out there, something calling attention to itself, which may require the forces to be

47

set in motion.   This way and that It turns, sluggishly at first, then with greater surety, focusing all Its powers on the source, like a searchlight piercing utter darkness.   Where is it, then, this annoying gnat of consciousness, this furtive itch flaring up within creation?   It will be found, it must be found; once the inquisitive process begins, there can be no stopping it.   Something is out there... and there it is, a tiny, dwindling, meaningless spark of life.   The situation may provide amusing possibilities, for there is no telling what may happen when Mind meets mind.

Sedona the fabulous lies ahead
Everything as I knew it would be
O, that such gorgeousness these eyes should see
In this realm to which destiny has led.
At long last the wish gives way to the deed
For years Sedona has beckoned to me
Promising not just bland reality
But the fulfillment of my inner need.
This is the chance for which oft I've yearned
To inhabit a land of true meaning
Where my soul shall undergo pure cleaning
Where I'll attain the higher state I've earned.
Never more life's crass material bane
Here the cosmic energies I shall gain.

It closes in, but not all at once, not as the result of plan, for this is the first, final, and ultimate Mind without thought, the Purpose without determination, the Creator without goal.   It sees all, and knows nothing; It is all, and is nothing.   Omnipotent, omniscient, omnipresent, yet It contains within Itself only chaos.   The light which can not illuminate, yet reveals all things, blazes from the farthest corners of time and space where the quasars erupt, incinerating galaxies and their myriad exotic denizens.   Untraceable waves of force sweep across the universe, passing eventually through the minute speck of material substance we know and call all there is.   Here there are stars and worlds which actually appear in our telescopes, an expanse covering billions of years and light years, a meaningless fragment of the totality.   Out of all this, one enormous, insignificant stellar cluster bends the waves unto itself, a trivial eddy within the penetrating vibrations, but it is enough.   As the power concentrates, it builds, feeds upon itself, grows into a whirlpool, swells to a raging torrent. Inexorably the force intensifies, narrowing into a tight beam as it does so. It probes now within this single cluster, searching for the source of the disturbance which has, unknowingly, shaken the cosmos.

I'm exactly the type who fits in here
One who's intellectually daring
Yet considerate and deeply caring
Expressing myself freely without fear.
I cherish politically correct views
I'm a nonconformist like all the rest
I stand for all that is socially best
I reject opinions that might confuse.
I've always sensed that life offered much more
Than the daily rat race I'm escaping
Forget the fools whose ways I've been aping
I've arrived to find my personal door.
Gentle Sedona is my chosen place
Wherein the world of the spirit I'll face.

Somewhere within this mass of matter, this conglomeration of cold particles and warm radiation, lies the source. The eternal gaze knifes through all, penetrating to the depths of every object in its path. How could it not? To that sightless eye, the densest matter is largely a vacuum, an emptiness held together by tenuous nuclear forces. And yet, if anything, the all-seeing Blind One sees too much, and therefore often sees nothing. Perhaps it is good that it be so; otherwise It might be driven to intervene in all circumstances, and the mad illusion of cosmic order would finally and forever disintegrate. These rare moments come, however. Somehow the right mind, at the right geographical point, calls down the powers. Even now It has located the planet. It peers closely. There are many minds down there, but just at this instant—for no humanly understandable reason whatsoever—only one of them counts. Even to the Eternal One, no reason is necessary. It continues with the search. Only a finite number of locations on the surface serve to channel its vision, and the goal should lie—such is the intensity of the signal—in close proximity to one of them. It examines each, spiraling invisibly over the seas and the lands, as relentless as the wind, patiently weaving Its web.

EERIE ARIZONA

Sedona's, the seat of cosmic power
Which unlocks the mysteries of the soul
Here I shall find myself, refashioned whole
Atop a majestic red rock tower.
Well equipped I come to this special land
I've brought my crystals and my gemstone beads
Which focus energy, acting as seeds
For the spiritual blossoming I've planned.
I didn't forget my paperback books
Collected in many a half-price store
 Volumes of vital esoteric lore
Purchased despite the sellers' sneering looks.
Books written by thinkers so in the know
That they're invited by every talk show.

One cusp of transmission attracts particularly strongly now. The Supreme Mind has identified the sole spot of current interest on all of this dark, whirling orb. The crucial point lies on or near the surface. That is good. Connection, if such be deemed amusing, will be easy. Such points can hang high in the skies over the planet, where living material seldom rises, where only wispy, vaporous forms routinely dwell; or they may lie buried deep within the mass of insentient matter, approachable only by the fluidic, squirming denizens of the lightless inner regions. Not so this time. The cusp is so positioned that it can be reached by virtually any animate form, including those which possess mental ability, however barely detectable. It knows that one such organism is on the way to this location. It could, without difficulty, track down this being, but there is no need. Already Mind senses, with absolute certainty, that the chosen one will come of its own accord. Not one erg of effort is required to bring it forth. Sometimes, the meeting develops this way. Perhaps one may envision the anthropomorphized image of a Great One relaxing, reclining comfortably while He waits. Misleading, even childish, this is, for during this moment of quietus unbounded energies are pouring into the focal destination.

My dog-eared, well-thumbed booklets tell the tale
Of a vortex found on the Hill of Stars
From which truth peeps through reality's bars
And through which the enchanted soul may sail.

50

SEDONA

The house of the Wilsons still stands up there
I gather those folk have long gone away
What became of them my sources don't say
But the gate stands open for those who care.
Initiates yearly flock to the site
To commune with nature under the moon
Evening falls quickly; I'll venture forth soon
The crescent moon rises this starlit night.
Loaded with all the gear I can carry
I'm ready, and in no mood to tarry.

The Ultimate knows, without knowing or caring, that It has impressed Its being upon this special place before. At some time in the limitless sweep of eternity, whether it be yesterday, at the dawn of creation, or far in the future at the end of all things, it has trodden here with the semblance of purpose. There had been another calling—several others—the most recent concerning the first of these inconsequential creatures to actually establish a habitat on the site. None had previously dared to do that. All the others had suspected or deduced something of the power which funneled through the spot and, while drawn to it, had instinctively chosen to stay away. On this occasion, it seems, there were four of them. Drawn by mundane aims, they lacked any knowledge of the gate. Until their predestined end they went unaware of its existence. Merely their continued, sentient presence at the location caused them to be noticed, leading to the critical actions taken. They hadn't understood what was happening to them, nor why (not that they ever really do), but it had happened, as it must. Since then no one has ever remained long, nor relatively few ever come near. None of these sundry details, of course, however relevant they might appear to the planetary dwellers, constitute matters of the slightest interest whatsoever to It which waits.

To the north the lights of Sedona burn
As I cross Oak Creek over the foot bridge
And commence the climb up the rocky ridge
Where the outlines of the house I discern.
The Hill of Stars and the Wilson abode
I tread at last upon this sacred ground
I gain the summit with a hearty bound

EERIE ARIZONA

Somewhere close by flames the magical node.
The Wilson structure appears but a shell
This ruin isn't what I expected
Its wreckage seems in no way connected
To the heaven I seek; rather with hell.
Whatever the cause, it's nothing to me
It's the Stones of Power I've come to see.

The subject arrives. Now the Infinite Mind can see it clearly. The Absolute Entity glances, casually observes as if with a shrug, knows all. It has always known. Organic, carbon, compounds of chemicals in semi-liquid suspension, superficial sensory apparatus; It reads the physical properties of the creature as if flipping through the pages of a book. The thing equates to the others that have come before. The Mind also sees into and through the nerve impulses and electrical currents which serve, for this lowly form, as a rudimentary identity. What It finds there is scarcely interesting, much less edifying. The subject possesses an extremely low-grade intelligence—nothing worthy of the term—characteristics unremarkable for this world. The tiny sparks of crude energy which course through its mammalian brain create muddled thought patterns which very much resemble those of previous visitors to this site. There may be some greater openness to outside influences in this case. The probability exists that the animal mentality encompasses a cryptic word. Perhaps that alone, or chiefly, has set the forces in motion. Then again, perhaps not. The Mind doesn't ponder the question, nor does It even decide not to ponder. Knowing all as It does, neither requirement nor necessity for thought pertains.

There loom the stones, those sentinels on guard
The ancient trio marking the lost gate
The path to unimaginable fate
Mystic red signposts, eternal and hard.
'Twas the Indians who erected them here
In strange ages before Atlantis dived
And the red man who from weird myths derived
The knowledge of He they adore and fear.
The Great Old One, the Ultimate Being
The master of all, the friend of the wise
He who I'll gaze upon with my own eyes

SEDONA

This night, all the beauty that's worth seeing.
It only remains to unlock the door
To speak with the god they call *Xenophor*.

It is done. Contact has been made. The opening word has been spoken. Everything falls into place now. The Great Old One—Creator, Destroyer, He who dominates and embodies the cosmos—Xenophor the Mighty has heard. His substance uncoils, expands to fill the gate, this vortex through which the dimensions plunge. He doesn't pass through the door; during one instantaneous flash of space/time He becomes the door. At that moment He has always become the door. The fabric of the universe, of every universe, shudders with vast waves of power sweeping across the patchwork of reality. A billion light-years away, on a forgotten planet in a dead galaxy, a curious statue, standing before a rubbled temple long abandoned by dark things, topples to the ground; in another mysterious quadrant, oceans boil on a green world; in still another, the lovely city of a writhing race of savants bursts into nuclear fire. Xenophor is the cause—the Cause—yet He notices not. The great and the small He sees, and right now He blindly sees, with full intensity, one of the smallest. The chosen one comes, hopefully, joyously, foolishly, it comes with mind wide open, defenseless. Its fate, ordained since creation, is at hand. This is an incredible, inexplicable marvel; yet Xenophor marvels not.

Intoning the words, I call out the name
From which peace, true life, and happiness flow
With sure strides between the red stones I go
To be kissed by He whose love is His fame.
Xenophor, come to me, your acolyte
Teach me the ways You deem holy and just
Grant me the wisdom to live as I must
Bathe my keen soul in Your exalting light.
I beseech, let my pilgrimage begin
Accept my soul, Xenophor, as Your own
Hold my hand within this trio of stone
That I may enter Your plane without sin.
I come to You humbly, not defiant
Regard me as Your noblest suppliant.

EERIE ARIZONA

Xenophor does not do; He perceives, and it is done. The power concentrates and, soaring to infinity, pervades the designated host. Had the mind of this pathetic thing grasped the situation, it might have understood, and the outcome could have been different. That occurs, occasionally, and can lead to fleeting episodes of interest. Here there is no understanding, no defense. The extra-cosmic invasion permeates the creature, overwhelming and illuminating every last bit of its substance. Its corporeal form, that lump of flabby matter, renders into its component molecules. The molecules break down to atoms, the atoms to subatomic particles, the particles . . . on and on the process continues, throughout the forever of a moment, endlessly. The subject acts and responds, after a fashion, but that is of no concern, nor even a distraction. Awareness, identity linger fitfully, although in time they, too, may be erased. Certain aspects of its being are immediately lost. Others may be thrown as scraps to the Favored Ones, who crouch hungrily beyond the rim of outer darkness. There remains the possibility that Great Xenophor may reserve certain portions to Himself, for His pleasure. Some of the more conscious fragments can be employed as trinkets or playthings. The Ultimate One, in His own way, is a collector of toys.

Horrors beyond belief I now behold
Torment lurks frightful between the three stones
Limitless power crushes flesh and bones
Surging from that Evil, heartless and cold.
There's only chaos, confusion, and pain
The energies destroy as they reveal;
Upon my doomed soul engrave His seal
My life, my shattered thoughts, flicker and wane.
To Sedona I trekked for happiness
To learn of a universe I abhor
In seeking the source of the golden door
I've found the truth of blackest bitterness.
Coming to hail the King of the New Age
Instead I confront His eternal rage.

MY WAR AGAINST THE INVISIBLES

The invaders came like thieves in the night. No one ever saw them, no one ever knew of them apart from their effects. They showed up the morning following the night of the meteorites, which can't be a coincidence; they came in something. Things fell to earth around there in the wee hours, and from those something alien hatched. I didn't actually know it at the time—I learned most of the sparse details later—for I was up in the hills on holiday from the big city, enjoying two weeks of fishing and other lazy recreation. We sojourned in the little cabin deep in the woods by the stream up from the mouth of Munds Canyon, I and a couple of friends, Mark and Buddy. A good time was had by all, and then that morning they went into Page Springs for supplies. That was the wrong thing to do, because I never saw them again.

By that evening I was really worried about them, but there wasn't anything I could do then since they took the jeep. The next morning, after frying myself some fish and heating a big biscuit, I set off on foot down the rocky four-wheel drive road to town. All that day I saw no one, which wasn't totally strange, but I'd expected to run across other outdoorsmen if not my friends. By following Oak Creek I reached the edge of the forest, where it gave over to farmland, before I sacked out again, very tired, confused, and remarkably low in spirits (I say that because I didn't know anything yet of what was coming). So it was one more morning before I hit the winding paved road out of the lowlands and made it to Page Springs.

Here began the heavy-duty weirdness. It looked like they were demolishing the town. As far as I could see the entire population of able-bodied men, a lot of women, even older children, were engaged in taking apart every structure in sight, right down to the outhouse. By observing a bit more I realized they were building something new, one big, long, rectangular structure, like a warehouse or factory building. They swarmed like perspiring ants over the shell of that edifice, which grew as I watched. Already others were working inside. My view of them was cut off as the walls went up.

I saw more. There were dead bodies in the streets, a few, being haphazardly collected at intervals. Most of the bodies were little children and old folks, and they looked messy. The scene was so freakish that I didn't think, but blundered way into it before I decided to feel afraid. Then I crouched against a smashed brick wall, my heart hammering, wondering what had happened, what was happening.

I backed out to the edge of town, hiding in the ruins of a torn down house, until a solitary figure trudged up the road toward me. He was a lean, weather-beaten old fellow who walked erratically, as if in distress, clutching one arm to his chest. At my hail he turned, made hesitantly for me. "What gives?" I cried. "Has the world gone nuts?" "Guess so," he replied. His hand, held tightly to his chest, looked funny, like he wore a furry mitten. I begged him to tell me what was going on. He told me, between gasps and groans of pain.

The invaders had come, invisible ones that dropped out of the sky into men's minds, occupying a corner of their brains, dictating orders. They wanted something done, commanded it done, saw to it that it was done. Those who wouldn't or couldn't work died in odd and unpleasant fashions. The surviving folks were being forced to build something, out of the available materials, a kind of manufacturing plant. He didn't tell me what it was for. Shortly he couldn't tell me much at all. His hand squirmed, and I saw that it wasn't covered by a mitten; his hand was a furry thing, an eyeless animal attached to his wrist with a nasty toothy mouth, and it was eating into him. He told me weakly that, unlike most, he'd resisted the sinister spell, so the Invisibles—that was his word—willed this creature onto his hand, just made it happen like magic. Then the mouth gnawed into a vital spot, blood spurted, the man collapsed. That's how he met his end.

I believed every word of his story, without reservation. Good Lord, after what I'd seen, why shouldn't I? Without missing a beat I took off at a trot down the highway to Cornville, intending to flag a car and escape to civilization, if there still was one. I began to have doubts, because an hour passed, yet never saw a vehicle on the road. That is, I didn't until I reached a certain point up on those open, wind-swept ridges, where I hiked up a slope and came across half a dozen wrecked cars and pickups all jumbled together. There was human debris mixed among the tangle of steel and fiberglass. I found out why. More invisible trickery, an unseen barrier laid across the road through which I could not pass. Nor, I gathered, could anything tangible. It affected vision, too, for the view beyond was blurred, misty, meaningless, the sort of distorted view one gets in a funhouse mirror. I walked far off the road, still met the barrier. That gave me the shakes. I was five miles out of Page Springs. How far did this murky wall extend?

I hiked it, kept going after the sun went down, just to be sure, and yes, it ran all the way around, a circumference of, I guess, about fifteen or sixteen miles. I was exhausted then, and tired, and hungry. I ate the last of the biscuit, washed down with my canteen. I pondered long before sleep overwhelmed me. As horrible as the situation appeared, one note of feeble hope occurred to me. Whatever had happened here hadn't happened to the whole world. That couldn't be, otherwise the aliens wouldn't require a barrier protecting their lodgment in Page Springs. It might not do me any good, but the real world was still out there.

This meant that, as it was likely to matter to me, the sole enemy was here inside, with me. Whatever must be done would be done here. I determined to do it, or to die trying. Having resolved, I slept, and in the morning walked back to town.

Why had I not been affected by the mind control? I could only take a stab at an explanation, but I figured my saving grace was previous isolation. Having landed, the Invisibles had gone after everybody they found, and they simply didn't find me. Mark and Buddy picked a bad time to intrude, right when things got hot, so I presumed they'd been sucked in. Maybe I could blend in, pass for one of the mental slaves, learn a thing or two, find a means of making a difference. It was a slender reed, but better than nothing. I tried it.

I strolled into Page Springs, casually dodged the construction teams, sauntered straight into the giant building and got to work. It was a factory of some kind, containing a series of assembly lines, extremely long wooden tables down which mysterious gizmos were being pushed, and added to as they progressed. I haven't the foggiest where that stuff came from; it didn't look cobbled together from local spare parts the way the building did, but rather like material provided from a technologically advanced source. The finished devices, collected at the ends of the tables by teams who carried them away for stacking at the end of the hall, were small machines that could be held in the hand, complicated instruments of convoluted metal casings with wires running all through them. I didn't know what they were, couldn't guess anything from their appearance. I would have bet they were weapons. The Invisibles were constructing these, preparing for the day when they sent their slave army out of the barrier.

To be precisely clear, the Invisibles weren't making anything; their human captives did the work. There were three hundred people in that vast, low-ceilinged room, each doing his minute part, utilizing a mess of common hardware tools to piece these objects together. Those people all looked dirty and weary; some looked sullen, even angry, but they all worked. I joined in, squeezing into line, staking out a space, began to fuss with the gadgets. There must have been a rule I was expected to know and obey, but I didn't know it and didn't care to obey, so I did anything that came to mind, sticking a wire here or there as pleased me. I'd be surprised if any of my productions operated properly.

At midday we were fed by human servants pushing trolleys laden with various-sized bowls of wheat porridge. It was wretched goop, but it filled the belly, as far as it went. Then back to work until dusk, when everybody at once, surely in obedience to a silent command, marched out of the factory and dispersed to the rubble of their homes, where they bedded down among the refuse of their lives. I went along with the bunch I'd labored by, which seemed to be the remains of a family and their immediate neighbors. We crouched or sprawled in the dark, with just a half moon to illuminate the pathetic scene.

"You don't belong here," said a youngish, sandy-haired fellow. I replied, "Nor do you. Why do you do it?" He said, "I have to obey them." "Who, the Invisibles?" "Yeah, yeah, that's right, the Invisibles." He groaned. "I can't see them, but they're there, always talking to me, telling me things. I hate it, but it has to be."

"And a good thing, too," cried another, an older guy with a scraggly, graying beard. "It's right to do what we're told. I'm happy about it." They had him lock, stock, and barrel. Curiously enough, despite his happiness he appeared in worse shape than anybody else present. At the time that didn't mean anything to me.

I turned to the girl beside me, a little bedraggled, but still a pretty girl. "Who do you agree with?" I asked. "It doesn't matter," she said hopelessly. "The monsters have got us. There's nothing we can do about it." "That remains to be seen," I said.

MY WAR AGAINST THE INVISIBLES

I slept, then woke at dawn, half expecting to wake up hypnotized, but I was my normal self. That was great. I woke because those around me were rising in unison, again obeying the silent command. They marched toward the factory, I tagging along. I was desperately hungry, but we received nothing but a swallow of water apiece. Then back to work we went.

Two bizarre deaths taught me a lesson. There was a frowzy woman at the next table over who worked more diligently than most, even humming to herself. An hour before our crummy lunch was served she broke down. It was as if she were all used up, had burnt herself out. She fumbled her application of wiring to machine, then staggered, then shrieked, "No, it isn't fair, why should it happen to me?" And then she literally fell apart. Bits of her started to come off, until she suddenly unraveled, disintegrating into tiny dusty chunks. She didn't bleed, she crumbled. So she was dead. There were plenty of sad comments, but everybody kept working. After lunch it happened again, this time to the older man who'd bragged the last night of his happiness. He screamed, begged for mercy, ran around shedding himself until he wasn't there anymore. This told me that, whatever the consequences of disobeying might be, too cheerful obedience was a lot worse, the effects more immediate. I debated how this knowledge might serve the cause.

That night I had a long talk with sandy-haired Charles ("Call me Chuck") and his pretty sister Marjorie. I'd discovered that they were still real people in a sense—their personalities and ideas intact—with the dominance of the Invisibles laid over to a greater or lesser extent. This meant we could converse pretty much like normal. I made use of that fact to get the goods on the situation. "What's it all about, Chuck? What are they up to?" "They want the Earth for themselves," he said slowly, like a thoughtful man puzzling out a tricky point. "They don't have bodies like we do, so they need us for all the grunt work. They jump from planet to planet, making the folks there build what they need, then move on to the next. Now they're here, and they're going to do the same to us. They'll always be hiding, but they'll be running the show, once they control all of us." "If that's the plan," I mused, "I wonder why they start off hiding in Page Springs." "Because," Marjorie cut in eagerly, "there aren't enough of them to control the world with their brains. They aren't that strong. They need the machines we're building for that." "Isn't it a joke," said Chuck. "I'm working all day, no wages, no benefits, to destroy the human race. It's shameful." "Now I get it," I said. "When they have enough machines, down comes the barrier, and their mind control reaches from one end of the globe to the other. After that there won't be any dealing with them."

"Isn't now," Chuck growled. "It stinks, but we have to work."

"I sure don't want to," said Marjorie, "but that's how it is. I know it's ridiculous. I hate them. They killed our little sister Tammy, just because she wasn't old enough to work. They made something awful grow on her. That's how life is, though."

Very earnestly I said to them, "Tomorrow I want both of you to do me a big favor. Each of you, when you're on the assembly line, do this for me: just once, screw up the job. If you're told to put wire A in hole B, do it another way, or break the wiring, or stick a pebble inside a case. Do some little thing just for yourselves, because you want to, because you can."

"I don't know." "I'd feel funny about it." "Somebody might mind." They gave me all kinds of answers, derived straight from their control, but their emotions fought for me. Both agreed to think about it.

I got results. I took a place across from them on the line, made regular eye contact, dropped suggestions. They would smile, glance at each other, do something wrong like naughty kids. They didn't exactly break the control, but they played with it, amused themselves, and in so doing accomplished a few acts of vital sabotage.

That night I praised them, joked with them, encouraged them without pushing too far. I was afraid they'd rebel against me if I drove them. Marjorie seemed—I really believed this—to take a shine to me. I didn't mind. I'd done a lot worse in my time. I advised them to spread the word of my cute idea, just for a laugh, if they didn't mind. Chuck was dubious about the enterprise, but Marjorie found it appealing, "as long as it didn't make for trouble."

The next day the other shoe dropped. It had to happen sooner or later. I'd been dreading something like this. How long could I wander about without drawing the attention of the invaders? In mid-afternoon I heard the buzzing in my ears, or in my head, a low, insistent drone which rose to a grating whine. I knew right then it was the mental power of the Invisibles. I also noticed, quickly, that everybody in sight sensed it. So it wasn't me in particular they were after; they were hitting the lot of us. Now why would they do that? I thought of a possibility. It was reinforcement, administered like

60

medicine, bad medicine in this case. If you're sick the doctor gives a big shot, then recommends a prescription of small doses to keep the first one going strong. That's what the Invisibles were doing, I concluded, or figured out as the process went on. It might be all the poor folks of Page Springs needed, but would it capture me?

I fought it in my mind, trying to beat it back without being too obvious about it. That sounds strange, but for all I knew the Invisibles could read minds, and I didn't want to think too loudly, if that's understandable. I waged the battle of the brain, guerilla-style. The force was amazingly transparent, only subtle, insidious, doing its best to become a part of me, to rearrange my views in order to corral them and bring them into line. There was nothing harsh or painful about it. It was as if I was considering another set of values, like a friendly conversation on politics or religion. Oh, I see your point; yes, you've got something there—say, that might be worth a try—I'll give anything reasonable a fair shake. Such thoughts swam within me, and they didn't sound evil or craven. An unprepared victim, like hundreds of Page Springs folks who awoke to the attack that first morning, could have fallen for it in a minute. The weak-minded would suck it up and feel righteous about themselves.

I remembered my missing friends. Mark and Buddy were tough, not likely to surrender readily, but they'd walked into the thick of the attack, when the aliens were pouring it on. I'm sure they were killed because they struggled too hard, fought too heroically for their souls. I waged war quietly. I didn't shout, didn't argue, didn't threaten, I simply shrugged and kept moving my hands like a willing worker. I even fitted a few devices properly, proving what a good boy I was. The whine turned into muted but comprehensible whispering, a reptilian voice hissing commands. I kept moving like a non-union employee, eager to get a good job done well.

The voice ceased, the whine returned, gave way to the buzzing, which stopped. I examined all the caves of my brain. So far as I could tell, I was unaffected. My mind was still my own, my purpose unchanged.

The Invisibles weren't so smart! In fact, they were pretty dumb, so smug and sure of themselves that they didn't investigate their results. Maybe they couldn't—maybe they had to sneak up on their victims to make it work (at least without the machines we were building, a scary thought if the Invisibles ever got loose in the world)—but whatever the reason, they'd screwed up badly. I was still the spy in their camp, designing schemes for undermining them.

I lost ground with my fellow conspirators, however. That night I found them dangerously obstinate, and guessed I had to just about start over again. I did so, only this time I knew what I was doing.

Here's the following couple of days in a nutshell. We went about our business, as the Invisibles wished it, trooping to work at dawn in our grimy, stinking clothes, the same we'd worn throughout, unwashed, crusted with perspiration. Water, for drinking only, was carried by slaves from Oak Creek, and little of that. Food dwindled rapidly. Either the Invisibles didn't care if we starved, or their plans were reaching maturity. Now and then the best and most pitiful workers blew up or fell apart, a taste of human destiny if the Invisibles got their way. We cranked out a ton of those machines, equipment for a small army, as if the aliens counted on swarms of new slaves soon. I brought Chuck and Marjorie around again, added everybody in our sleeping group, set them to passing the word at every opportunity. Each one of us talked to several—just throwing out ideas, you know, take them for what they're worth—and everybody we talked to were encouraged to pass along the message. I relied on the power of mathematics to spread the word: two, four, eight, sixteen, on and on, until everybody heard. Surely it didn't take with some. I heard arguments, nasty comments, threats to "tell." I also saw many quiet nods and secretive grins. Rather than making waves, I set in motion ripples that could pile up into a tidal wave when the time was right. In the end the request was always the same: keep playing along, agree to every mental command, don't fight it or talk back, but disobey it, be subversively creative with the machinery. The Invisibles were clearly counting on that stuff. We must see to it that it let them down.

During those days there were dim flashes of light in the sky, like sheet lightning, and muffled booms from all directions. That had to be the fine warriors of the human race, God bless them, battling to break in to us. Nothing came of it, though. No one came. The alien barrier held firm. We were on our own.

On that last afternoon we received another dose of mental reinforcement. It didn't affect me at all—I'd figured it right—but what really mattered was how it impacted the rest. There were some waverers, more than a few I admit, but with lots of them the relapse wasn't severe, nor did it last long. It didn't take with Marjorie one minute. She stuck to me, collared her brother and straightened him out, and what with one thing or another by that evening we were solidly on course, as if the Invisibles hadn't tried their dirty tricks again.

I set Zero Hour at nine o'clock in the morning. Everybody who was ever going to matter got the message. I felt a curious, breathless sensation in my head, rather than my chest, an oppressive feeling which told me that our enemies were already on the move, perhaps suspecting something. That couldn't be helped. Came the moment, and I leaped onto the work table, at the top of my voice declaring a strike. "Stop working," I thundered. "All of mankind are counting on us. No more fooling. Spit out the Invisibles! Smash the machines!" Every device within reach I stomped or kicked to the floor. Marjorie jumped up with me, grasped my hand, added her voice and her feet to mine. "Death to the Invisibles!" she cried. Chuck echoed that call to battle, his strong voice rolling across the factory floor.

Hesitation, a frightening beat of ghastly silence, then hubbub and frantic commotion as scores of mental slaves threw off the weakened chains of their minds and got into the act. They shouted, bellowed, destroyed. Hammers, screwdrivers, monkey wrenches crashed down upon the horrible machines. Wires snapped, casings split, guts of metal tumbled out. Inside of a minute the entire production system was completely wrecked. The place was a shambles of ruined, bent, crushed metal fragments. The far corner of the factory caught fire, set ablaze by a patriotic arsonist.

The Invisibles struck back. Oh God, it was bad, worse than anything I'd felt yet. They came after our brains with red hot needles of unseen energy. That, I'll bet, was how it was that first day in Page Springs, and happy I am I wasn't there then, only had to experience it once. They hit back with fury, a genuine sense of blood-red anger knifing into my mind. Within seconds we learned that our would-be masters were playing for keeps, willing to kill those they couldn't dominate, maybe lusting to kill. They just about bowled us over with their counter-attack. Strong men fell to the floor crying, I staggered, Marjorie screamed in agony, the real thing—because it really hurt—and for a second we were checked. We were also aware, understanding as much as we could, united and fighting mad. We beat back the psychic shock wave.

Then came round two, when it seemed the Invisibles tried to murder as many of us as they could, probably to cow resistance. Here, there, at random, hideous growths sprouted on certain unfortunates, things like parasitic animals that attacked their human hosts. Maybe a dozen went down screaming or moaning. Chuck, to my horror and disgust, was one of these. I'd thought him tougher than that, but I can't make big statements. I don't know that it made any difference. It could have been luck of the draw. I don't think our opponents accepted defeat yet, but I'll never know that; either they were making examples of a few, or they couldn't handle us all at the same time. Anyway, a lizard thing grew out of the side of his face, bit into his neck, and that was the sad end of him. Marjorie gushed tears, hot, furious ones. "Death to the Invisibles!" she shrieked, and countless voices maintained the chant. Boots ground on metal parts. Debris was knocked off the tables. Gray smoke clouded the rancid air.

The vast majority of us still lived, healthy, sane, and uncontrolled. Whatever happened to us, victory was almost ours. The Invisibles played their last hand. This is the especially tragic part. There were those among us who had failed to break the control, or who were so eaten up by its power that they hadn't tried. They didn't have the numbers to fight us, but they could still serve their masters with their bodies. Now they seized the remaining intact alien devices from the completed stack, held them before them like the monstrous weapons they were, and prepared, as must be the case, to use them to re-enslave their freed fellows. Of course we couldn't stand up to that, of course we couldn't reason with the deluded ones; they were too far gone, so we did the only thing we could. I was neither the first to realize the dilemma nor to advocate the solution, but I was right in there, bawling soon enough at the top of my lungs for necessary action. "Kill them!" We did it, and I'm sorry, but I don't know what else we could have done. I pray we didn't kill anybody on our side by mistake. To pick up a machine, for any reason, was to invite an immediate death sentence. We slaughtered them all; every man or woman who snatched up one of those objects perished, and went fast. It was a messy, bloody brawl, which didn't stop until the final slave hit the dirt, pummeled and broken.

And with that the battle concluded. I didn't know it was over yet, though I sensed a sudden lessening of tension in my mind, a lightening of spirits which had been furtively depressed. Looking back on my feelings throughout those days, I believe the energy emanations of the aliens had been affecting me since I'd approached Page Springs, and I'd grown unconsciously accustomed to them. Now I felt joyous, light of heart, springy in mind. Marjorie came to me from the scene of her last fight and wrapped her arms around me. I held her. All over the wrecked complex our people were acting as if they were finally able to take a breath and relax from the nightmare.

Our instincts proved true. We had won. The Invisibles were gone, departed from our minds, vanished from the Earth, as we shortly learned. In another hour an avalanche of military vehicles and troops charged into Page Springs, our first realization that the barrier was down. Indeed, save for the trampled remnants of alien technology, no evidence remained, or was ever found, that the invaders had even existed. I suppose it would be that way. It's fairly certain they didn't have bodies of their own, so once flung out of ours they had no place to go except Hell. I guess we did for them.

We were safe, we citizen soldiers, and the world was safe. That's all. I don't know any more about those grim days than anybody else, don't know as I ever will. That's the whole story of my war against the Invisibles.

THE DIARY OF PHILIP WYLER

From the notes of Professor Anton Vorchek, author of *Cryptica*, etc.)

It is a curious tale that I here report, one providing few definite answers, but many entertaining questions, of a sort dear to the hearts of students of the weird and the mysterious. There has come into my possession the diary, along with a few personal effects in the form of enclosed private photographs, of a man named Philip Wyler, who for a period of some months several decades ago kept an account of his life and observations in a bulky loose-leaf notebook. He opens thusly with an entry dated May 25, 1947:

"I begin this strange record of recent and unfolding events because I have reason to believe something dreadful, something monstrous, is going on here. Even now, after all this time, I can't be certain of anything, but the implications are staggering, for me, for the world. From this point I must keep track daily of all odd occurrences, until I have enough information to justify action."

Note that this is not the typical diary, the formless study of an obscure life, but a history with a purpose. Mr. Wyler had experienced something which he feels obligated to set down for posterity, therefore he writes. In order to understand the context of his writings, one must know a little more about himself and his situation. Fortunately he provides a bit of this in a sort of preamble, which also serves to bring the reader up to date on the matters which plagued him.

Philip Wyler was a commercial writer, one of that breed of advertising men, copyists and proofreaders who earn a living from putting into legible, coherent form the ideas and scribblings of others. I take it that he garnered a fair income via this method; approaching middle age, I suppose, with a wife, Margaret, and three children, the older boy well into adolescence, yet there is no sense throughout his chronicle of financial hardship. That January he had taken a position in the public relations department of a major company, the Fairbank Processing Corporation, located in southeastern Arizona, which firm had to do with treating certain chemicals, or chemically treating other substances, for sundry mining related activities. It was a big operation, with a sprawling central complex marked by two perpetually steaming smokestacks, surrounded by the beginnings of suburban living quarters for the employees. While not an engineer himself, Mr. Wyler took it upon himself to learn more than the rudiments of the business, which knowledge enhanced the performance of his salaried task.

He lived with his people in company housing by the banks of the San Pedro River. Photographs inserted into the diary, stored inside envelopes within the notebook sleeves, show views of a modest frame house, typically sturdy architecture for the time, one snapshot exhibiting a quartet standing in front of the little yard: a smiling, pleasant-faced brunette wearing a simple flower-patterned dress with shoulder pads; three youngsters of various ages and sizes, the infant girl and the two boys; and a stout, sandy-haired fellow who is surely the diarist. He tells us little in his initial summary of family matters or job concerns, save to note that all seemed well. Mr. Wyler evidently preferred to get to the meat of his narrative.

The first evocative incident occurred (as he later established, after he began to worry) on February 27th. That afternoon one of the head engineers, a gentleman named Benjamin Garcia, suffered a spastic seizure which caused him to collapse, twitching and moaning, while crossing the secretarial offices. A crowd of concerned women gathered; Mr. Wyler happened to be passing as a team of company executives pushed through the onlookers with the senior company doctor, a Dr. Withers, who dragged on a rolling cart a steel canister with rubber hoses and face mask. The mask was applied to the sufferer's mouth and nose, the tubes connected, gas pumped from the canister. Within seconds Mr. Garcia had recovered, apologized for his public display, gone about his business. In subsequent weeks he was occasionally observed drawing breath from a curiously complicated inhaler.

In the minutes immediately following the engineer's attack Mr. Wyler noticed something which struck him as odd, although he read nothing major into it at the time. The cart with the canister had been left behind. Perusing this, it struck him that the metal cylinder was marked with a red circle at the top, precisely like the labeling of certain canisters which contained powerful industrial chemicals. Puzzled by what seemed a lapse in company regulations, he casually turned, ever so slightly, the knurled wheel on top and sniffed at the forthcoming vapors, expecting, under the circumstances, the odorless emission of oxygen or similar healthy agent. Instead he whiffed, and quickly drew back from, the unmistakably acrid odor of sulfuric acid gas, a deadly poison, and exactly what he had understood the red marking to signify. He could not fathom this discovery, could only wonder idly how the canisters had been switched so fast under the circumstances. Certainly Mr. Garcia had not inhaled, nor benefited from inhaling, that incredibly toxic substance.

So it began, the little things, the rare but recurrent situations giving rise to questions and dismay. On March 23rd, called to attend an office meeting related to sales promotion, Mr. Wyler observed both chief engineers, as well as the vice-president in charge of operations, using the odd inhalers. He contrived to ask the doctor about this, expressing wonder that so many company men should suffer from similar ailments, opining that the air in the vicinity of the complex must be bad. Dr. Withers brusquely dismissed the concern, stating that several employees were prone to severe allergies of a sort quite common in that region, where the close presence of pollinating flora from river bottom, low desert and high mountain forest could foster troublesome physical reactions. The ad man accepted this, though he pondered the nature of an allergy that exclusively struck important officials.

Already, on March 14th, another discovery had intrigued him. There were two conical buildings on site, very much different in structure from all others, joined by a covered and enclosed walkway, all fashioned of cement, with single doors in each building but no windows, the entire mini-complex surrounded by a gated chain-link fence. The diary contains a single photograph of both; interesting structures they may appear, though with no signage or other indications of function. Mr. Wyler had been told that dangerous chemicals were mixed and stored in these remarkable edifices, with no one being allowed to enter without authorization and need. One day he chose to do so, out of sheer curiosity, when FPC president, Arthur Cunningham, and his second head engineer, Morris Roberts, emerged and departed hastily, failing to secure the gate. Mr. Wyler amused himself with thinking that he merely sought to increase his useful knowledge of profitable processes. He managed to get into one building before he was stopped. The pointed-domed structure did not contain anything like what he had come to expect, at least not the large, central room that he glimpsed. An educated man, he recognized the scattered array of lights on the walls as forming a kind of planetarium, with minute lights representing stars and planets. Each light had inscribed beneath it (in bas relief, as I deduce from the description provided) a series of symbols which Mr. Wyler did not recognize, but which he guessed were scientific in nature. From its location in the astronomical set-up he determined which was the Earth, spied a series of fine wires stretching from it to another light far across the ceiling. He could not determine what that light was meant to be, given its position in the scheme which appeared to place it, as he grasped the logic of the display, beyond the Solar System.

This much he saw, but no more, for at that moment two armed guards appeared from an inner chamber and rudely hustled him outside. Mr. Wyler's congenial snooping caused a storm, first with his immediate superior (referred to only as Seabright), then with the company's upper echelon. He feared, on the instant, that he was to be fired. No less a worthy than Cunningham intervened, counseled discretion and coolness, urged the inquisitive subordinate not to worry, but to obey rules in the future. The big boss asked many questions of him relating to what had been seen, then with an air of graciousness explained all. Mr. Wyler was informed that he had glimpsed an abstract, schematic layout of nationwide company installations and suppliers, with wires linking those which required regular commerce with one another. Mr. Wyler nodded and smiled and agreed with everything he heard, only in his heart he doubted the whole presentation. He had seen what was in there, and he had paid visits to planetaria in the past, and he could not shake the conclusion that the strange building contained something more in line with his conceptions than anything he was being told, regardless of the eminence of the source.

It had only been luck that got him that far; Mr. Wyler never entered the building again, nor did he ever have a chance to penetrate its twin. Conversation with a neighbor—this man identified as "Mike", a long-time employee whose son played with the Wyler boys—led to the theory that the second conical structure contained

70

"what might be radio or radar equipment." Mike had seen such instruments being carried in during the construction of the unusual buildings. "He told me," wrote the diarist, "they were erected at the end of the war, when new management took over. New management indeed; who are they, and who do they work for?" With this statement he anticipates himself. He relates that Mike now considered the plant "a strange place to work," that he and others were puzzled by the behavior and methods of the recent owners. "He said there were fewer restrictions during the war."

I have two snapshots from the notebook providing views of the San Pedro River as it appeared then. The first extends from the old road bridge to the railroad crossing, the second from the elevated track to a point facing north up the river. In those days the heavily utilized watercourse resembled a nondescript canal, its banks straight and narrow. On the evening of April 18th Mr. Wyler claimed to have experienced a weird adventure at the scene of the photographs. Taking a stroll with his younger son Bobby (which gave the father an opportunity to mull over a fresh marketing ploy), they crossed under the railway trestle where it rose above the bottomland, then halted abruptly at sight of the river. Something was going on in the water. The surface frothed, seethed, followed by the irruption of three distinct, faintly luminous objects which rose into the air and drifted or soared above the cottonwoods before disappearing from view in the direction of the facility. Mr. Wyler described them as glassy or very shiny metallic globes. Of course he had never seen the like before, would have doubted his senses had not his son also seen the apparitions. The adult chose to say nothing of the experience, counseled his son likewise to silence, but he learned that his advice had been ignored. About two weeks later he overheard the boy bragging to friends about his knowledge of "big bubbles in the water," and within days the stretch of river adjoining the plant had been "closed by administrative authority" due to unspecified health hazards. The territory was heavily patrolled, and Mr. Wyler never saw the river again save from the road bridge, which naturally could not be closed.

At this time the author's ideas concerning the place and its doings become truly interesting, as well as bizarre. The last paragraph of his summary reads: "It's crazy, but I can make everything fit. I thought of spies, or secret government work, but none of that will do. I laugh at myself when I imagine another possibility. I've read Wells, and some other stuff in that vein. This isn't the same, but I can make the connection. What if they're Martians? What if those in charge of this project are extra-terrestrial beings, disguised as men, living among us and acting for ends of their own? It really explains everything. When they get sick, or can't tolerate our atmosphere any longer, they need a whiff of their own air, which is poison gas to us, not much different from the stinking smoke that belches daily from the stacks. Maybe they spew that stuff deliberately, because it suits them. They come from another planet, with which they must communicate; the purpose of the two buildings. They are masters of strange machines or devices, like the San Pedro globes. I can almost believe it. If it isn't something like that, then I'm going nuts . . . but Bobby saw his "bubbles." I won't forget that."

Mr. Wyler, in his first daily entry dated May 26th, informs us that he had a long heart to heart talk the previous night with Mike, whom he felt he could trust. Apparently his friend did not take well to esoteric hypotheses; certainly this one left him cold. "He says there's a rational explanation for everything. Big factories these days are all spooky places, with lots of gizmos and goofy rules. He's seen it coming for years. Who understands everything these days? Each week we hear of amazing new developments, stuff that's secret one day, proclaimed the next. As for the river event, he says Bobby is more right than I. The company is constantly pouring junk into the water, lately more than ever, and it wouldn't surprise him if there are bubbles now and then. In the end he thought I was joking about Martians, pointing out how they'd have to get here somehow. 'An invasion would stand out like the toad. They'd come in rockets that everybody could see, not just appear here looking and talking like us. That simply wouldn't make sense.'"

Mike seems to have been a stolid, no nonsense sort, with sound ideas that did not cut the mustard, as they say, with Mr. Wyler. The diarist recorded faithfully his observations, which quickly acquired a darker tone. "June 2: Visitors at the plant—closed limousine, blackened windows, occupants never seen—stacks emit greenish, rancid vapors—no one ever seen such." "June 7: Mike dead, drowning accident—body fished from river—what was he doing there? He told me last weekend he'd been talking about our discussion. I didn't care for that." "June 9: Mike buried in sealed casket at the old cemetery on the hill down river. His family have been paid big bucks, are clearing out, Maggie reports." "June 15: New restrictions—running the place like a concentration camp—told my vacation put on hold; supposed to start next week. 'Big new campaign'—first I've heard of it—is it a blind? See what develops. I ask myself why they want to hold me here."

"June 30: They're being taken into the other dome." According to Mr. Wyler, individuals among the low level personnel ("those not of the inner circle") were being granted admittance singly for purposes which were either not specified, or for stated reasons which did not impress his suspicious mind. Even certain family members were being led within. All emerged in due course, and in each case the critical observer professed to find them changed. Their characters had altered subtly, their behaviors assumed a new and frightening cast. He thought them now moody, secretive, quietly hostile, and he convinced himself—states this more than once—that their freshly repulsive attitudes appeared directed chiefly against himself. He found himself increasingly alone, cut off from his fellow men, shunned by those who formerly welcomed his company. His speculations as to the import of all this attained new heights of wildness. The term "brainwashing" had not yet entered the public consciousness, but what he deduced sounds like a forerunner of that idea. Human minds were being modified or controlled or replaced for sinister reasons. The indoctrination or alteration of mentality included a prohibition on congress with him. From July 23rd: "Why do they not take me? Perhaps awareness breeds resistance. After all, they killed Mike. Maybe he believed more than he let on."

Mr. Wyler resolved to get out with his family before the perceived danger overwhelmed him. As he tells it, he waited too late. "July 29: Sat down with Maggie and tried to make her understand. Before I began talking realized something was wrong. Her facial features—posture repelled—her silent indifference, utterly uncharacteristic, gave rise to hideous thoughts. Such a good mother, but she held Katie like a sack of potatoes. Asked her if she'd been inside. She said, 'What of it? It's a marvelous presentation.' Demanded that Phil, Jr. stay to hear. He refused, bluntly, left the room when I ordered him back. Maggie admitted he had accompanied her. Dread that they are lost to me.

"Later: They're packed and leaving, all of them. Maggie said they're going to her parents, but it's a lie. She took the kids in the good car, but didn't turn onto the road at the end of the lane—turned left, into the complex—saw the car parked at the far end of the project—leaving me, but not leaving them."

EERIE ARIZONA

The final entry, from August 6th: "Alone among these strangers. They become more blatant with each passing day. I've learned all I can—can't remain here—will head back east, talk to someone, anyone. I'll slip out like a thief in the night." On that ambiguous note the diary concludes. No marginal notation, no inclusion, hints at a date subsequent to that entry. One must turn to other evidence in order to determine whether or not Mr. Wyler followed through on his plan, or even whether the forces he professed to fear intervened.

The diary rests on the desk at my side. It is genuine, by which I mean that I have had its physical substance tested: paper, ink, brand of notebook, the material of the photographs; and it holds up as an authentic document of the period. What is the earnest researcher to make of such a manuscript? Perhaps the initial response should be to deem it a private joke, or the rantings of a disordered mind. Beyond that stage, what endeavor serves? Clearly one must investigate, to the extent that evidence allows, in order to seek confirmation or falsification. That is the scientific way. In our later, more credulous times, one could create a popular career out of peddling such material uncritically. That is not my way.

I have formed a general theory, built upon a foundation of arcane and murky cases, which appeals to me, though I can not establish its verity. It tickles my fancy, if you like. My theory is this: the world and the universe in which we precariously exist is both more impossibly complex, and more impossibly strange, than conventional notions of truth and reality have ever prepared us for. There are things that can not be which are, things that must be which are not, and what we consider normality is merely the infinitesimal dividing line between the two. That which exists does so though we refuse to conceive it; forthright answers fail us though they scream out for acceptance. I have seen this pattern in my work over and again, until I have reached the point, in a given case, that I no longer seek solution, but only meticulous description.

This is true in the case of the tale told by Mr. Wyler. Naturally I have pondered, have investigated. His story is old now, a matter for historical analysis. Given the truth of his claims, what consequences for the future, the future from the standpoint of 1947, should one deduce? Martians, or mysterious aliens in general, have not obviously taken over or even made themselves definitely known. The history flowing from the diary is not overtly our history. On that basis alone most would dismiss it as the product of a broken mind.

74

I have taken the matter further. I looked up the Fairbank Processing Corporation. There is copious information available, none of it remarkable, in the Phoenix Court of Records. I sifted those papers with my own hands. FPC, founded 1912, established in Fairbank, Arizona (which was a formally incorporated city for a while), operating in conjunction with mining facilities in Bisbee, Benson, and Sierra Vista; later expansion as a regional concern; so much could be expected. I find itemized statements referring to lucrative government contracts from 1942 to 1945; again, all is proper. Much is made, in happy fashion, of the change of ownership in 1946, and there are indications of sadness seeping from the papers in later years, leading up to 1972, when the company closed its doors. Yes, the Fairbank Processing Corporation is no more. Some holdings were bought out at that time, but the main plant at Fairbank, on the banks of the San Pedro River, was abandoned. Where is the cosmic conspiracy to be gleaned from this dry account?

Lately I visited the site. Few traces remain. The old bridge on the road to Sierra Vista, and the rusting tracks on the forgotten trestle, appearing much as they did in the photographs, still cross the river, but little else may be discerned. The location has been absorbed by the San Pedro River Conservation Area, a federal preserve devoted to rejuvenating the pristine splendor of that riparian region. A relatively recent newspaper report, from which I kept a clipping, describes the dynamiting of the ancient smokestacks as part of the land reclamation strategy. The river, released from its civilized stranglehold, has been allowed to assume its natural, winding course, while the animals and the birds have crept back in. They have crept into the old factory and town as well. Fairbank is a ghost town, a collection of tottering wooden structures, a couple of standing stone edifices, and much Twentieth Century debris. There are no Martians there, no concealed spaceships—at least I do not think so—no freakish machinery to astound and defy the researcher. I found two large concrete circles within the sagging old gate of the former plant, less than foundations, items which prove that interesting structures stood there, yet nothing to support a lurid tale. Records do refer to the twin storage domes used for hazardous chemicals. Should not that be good enough? Our world remains intact, in some ways better than it has been, while the FPC is gone.

I could leave it there, save for one blasphemous, infuriating finding, of a sort that must forever stump me, yet which must ever nag at the logical centers of my brain. There is a mystery, one I do not like. To this day I can not verify the former existence of the man Philip Wyler. I have entirely failed to turn up any documentary evidence of such a fellow having lived and worked for the Fairbank Processing Corporation, nor of his subsequent history. This is the single most peculiar aspect of the case, for all who live in this age are smothered in a web of revealing paperwork. All who breathe in the civilized world leave fingerprints where ever they go. I have looked everywhere. The diary is frustratingly reticent about the fellow's background (no surprise, for it was never intended to stand on its own), but the company records survive in apparent completeness, and there are county records, state records, national records, all of which should tell a confirming tale. Old FPC files contain references to names incorporated within the account: there was a company president named Arthur Cunningham, engineers Benjamin Garcia and Morris Roberts, a Dr. Withers, a Seabright; deceased now, they live on in faded text, but there is no Philip Wyler listed in the rolls from that period or any other. Government files exhibit the same impossible lack of what should be routine data. By the way, while various "Mikes" worked for the corporation then, there is no supporting documentation to show that one died of any cause within the period in question. What of him; what of the diarist Philip Wyler, writer of advertising copy, his wife Margaret, their three children?

Thus stands the case. The diary came into my possession as the result of a bequest from a colleague, since passed on, a fellow researcher into the extraordinary who held it among his papers. Nothing in his collection, now part of my own, clarifies its provenience. No evidential pathway remains open to me. Stark mystery reigns supreme.

AMONG THE HOODOOS

So the fall of evening found me in my little rented car creeping up that icy road in the Chiricahua Mountains, far from the welcome lights of civilization, smothered in darkness save for the stabbing illumination of the vehicle's headlights. They showed me the narrow blacktop passage dead ahead, peaked around winding corners and picked out overhanging branches of the pressing, shadow-shifting trees that huddled despairingly in the snow. It was cold in that car, though I was heavily bundled, and colder outside, the cruel, clutching kind of cold that breathes frost on the windshield between swipes of the wipers. I could only make it up there because a snow plow had gone before me at some point in time, maybe a day or a week before, rendering the lane barely negotiable. I cringed when the asphalt gave way to dirt, but it was hard-packed frozen earth, and I didn't have to decrease my already pathetic speed. The directions received via prior communications proved accurate—I knew where I was—and shortly I pulled above the gloomy tree-line onto a wide, undulating plateau.

From there I could see a far ways. The stars gleamed above me, quite a lot of them; dim heaps of mountain crouched at the limit of vision like quiescent prehistoric beasts; and a lone, bright light burned directly ahead atop a steep mound. As predicted, the now straightened road carved an arrow's path to that spot, as did I. I'd traveled a great distance to reach it, counting on the effort proving lucrative. As I neared it I thought for a moment that the trees encroached again, for large black shapes came at me from both sides. Then I thought for an instant they weren't trees but something more, living things of unexpected size oddly in motion, only that was nonsense, for they didn't move, and they were just rocks, stone figures like the fabrications of a mad sculptor's worst nightmares. That fit too; I had heard that this was a picturesque locale.

I pulled into a big clearing among the weird stones, saw a few trees, a few cars, and a couple of structures. One, surely my destination, was an old two-story house of wood with many shuttered windows, bar the one on the upper floor from which the glaring light radiated. I guessed that house had been there since the olden days. It had that look to it, like something dropped out of a ghost town, only it looked a little bit lived in. The other structure suggested the ephemeral, a metallically shining trailer hitched to a big, clunky prime mover. That stuff was certainly new.

I parked with the other cars, got out, scouted the place, checking by habit for anything out of the ordinary. I didn't expect trouble, but in my business it pays to be wary. I carried two items of consequence on my person, one of them being a gun (again, habit), which need not come into play should that night prove profitable for all concerned. I trudged to the door with my penlight activated, following a sort of path in the snow, shook off the clinging powder from my boots on the porch. No buzzer, so I put to quaint use that old-fashioned brass knocker. Counting puffs of vapor from my nose and mouth, I reached nine before the door squeaked open.

There appeared in a bath of yellow electric glow a frumpy old woman with stringy long gray hair, too much make-up, and an unflattering purple dress dangling rhinestones from every fringe. I snapped off the flashlight. "I'm here to see Mr. Thrushwaite," I said.

She pointed a fat finger at me, said in a whiny old voice, "Are you the one? Did you bring . . . it?" I don't hand out information to anyone, so I fired back a question, "Who are you, the housekeeper?" She got all huffy and stuffy on me, snapped, "Certainly not. Our host has dispensed with the hired help. Well, there's Hugo, of course. Otherwise there are only guests here. Young fellow, I am Madame Larisha. I hope that name means something to you."

It didn't. I brusquely pushed past her into the hall. I was freezing out there. It was deliciously warm inside. I threw off my jacket onto a lacquered wooden chair, unbuttoned my jacket, kept it on. It contained my goodies. "Tell Thrushwaite I'm here," I said, "or tell this Hugo to tell him. I don't care. I'm Harrow, John Harrow, and I'm here by request to complete our financial transaction."

Madame Larisha seemed thrilled by my news, but she didn't push me anymore. Instead she led me around a turn of the hall to a door opening into a large, inviting room. "Wait here," she said. "Our host will join us shortly. I will let him know of your arrival."

Unless he was a dope he already knew, but I could wait a little longer. I entered the room. It was a combination den and library I guess, very cozy, much ornamentation and antique furniture, a crackling fireplace, lots of books in shelves along three walls. The reading material didn't look like current best sellers. In a comfortable seat by the fire slouched an astounding beautiful young girl, a petite blonde who might have stepped out of a fashion magazine, smoking a cigarette and languidly flicking through the pages of a book. She casually dropped the volume on the floor and turned bored eyes upon me. She looked, shrugged, said in a pretty voice, "You're the courier, I suppose."

"Sure enough. I'm Jonathan Harrow, sweetie, and pleased to make your acquaintance. I didn't expect anyone like you here."

"Neither did I," she drawled. I could tell she was already tuning me out. That annoys me.

I sat down in a matching chair opposite her. It felt good. With the chill leaving my bones, another need loomed large. "I could use a bite to eat, babe," I said. "How do I arrange that?"

"You don't. Mr. Thrushwaite will in a few minutes."

"You got a cigarette?"

"I have plenty, thank you."

I had my own. "Do you know what this is all about?" I persisted.

"No."

Okay, I got the point. I got up, intending to wander as I pleased, met a big guy coming through the hall door. I didn't get out of his way, he didn't move out of mine. We faced each other, I with studied belligerence, he with what seemed honest amusement. He was tall, mature, lean but solid, immaculately dressed like a true gentleman. I don't meet many of those. He wore an expensive suit, a soft, clean hat, and his boots were polished leather, the real deal. He had a little manicured beard, a hawk nose, and eagle eyes. He said, "You must be our important visitor. We have ardently awaited your arrival." He spoke with a tinge of foreign accent, but his English was better than mine.

I said, "Thrushwaite, let's get it over with, do the deal, and I'll clear out."

The girl snickered. The man replied, "A case of inappropriate identification, sir. I am Vorchek, Professor Anton Vorchek, invited here as were you. Miss Delaney, whom I presume you have met, accompanies me. Our host calls for dinner. He is, as of this moment, aware of your presence, and will surely see you."

"He'd better," I growled. This was too much time wasting. Still, "I'm starved," I announced. "Lead the way, Professor."

The Delaney babe, who I soon learned was named Theresa, fell in behind us as we wended down a couple of corridors to a cramped dining room (made bearable by a space heater) separated by a counter from the kitchen. Madame Larisha was already seated at table, which had settings for four. "One other, Hugo," Vorchek said to a short, chunky, mean-looking goon behind the counter. The goon ignored him. I plopped myself down at an empty plate. Another guy entered from the hall. He was kind of old, really skinny, dried up, with glaring eyes, shabby. He wasn't a patch on Vorchek, but I figured him before he nasally cried, "I'm Lawrence Thrushwaite. You're Harrow?" "Yeah." "Do you have it?" "Yeah." "Let me see it."

"Let me see what you've got," I said coolly.

"Come upstairs."

"After dinner," I responded.

Thrushwaite rolled his eyes, motioned to the goon. "Hugo, serve them. I'll not eat." He stood by me, pulled a roll of bills from his jacket pocket, pushed it at my face. "Here, it's all there. Now give it." I took the money without counting it. Maybe later, but they were the right denominations of bills, and it was a big wad. I reached into my jacket and pulled out a modest, flat package, taped in brown paper. Thrushwaite seized it, scuttled to the counter. Hugo served a passable beef stew with salad, placed a bottle on the table. We helped ourselves to the wine.

Hugo receded into the kitchen, clattering dirty cookware. Theresa chowed down, I coming up a close second. Vorchek fussed with his food. The old bag watched Thrushwaite. He tore paper, talked to himself.

"This is it," he muttered. "I know this thing. The description matches, the materials are genuine. The base metal is gold, the jewels perfect green emeralds. The inscriptions are as foretold by my sources. I hold it in my hands. Madame Larisha, we may commence."

Vorchek swallowed a tiny bite, leaned over confidentially and said to me, "Many men have sought that prize, Mr. Harrow. I wonder how you came by it."

"Don't ask me," I said. "I'm just the delivery boy. That's my trade, how I pay my bills—big bills—I deliver goods, no questions asked. Talk to your buddy."

"I wonder," Vorchek continued, "about the current health of the former owner."

"I wouldn't know," I said. "Drop it. That's not part of the deal."

"Thrushwaite said, "Let it lie, Vorchek. That's no concern of yours. What matters is that I possess the legendary Cross of Xenophor, and that you can translate the words written on it. Look at it, Vorchek."

The professor turned in his seat, appraising the object with a glance. For the first time I saw it. It was a beauty, about nine inches by four, studded with winking gems both lengths, with lots of ornate scratchings in the gold. That didn't resemble any writing I knew, but then I guess it wouldn't, given what I'd just heard. It looked a valuable piece of merchandise, much fancier than anything else I'd seen in the house. Maybe Thrushwaite kept his collection in the trailer.

Our host left us then, curtly calling Hugo after him. Madame took off after them shortly thereafter. Vorchek came across as a decent sort, even if I wasn't especially tempted to trust him, so I casually asked, "What goes on? Is Thrushwaite a hot shot smuggler?"

Vorchek chuckled. "Heavens, no. He is a student of the occult. Madame Larisha is his close colleague. The cross is an ancient talisman, reputed to possess great power. I dare say they mean to try it out."

I grinned. "You're kidding?"

"He's not," Theresa said loudly, with warm emphasis. "The professor wouldn't get involved with such weirdoes if he didn't think there was something real going on."

Vorchek smiled, very pleasantly. "You know me too well, my dear. Sir, having received my invitation, and the reason for it, I chose to come in order to establish two facts: the genuineness of the fabled cross, and the use to which it will be put. The first point I consider adequately confirmed. Thoracrates, in his *Dark Jubilations*, describes well his hoary find, considerately incorporating a detailed drawing."

"He one of your friends?"

"A remote colleague, long deceased. He, and others, write of the object's curious properties. Mr. Thrushwaite intends to test it. How, I do not yet know."

"Good enough," I said, pushing away my plate. "I'm out of here."

"Good riddance," whispered Theresa, hunched over her bowl of stew. I ignored that crack, got up with every intention of dashing out.

"Do not be in a hurry, young man," advised a genial Vorchek. "You may find much to amuse you here in the days to come."

"No chance. I never stay put for long. That's not good for business, you see."

"Pause, briefly," he said, "to look out the window, and you may see."

I frowned, obeyed, stared with mounting anger and frustration at the sight I beheld. Snow was coming down in buckets, and I realized now that I'd been hearing for some time the whipping of wind. It was outright storming. No chance, I realized, of ever negotiating that tricky road in these conditions.

I swore. Theresa blinked, laughed out loud. I said, "Thrushwaite will have to put me up until morning."

Vorchek said, "At the very least. Have no fear, for there is plenty of room to accommodate you, nor do we lack for essentials."

Thanks for nothing. Getting to brass tacks, I eventually crossed paths with Thrushwaite again, he being mighty disturbed that I was still there, becoming a deal more so when I made it plain I was to be another guest for an indeterminate while. He acquiesced because he had to, but he made it real clear that it wasn't what he wanted. I got to bunk in a crappy downstairs room that, so Hugo told me, was the handyman's quarters. That was the first time I'd heard the voice of Thrushwaite's ape. That's how I thought of him. I sensed danger there. His voice was heavy, coarse, uneducated.

So I spent the night. I rose early, as is my way, dressed with every layer I'd brought and went outdoors. The sky had cleared, looked an intense blue, the air biting cold. Snow lay thick on everything, a charming wintry scene that curdled my mood. My car sat axle deep in the stuff. I wasn't getting out and back to civilization until somebody with heavy duty machinery unburied the road. I meant to ask about that pronto.

Only now did I realize what a strange place I was in. The old-timey house on the hill with the thicket of spruce pressing close was dramatic enough, but there were other features to this terrain that truly startled. It was as if we were surrounded by an army of huge stone monsters. In every direction, save for the house and the trailer,

I spied ominously suggestive shapes of rock standing tall, much taller than a man, wearing wigs of snow and leering with implacable hostility. That last was a foolish conceit, yet many of the formations, with their odd protuberances and cracked lines, did appear to possess harsh, rough faces. I felt enclosed by enemies, a rotten feeling under those conditions.

Vorchek said, "Majestic, is not it?"

I spun round to face him, surprised that I hadn't detected his approach. He had come out right behind me, heavily dressed for the occasion, still looking smart. I asked, "What is all this, Professor?"

"Behold the wonders of the Chiricahua Mountains, young man. Millions of years of volcanic activity built up dense masses of hard deposits, millions more eroded them into the intriguing shapes you see. Quite attractive in their own way, I grant you, though cruel to the overly imaginative, like denizens of a nightmare."

"They're just rocks," I said.

"Hoodoos, Mr. Harrow," Vorchek replied. "This type of mineral structure is colloquially referred to as hoodoo. Whoever invented the term was also spooked by them."

"I'm not spooked."

"Come to breakfast, sir. We may leave our stony friends to their own devices. They do not mind. They are extraordinarily patient."

The professor and his girlfriend, if that's what she was, were whipping up a meal for themselves in the kitchen, a little feast to which I was invited. Over breakfast we talked. Vorchek asked a lot of seemingly casual questions at first, I infrequently responding. Theresa, who looked mighty fetching so early, said bluntly, "You've got to be some kind of criminal." "A malicious accusation," I said. "What are the charges?" She snipped a slice of crisp bacon with her perfect teeth, said, "Robbery and smuggling." "False in both particulars. I don't care for the authorities hanging over my shoulder, and I take it hard if somebody gets in my way, but I walk the line, just enough to get by. That keeps me healthy and free."

Vorchek said, "An admirable philosophy, sir, one of which I can approve, within limits. At times the deed requires an unconventional approach. I am aware of the necessity."

"Are you ever," muttered the girl.

The professor chuckled. He did that a lot, making me think other people tended to amuse him. That was probably why he kept her around, if not for the obvious. He said now, a little more soberly,

"I hope, Mr. Harrow, that you have not bitten off too much on this occasion."

"Call me John," I advised. She subsequently did at whiles, he never; the stuffy, prim and proper kind of guy. I said, "I'm here on business, that's all, no great mystery. Not that it really matters, but I wonder what's in it for you."

He told me, "Why, business, of course, what else? Does not it always come down to that? Mr. Thrushwaite has embarked upon unusual research, with lofty goals in mind. He wishes, with the aid of his kindred spirit Madame Larisha, to test the veracity of a most peculiar Indian legend. They require my services to translate the inscriptions on that valuable object which you brought. I have already been paid a princely sum to do just that."

I grinned, shook my head. Lighting a cigarette, I stabbed in the dark, said, "That won't do. You could work from your comfortable office. You and your sweetie don't have to rot in this freezing wasteland."

Theresa started to sneer, but Vorchek cut her off with a booming laugh. "Excellent, sir. Our host recommended precisely that. I chose to come here, and Miss Delaney kindly agreed to accompany me. I wish to observe the proceedings."

"What's going to happen?"

"Why not ask the learned Madame?"

She had entered from the hall. "I will accept a cup of coffee," she said wearily. I didn't guess she'd been to sleep. She was dressed in a ragged robe, her slippers flopping on the wooden floor. "What are you talking about, Vorchek?"

"Matters of grave consequence, perhaps," he replied. "Mr. Harrow is keen to learn of our affairs."

"That is none of his concern," Madame Larisha said. "He shouldn't even be here. His presence fosters complications."

"Sorry, lady," I sneered. "I'm unavoidably detained. Have your boss call a helicopter for me."

Then Thrushwaite came in, fully dressed. "Are we ready?" he snapped. He dismissed the suggestion of breakfast, whining, "No time for trivialities. There's work to do. Vorchek, I want you now. The cross is in the laboratory, where it will remain. Do what I've paid you to do." The professor nodded, rose. Thrushwaite added, "Madame Larisha, let us repair upstairs to continue preparing our notes. You two—" he meant Theresa and me—"amuse yourselves.

Keep out of the way."

When all had vacated the room except the girl and myself, we went on with our meals. I attempted to engage her in small talk, chatting archly in my customary way, but she wasn't having any of it. I didn't appeal to her at all. That was a shame, because I could have given her a squeeze. Finally she dumped her dirty dishes in the sink, announcing, "I'm checking out the lab. At least the professor's a familiar face. Interested?" Scarcely, but it was better than suffocating boredom. When she was ready I trooped along after her.

The girl led me outside, then to the trailer. So, that was the center of operations. The door was locked, but Theresa's banging brought a prompt response from the sole occupant. The affable Vorchek let us in, seemed wholly unconcerned by our intrusion. In fact, "Enter and welcome," he said, puffing languidly on his pipe. "This is a cold and lonely edifice. I would rather talk to you youngsters than to myself."

The place was a standard trailer, like somebody might live or travel in, but it had been turned into an office of a sort, with papers and books scattered willy-nilly, and other stuff that presumably justified the designation of laboratory. On a built-in counter and an installed desk I saw rock samples, a strewn assortment of picks and other tools, and the cross, the Cross of Xenophor which I had conveyed from a far land to these odd people. Vorchek resumed his seat in a swivel chair before the thing at the desk, without further word began scanning old documents, studying the cross, scribbling in a notebook. Theresa sat by him, I remaining standing. Shortly he commenced to mumble, "Thoracrates did not lie. This is powerful magic, if that be the proper term. This can truly make big things happen. I wonder," Vorchek continued, speaking louder, "if this can connect with the Apache tales."

"The cross hails from Europe," I pointed out. "It can't relate to anything here."

Vorchek looked at me, said, "That remains to be seen, Mr. Harrow. Europe—Hungary, I believe?—" I nodded stupidly—"is merely a way station in this object's long and mysterious career. I know quite a bit about it, you see, although I have never laid eyes on it until now. It was known in the Rome of the Caesars, referenced by Egyptian scribes of the elder dynasties, reputed to antedate them by half-forgotten eons. If the olden account of Jacob Bleek be accepted, then no less a scholar of antiquity than Maltheus the Wise placed its creation at the hands of the Rhexellite wizards who plumbed the arcane arts millennia before the history we know. This cross has been practically everywhere. Even if this be the first time it has graced our shores, its power holds true where ever it resides."

"Thank you for explaining everything," Theresa said in a deliberately silly voice. She shook her head. "I still don't get, Professor, what it's supposed to do."

"Open a gate," Vorchek replied, "which has been shut for almost as long as the memory of man recalls. Here is the simple version of the story. The Chiricahua Apaches, who once dwelt in these mountains, told tales to the first Spanish chroniclers who accompanied the Conquistadors, tales derived from still earlier tribes who lived here until the later migrants destroyed them. They considered these mountains a holy place, a magical land touched by the Gods. They believed that among these peaks existed one of the Gateways of the Gods, those curious, mythical portals through which the celestial Great Ones pass from Their unimaginable domain into our own. From the outer dimensions They could come and go as They pleased, and also could a clever man, one steeped in ancient lore, utilize the passage into the unknown if those Others allowed. There are legends, often rather grim ones, of such traffic.

"However, we are told, via differing oral formulations, that the Gods took offense at evil deeds, or were angered by hubris, or acted through sheer maliciousness, and that they punished horribly the ancient ones who worshipped Them at the Gate, and They sealed the Gate, and They placed at the closed entrance a frightful guardian, an entity of virulently nasty power called into being by the Gods for the sole purpose of defending the opening against any who would henceforth seek to disturb it. So terrible is the creature that it can not be bested by mortal means, nor will it condescend to treat with those who would implore its forbearance. Therefore, since primordial eras the Gate has been shut, likely to remain so, lacking extraordinary measures."

"But the cross is that measure," Theresa cried.

Vorchek said blandly, "That is currently the working assumption around these parts."

"It's rubbish," I blurted. "I still don't catch the connection. You can't possibly believe all that. I mean, you're a professor." I paused significantly. "You really are, aren't you?"

He grinned, leaned back in his chair, stroked his beard. "More or less."

"Well then, you ought to know better. What difference does the cross make?"

"Not just any cross, sir, but the Cross of Xenophor." Vorchek hefted the thing, turned it toward the light. That was a pretty bauble. "Behold," he said, "a surviving piece of Rhexellite sorcery from days of yore, dating so far back that conventional historians refuse to credit the possibility. My esoteric sources tell me that those primeval wizards fashioned a device, imbued with cosmic power, that in the hands of adepts would communicate with great Xenophor Himself, the Master of all power, the ultimate Power embodied."

"Never met the fellow," I sneered.

"I hope you never do," Vorchek replied, "if legend speaks true. No one ever wins any game in which Xenophor is a player."

Theresa said, "Thrushwaite obviously disagrees."

"The man cavalierly flirts with peril," said the professor, "if I do not mistake him. His intentions are obscure, but troubling."

"Why help him, then?" I asked.

Vorchek stared at me like I was an idiot child. "I want to know what is going to happen," he said.

Thrushwaite stormed in, his old lady in tow, ranting and raving like a lunatic. "Get them out of here," he said of Theresa and me, "and keep them out. They aren't part of this. I won't have you handing out my secrets."

Vorchek said patiently, "Before I may tell them all, you must first be more forthcoming with me. We must talk, sir. My labors for you are complete. Mr. Harrow, Miss Delaney, leave us now. Go out and enjoy the view." Before we left them Thrushwaite curtly informed me that a snow plow would have cleared the road by next morning.

That suited me fine. I figured that I was trapped with crazies, a category including Vorchek, and all I wanted was escape and the leisure to enjoy my loot. That left a dull day to kill. I didn't approach the trailer again, partly because Hugo guarded the door after that episode. Maybe I could handle him—I calculated the odds—but there was no need. I had a hot girl to talk up, but no matter what I said or did she gave me the cold shoulder. Her biggest problem lay in taking her pal Vorchek too seriously. If that sort impressed her, then I didn't have a chance.

The girl and I shared lunch with Madame Larisha, opening cans of spaghetti and heating the goop on an electric skillet. I found Thrushwaite's liquor stash, broke out a bottle of booze for us.

Madame hit it hard. I gathered from her loose comments that she was totally under Thrushwaite's spell, yet somewhat concerned about his plans, whatever they were. After lunch, to my surprise and distaste, she followed me outdoors as I filled the time with a modest hike about the frigid perimeter of the property. She actually took pains to make herself pleasant to me. I noted with amused disdain that she had applied her pancake makeup even more heavily.

I wandered through the snowy paths among the hoodoos, always keeping the house on its hill in sight, making no allowances for her earnest attempts to keep up. She managed. The vistas were all impossibly weird, with those hundreds of hideous stone giants frowning and leering down at me from every angle. They got under my skin. They never moved, of course, hadn't for a million billion years, but I got the feeling they were crowding me, closing in when I wasn't paying attention. I got to peeking out of the corner of my eye, trying to catch a motion that ceased the moment I observed directly. I knew that was stupid.

Madame noticed, snickered in her old, batty way, her breath smoking in condensing puffs. "The warriors of the guardian," she said. "That is what the red men called them. He sleeps under the house, surrounded by his servants, ready to act and to command them against those who would violate the gate. We must, therefore, command him, if we wish to triumph unscathed."

"Under the house?" I cried. "That's a spooky coincidence."

"Not at all. The rancher who raised the house a century ago put it there deliberately, to mock what he deemed a vile superstition. They say he came to a bad end. I believe that. Power rests unquietly beneath the mound. That is a curious formation in its own right, an upwelling of granite protruding through lava layers. So say the geologists. It is, in fact, the tomb or vault of the guardian, a fabrication of forces that stride between the spheres. He waits within, eager to come forth when necessary, or when called."

"You wouldn't want to wake him," I pointed out. "Just put him out of the way, if I understand you people correctly."

She chortled, "If you do." She sat down abruptly in a pile of snow, floundered, adding with a flutter of her hands, "That's why we took over the place, cheaply too. It is down there now, ready for us." I wondered what Thrushwaite thought of having a lush for his assistant. After I got her walking again I excused myself, dashed back to that wretched old house.

AMONG THE HOODOOS

When I arrived Vorchek and Thrushwaite were out in the lot shouting at each other. My host, at least, was engaged in a screaming match; the professor, to be fair, seemed to want to discuss quietly, but the other wouldn't have it. Thrushwaite yelled, "The key is mine, thanks to you. Only a fool would oppose me openly. I will have it up this dawn, and the gate will belong to me, and the power of the guardian. Then there's going to be some real changes in this world!" He stormed into the house.

Theresa appeared from the woodwork, joined Vorchek. So did I. "A falling out among thieves?" I said.

The girl said acidly to me, "The plow will reach us in another hour. Why don't you get lost at the earliest opportunity?"

"Your wish is my command."

"Reconsider, sir," said Vorchek. "The matter gets out of hand, quickly. Mr. Thrushwaite knows what he wants to know. Unfortunately, he is not the man to wisely utilize dangerous knowledge. He is, I discover at last, what I term an 'aggressive utopian.' He desires to grasp the ancient power dormant here, awaken it, master it for earth-shaking ends. Not since Thoracrates wielded the cross in the time of the Roman Emperor Egabalus has our planet seen such a transparent attempt at magically inspired enslavement. The power is genuine. The consequences of its unrestrained use are unknowable."

"I don't buy it," I stated, "and it has nothing to do with me. I have what I want."

"If he has his way," Vorchek pressed, "you may not rely on the ground beneath your feet. I implore you, Mr. Harrow, to stay with us another night, until this ugly business be resolved." About to object, my words were cut short by his hailing of Madame Larisha, who showed up just then. Vorchek demanded, "You must stop him, Madame. He has told me. Had I realized before, I would not have cooperated with this scheme."

She stopped short, smirked nastily. "Then it is well that you did not know. Mr. Thrushwaite is a great scholar, bold in mind and learning. He and I shall realize our dreams. Tonight we perform the ceremony of opening and awakening. Come the new day, the appointed tasks commence. That will be a hard time for our enemies."

"I am not your enemy—" Vorchek began.

"But you are, Professor," cried Thrushwaite from the porch.

Hugo stood behind him, a heap of grinning beef. "I can't allow you to interfere. Once it is done, you will crawl at my feet willingly. Until then, I must limit your activities. Hugo," he said in the tone of an order, "take them, Vorchek and his girl, take them to the rear storage room and lock them in." He glared at me. "That one too. Shut them in, keep them in."

What Theresa said at that point would have given me the giggles if I hadn't been so angry. Her spitfire protest didn't cause a quiver in the gun Hugo aimed at us. He snarled hoarsely, "Inside, all of you." To me especially he warned, "One move and I blast you."

I knew he was dangerous from the start, but I let him catch me flat-footed, with my pistol tucked under my effects in the servant's room. He had us for sure. I went stiffly, showing my hate, but I went, as did Vorchek and his honey. In a minute we were trapped inside a filthy hole, a kind of indoors shed with a single overhead bulb, rough benches, a collection of junk, a couple of shovels, one locked door and no windows. "It pays to keep alert," I grumbled.

"What happens now?" Theresa asked.

"I did not foresee this development," Vorchek admitted. "We are in a bad way. Mr. Thrushwaite and Madame Larisha will carry out the experiment with the cross. There is no reason—thanks to me!—that they should fail. If they do control the power of the guardian and the gate, they can do as they see fit, which is too ghastly to think upon."

"We'll figure a way out," I said. Minus the mumbo-jumbo, the situation was still little to my liking. I intended to break free, knock some heads together.

We rotted in there all afternoon. Occasionally Hugo jeered at us through the door, letting us know that his vigil continued. We heard when the snow plow arrived, the mechanical grinding of engine and gears that told me the road was finally clear. Then we heard the blasted thing drive away. Before dusk we heard something more, voices raised in unison, a cracked, warbling singing or chanting, sounding distant but distinct, recited in a foreign tongue. I knew those voices: Thrushwaite and the hag, acting out their nonsense in the trailer that lay near the wall of our dungeon.

Vorchek said, "The conjuration begins. It is going to happen." I replied, "Forget it, it's kid's stuff," but hard on my words something did happen. The room shook, a rocking vibration that traveled under us, swept away our balance. Theresa sat down hard, Vorchek grabbed a post, I went into a crouch. The sickening motion swayed us back and forth, as if we were on a ship at sea in gale force winds. Then it stopped, but quickly came more chanting, and a new sound, a noise like excavation underway somewhere below. I heard a rumbling, a sliding, a crashing of rock. "Vorchek said, "It is awake, and burrowing its way out of the mound."

"It can't be," I hissed.

Came yet another sound after an apparent pause, this emanating from the direction of the trailer: the sound of metal tearing, thin metal shredded into strips. Muffled gasps, more chanting, at a frenzied rate this time, and then I heard Thrushwaite's voice loudly barking unfamiliar words, speech in freaky syllables that gave me the creeps. Even more horrible was the voice that answered him.

I didn't understand a word of it, yet what I heard scared me more than it puzzled. Damn me, but that voice didn't sound human. I began to second guess myself concerning what everybody had been telling me all this time. I turned to Vorchek. He said, "We must escape from here now, or there is no hope."

"I'm convinced of that much," I said in a whisper. Still very quietly, I went on, "Here's the deal. We need food, see? We haven't eaten for hours. Kick up a fuss, keep at it until Hugo opens that door. You two stand over there in the corner. I'm asleep, see? I'm sick, I'm out of it. I'm here; don't look at me, don't talk to me. Ignore me completely. And you be sure to say when. Got it?"

"We get it," Theresa said. Vorchek nodded. We discussed the details until I knew they had it right.

They both went after the door with their fists, moaning and complaining. Hugo cursed them, he threatened them, finally—just to spare himself the grief, I'd guess—agreed to bring something. I made myself ready, folding myself up on a bench to the left of the door, face to the wall. My fellow prisoners assumed their station way to the right, seated at another bench, as far from me as they could go. We waited.

During those nerve-wracking moments I heard something else that gave me the willies. That other, that hideous voice spoke again. It hurt my ears. Vorchek muttered to Theresa, "It demands a fee. Payment must be offered and accepted. It will not cooperate without such." The professor could understand the lingo. That was no time for curiosity, but I burned to ask him what it wanted. I made out, barely, Thrushwaite agreeing—sounds of muted argument—then an awful, enduring scream in a scratchy female voice. At first calling up ideas of terror, the scream as it continued gave way to stark indications of monstrous pain. It trailed away into choking gasps, subsided into dreadful silence.

Footsteps, keys rattling at the door, and I heard the door rasp open. I pressed my face to the bench. I detected the odors of hot food, maybe soup. Hugo's uncouth voice said, "What's his problem?" Footsteps, a sharp poke in the back. "Get up, fool." I moaned, shifted a little. Hugo laughed gruffly. He said, with his voice turned away from me, "This will hold you, until it's all over."

Vorchek, very distinctly, said, "When."

I came up off the bench like a buzz saw, with a shovel in my hands. Hugo scarcely had time to react. I clipped him up the side of the neck and he went down like a dropped potato sack. A single big bowl of steaming liquid crap went spinning and splattering. His gun fired aimlessly, then bounced to the floor. A fast glance assured me he wasn't getting up again.

"Everybody okay?" I cried. They were. Both shot to their feet. Theresa asked plaintively, "What's been going on out there?" I cut her off, asking authoritatively as I collected Hugo's weapon, "Can either of you use a pistol?"

The girl stepped forward. "I'm an ace."

"Good. You know my room. Find my gun, and you two follow when you're able. I'll take this one."

Vorchek strode forward, took me by the arm. "What do you mean to do?"

"Ensure my safety." I checked the gun in hand, made certain it was primed.

Hard on the heels of my reply came the roaring of an engine, followed by the growl of machinery in motion. Vorchek reached for a flashlight and dashed past me into the hall. The girl and I raced after, caught up with him on the porch. I couldn't believe it. Thrushwaite's trailer was slowly trundling down the road. I noticed a big gash in the side facing us, where the thin siding had been torn away. It reminded me of what a mountain lion had once done to my tent.

"Look there," advised the professor. Something dark lay in the trampled snow by the edge of the house, near where the trailer had stood. We approached it. The thing was out of shape and fragmentary, yet from bits and pieces of clothing and a handful of face I recognized the remnants of Madame Larisha.

"Vorchek said, "He sacrificed her. Knowing him as I do now,

that may be the only reason he included her."

I sighed. What a place, what a bunch. I decided I needed a long vacation. "Anyway," I said, "we're all right. Call the police if you wish. I say we vacate the premises."

Theresa obviously preferred my plan, but she turned to her man for his response. He gazed at the body for long moments, then snapped alert. "Impossible!" he roared. "Understand this, Mr. Harrow, whether you believe it or not: the guardian is awake and aware, and active on our planet. Our insane host called it up to do his bidding. Look there, down the slope past the parking lot." My God, how had I missed that big hole, like the mouth of a tunnel, with chunks of solid rock scattered before it? Of course I knew: it hadn't been there before. Vorchek said, "It burrowed out of its granite shell, clawed into the trailer—perhaps the door was too small for it—treated with Mr. Thrushwaite, munching on Madame Larisha in the meantime. Now man and monster are driving away from us. With such power at his beck, why would he run?"

"Thrushwaite heard the shot," Theresa opined, "and maybe more. He guessed we were loose."

"And might interfere," Vorchek surmised, "which indicates that his incantations are not complete. He is buying time. It fits. We must pursue, overtake, defeat."

"You can't be serious!" I screamed.

"Miss Delaney," He said crisply, "fetch Mr. Harrow's gun. I will pull your car around. Sir, you are a free agent, but I beg for your help."

It should be clear that I refused, that I laughed at him, mocked his fears, laughed at them all and scooted out of there in my own good time. Of course that should be the rest of the story, but with all that talk of guardians and gates, of magic crosses and spells a kind of spell possessed me, and I didn't forget the telling sound effects, either. In a minute we were packed into Theresa's sporty coupe, she at the wheel, I at the passenger window, Vorchek squeezed between, barreling down the dark, precipitous mountain road after the madman; after him, and perhaps—if the professor was right—whoever kept company with him.

That girl drove like a demon on that rugged road, granting me a few unwelcome thrills at sharp curves. We hurtled through a murky wonderland in which images flared in the headlights and then vanished forever. In my state of mind I didn't credit half of what I saw, the way those hoodoos seemed to shift and shimmer and lurch forward from

93

the sides of the road where the snow had been heaped in low walls by the plow. I hadn't remembered them standing so close to the track, nor leaning into the road in the menacing fashion they did now. Then one toppled forward, crashing to earth across the bare dirt, almost completely blocking the way. That thing must have weighed tons. Theresa shrieked, but she spun the steering wheel until I thought it would break off, ricocheted off the snow bank, whipped us back onto the road like a pro. I overheard Vorchek say to himself, "It could be coincidence."

No sooner had we struck pavement than our lights picked up the trailer dead ahead. The obvious question arose in my mind. "What now, Professor?"

"We ram him, drive him off the road."

"That's nuts," Theresa exclaimed. "He's ten times bigger than we are. Besides, do you have any idea what this car is worth?"

"He dare not risk it," Vorchek replied. "Bring him to a stop, whatever it takes."

The girl said something grossly unladylike, gunned the engine. I would have argued the point if granted the time. Instead I braced myself as the rear end of the trailer swelled to fill my vision. It began to swing slowly through a switch-back. We impacted, a bruising jolt, catching it near the left rear wheel. We bounced, our right front sorely crumpled. Theresa regained control, poured it on once more. Again we struck, and this time our prey ground to a complete halt.

At Vorchek's command our driver stopped the car. The headlight beams still slashed the darkness. "Everyone out," yelled the professor. "Mr. Harrow, oblige me by subduing Mr. Thrushwaite. Surely you can easily take him."

I could do that much. Out I went, Vorchek tumbling out behind. I dashed to the side of the trailer, inching toward the cab. The driver's window was rolled down. I was almost alongside when a pistol protruded from the interior. I darted back as it fired. So he packed a piece as well. Another shot boomed from my left and rear; I snapped back a glance, saw Theresa in fighting stance. I rolled to the ground, sprang up before the windshield, hearing Thrushwaite's screechy voice crying, "It can't be! I'm so close! It mustn't be! Just a little more time!" I fired, one shot dead center, and the human shape in darkness behind the wheel jerked, sagged into a motionless heap.

As I checked Thrushwaite's vitals (a mere formality in his case) I heard a shout, almost a scream, from some point behind the cab.

Theresa cried, "The professor is in trouble!" and scampered around back waving her gun. I dashed after her, my thoughts spinning like an exploding galaxy. "Isn't it over? Shouldn't it be over? What, really, could harm Vorchek now?" The rear of the trailer had slued off the road, the back door barred by tenacious branches, and as the girl exclaimed, "It's locked!" I could shoot it open, but that risked injury to the man inside. I pondered for an instant, noting with a thrill of genuine fear the looming presence of two hoodoos very close in the darkness. I hadn't remembered any down this far.

"This side is bashed open," I yelled, charging around to the gaping hole. A hideous voice assailed my ears. Light flashed within that black maw; a flashlight in hand. It was Vorchek, crouched against the desk, staring into the hollow space beyond my vision. I sprang inside, landed in a squat, saw what he focused upon. My brain went hot and dry like an over-baked potato. It couldn't have been a live thing; nothing looks like that. How could it be alive, yet not resemble anything I'd ever seen or heard of before? I fired once, twice, emptied the pistol, and the indescribable form, not quite the same from one moment to the next, turned from Vorchek and came toward me, or extended itself, or protruded something, in some fashion became agonizingly nearer. I heard another scream. I'm afraid it was my own. The thing spoke—was there a mouth in that mass?—my mind began to unravel.

Vorchek held up a hand and loudly uttered gibberish, three unique words or weird sounds. To his chest, partly concealed in his open coat, he clutched something that gleamed in the wavering light. His utterance had an immediate effect. The sickening lurker in the trailer contracted—yes, that's the word—folded upon itself, red eyes blazing as it hoarsely croaked and bellowed, appeared to move sideways—move, not step—then was just gone. There was only Vorchek and I in there, with Theresa's wondering face peering through the gap at us.

She called, "You got it under control, Professor?"

A hoodoo crashed to the ground at the tree line. It made her jump. I laughed crazily.

A little later, after a lift back to the empty house, I reclaimed my rental car. Vorchek, from inside the girl's coupe, said, "I suggest that we go our separate ways. This episode has been debilitating enough, without compounding the adventure by broaching the subject to the authorities. I presume, Mr. Harrow, that you are not officially here?"

"I'm already officially gone," I said. No one had mentioned it, but even in the dark I could tell that Thrushwaite's house was sagging, the walls leaning in as if its foundations had been undercut; foundations of solid granite. I didn't mention it. "Nothing happened here. I can tell that lie with a straight face."

"That is wise. Miss Delaney, let us go."

"See you, Johnny," she said with a flippant wave.

"Hey, wait a minute," I cried. "We're forgetting the Cross of Xenophor. What about the cross?"

Vorchek clutched protectively at a bulge in his coat. "What about the money?"

I grinned. I hoped he was a saner man than our late host. "You folks take care," I said.

Theresa gunned the motor, and they sped away down the treacherous mountain road.

A CHANCE RESULT

So the foolish will say that Vorchek was right, or that there was something to his crazy ideas, but I'm not buying it, despite Morrison's death and what happened to my carefully managed project. No, they will never convince me, because I know Vorchek's type: the wild claims, the scattershot analysis, the grabbing for any iota of data to prop up his bizarre theories; these are the stuff of kooks, and Vorchek, I say, is their king. Professor Vorchek he styles himself; professor of what, expert in what, I want to know. He's just another charlatan with big ideas, who if he spouts enough rubbish often enough, cherry-picks enough evidence, will seem to come up with something, if only by chance. Truly it was a series of chance results that wrecked all my hard work, leaving tragedy in its wake and Vorchek crowing like a loon. I guess those things crow.

Good Lord, was it only two months ago that I, Arthur Lonin, chief anthropologist at NAU, was working happily away on a useful prehistoric find in the outback beyond Sedona? Into the wilderness of the justly famed Red Rock Country I went with my team of shabby graduate students, there in the forests behind Wilson Mountain, into the gloomy vastness of Secret Canyon, there to grub up the relics of a pristine Indian site dating from the era of the pueblo builders. An adventurous hiker, exploring off trail, had initially come across the signs six months before, kept his find considerably quiet until he contacted my department at the university. Seizing the opportunity (these don't come up too often any more), I swung into action at once, established the location, scouted the clues, organized my party and got to work. Once we left the dirt road below the mountain we had to pack in everything on our backs, but we were good for that: I and my colleague, Willis Morrison, desired the glory of first publication rights, while our quintet of students wanted the break from routine and the extra college credits. A fair deal for everyone, I'd say.

We set up a camp sufficient for three months, requiring mere weekly trips to the outside world for replenishment of perishables. Morrison and I got along pretty well, though he was a bit too much of the old school, dig 'em up, record and move on crowd, lacking the knack for in depth theorizing. Our work gang were all right, about what one gets these days, slap happy youth overly addicted to mutual groping and their blasting radios and glued-to-the-ear cell phones, none of which (I'm sorry to say, hah hah!) functioned well in that region sheltered by a billion tons of orange sandstone cliffs. We got fairly down to business in short order, began bringing to light the time-ravaged remains of that ancient, primitive culture.

The location lay against the western wall of the canyon, within a kind of pocket, a subsidiary box canyon that resembled a circular limestone amphitheater. In the cliff face above stood a long known, well preserved ruin, a fine ring of rocks most likely used as a storage bin for grain. Our work focused on the canyon floor, where lay the vaguely dated new site, which I deduced might be the primary habitation. Morrison wasn't so sure. "The architecture doesn't match," he noted, and I couldn't disagree, save to point out that actual living structures might have been erected with more and different care. "It's a valid starting point for discussion," said I. What we had to work with were foundations, quite extensive, much of them along geometrical lines, several rounded, with the debris of higher walls and stories, and a mass of commingled artifacts. On the surface, the highest level, we found a plethora of characteristic stone tools which placed that living floor in the earliest Anasazi period. That intrigued me, because cursory test digging illuminated lower levels, many of them, which appeared to date a lot farther back that I would have *a priori* reckoned.

That work was my style of joy, what I lived for, what I'd built my reputation upon. I'd pull up the stuff, measure everything, go home in the end to piece together my report which strove to place the site within the contact of the greater southwestern culture of long ago. Simple, elegant, informative, useful; that's the way it's done (certainly the way I do it), and that's the way we learn. Hard work, under those conditions, but never doubt that the advancement of scientific knowledge brings its own rewards.

Into my tidy, carefully orchestrated set up dropped one Anton

A CHANCE RESULT

Vorchek, professor of whatever, hailing from a chintzy Phoenix college of no great standing. He appeared that morning, dressed as for a tourist's safari, in khaki suit, matching tie, bulky boots and broad-brimmed floppy hat, and carrying two-handed a big, over-stuffed attaché case. That he swung onto a large rock outside my tent, plunking himself beside it and introducing himself with a wearily outstretched hand. I perfunctorily shook it, asked, with a show of frosty politeness, his business.

"It is like this," he began, in excellent, precise English, though with a subtle trace of indefinable accent; "I come to see you—Doctor Lonin, I presume?—on matters of scientific import. I read about your work, naturally, and I am intrigued to discover that, as I suspected, it crosses mine."

"I don't see how," I replied testily. Morrison joined us, the students pausing in their labors to gather round. I continued, "We've permits for digging here. Have you?"

"What I do not have," Vorchek said, "I can acquire, as needed. Grunt work, as they say, is not my line. I pursue what may be styled, for want of a better term, a problem in physics. For many years I have studied the vibrational energies thought to emanate from this region. Surely, Doctor, you have heard the popular tales, and a man in your profession must be aware of the lingering Indian myths surrounding the area. There are forces operating here, perhaps in this very spot. That subject, sir, I vocate."

So Vorchek was a New Age nut. I should have known one of those would pop up. I suggested, with even more iced courtesy, that he was unlikely to find much of scientific content underlying his presumably devout passion. "The only oneness we've got here is that of exacting team effort and dedication to logic."

"That is music to my ears," he responded, rising with the words and opening his case. From this he shortly extracted a curious instrument, a boxy metallic device mounted atop a camera tripod. "I follow the evidence. This meter, constructed according to principles of my own devising, registers ethereal influences radiating from planes of existence beyond the norm. Let me show you." I started to say something quite warm, but he was awfully quick on his feet. In no time his machine was merrily humming, powered by a hand-held rack of three wired batteries. Then it began to click like a Geiger counter. He swiveled the meter back and forth on the tripod head.

"You see," he explained, "three separate nodal points, one

emanating from up canyon a good ways, another to the north and down (far beneath the surface, I think), and the third—just so—the third and most powerful, from right here." Indeed, the machine suddenly chirped loudly and rapidly, a grating sound.

"There may be uranium in these rocks," Morrison suggested. "Interesting, I dare say, but not our line." I echoed him. My students, I'm sorry to say, seemed keen on that meaningless display. They began asking questions of Vorchek, the sort of questions inspired by reading of cheap paperbacks rather than textbooks. I ordered them back to work. They went, with sullen faces.

Vorchek chuckled. "They are young," he said breezily, "their minds not honed to critical thought. They believe, rather than reason. Fortunately, we do not suffer that malady. Gentlemen, proceed with your work—" the nerve of the man!—"yet attend to the forces which stir here. Let us not stir them up, until we understand." He told us he expected to remain in the vicinity for some time. So saying, he packed his gear and left, pushing through and disappearing into the scrub.

Morrison laughed, saying, "We'll have hippies camping here before long, trying to invoke the primordial wisdom of the Red Man." I said, "Maybe I can talk to somebody about him."

I didn't, because I hoped that was the end of the professor's intrusion. On my next foray into town, desiring to kill an hour before charging back into the wild, I looked up Vorchek's bona fides via wireless. Well, he had published a lot, most of it pretty strange sounding stuff; some about what I expected of him, but certain articles had appeared in small but high grade magazines, suggesting a reputation not wholly rock bottom. I deduced that he was the real thing, with a bee in his bonnet. I have known other such.

Just by chance I ran into him that day, spying him at an open air Sedona eatery where he sat at table under the awning with an absolutely delicious young girl. She was a blonde, flashily dressed type, haughtily smoking a cigarette while Vorchek leaned close to whisper something. She tossed her long hair in an arch manner at what he said, grinned. While I stared at her, Vorchek just happened to glance up and saw me. I, of course, would have hurried by, but at his annoyingly friendly invitation I had to join them.

He introduced us. "Doctor Lonin, my private secretary, Miss Theresa Delaney." Why didn't I rate a secretary like that? Why did he? Life can be so grossly unfair. "We have been discussing your case," he said.

"My case?" I replied with a forced laugh. "I didn't know I was one or had one."

Said Theresa, with absolute assurance in her sultry voice, "You're going to be one if you don't listen to the professor." Vorchek interjected good-naturedly, "Well, that remains to be seen," but the girl went on, "If he gets mixed up with that nasty stuff, there's going to be trouble."

I asked, with bite in my tone, "Who's going to make the trouble?"

Here Vorchek weighed in, overriding his companion's intended retort. "If my research is correct," he said, "you will. Sir, I believe you operate according to false premises. I have taken the liberty of examining your background, and that of Doctor Morrison. Geology is his strong suit, I believe? Surely, then, he has sent up warning flags concerning the strata in which you are excavating."

I had to hand it to Vorchek, who was one smart cookie in his own way: he had squarely fingered a curious matter that had quite puzzled Willis, who had already broached to me his querulous concerns. Weeks before he'd advised me, "There's something wrong, chum, with our on-site dating. From the surface artifacts you deduce an age of seven hundred to a thousand years for this entire structure?" "That's about right," I said; "perfectly conventional, in line with numerous known locations." "Well, that isn't panning out here. These lower levels are intertwined with bedrock, placing them back many thousands of years, if not more; much more, I'd say." "Intrusion of construction into older strata, maybe." "It had better be," said Morrison, "or otherwise everything is completely out of whack here. I just don't get it." Nor had he resolved the conundrum at this time.

Before Vorchek and his lady friend I held my peace, merely allowing that initial results are often problematic. The professor would have none of that. "My dear sir, geological dating these days is a science, not an art. I have in my files potassium-argon readings from those layers, samples derived from various points in the canyon. There is no doubt that the lower remains date back into the Pleistocene, at the very latest. That accords with my theories, scarcely with your own."

I might as well get this over with. "What are your theories, Professor Vorchek?"

He beamed like a man ever prepared to ride his hobbyhorse. "There was a much older culture existing in Secret Canyon, and probably for a long ways around, than current archeology accepts. The inhabitants were probably human, in their essentials, although given the remoteness in time one may wonder. Given their location they probably tapped or connected to the strange forces at work there, for a purpose that the hard data will not as yet reveal. Those forces still function to some degree, as I have established, and your presence and activities may potentially fuel the powers, perhaps awaken them."

"That's a pile of probabilities," I shot back, "without one solid link in your chain. You said the 'hard data' won't suffice at this time. What else is there?"

"I perused the records of Yavapai myths," he replied. "There is an especial tinge of weirdness to their accounts. They speak of the 'Teritreki,' meaning 'Those Who Came Before,' a majestic race of demi-gods who once dwelt in this part of the world—children of the Gods, who communed with Them and dealt with Them—the ancient Gods who came to earth in this land from celestial spheres via gateways of mysterious power. According to legend (which the present day Indians claim were old when they first heard them), the Teritreki dabbled too greatly with these forces, rubbing shoulders with those Gods to their detriment. Eventually the baleful influences of the place overwhelmed them and wiped them out.

"Who knows what survives from those olden times? Something still lurks out there, in the rocks, in the air. The common folk sense it, make up happy stories about it. We need not fall into that trap, nor the equal error of disbelief. We must not."

Okay, now I knew. "That's enough," I said, getting up. "I must get back. Believe what you like, Professor, but don't pester me or my people. We have real work to do."

As I strode away Theresa called after me, "You'll be sorry."

It was just my rotten luck that one of my students was the superstitious sort, a girl who, I guess, had picked up some of Vorchek's nonsense. We professionals do get those types, though they usually aren't drawn to nuts and bolts archeology. This girl, Sandra, had a dream that next night, after putting in a good day of digging into the next lower level, an impressively large one revealing intact walls and foundations of well-preserved granite blocks, hardly the norm for classic pueblos. This, and the silliness in the air, must have set her off. In the morning she blabbered the whole thing to her fellows. Sandra declared, "I woke up, exactly like really waking, and I was right here in the canyon, only the vegetation was tropical rather than semi-arid, and instead of ruins there was a beautiful white city filled with people. It was night, but the moon was up, a full moon, and all the people were illuminated by that and lights on the walls, flickering globes that blazed without visible flame. The inhabitants looked a bit like Indians, but they were tall and lean, and the old men had long beards, and they were all dressed in white robes. Hundreds of them gathered in a big round room, kind of like that wrecked kiva we dug up yesterday, but it wasn't a place for games. No, there was a black stone structure in the middle, like a walled altar with open doorways, and the old men gathered before it, and they chanted in a strange language.

"Then came light out of the altar, a greenish glow that grew and shot out of the top to the sky like a searchlight. Everybody bowed down, mumbling, and from the glow I saw eyes emerge; definite eyes, only a lot of them, many eyes without a face. Just then I understood that those folk knew I was there. They turned to me, smiling, grabbed hold of me and began pushing me toward the altar and those eyes. I screamed and woke up for real, feeling sick to my stomach."

Such was Sandra's charming tale. That bugged me already, because several of the staff seemed to pay her unwholesome attention, as if what she said mattered a damn. I surely could have whipped her into shape (she had a foolish crush on Morrison, which might have counted), except that I quickly received my next, shall I say, bad break. Mark Lessingham, my best student, took a fall late that afternoon which put him out of action with a broken leg. He was at the top of the excavation, over the deepening pit, in the gloom evoked by the steep canyon walls, and I guess he tripped. Hey, it happens, that's the human condition. Everybody slips up sooner or later. Unfortunately Mark (a sound fellow, I thought) made a big to-do about not having fallen, but of having been yanked down by something he couldn't quite see in the dim hole. Idiocy, of course; there was no animal down there, nor anyone else, but he persisted in his story against all reason. We had a devil of a time hauling him out to town, and as it developed Sandra had had enough, so she packed up and bolted, leaving me down two. I called from Sedona to the university for replacements.

Morrison said that night, "We've got a mess on our hands. This one isn't stacking up. Art, just between you and me, I've got a creepy feeling. I don't know what to say, but keep in mind the need for reconsideration." I considered myself enlightened.

Two mornings later a single warm body arrived, Tabitha Blake, a short, hunched-shouldered girl with a brunette mop of hair who dressed even more the drab than was customary among her set. With her head bent and a cringing demeanor she addressed herself in a low, whiny voice to Willis, got absently to work. They sent me one girl. Bless them, but I'd lost one heavy lifter, and she didn't even live up to Sandra's standard. I ignored her, and she kept out of my sight most of that day.

Vorchek popped out of the woodwork again. Trooping out of the bush at midday like a Great White Hunter, encumbered with more gear, he sought Morrison and me. "I heard about your difficulties," he said airily. "I manage to avoid surprise. Miss Tompkins—Sandra Tompkins—told all, a stirring tale certainly. Her hallucination, if you wish to deem it thus, mirrors adequately certain folk renditions in my files. You might find that meaningful."

"What is the point, Professor?" Morrison asked, without challenge, as if he desired an answer. That infuriated me. "There is none," I snapped. "We had a goofy girl and a clumsy guy." Morrison glared at me, said, "I'm open to opinions on geological matters."

Vorchek shrugged. "I bear you opinions galore, while I continue to wrestle with data. Too bad, by the way, about Mr. Lessingham's accident. He places a curious spin on the tale, does not he?"

"Doctor Morrison, your professional misgivings are justified. The dates will not match, because in this case geology and conventional archeology do not mix. This site, the stub of a great Teritreki ruin, is far older than Doctor Lonin can allow. Incredibly older, and more evil, as we understand these obscure conceptions. The latent forces here are inimical to human life. Those who came before learned that. They are gone. The Indians, after horrid experience, learned to shun the place. Until such time as our knowledge and wisdom surpasses the contemporary, I urge you to do the same."

"Nothing's wrong," I insisted. "We've had some chancy nuisances plaguing us, nothing more. Speaking of nuisances, I don't appreciate your presence, Vorchek. I've got a permit for this place, which makes me responsible for who comes and goes. Do the latter, if you want to satisfy me."

He smiled sadly. "I camp up the wash, a quarter mile away. There I find a significant aura of disturbance, although your site gains by the day. You can find me readily enough. I will be in touch."

Little did I know how much the old fox was playing his tricks on me. I got a shock that evening that just about blew me out of my boots. I sauntered up to the campfire, where the others were already eating, to overhear Tabitha huddled in whispered conference with two of my students. What she was saying so outraged me—it sounded like a page torn from Vorchek's play book—that I with difficulty restrained myself from calling her to account. I needn't have held back, for as I glowered at her across the fire, I got a good look at her for the first time. She was sharing a cigarette with Brittany, which galled me as it was, but by the glow of flames I saw her truly, her familiar face leaping out at me. Tabitha was in fact Theresa Delaney, Professor Vorchek's haughty girl Friday. He had slipped a ringer into my camp!

Biding my time, I collared her afterward alone. "Theresa," I bellowed, "I can have you arrested."

"For what?" she replied archly, without shame. "You've gotten work out of me. Doctor Morrison hasn't complained."

"He's not himself these days. Neither are you, apparently. You've come down in the world of fashion. What are you doing here spying on me?"

"Spying on you."

"What secrets and profound revelations will you carry back to your master?"

"I don't have to," she said with a grin. Theresa produced an oblong device from one grungy pocket. "We communicate by walkie-talkie."

"You've done too much ridiculous talking to my people," I sneered. "Trying to win them over to your crap, are you?"

"Not at all. I pumped them for information, and heard an earful. They talk among themselves, just not to you. They know that's a waste, but they're picking up on stuff. It's like the professor says, some people sense it, some don't. I don't, much—you don't at all—the boss feels plenty, and others here. Something's about to happen."

"Get out."

"At this time of night?" She raised her hands in mock dismay, then activated her device. "Come on, Artie, be a sport. Hello, Professor. It's gone bust. Collect me in the morning."

A squawking, but hatefully familiar voice, replied, "Quite so, Miss Delaney. Be sure to acquaint the good doctors with your observations. Out, and sweet dreams."

I refused to listen to her snide insinuations. Morrison, when he learned of the exposure, laughed nervously. "Maybe we could use advice," he said. Theresa slept that night in her tent, apparently without further attempts to stir rebellion.

Vorchek showed at dawn. I expected an apology. He never thought of it, launching instead into one of his diatribes. After a tete-a-tete with his secret agent he said to me, "You really ought to speak with your folk. The impressions pour in fast. Miss Delaney tells me that she derived from their conversation decisive descriptions of awakening imagery, visions of old, as well as clear-cut references to certain crucial words. She mentions 'Teritreki,' the term 'Xenophor,' and the oblique concept of 'Dyrezan.' This is serious. I know those words, comprehend somewhat their meaning. Do you, sir?"

He startled me. "Xenophor, yes. An Indian god, that's all, a fairly disreputable one. They had a bunch. So what? Paganism is dead in these parts."

"Perhaps, Doctor Lonin, but not what lay behind it. That lives forever, best for us when dormant. Xenophor, you should know, is a deity recognized in many regions of the earth, often by that name, always viewed in the same wary light. Do not set off an explosion of the cosmic forces."

"Good-bye, Vorchek." He departed with his girlfriend, who had already somehow managed to shed most of her rags, unduly stimulating some of my team.

A bad day was coming. How could I have predicted what a series of entirely meaningless events would bring? I have learned that there is no meaning or purpose to life, only chance and luck, usually lousy. Here's how the day went. Over breakfast I held an informal chat with the gang, wanting to find out how much this garbage troubled them. I didn't enjoy the results. Yuri, the most intense thinker and hardest remaining worker of the bunch, delivered a rousing rendition of his "latest" nightmare, in which he found himself standing at the edge of the excavation pit, which transformed before his eyes into a thriving scene of blood and horror. Ghostly shapes slaughtered a human victim in a stone enclosure that sounded an awful lot like Sandra's altar. Weird light pervaded the scene, and from that rose into the black sky a "screaming mist." Much obliged, Yuri. Cindy Tolleson told a creepy tale drawn from her dreams, of having been drawn into a dark chamber where the phosphorescent images of multiple eyes glared at her, and a ghastly inhuman voice intoned her name, strangely pronouncing the syllables as it called her deeper into endless darkness.

Okay, so Vorchek and his girl had infected them, excited their subconscious minds; just that, no more, too bad they happened to dream the stuff and remember it, too. Another bad break for me and discipline, but so it goes when blind fate turns against one. More devastating by far was Willis' alarming attitude. "I'm not the impressionable type," he asserted, "and I don't dream—never—but I do here, recently. It was especially disconcerting last night. They came for me in the dark, those strange men—I guess they were supposed to be Indians, although their racial characteristics were distorted; a bit too prognathic for my tastes—and they dragged me from my tent. I yelled for help, but no one came to save me. My captors forced me over a rise to that shining stone city, where the folk gathered in the giant kiva howled, calling my name and crying another name, a very peculiar word or words. What was that? It was Greek to me, started with a 'Z'; like 'zenie' . . . 'zenie for' . . ."

I stopped him right there, seeing the eyes of the students blaze in astonished sympathy. Oh yes, Vorchek had laid the groundwork very well indeed. I said, "We can't afford to give in to rank superstition. That surrenders all we stand for. Vorchek's machinations, and a couple of irrelevant incidents, have us on edge. Shake it off, all of you. We have great work ahead of us, weeks more of genuine research. Let's make the most of it, and in the right spirit."

What could they say? What could they do? They went along, their emotions black in their faces, but they heeded me one last time. Afterward I came hard at Morrison, warned that his weak response to events threatened the expedition. He apologized, though his heart wasn't backing his words. I hoped he was level again, because I needed to run up to Flagstaff that morning on administrative matters, and I counted on his firm hand.

I got up to the university around ten, dealt with paperwork, thought I'd check on my ailing student Mark. Evil tidings awaited me; the anthropology department, in fact, was abuzz about him. It turned out that his injuries were worse than I'd realized: Mark's thigh-bone had been wrenched from his hip socket, requiring costly repairs and medical services, to be charged to us, of course. I'd deduct a week or more from our excavations to cover the bill. Frustrating, naturally, and infuriating as well, because just by chance his damage corresponded loosely with his silly tale. I didn't even bother to see him personally, not wanting to hear more.

EERIE ARIZONA

I returned to the ruin site by three, hot and bothered by my hike on that warm afternoon. Perhaps the heat wearied the others as well; certainly they hadn't accomplished much while I'd been absent. I got them moving again, kept them at it until five, by which time my energy also flagged, so I called a halt for the day. Something was in the air, everybody in a bad mood, and I felt like I was fighting against something, struggling against amorphous hostility and clinging torpor. A good night's rest and a stirring pep talk, I thought, would supercharge the team into renewed endeavor, so long as Professor Vorchek held off.

He did. He didn't show any more that day, thank God. That could have made a difference, given time. Over our rations, around the fire, with a cool breeze rustling the dry juniper branches and the red cliffs looming in a wide ring, I led the discussion on the day's attainments. We'd broken through another level, partially exposing two extremely old but nicely constructed chambers of basalt. I thought the architecture impressively novel, praised the work, bragged of the possibilities. Morrison glumly seconded my views. The students stared blankly into the flames or buried their eyes in their plates.

I wish I hadn't been so tired that night. If I hadn't felt so worn out I'd have stayed up late, checked everything, maybe caught on to what was coming, been in a position to prevent it. That would have constituted luck on my side, something I deserved by then. It was not to be. The final curve was pitched.

Infinitely drowsy, I retired to my tent when the others did, dozed briefly (starting awake when I thought for a moment that someone had laid a hand on my shoulder), then sank into deeper slumber. Now here is the kick in the head: I dreamed that night. It began oddly, with my dream-self waking up, in the tent, in the dark, all appearing normal, only with an overpowering sense of imminent danger closely pressing. I sprang up, went forth from the tent in my pajamas, to find the rest of the group already out in their night clothes, mostly tee-shirts and shorts save for Morrison, who wore a woolen robe. Only he spoke as I approached, saying in an awful strangled voice, "It comes from the dig."

His words sounded strangely portentous, like a pronouncement of doom. What did he mean? I meant to ask, but at the words I, with dream omniscience, understood. A silent force called from that direction, an urging onward toward a location out that way. Even as I thought this Morrison and our students began to shuffle awkwardly toward the ruins hidden in darkness and screening shrubs. I intended to stop them—or something in my mind screamed that I must—but having joined them I followed along, saying nothing, nor any longer thinking to do so. It felt proper and right that we went as we should, into the dark, without lights or discourse.

We pushed through the clinging undergrowth, which did not scratch or tear at us, for it bore soft wavy fronds rather than cruel thorny branches. As we easily made our way a glow began to gently radiate from our front. It grew brighter; we beheld through the alien trees magical towers of gleaming white stone; we emerged into a broad clearing on the edge of the fantastic city standing against the ring of cliffs. By night it teemed with life and sound and curious light, the surging of the populace out of doorways and through the gates of wide avenues. Strange men they were, and their women, robed white in cloth of silk and gold, speaking among themselves in sibilant voices distressing to the ear. We joined their throng, passing along the lanes of the city, encompassed by the hordes that jostled among themselves, yet neither touched nor spoke to us. Indeed, though they noted our presence, they stood apart with deliberation from us, as though we were either abominably unclean or specially favored.

And we entered the great round court or plaza, with the dreadful altar before us, and the crowd drew back to fashion a path forward for us, one on which we were loath to tread. Surely all the evil of the world and the universe reposed in that hateful edifice or reached out through it. Mysterious colored lights twinkled around it like fireflies, while from within a pale greenish radiance flowed.

Gathered near the altar stood a band of ornately attired elders, intoning a meaningless chant or song in their hissing speech. When those men concluded others advanced on us, strong, powerful young men unarmed but adorned with silver helmets and bearing large oval shields of bright steel. With these they, unspeaking, drove us down the lane of robed flesh to the altar. We held back as we might, resisted frantically at the last, and only then did they lay hands on us, propelling us toward what I knew to be unexplained, and unexplainable, doom. I heard the voices of my fellows, crying out and yelling in terror. I heard likewise my own voice.

It was Morrison that they first brutally shepherded, unsparing of force, into the structure. Gagging on a scream through clenched teeth, he stumbled into the now flaring opening. I saw within something, I know not what. It was a matter of seconds, but Morrison was not alone in there. Eyes peered at him from all sides, eyes swarmed him like bees, tendrils of darkness enfolding him. He vanished; not receding from view into the interior, but just gone, ceasing to be. As he did so a black cloud like smoke or roiling dense vapor rose from an opening in the peaked roof, and that cloud shrieked as it churned and spiraled in a voice like Morrison's.

Then I truly awoke, my face in the dirt, my body half in, half out of my tent. Yuri, lying near the dead fire, pushed himself up on his elbow, groggily shaking his head. My other students staggered immediately from their tents, disheveled, staring uncertainly about. I leaped up, ran to one other tent, peered inside. "Where's Willis?" I demanded.

Mary Gale asked in a hushed voice, "Did they really get him?" I told her to shut her nonsense, ordered them all to help me search. For no good reason I lead the gang to the ruins, pushing this time . . . well, just pushing through the snaky, poking thorns and hard branches, unmercifully wounding myself in my haste. The single weak flashlight among us (I forget who thought to grab it) probed the scene. There we found Willis all right, at the bottom of the pit. One glance told me he was as dead as a man can be.

We returned quietly to camp. As we arrived harsh twin beams stabbed at us out of the darkness before the dawn, dazzling our eyes. A young feminine voice wafted from the murk, saying, "I hope we're in time." I recognized it at once. Within moments Theresa Delaney strode into sight, clutching a huge flash, followed by her similarly accoutered mentor Vorchek.

He said to me, abruptly, "I did what I could. So soon as my instruments detected that incredible energy surge I knew it meant horrific peril for someone. I tell you, Doctor Lonin, that I have never seen readings like that. I have another device—quite a tricky machine—which, in unison with the requisite olden phrases of Dyrezan, can minimize the worst of the material manifestations. Having activated it, we came here at once. I did what I could. Was it enough?"

Was it enough? "There's been an accident," I croaked. If I weren't a civilized man I would have killed him on the spot! Professor Vorchek, you phony, you braggart, you double-dealing, sneaky liar: you did nothing.

That is my official answer. I had a bad dream, a heavy duty

nightmare. Okay, so I wasn't the only one; all of my students (the sweethearts, ex-students now) had tales to tell, and by the time Vorchek was finished with them, his damned note-taking, with Theresa bobbing about with her pad and pen, their stories and mine all sounded an awful lot alike; but it meant nothing, because it was just a dream, the idea planted in my overtaxed brain by Vorchek's previous mewlings. It was just chance that he got a wild hair and came running, solely because one of his stupid quack machines went on the blink about then. He achieved nothing, save for impeding the investigation into what really happened that night, the objective fact of Doctor Willis Morrison's unfortunate demise.

Vorchek got in the way, every way he could, then and later. I know he talked secretly with certain Forest Service personnel weirdly sympathetic to him—I heard this later, through the department grapevine—got my excavation contract aborted. I'll publish what I have, which is scarcely adequate, avoiding any mention of amateurish rantings. I'm told that a certain area within Secret Canyon, west of Sedona, out in the wilds of the Red Rock Country, is temporarily restricted to visitation, including honest professionals doing their jobs.

Self-serving interference, bad breaks, and chance results: those compose the real story of my wrecked project, including the final chance result, the most pitiful of all. Willis died, and I'm sorry about that, but it's pointless to ask, as Vorchek did, what Willis experienced that fatal night, because we don't know anything of the kind. Who says he dreamed? He isn't telling. I say he woke up and chose to examine the site, something he and I did frequently, a task I might have performed if not worn by weariness. Refute that. He should have taken a flashlight with him, but I guess he thought he knew the ground. Refute that. He fell in, got himself killed. It was a big, deep hole, where a fellow could break his leg, or his neck, or any other part, for that matter. That's what happened. Refute it; let me hear you try.

It was only chance, no matter what crazy conclusions the esteemed Professor Vorchek chooses to derive from the autopsy. I say it was a big drop, a good twenty-five feet by then. A man can get pretty broken up from such a tumble. I can ignore Vorchek's opinion. I may not be a medical researcher, but neither is he. I grant that Morrison's body wasn't just damaged by the fall. I saw it lying down there, crushed beyond recognition, its soft tissues and fluids splattered against the walls of the dig. Horrible, I admit, but where the necessity for invoking the supernatural? In the results of any event, any accident, there is a permissible range of probabilities. Morrison's end simply pushed probability to the limit. It was a most disagreeable chance result, and nothing more.

THE MYSTERY OF THE INNER BASIN LODGE

"**I**t seems that our affairs grow increasingly complicated," observed Professor Anton Vorchek, stroking his beard with irritation as he waited with his lovely assistant Theresa Delaney in the crowded hotel lobby at the foot of the snowy mountains. Activity bustled there that night, most of it to no apparent purpose, while with the passage of hours the lack of useful information began to grate. "By this time," Vorchek continued in his well-modulated, slightly accented tones, "I expected to be up there in the thick of entertaining matters."

"It was a dopey idea in the first place," said Theresa, with an annoyed toss of blonde locks the color of ripe corn, "to hold a conference in a hopeless, out of the way wilderness like this, in the middle of winter yet. Why don't we buzz off and get back to civilization? Obviously it's all gone wrong, and somebody should have planned for that way ahead of time."

The professor concurred, in part. He had been called, along with a number of other notable scholars, to attend a symposium on unusual questions relating to the science of physics. Grand ideas were to be expounded at the conference, which had been convened at the isolated Inner Basin Lodge, deep within the enfolding circle of the San Francisco Peaks north of Flagstaff, Arizona. Facilities had been assured, all amenities guaranteed for the duration of the gathering. At the moment it was possible to conclude that all factors had been considered other than, inexplicably, the weather. It was snowing here on the outskirts of the city at an elevation of 7000 feet, and very cold. Up above at the lodge, 2000 feet higher, the conditions were presumably more severe still. That seemed to be the prevailing rumor anyway, as word trickled from hotel employees and spread among the

113

tourists rooming there or pausing from their journeys in that pleasant, well-heated lobby. Whatever the case, it did appear that something had gone wrong. Vorchek received assurance that the other guests at the conference had gone up before him (he running seriously late while Theresa spent a ridiculous amount of time preparing her wardrobe), that all had been well that morning, but that the situation had changed suddenly. Communication with the lodge had broken down; the telephone was out, no link to the earlier attendees functioning. The ubiquitous cell phones failed to bridge the gap. It could only be assumed that a fierce storm had visited the Inner Basin, blanking out any technological connections.

So it might prove, yet the development irked and troubled Vorchek. Not truly a physicist, but rather a student and investigator of scientific arcana, he had been promised great revelations and unique insights should he attend. Therefore he made for this desolate region, at this odd time of year, with his young, beautiful but exasperating companion in tow (she insisting on coming, then complaining unceasingly), only to be left cooling his heels in this mercifully warm hotel lobby.

Theresa, heavily bundled in her expensive, newly purchased winter attire, a magnificent fur coat and sleek black boots which drew many a head, stepped outside in a huff to smoke a cigarette. Vorchek thought to join her with his pipe, chose to tarry within awaiting fresh word. It came presently, but Theresa was the first to glean the arrival of news. A man entered by the main door, breezing in without pausing to stamp the ice from his boots, making for the front desk. The girl reappeared right behind him, skipped to Vorchek and said, "He's got something to say about the lodge. He knows a thing or two." Vorchek sidled through the throng, listened with seeming casualness to the report. There was a big storm up there, much ice and snow; power and phone lines down; a tricky and momentarily tense situation, but no cause for alarm. The current tenants of the lodge enjoyed an array of emergency or backup systems, all operating, no need for any thoughts of rescue or aid. They would dig themselves out in a day or two. It would be a total waste of time and resources to send anybody for them. The man made that point repeatedly.

Having delivered the message the man started to leave as he had come. Vorchek collared him by the door, said, "Excuse me, sir, but I could not help but hear. You have come from the lodge, I take it, which surprises me, for I knew of no way up or down under these conditions. I am interested, for I desire to get there."

"Out of the question," growled the fellow. He was a dark man with hard mouth and eyes and, as it seemed, a surly disposition. "You misheard. I haven't been there. It's impossible to reach the lodge until the road is cleared, which can't be until morning at the earliest. Besides, the site has been rented for special purposes. Tourists have no business there."

"I am no tourist," replied the professor with an emphatic flash of teeth. "I did hear most accurately, by the way, what you told the manager. I am Professor Vorchek, and I have business there. I am expected."

The man stepped back, startled, cried, "Vorchek? You're here? But I thought you were with the others!"

"I was detained. Now, sir, I wish to know how matters stand."

The man paused, blew on his hands. "Forgive me, Professor. You surprised me. You are very much expected. Oh, yes, I am Richard Dassin, Doctor Dassin, the organizer of the conference. I chose the attendees. I especially wanted you there."

"Dassin? I do not know the name. I understood that Doctor Wembley convened this gathering."

"Ostensibly, Professor. Wembley is a decent old fellow, with a weighty reputation. Questions of physics were—are—on the agenda, but not his sort. More in your line, I'd say. I've been working on a project of esoteric possibilities, knew that a mind such as your own would be vital to its success. Still is, despite everything; I'll be damned, but I should have checked the guest list before we began. The others might not be enough."

"You speak mysteries," said Vorchek. "What did you want of me, and what can I do about it now?"

"I want your mind," said Dassin, "and you can do much. It is the unusual that we investigate. All right, we can get up, and tonight. I came down the ski lift. It's in perfect shape, entirely safe. The weather has moderated. I'll return the same way, with you as my guest."

"Excellent, Doctor. That beautiful vision by the flowerpot is my assistant. I shall collect her and we may commence the expedition immediately."

Dassin, scarcely bothering to suppress a sneer, exclaimed, "That one? We don't need her. My invitation extended to you only. She can take a room here."

"If the lift holds three," replied the unflappable Vorchek, "then three will go." Dassin acquiesced ungraciously, urging speed. The professor went to Theresa, explained as much as he knew, added, "Fetch the little bag of necessities. Just that goes with us. Cosmetics do not count, nor a wardrobe sufficient for a fashion show. We travel light, and we travel solely for knowledge. Apparently there are unconventional aspects to this business, Miss Delaney. I would know more."

Theresa sighed. "What are we getting into now?" They left the warm lobby with Dassin, stepping into the frosty air. Vorchek clamped his broad-brimmed floppy hat down over his brow. The girl retrieved the bag from her sporty coupe, then the trio marched through snow across the dark road to the lower tram station. Lights gleamed within, the cable car open and ready. They climbed in, seated themselves, with Dassin at the interior controls, from which he activated the mechanism. Electric motors whined, vast wheels turned, the cable stretched taut, and with a jerk and a groan the car began its ascent.

Said Dassin presently, "It was my good fortune, Vorchek, that I ran into you. I came down merely to alieve worry, so that my guests shouldn't be disturbed by meddlesome interlopers. I don't care for outsiders getting in the way. If I hadn't found you, then you'd have missed all the fun. It's a lucky break."

The car rose through mist, the outer world invisible, the sole reminder of connection the occasional bump as the aerial conveyance clanked over the towering cable supports. Vorchek said, "I am not familiar with you or your work, Dr. Dassin. What brings you here?"

Dassin laughed. "Well might you ask, Professor. The place brings me. I'm studying unexplained energy emanations from the bottom of the Inner Basin. There's something in your line. Doesn't the unexplained fascinate you?"

"I have dabbled in such subjects, Doctor. Is there anything about this locale that should especially pique my curiosity?"

"I should think, Vorchek, I should think. The Inner Basin has long been understood as a primordial caldera, a crater formed when a gigantic volcano blew its top. Interesting enough, I suppose, but false. I've deduced the truth, from scientific delvings and old records: it's the site of an ancient impact by a very large object, possibly meteoric, although certainly not metallic or stony. It was something otherwise, something beyond conventional understanding. Geologically speaking the event occurred only a short while ago, a few thousand years perhaps. Whatever crashed here has left traces, peculiar energy traces. I've been working on it at the lodge, which lies at the bottom of the crater. I have reason to believe—very good reason, in fact—that I've cracked the mystery. I know what's going on here. Our colleagues have already proven immensely cooperative in my research. You were intended to be with them at the time. You can still contribute."

"How may I be of service?"

"All in good time, Vorchek. I'll put you to use once we arrive. The others . . . the others can explain it to you. You will find them most illuminating." Dassin laughed again. He seemed in rare good humor.

Theresa whispered to Vorchek, "I don't like this guy. He's up to something. You'd better watch him."

Another bump and the car ground to a halt. "Everybody out," cried Dassin. "Let's join the festivities. The lodge lies directly ahead."

They stepped into the shelter of the upper station, exiting from there into fierce cold. Snow lay on the ground, but not a lot, and the mist had cleared at this elevation. The stars in their multitudes burned steadily overhead, while only darkness met the gaze elsewhere. The great walls and peaks surrounding the Basin cut off distant views in every direction save up. Nearby loomed majestic stands of old-growth conifers. A hint of dark structure could be discerned.

"Has everybody gone to bed?" asked Theresa. "Why aren't there any lights?"

"My colleagues keep early hours," Vorchek observed. "Not typical behavior on their parts, I would say, if they wrestle with mysteries."

"They've been working hard," said Dassin with a grin. "Feel free to rouse them, if you can. I'm sure they'll be pleased by your company." He urged them to go on ahead while he looked after the cable car and its controls. This Vorchek and Theresa did, tramping across the thin snow, carefully negotiating patches of slick ice. The branches of the many trees bore coatings of frost, but little snow.

"I detect precious few evidences of a major storm," noted Vorchek to his companion. "I see no cause for enforced isolation. That puzzles me. Indeed, my dear, something odd is going on.

Bring forth the flashlight. I want to see into what we are getting."

Theresa extracted the little pocket flash from her bag, flicked it on. The white beam shot past the trees into the edge of a vast clearing, where stood the lodge, a two-story structure of native timber. It looked an old building, though in fine shape, befitting a popular retreat for the cross-country skiers who flocked to the Basin when the proper conditions lured them. By the light they spotted the cluster of shiny cars and four-wheel drive vehicles in the lot, with several sets of tracks leading to the big double doors.

Inside they found themselves immediately within a largish den with many plush chairs arranged around a fireplace, all overlaid with trivial evidences of recent occupancy. Theresa made a cruel comparison between this and the bright, cozy lobby they had vacated below. This room was empty, dark and cold, silent, with mere embers gleaming in the sooty grate. Vorchek located the wall switch for the lights, tried it. The room stayed dark. "So the electricity is out," he said.

"Too bad about that," announced Dassin, a featureless silhouette, from the doorway. "We blew the circuits in the midst of our endeavors. It's not very convenient, I'm afraid."

"Where is everybody?" demanded Theresa. "I'd like to talk to someone."

"As would I," said Vorchek. "I know Dr. Wembley. He should not take it ill if I awakened him."

"Actually," said Dassin, "that won't be necessary. Now that I think of it, they're all downstairs. There's a kind of basement, you see, which we've converted to our needs (used to be a storage room in the days before refrigeration), and I'll bet you any money they're still there. Check it out, Vorchek."

The professor nodded, stepped warily toward the indicated door, Theresa close behind. He called, "Dr. Dassin, are you coming?" But Dassin had disappeared again, this time without a word, so the pair descended by themselves the flight of creaking wooden steps. The narrow passage led to an expansive subterranean cavity with a concrete floor, empty save for a grouping of curious objects huddled in a circle at the center. Strange abstract designs were scrawled on the bare wooden walls and ceiling, a discordant, overlapping mass of exotic or geometrical images. The girl's flashlight revealed what the objects were: a ring of eleven men, lying sprawled on their backs with their heads radiating from the central point; mostly elderly men, snugly clothed, lying as if sleeping, yet that in their postures suggesting more; lying there motionless, mouths agape, eyes staring dully, features sunken. They were all clearly quite dead.

The voice hissed from above. "Come up when you're ready, Vorchek, and don't be foolish. I'm prepared." The professor and Theresa quietly conferred; at his insistence they mounted the steps and rejoined their host, who now held his own flashlight in one hand, a pistol in the other. "Yes, Vorchek, it's as bad as that. You walked blindly into a hopeless situation. Obey me or I'll kill the girl. I don't need her. Too bad about your bimbo, but you would bring her."

Theresa said something rude, at which Dassin chuckled. Vorchek asked coolly, "What is your game, sir? Why have you done this?"

"I haven't done anything. My hands are unstained. It's my show, however, and I want to tell you what happens next. You're a scientist; you deserve to know. Sit down, both of you.

"It's like this, very simply. You and I are kindred spirits, Vorchek, both seekers after arcane marvels. I found one here. I discovered that weird forces were filtering up from deep below the crust at this site, from the very epicenter of the primeval impact. Something came to earth here long ago, arriving violently, wrecking these mountains and probably the plains beyond for a hundred miles or more. This region wasn't always as desolate as it is now. The celestial visitor, however, was much more than a meteor. I don't think it was material in the way we understand the term; it surely left no direct physical traces, which naturally led to the spurious theory of vulcanism. It was a vessel of some kind, a container of force and energy, composed of such, holding within itself the concentrated essence of same. The vessel, I deduce, broke apart or vaporized or was somehow destroyed on impact, but—this is the critical point, Vorchek—the contents survived.

"Those contents, I found, were far more than the chaotic energies which operate naturally in our universe. They are organized, coherent, purposeful. Hence, they must be intelligent. Working along those lines I set out to do what no one, except perhaps yourself, would ever have considered: I made contact. There are ways, means known to the savages who once reigned in these parts. I studied the legends of the Yotapai, the older tales of the Anasazi, found clues, descriptions of rituals. I commenced putting those into practice. Some detail had been lost over the years—no single document told me everything I required—but trial and error saw me through, as it ever will in science.

"I have spoken to them. Tonight I have seen them; I and the others. We saw. Pure beings of immateriality, what one might call ghosts. There are stories about that, even popular tales that the lodge is haunted, which I now accept for what they really are. Call them ghosts, if you will, but know them for entities of a higher plane, one which lords over our own, a sphere whose denizens can wreak their will in our own if they choose. These pioneers, or castaways, these visitors are inclined to assert their will, to reach out and grasp for what they need. That is energy, specifically mental energy, in as pure and as concentrated of a form as possible. They must have the basic force underlying keen intelligence in order to achieve their aim, which is to reconnect with their domain, possibly to return to it. I learned that much, so I arranged that the best minds available be brought here for their disposal."

"Professor," cried Theresa, "is any of this possibly true?"

"I think so," answered Vorchek. "I have heard of similar cases, though none quite so devilish. Dr. Dassin, you mean you fed the brains of our esteemed colleagues to these mental ghouls!"

"An ethereal process, but you've got it pretty much right. My new friends are most grateful to me."

"But why, Doctor? What is in it for you?"

"Knowledge, Vorchek, an answer sufficient in itself, knowledge of ultimate realities beyond the ken of mortal man. Then too, my friends have promised much to me. They assure me that they will teach the method of translating myself into their world, thereby enabling my mind to penetrate the shroud veiling their mysteries, thereby allowing my corporeal body to span the dimensions. Isn't it enough, Vorchek? Isn't it worthwhile?"

"So what happens now, sir?"

"That should be obvious," sneered Dassin. "I shall instigate the ceremonies once more, on your behalf. Those dunces on the floor below cooperated for a lark. Will you do the same, for the advancement of science?"

"No, I will not."

"You better believe he won't, buster," snapped Theresa. "The professor isn't dumb enough to play your game. You'll get nothing from us."

"I want nothing from you, lady. You're excess baggage." Dassin said to Vorchek, "Your cooperation is unnecessary. I will do the deed right here, alone if you like. Clear out if it suits you. You can't get away, you can't run far enough. High tail it, Vorchek, while I laugh at your pathetic struggles. The forces shall be released, shall come for you soon. They'll find you a choice morsel. They'll savor the delicacy I offer them."

Vorchek edged away toward the door, keeping his tall frame between the gun-wielding man and Theresa. Dassin chuckled, waved them off, headed for the passage into the basement. Once outside the two fugitives made a beeline for the upper tram station. Theresa asked breathlessly, "Are you sure he isn't crazy?" Her companion replied, "Much worse, Miss Delaney; he is obsessed. I will refute his claims later, if I can. For the time being, treat them as deadly serious." They reached the small structure, dashed inside. Theresa focused the flashlight as Vorchek examined and fumbled with the controls. "Useless," he said at length. "There is no power. Either I am too ignorant, or Dassin did something to the machinery. He did linger, as I recall. We can not descend this way. Our only chance is by the road."

They returned in a rush to the parking lot, peered into each vehicle. "No keys," observed Vorchek. "My dear, do you know how to hot-wire one of these?" Theresa smiled and spread her hands. "I can swing it. This one's open. Give me a minute." She crawled into a fancy van, tinkered underneath the steering wheel. The engine fired, turned over. "Hop in, Professor. We're blowing this joint."

Scarcely had they begun to pull out of the lot than the earth shook, and a low rumble reached their ears. A faint, sickly yellow radiance oozed from the lower windows of the lodge. The van expired on the instant, its headlamps extinguished. Nothing would make it go. "Dr. Dassin has commenced," said Vorchek. "I should have expected this side effect. So be it. We walk, and good luck to us."

They got out of the dead vehicle, ran against a sudden, clawing wind for the road leading down the mountain. "Twelve miles I think," said the professor. "A poor chance, but the only one we have got. Are you prepared for the journey?" Said Theresa, "More than I am to stay."

Complications ensued very fast. As they marched down the slope, bracing themselves against the wind, hands tucked under their arms against their bodies, Vorchek began to exhibit signs of distress.

He would halt suddenly, then stagger on clumsily, turning about at times as if unsure of the direction. The clearing left behind, the trees pressed closely by the side of the road, the surface firm and smooth, with little ice, yet Vorchek had difficulty maintaining his balance. They had gone less than a mile when he stumbled and fell heavily against the trunk of a blue spruce, his hat toppling onto the frigid ground.

"What are you doing, Professor?" demanded Theresa. "What's the matter?" And the cool, staid, steady Anton Vorchek turned wild eyes upon her.

"My God, Theresa, my God, doubt not Dassin's rantings; believe, for I can feel it. His discourse was most accurate, most precise. Those things, those hideous monsters from some mystical hell, intrude into my mind!" And resourceful, masterful Professor Anton Vorchek screamed.

Theresa clutched at him, pulling him to his feet as he would sink to his knees. "Come on, Professor, it's our only hope. We must keep going." With an immense effort Vorchek rose, stood stoutly, placed one foot forward, then another. "I can hear the chant," said he, speaking as if in a dream, "Dassin's chant, so far away, yet I hear it as if he whispers in my ear. Other sounds, too, something that might be a mockery of speech; a humming, a buzzing, insane noises, yet with a logic to them, like speech. Something speaks to me, many voices, speaking inside my mind, telling me to halt and surrender to them."

"Don't do it," pleaded Theresa, with tears freezing on her cheeks.

"How can I resist?" he panted breathlessly. "It is no longer my mind. My brain, all that I am, belongs to them. They seize it, piece by piece, making it over for themselves, rewriting the electrical impulses that are Vorchek; that were Vorchek."

"Keep going, Professor. Easy now, don't think, just walk."

"But I must think!" Vorchek bellowed, shaking off the girl's tender hands. "If my thoughts cease, then I cease to exist! It must not be!"

Then Theresa saw that which stifled her heart with fear. Vague, shimmering, luminescent shapes approached from all sides. "Oh, Professor," she breathed, "we've got trouble now." The things looked like . . . well, one would be hard pressed to describe exactly what they looked like. They did not resemble anything Theresa had seen before. They were, and they were unspeakably horrible, and they flitted between the trees, and through the trees, their opalescent substance slipping like living mist through the solid obstacles. They gathered round, reached out skinny, misshapen arms toward the desperate man. "It is the end!" shrieked Vorchek as he sagged limply to the ground, coming to rest in sitting position against a slender aspen. The girl hesitated for an unendurably long moment as the things thrust hideous faces into that of the stricken man. Then she screamed helplessly and plunged into the throng, feeling nothing tangible except for Vorchek, whose hands she seized and tightly held.

"Ignore them, Professor," she begged, "fight them, reject them, think of me, listen to me. Don't give yourself to them." The oddest thing happened. Vorchek rallied. Awareness crept back into his eyes. His flaccid features worked, regained vital character; he endeavored to speak. He croaked words, unintelligible syllables certainly, as if his tongue refused to obey, but with a hint of straining mind behind them. And the ghastly, hazy shapes wafted away, as if blown on the furious wind, which began to abate that very second. When Theresa raised her head and opened her eyes she could not see anything to oppress or terrify her, save the vision of her mentor in a state of prostrate weakness.

Of uncanny horrors, that was the last they experienced that night. Perils remained, for the descent of the mountain in darkness and cold was long and dangerous, and hours before they reached the main highway and spied the lights of civilization they were almost frozen through. Make it they did, however, and Vorchek, already regaining his composure and aplomb by the time they reached bottom, soon recovered to his usual debonair self.

The various media reported on the tragedy of the Inner Basin Lodge, a few suggesting mystery, most opining vaguely about accidental poisoning or unhealthy emissions from faulty gas heating. All stated accurately the dreadful news that several of the greatest minds of science had perished. Their names were listed in the papers, along with their full honors, awards, and achievements. The names included that of Richard Dassin.

Professor Vorchek, sipping wine between puffs on his pipe in the happy surroundings of Theresa's luxurious apartment, rustled the newspaper and said to her, "Considering what transpired in the end, Miss Delaney, I can not be surprised to read his name here. Those beings were denied the final prize they sought, yet they are greedy, so they turned upon the keenest mind within range. I wonder if the esteemed Dr. Dassin lasted long enough to know what was happening to him. I hope he did. Oh, I wish I had not said that; pretend I did not. All is in the past, and all is well, thanks to you, my dear."

"Of course," replied Theresa. "I'm pleased to hear, I'm glad you're well, it's all my doing; but what did I do?"

"Like the mountain, sweet Miss Delaney," he said, "you were there. Given my subsequent studies I understand all. It's here in this volume I brought with me. Read it if you wish, perhaps when you can not sleep."

Theresa picked up the ominously large and age-frayed tome, flipped through it, tossed it onto the coffee table. "Why don't you summarize?"

"Very well, as you request. The book concerns the ancient rites of the Yotapai, the people who inhabited the area around the Inner Basin in ages long gone. One of their "medicine" ceremonies involved a worshipful approach to the so-called spirits of that place, who were said to respond to the right kind of incantation. The formula is complex, surprisingly so for a primitive tribe. It must have taken them centuries to work it out, or perhaps the Yotapai derived it from their still more ancient predecessors. I am convinced, by the way, that Dr. Dassin employed a rationalized version of this same rite.

"According to early testimony, the priests of the tribe, the shamans (their best minds, you see) would convene a council within the Inner Basin, in order to call up the mystic forces lurking there. Rather like Drs. Dassin and Wembley and the rest, but with one enormous difference: the Indian grandees always came with and were attended by their lesser acolytes, who never took part in the ceremony in any way, but merely observed and—very important this—intervened if matters got out of hand. They acted to support their masters by aiding them in retaining a thin but firm connection to material reality, lest the minds of the shamans be absorbed by the frightful energies they confronted. Think of it as akin to the lowly slave who whispered words of harsh reality into the ear of the triumphant Roman conqueror. This system worked reasonably well for the Indians and, as you have proven, it worked pretty well in my case. Thanks to you, I am still here to propound intelligently upon the matter. That is the whole story, I believe."

"Not quite all," said Theresa. "There's still those horrible creatures of the Inner Basin. What became of them?"

"Nothing at all," Vorchek replied soberly. He drew on his pipe, drained his glass, adding, "They remain up there, to my knowledge, as immaterial and as potentially menacing as ever. I gather that true danger exists only when the entities are summoned, therefore I recommend a hands-off policy in the future. If they are not called, they can not bite."

THE LEGEND OF THE VULTURE MINE

"It's hot," complained Theresa to her companion, "and it's dry, and it's dusty, and there's no water anywhere, and it's hot, too. Of all the places to drag me, you have to pick a spot right in the middle of the worst desert for a hundred miles around."

"My dear Miss Delaney," replied Professor Anton Vorchek to his charming assistant, "you do this lovely locale an injustice. Here are we, a scant few miles from quaint old Wickenburg—a fine specimen of preserved frontier town, where you seemed to enjoy yourself very much—at the site of the historic human endeavors which built that town. This is where it started, in this very spot. Once upon a time thousands of dedicated men toiled unceasingly here in hopes of enriching themselves, and quite a few succeeded, thanks to the millions of dollars of gold and silver which this bare earth disgorged. Where is your romance, child?"

They stood atop a bleak hillside, one of many under an intense and withering sun, gazing upon a landscape littered with the debris of a former age. Decrepit wooden shacks and ruins of larger structures composed of worn stone and corroded metal sprouted from the cactus-strewn slopes. A single road wound away into the shimmering distance, vanishing among the ridges to the north where loomed the ominous heights of Vulture Peak.

"The Vulture Mine, they called it," Vorchek continued, in his well-modulated, faintly accented English. He paused to remove his broad-brimmed hat and wipe his streaming brow. "Well over a hundred years ago Mr. Wickenburg struck his fabled lode right here below us. He made himself a fortune, then lost it all, but at least he got an entire town named for him, which is not the worst road to

127

immortality. Such stories they tell of this place! I do not wonder that people come from miles around, eagerly paying money to see it. Here, take a look at this brochure."

"I picked up one of my own, thank you," grumbled Theresa, who was hopelessly overdressed for the occasion. She would come attired in her prettiest dress, and wearing expensive designer's shoes more suitable for a night out than a stroll through cruel desert. She had brought a proper bonnet, though, one which provided plenty of shade for her fair features. "It's a mine," she said, "that's all. Wickenburg is nice, and old-fashioned, and it has a cool museum. This is horrid, and abandoned, and I'm not surprised."

Affably replied Vorchek, "The rare metals, indeed, eventually gave out, so the miners left, but their history remains behind them. See the wreck of the Assay Office down there? Constructed it is of gold and silver ore; low grade, unfortunately, or we could spirit away samples. Over there still stands the Hanging Tree, where many a scoundrel met his deserving fate . . . for spiriting away samples. And here, at our feet, is the awesome mouth of the mine itself."

The professor referred to the gaping dark hole in the hillside, next to a crumbling edifice where they currently sheltered. The ancient building contained the vast diesel engine, resembling a docked submarine, which once supplied power to the excavation machinery. The entrance to the mine disappeared into the earth at a steep angle, nor could anything within be seen beyond a few yards.

"Don't even talk to me about this mine," Theresa implored. "I don't like the looks of it, I don't like your plan. Is it really necessary?"

"It should be rewarding," Vorchek assured her. "We will find out momentarily. Our host approaches now."

A man came trudging steadily up the steep path from the visitor's center, carrying a large quantity of gear. He arrived, an older, heavyset fellow, perspiring heavily, wearily blowing out his breath. "Professor Vorchek, Miss Delaney."

"Mr. Cartwright," cried Vorchek, extending a friendly hand which required shaking. "So good of you to come, and even better to serve us in this fashion. I see you have brought the supplies for our journey. I can not tell you how pleased we are that you afford us this courtesy, far beyond what you offer to simple tourists."

"It's my property," responded Cartwright, "and it's my responsibility if anything happens to you down there. I reckon I'd better accompany you."

THE LEGEND OF THE VULTURE MINE

"And personally guide us through the mine," added Vorchek. "No small boon, that, for which we thank you."

"Yeah, thanks," muttered Theresa.

"It's not often that tourists ask to enter the mine," Cartwright noted. "The look of it scares them. Kids, now; kids love the idea, because they don't know any better. Of course, I don't allow that."

"We are not tourists," Vorchek assured him. "This is research, as you already know. We mean to investigate certain unusual aspects connected to the history of this place. It is necessary that we visit the lowest depths."

"So you say. Well, you're paying for it."

"I'm paying for it," Theresa pointed out.

"It's a long walk down," Cartwright cautioned, "and a longer walk back. We'll be descending three thousand feet. You need to be in good shape for that."

"We are that," replied Vorchek. He hefted his camera bag. "Let us begin."

Cartwright fitted them with miner's helmets, then donned his own, testing the built-in lamps. With everything square, he led the way into the black hole of the tunnel. Just inside they encountered remnants of the trolley tracks which once carried carloads of workers into the bowels of the earth. The trolleys were long gone, the tracks rusted and loose. Theresa opined that life had actually been easier in the old days. At least they didn't have to hike in and out every time.

Except for the abandoned tracks, very little remained to suggest the artifice of man. Here and there a few sagging wooden beams told the tale, but otherwise this might have been a natural, if plain, cave. They walked along a gently inclined passage, which revealed to their headlamps regions of brown earth and gray limestone. Cartwright pointed out, early on, the faint chisel or drill marks in the rock, which his charges dutifully acknowledged. There really wasn't much to see.

They came to a broad staging area which opened upon three narrow tunnels. Two of those ran level to the left and right; the third descended sharply before them. "That is the one," said Vorchek. Cartwright shrugged his burly shoulders and trooped down the designated passage, the professor right behind him, Theresa bringing up the rear. From this point forward they felt a genuine sense of how much they were losing in subterranean elevation.

"At least it's cool down here," said Theresa. "It doesn't seem like summer."

"It never does," muttered Cartwright. "It's always about seventy degrees. Otherwise nobody could ever have tolerated the work."

Cooler, perhaps, but it was an oppressive realm. The walls pressed close, the ceiling of the tunnel closer. Vorchek, a tall man, almost had to stoop. The air in the passage was stale, tasting of dust. Once, their host informed them, a ventilation system had circulated air from the upper world, but that equipment had been torn out decades ago, along with everything else. Too bad, he said. It would cost way too much to refurbish the tunnels, in order to make them a paying attraction. And then there was the safety factor; to render the place fit for casual visitors would cost millions, and where was he to get that kind of money? So no one ever came down here, and it didn't normally matter how foul the air was.

They ate from their sack lunches at another tunnel junction. Cartwright had provided ham sandwiches with mustard, one big can of pork and beans with plastic forks, and bottles of soda pop. He produced an old-fashioned kerosene lantern, so that they could conserve their headlamps. They sat against a stone wall on a rough, fallen beam. Overhead a decrepit wooden arrow indicated the downward trail. Painted in red on the crude sign were the words "Mother Lode."

"Tell me, Mr. Cartwright," Vorchek said conversationally, between mouthfuls of sandwich, "what you know concerning the story of Jonathan Paully."

"Paully!" cried their guide. "Boy, that takes us way back. That was about the time the mine closed down."

"It was precisely that time."

"I suppose it was. How did you hear about it? Not from any brochure of mine, I'll bet."

"No, but I have read his statement."

"I haven't," piped up Theresa, who had given up on her beans, those not her idea of suitable cuisine. "Is that what this expedition is about? You never tell me anything, Professor."

"It is what led me here."

"That's a shame," said Cartwright, "because there's nothing to it."

"It is a signed and witnessed affidavit," Vorchek observed.

"It's nothing more than an ignorant miner's tall tale," their host insisted. "Get a bunch of hard men, drag them out to the middle of nowhere to work like slaves, with nothing else to do in what little free time they have, and you're going to get crazy stories, lots of them.

Paully's is just one more. If I'd known that was what you were after, I could have saved you a lot of time and sweat."

"But what is the story?" asked Theresa. "It must be something pretty weird, to catch the Professor's attention."

"It is, rather," said Vorchek. "Weird enough to shut down a multi-million dollar operation. There were real world consequences, which should not be ignored."

"It's nonsense," growled Cartwright. "Kid stuff."

"Tell it to Miss Delaney, sir, as you have heard it."

"All right, if it'll help pass the time. You see, ma'am, Jon Paully was a young fellow, a new man, green I imagine, probable not a stable or reliable type. The sort who would make trouble, stir up a fuss, get carried away with his silly tales. One night, while digging in the lowest shaft—where we're heading, I understand—he claimed to have seen something.

"This was back in '26, and it was the last season of excavation, for what that's worth. Paully was the leader of the lowermost crew, although I can't guess how such a scamp got that post. He and six others were working at the three thousand foot level, when one of his men—he claimed—heard something ahead, through the solid, unexcavated rock wall. This is the story he told. They were spooked by it, thought it might be miners' ghosts or some such thing. That's how they thought in those days. It was a creepy, crying kind of sound, he said, like nothing no one had heard before.

"In Paully's version, he insisted they keep digging, and with gold at stake, he didn't have to argue too much. They kept at it, and nothing happened right then. Over the next few days they occasionally heard the noise again, always ahead of them, and getting louder as they went along. Toward the end, according to the tale, they thought something was starting to dig toward them, to meet them, halfway like. The men didn't care for that one bit, but hero Paully kept them going. Then, without any warning, they broke through into a passage nobody knew anything about, one that wasn't supposed to be there."

Cartwright swigged his soda. "It was a tunnel, sure enough, which went back as far as their lights would shine, but it wasn't one of theirs, and, as they soon learned, it didn't appear on any map of the mine layout. Of course it must have been a cave passage (this part of Arizona is honeycombed with caves), and after a bit of surprise that should have been the end of it. I'd think they might have used it to get to the gold more easily. That would make sense to me. Paully,

131

however, must have had other plans, judging from all the confusion he caused.

"He said they explored the passage, and he said it didn't look like a natural feature or a regular excavation. He said there were scratches on the walls, where it looked like somebody had been scraping the tunnel out with his fingernails. He's talking about solid granite! There's a nutty story for you. He said the tunnel went down a spell, then looped back around an igneous deposit. That's volcanic rock, young lady."

"I know that," said Theresa.

"Sure you do," agreed Cartwright, congenially. "So, at the end of the loop they came to a dark drop, where the tunnel opened up into a huge chamber, so big they couldn't see into it, to the other side or to the bottom. They'd come to the end of the trail, and that should have been the end of the story, but that still wasn't enough for clever Paully. It wasn't satisfying to leave it there, so he added the rest, and it's the ultimate whopper."

"So what happened?" asked Theresa, with a note of insistence in her voice.

"What happened, he said, was that something crawled up out of that endless chamber, and chased them." Cartwright laughed boisterously, spilling his drink in the process. "Now, this is how he told it, if I recollect correctly. They heard a sound of crawling and scraping, coming up from below, and when the men cried out, and began backing away, they heard that awful wail again, only much louder than before. Something that was impossible, that shouldn't be real anywhere, was close by, and then they saw what it was. Paully says that little men began to climb over the lip of the drop, strange little men creeping into the glare of the lights. By 'men' he meant they were kind of shaped like us, with heads and arms and legs, but otherwise there wasn't too much human about them. I guess there was more insect in them than man. They had shells or scales instead of skin, and weird joints, and claws instead of fingers and toes. They had no hair, but they had big mouths full of teeth that looked just like their claws. Also, he said they didn't have any eyes at all. Can you picture something like that? I have a little trouble myself, and I wonder how Paully cooked up such a tale. You can bet he was a hard drinking fellow.

"Well, as the story goes, the bug-men attacked the mining party. The men didn't try to fight back, just to run, which is how they came to

132

lose one of their number. Those creatures grabbed him with their claws and dragged him back toward the edge, while Paully and the rest took off and left him. Paully says he tried to stop the flight, but you can't take any of this part seriously. They left the guy there, screaming his head off, while they ran like maniacs for the surface. By the time they reached the top the story had spread throughout the mine, and everyone was trying to get out. That was all of it, until the next day.

"They returned, a tough gang of them, armed with guns and dynamite, with Paully leading the way. They found the mysterious passage. Its existence is supposed to be fact—maybe so—maybe we'll find out before long. This time, according to Paully's statement, he noticed something he hadn't seen before. There was a kind of wet-looking or slimy substance sticking to the ceiling of the tunnel, glistening in the lights, that they couldn't have missed the first time around, but seemed to be growing and bubbling there now. We're told it was dangerous: one man touched it and it burned him, and they had to carry him away, and I believe he lost his arm. I don't believe it, but you know what I mean. We're told this. That was almost enough for them right there, but Paully says he pushed them on to get the job done. As they reached the big drop the bug-men showed up once more, and the miners' posse had a fight on their hands. The little monsters were hard to kill, but they would crack and break if shot at a whole bunch. Paully's men destroyed them all, taking their own licks in the process, then set their dynamite charges and cleared out. The homemade bombs went off and sealed the mysterious chamber for good. After that they returned to the head of the unknown tunnel, being careful to avoid the nasty stuff on the rock over their heads, and set off more charges, which blocked the passage permanently.

Cartwright shrugged his shoulders. "That's all the good parts of the story. They all came back, mission accomplished, and that ought to have put paid to the story, but so much talk had gotten around that it wouldn't die. I guess they were all a lot of superstitious coots."

"So the mine shortly closed," Vorchek put in, "because the owners had such trouble finding men willing to work the lower levels."

"The Vulture Mine had been running lean for years," Cartwright pointed out, "and they were digging deep as it was, for diminishing returns. I tell you it just wasn't worth the trouble anymore. No matter what stories they told, if there had been a pile of gold down there, somebody would have been eager to pull it up."

"To be sure," Vorchek agreed, in a diplomatic tone. "Thank you, Mr. Cartwright. You have encapsulated the basics of the Paully account quite well. It only remains for us now to visit the scene of the action."

"We're going there?" asked Theresa, with trepidation. "Now that I've heard the story, I'm losing interest."

"Surely you jest, my dear," the professor responded good-naturedly. "This is where the fun begins. Let us move on." After some querulousness on Theresa's part, and further chortling from Cartwright, they got underway again. As they descended Vorchek spoke quietly to his lovely companion. "Paully's tale was confirmed by several others witness to these events. Allowing for that, our host has presented the case fairly. Given that, I want you to bear certain facts in mind. Firstly, the unusual substance which appeared between the expeditions, the slime clinging to the ceiling. That may be important. Secondly, the fact that the unexpected tunnel was, in the end, blocked from both sides. That may indicate the possibility of further discoveries. Finally, what happened to the man who touched that material. That is suggestive." Theresa demanded more information, but she didn't get it then.

Down they marched, at a gentle yet constant angle, until they came up short against a rough mass of stony debris entirely blocking the passage. "End of the line," declared Cartwright. "I don't know what else you could have expected. This is where Paully set off the last charges closing the tunnel. See the powder marks on the exposed surfaces? If this is what you wanted, you might have taken my word for it. I've seen this in the past, and probably nobody else since those days."

"I would not have doubted you," Vorchek said absently. He examined the blockage for a moment, then opened his bag. He drew forth two small spades, the sturdy sort employed by archeologists in their professional work. "Miss Delaney, we shall excavate this promising site."

"We'll never dig through that!"

"This barrier is crumbly, and I suspect not particularly thick. The dynamite charge necessary to create a major block would also have brought the roof crashing down on the miners. We will make headway. Mr. Cartwright, I have a third tool. Will you join us?"

"I'll sit this one out, Professor," replied their host. "You two can hog the fun." He sat back, popping open another can of soda.

134

"In that case," Vorchek said amiably, "I can still appreciate your honoring us with your company."

"Yes, we really appreciate it," said Theresa, in a flat voice.

Digging commenced. The professor and his assistant hacked away at the loose soil, by degrees hollowing out a wide hole. At times they had to extract bulky stones, but in general they made good progress, having little difficulty advancing. Occasionally quantities of dust sifted down from above, spooking Theresa no end, though Vorchek only chuckled and admonished her to continue. Before she could reach a state of utter rebellion they had broken through to the other side, and presently they had carved a passage through which a human being could crawl.

"Well done, Miss Delaney," said Vorchek.

"That was easy!" she replied. "I hardly worked up a sweat."

"But of course. I never underestimate your capabilities. Mr. Cartwright, we shall proceed. Surely you are interested?"

Cartwright had risen and joined them at the narrow mouth of the tunnel. "You're something, Professor. You actually did it. Yeah, I'd like to see it. Nobody's been inside there in eighty years."

They squeezed through the fresh opening one after another, Vorchek, Theresa, then Cartwright. Heads dipped and lamps bobbed, revealing the primal interior. The tunnel which lay before them had surely never been gouged by the crude implements of man; these walls were polished and free of dust, the naked stone gleaming iridescently. All surfaces were completely dry, however, a point which the professor noted aloud. They advanced slowly down the passage. Presently they encountered a scattered array of gray bones. Vorchek stooped to examine them.

"Is that the guy who got caught?" Cartwright asked, with some trace of wonder in his voice.

"No," said Vorchek, after a pause. He picked up one and peered at it over his glasses. "It does not appear to be human."

"One of the creatures," whispered Theresa.

"Undoubtedly. This is an excellent development." He studiously photographed the bones.

As they marched on, they came across other remains, including an intact skull, which they found at the base of an igneous outcropping at the point where the tunnel began to curve. The unusual appearance of that skull caused them all to hesitate, and visibly affected Cartwright.

"That's enough for me," he said shakily. "Whatever has been going on here, I don't want any part of it. Let's clear out."

He received no answer, for at that moment, just as Vorchek snapped another picture, their collective attention was focused upon a sound which suddenly emanated from immediately beyond the radii of their lamps. A large, heavy sound, as of something big moving quickly toward them; they froze, staring hard into the farther darkness. Vorchek deftly pulled his assistant to the back of the line.

"I was right," said he. "Get going, girl; run as fast as you can." Without a word she obeyed. As she made her unplanned departure Cartwright started to react angrily, but he never had the chance to fully express himself. At that precise moment something came into view just ahead.

Something oily and liverish rapidly squirmed down the tunnel toward them. A great mass of pearl-colored matter, horribly alive, lunged forward. Cartwright screamed like a beast, tried to turn and flee, but found his path of retreat blocked.

"Sorry, old man," cried Vorchek; "it can not be helped," and with those words he shoved his frenzied guide at the quivering, onrushing mass. Then the professor turned and fled, ignoring the shrieks which peaked in a mad crescendo of fear behind him. In what might have been record time he attained the mine proper, where Theresa had dutifully waited.

"Give me a hand with this," ordered Vorchek, as he removed from his bag a complicated device, a bundle from which protruded wires and a timer. "Explosives did the job once. They should serve again."

"But Cartwright?" Theresa cried.

"It got him. He was too slow."

He set the timer, flicked a switch, and then urged his companion up the passage. They could hear something approaching from the cave passage. There came a reverberating boom, followed by a rush of warm air, and silence. After that they heard only the sounds of their own footsteps.

Much later, under very different circumstances—in the spacious, well-lit living room of the professor's isolated desert house, where he relaxed with Theresa after dinner—Vorchek refilled the girl's glass, sipped his own brandy, puffed affably on his pipe, and expounded, thusly:

"As you surely realize, Miss Delaney, I do not make a habit of pursuing tall tales from the old frontier. The Paully story, which came to my attention quite by chance, intrigued me because it seemed to offer so many parallels to older—much older—accounts of apparently greater weight. Bear in mind the salient facets of the case, as I understood it before. These are the underground setting, the report of the strange humanoids, and reference to an unusual, growing substance adhering to subterranean walls.

"I was aware of a series of claims, stretching back into antiquity, which might cast light on Paully's affidavit. There is the familiar account in Herodotus, in which he refers to the troglodyte worshippers of the 'Serpent in Darkness,' who lurk under the Great Pyramids and feed upon tomb robbers. From medieval Ireland we have the purported biography of Father Michael, who dared defy 'the men who are not men, dwelling in deep burrows, who follow the slimy snake as it slithers through Earth's bowels.' From Munich, Germany, of a surprisingly late date, I found a newspaper report of an irruption of the 'Ancient Worm' which the superstitious believe gnaws through and devours solid rock, tended by its repellent guardians. Parallels, as I say; there is a pattern to all this, and I wanted to know what it signified.

"Then there is that suggestive fragment from the lost manuscript of Jacob Bleek. I shudder to think how he acquired his information, but he was aware of these legends and, if I have interpreted rightly what survives of his writings, he had reached definite conclusions. There did exist a race of vaguely manlike beings inhabiting the great unknown below our feet. Perfectly adapted to such a life, they throve all over the world, creeping through the global network of what we now call karst strata. Their existence, probably their reason for existence, is bound up with the growth, nurturing, and even worship of worms, snakes, or serpents, although the genuine object of adoration was probably ill described by those terms.

"I had to find out. Here was the Vulture Mine, right on our doorstep, with this delightful tale connected to it. I remembered the sealing of the mysterious passage at both ends by Paully and his gang, and his mention of the slimy matter growing on the ceiling. I deduced that the 'worms' were propagated in this manner, and therefore it might still be possible to get hold of a sample of the material. That is what our expedition was all about.

"For what it is worth to you, I did not expect to encounter more than the insect beings, which I thought my explosives would handle. That the slime had festered in the sealed tunnel—that it had fed upon its trapped worshippers, remaining in the passage, absorbing mineral nutrients from the walls—that it might grow to such size under those conditions; I did not adequately plan for any of that. Why did not it escape over the years, by using its corrosive substance to burn a hole? Perhaps it truly needs its faithful, is fundamentally helpless without them. At any rate, once I realized what was happening, my first thought was for your safety, so I chased you away, and therefore you missed the dramatic, heart-rending finale.

"When all is said and done, the business worked out rather well. I have my pictures, and my intellectual confirmation. While I did not collect a sample of that nasty slime, I did manage to make off with a unique bone, which I shall add to my collection. I have verified the old tales, which is not bad for a single day's effort."

"Don't forget what happened to poor Mr. Cartwright," said Theresa. "He paid a big price."

"A price often paid for the advancement of knowledge," Vorchek sagaciously observed, "even though Mr. Cartwright, sadly, shall never receive the credit due him. You agree, I trust, that he ought to remain a 'missing person;' it avoids the necessity for tiresome official explanations. Most regrettable, his fate, but I want you to know (I think this will ease your mind) that he did not die in vain. His valiant sacrifice made possible my own escape, along with my photographs and specimen. As a result I now possess considerably greater data on a thrilling subject, and I still retain my own life. That is, almost, the best of all possible worlds."

THE REVENGE OF THE PAST

Said Professor Anton Vorchek to his lovely young assistant Theresa Delaney, "I have before me a series of newspaper clippings which indicate curious developments in a small community west of Phoenix, out in the desert on the edge of the valley. It sounds like it might be something right up our alley. Shall I tell you about it?"

Replied Theresa, "Only if it doesn't involve anything really weird." She said this with a sinking note in her pretty voice, for she knew too well his keen fondness, verging on obsession, for strange mysteries, to which he had devoted an unhealthy proportion of his career. He had invited himself over to her upscale Scottsdale apartment without warning, proclaiming interesting tidings.

He answered with a disarming air, "Nothing very out of the way, my dear; perhaps a few unusual elements," at which Theresa sighed, leaned back heavily into the soft cushions of her sofa, lit a cigarette and said, "As I suspected. Okay, hit me with it."

Vorchek launched into his dissertation with alacrity. "This concerns a recent suburban development called Saguaro Canyon Estates, located in the shadow of the White Tank Mountains. Although the name may mean nothing to you" ("It doesn't," she admitted) "you know the area. We drove around there last year for a Sunday excursion among picturesque groves of orange and grapefruit trees." ("That I remember. It was nice.") "Well, the trees are gone, leveled by the developer, who has scraped away unwanted nature and replaced her with fully functional concrete, asphalt, and stucco. Quickly done the deed, and now upwards of five hundred inhabitants dwell where quail and coyotes once roamed."

"Too bad," said Theresa with a languid puff, "but there's nothing unusual about that in these parts. That, Professor, is standard procedure nowadays."

"So it is, Miss Delaney. There is nothing overtly unique about the place. It follows form. The very name, Saguaro Canyon, is a misnomer, for the dwellings are located on a flat plain, with the namesake cacti uprooted and discarded. Here is a street map provided by an ever helpful real estate office. Note the fanciful, and wholly meaningless, designations: Cactus Avenue, Coyote Lane, Farm Trail, each referring, if to anything, to what has been swept away, replaced by artificial landscape containing none of those items. The community, unincorporated as yet, approximates the mean of its kind. There has, however, been recently another sort of development there."

"Your sort, I'm afraid."

"I think so," Vorchek responded brightly. Then his precise, well modulated, slightly accented voice turned serious. "It appears that we have come across a case of a haunted development. Does not that excite you? Strange things do arise among the commonplace. These cuttings tell the tale as I know it yet. This first one, dated a month ago, derives from the small press local paper serving the immediate region. *The White Tanks Gazette* reports claims of disturbing sightings made by the denizens, tales of ghostly presences, sinister shapes glimpsed in the night, human figures spied amidst shadows, vanishing when approached. Here are three more such stories from the following week. Two weeks ago our big city paper got into the act, mentioning these accounts and adding more. Since then we find a constant stream of suggestive information. The question is, what do we make of it?"

"It could be a publicity stunt," Theresa pointed out. She stubbed out her cigarette and said, "People are attracted by this stuff. Look at you."

"My interest is professional," said Vorchek. "Pass the wine, will you? Ah, thank you. Of course you may be correct, only these reports derive from various citizens, none of them obviously connected save by geography. I think they believe what they tell. That being so, I provisionally accept the reality of the phenomena. Given this, I wonder why these events have arisen there, and done so now. As to the first part I reach no conclusion at this time. Casual study informs me of nothing startling in the history of the locale. It has been farm and ranch land for well over a century, before that the haunt (if you will pardon me for putting it that way) of Indians dating back to prehistoric times, all typical around here. That point I reserve for further investigation. Why the now is readily apparent, for no unorthodox tales stem from the period prior to the construction and populating of the community. Therefore I deduce the latter piece of the puzzle with minimal effort, and we need only focus solely on the former."

"Which means what in the real world?" Theresa demanded.

"We pay a visit to Saguaro Canyon Estates, where we observe and learn."

This they did, driving out in Theresa's sporty foreign coupe, insinuating themselves into those bland streets and among those pebble and gravel landscaped lawns as reporters, said tactic serving to open doors for them, although they scarcely looked the part. Professor Vorchek, nattily dressed as always, went forth in his blue corduroy with stark red tie, a felt hat riding high on his broad forehead. An imposing middle-aged figure, he stood tall and lean, hawk-nosed and eagle-eyed, his well-groomed, iron-gray beard accentuating his formidable appearance. Theresa was another matter. She looked as if she had stepped from the pages of a fashion magazine, she the top model in her sashed crimson dress, matching floppy hat loosely enclosing her piled yellow hair, and jet-black boots. She carried pen and pad, which presumably clinched her pose as reporter's assistant. It may be that she from some drew more eager attention than Vorchek.

Many, even most, local citizens had seen nothing, though all had heard much, but the residue had thrilling stories to tell. Said one balding older fellow, speaking mainly to Theresa, "I returned home at dusk, having finished a walk along the big wash—the deep gully on the west side, just off Gila Ranch Lane—and was going in when I noticed a glow coming from the back yard. I stared through the glass door. It was weird, like I was watching a silent movie projected on fog. I saw shadows of men jumping around, moving fast, acting like they were dancing or fighting, or maybe some of both. Then it was like they all came rushing at me, attacking me. I let go of the curtain and stepped back, really scared. Nothing happened, though, and when I peeked a little later nothing was there." Said an elderly woman, who coldly ignored Theresa but fawned over Vorchek, "I took my little dog, Charlie here, for a late walk in the direction of the mountains. When I first moved in I was afraid the coyotes would run off with Charlie, but somebody got rid of them for us, so it's all right now. It was a balmy evening, just the one for a stroll. We crossed the ditch and

141

circled around toward home. About a block down the way I saw something moving beyond the street lamp. I couldn't see it properly, thought it might be a group of strollers, then feared it was a pack of coyotes, no matter what I'd been promised. It wasn't, but I don't know what it was. I'm sure it was one thing rather than a group, but it looked awfully big, and every bit of it was moving every which way. While I watched it disappeared, only it didn't go anywhere, it was just gone, if you know what I mean." Claimed a youngish man, "My girlfriend and I went for a cruise in my four by four, driving through the gate at the end of Sedley Springs Road. This was late, after a party in town. Yeah, we'd been drinking some, but we saw what we saw, and heard it too. There were lights moving out there, so I drove around that way to see what was going on. We went down an incline and up the other side, but by the time we got up the lights were gone or put out. That's when we heard stuff, though. I killed the motor, stopping in the dark with my headlights out. Then we heard the talking, or the singing, or whatever it was, kind of singing voices rattling away in the darkness. They didn't sound English, or Mexican, or anything I've heard before. It was creepy, because we couldn't figure out where the noise was coming from. It sounded like it was coming from everywhere, even beneath us at times, like from deep in the ground. Wendy (that's my girl) got scared so I cranked up and took off back for pavement. I don't know what it's about, but that really happened."

Vorchek and Theresa collected these stories, plus a fair dozen of similar caliber, then stopped in at the real estate office to speak with the man on duty. This Mr. Holloman proved friendly and loquacious. After a lengthy housing pitch he said, when pressed on the issue, "We've got something for everyone here. We even provide our own ghosts. That shouldn't be a surprise, because there's lots of history here. The Gila Ranch ran cattle round about until the forties, when the springs were diverted for the orange growers. We've got the springs dammed for the central pond now, Saguaro Canyon Lake we call it. There's plenty of Indian tales as well, stuff going back a long way. Take a look among the rocks in Johnson Creek and you'll find petroglyphs, prehistoric Indian signs, lines and squiggles and stick pictures of animals. A lot of them have been defaced lately, though, what with all the people pouring in these days. It can't be helped. Anyway, with all those dead times stacked up here, you'd expect a few ghosts to wander, wouldn't you?"

THE REVENGE OF THE PAST

Vorchek lived in an ancient, gloomy house located on a lonely hill overlooking the valley from the north. There he dwelt, and in that two-story habitation, dating to the days of the earliest homesteaders, he also worked when away from the university, maintaining within a large private collection of esoterica and the massive array of books and papers that constituted his stock in trade, the artifacts and lore of elder times. That night he and Theresa repaired there after a sumptuous restaurant dinner to collate their acquired information and reason from it. She sprawled in a hoary old overstuffed Victorian chair while he sat at his scarred roll-top desk, thumbing through his notes. Mused Theresa, who was independently wealthy, "It might be worth my while to buy property out there. Public foolishness can make for good investment." Vorchek, who had to scramble for every penny of grant money and teaching income, said with emphatic disdain, "Foolishness is a common enough commodity, my dear, but do not count on it just yet."

He pondered silently for a spell the transcripts of spooky tales taken down by the girl. When he spoke at last he asked, "Did you notice, Miss Delaney, the occurrence of pattern in these reports?"

"Not much. Everything supposedly happens around the Estates at night, which is the only link I see, but they're spread out all over the community, and the events described vary quite a lot. If genuine, the manifestations assume several forms."

"So far, true. However, in eight of these cases there is reference to a particular, narrowed geographical location. I mean what Mr. Holloman calls Johnson Creek. According to my topographical map that is a long, wide declivity, normally dry save in times of flood, running down from the White Tanks and sweeping along the western edge of the development. As I reconstruct the matter, all these casual mentions of 'the wash,' 'the ditch,' 'the gully,' and so forth refer to Johnson Creek. Our hirsute pickup driver and his lady friend, I deduce, drove across the same. It may be telling that the place comes up so often. If there is a definite focus, that may be it."

"It's a dry wash. What's the deal?"

"We must find out. Miss Delaney, sleep here tonight. I will take the couch, if you insist. Tomorrow morning, first thing, prepared for hiking, we visit Johnson Creek."

Full light found them standing by Vorchek's van before the closed but unlocked gate at the end of Sedley Springs Road. He opened the gate and ushered Theresa through, insisting that they walk the ground

143

rather than drive it. "I must be free to observe," he said. Both dressed more functionally on this occasion, she marching down the dirt road carrying a heavy canteen and a backpack of snacks, he sporting a large old film camera (a Minolta Srt-102, practically an antique), a knapsack filled with lenses and other gear. They went among various types of cacti and hardy desert plants such as palo verde, mesquite, and intrusive salt cedar. Their tough boots crunched on gravel and crumbly red earth.

Within a hundred yards or so they attained the bank of Johnson Creek, a sharp drop onto a broad, flat floor of jumbled white granite boulders and copious sand. The road passed across a kind of ford which cut through the elsewhere formidable cliffs. "We will descend and walk south through the wash," decided Vorchek, "our route paralleling the nearest street. Queried Theresa, "Looking for what, pray tell?" He said, "Anything more than the usual debris of nature."

They looked as they trudged, and among the (very infrequently) runoff-scoured landscape of the channel they did happen upon plentiful evidence of recent human visitation. Here and there, at choice spots, shattered beer bottles sprinkled the stones, crumpled beer cans winked from the sand, while discarded candy wrappers scuttled over the ground, propelled by a light wind. Wadded, greasy fast food bags teetered with the breeze. Asked Theresa, "Did we walk a mile for this evidence?" "It may be suggestive," replied the professor. His tone was casual, but he snapped pictures of the litter with his trusty Minolta.

They found more, something older, more inherently intriguing. They came across a handful of the petroglyphs said to grace the locale. On dark slabs of rock, far up the slope above the currently nonexistent water line they observed incised patterns of intricately intersecting or wavy lines, with one panel presenting what might have been crude images of deer, a creature still plentiful in the mountains. Many of these markings exhibited signs of cruel effacement, chunks chipped or gouged out of the ancient decorations, or vulgar modern graffiti scrawled in paint over the antique art. Theresa asked, "Is this it, Professor, what you're looking for?" "Perhaps not," he muttered, "but it gives me cause to wonder."

The greatest grouping of images, as well as the most damaged, lay within a rocky, litter-strewn natural amphitheater, the lie of the terrain modified by ruinous walls of stacked stones and crumbling mortar, clearly the work of prehistoric artisans. There, taking seats on boulders, Vorchek and Theresa tarried to eat and drink and refresh themselves. Then, while she continued to relax, he ambled about the place taking photographs, pausing at times to change lenses. When Vorchek returned to their impromptu camp he saw Theresa throwing away a stubbed out cigarette. "Do not do that," he cried. "It is naughty, little girl, possibly unwise. Pick it up, and be sure to leave no traces. I have a mind to clear this site before we leave." He sat heavily, took out his pipe, fired it and puffed absently. Theresa asked presently, "Are we on to something?" He said, "I do not know. An idea occurs. It is shaky, though, the notion of a singular effect based on ubiquitous causes. I like not that, and yet it is an answer."

"I am convinced," he went on, "that forces have awakened here, in this vicinity, perhaps this very spot. I examined the surviving petroglyphs about us. They are unique, incorporating designs of a cosmic nature: sun signs, spirals, star bursts, and the like. What you see on that black slab across the way is the remnant of a humanoid figure, extremely scarce in these parts. These elements are indicative. I deduce my next line of research."

Before departing they cleaned up the contemporary rubbish, hauling it to a public bin in a crammed plastic bag. The professor dropped off his companion, returning to his house and books alone.

Two afternoons later he appeared at her door, waving a newspaper. "Further developments," he declared, "exceedingly distressing ones, telling me that a baleful process augments itself. Read this, my dear, and comment." After attending to the demands of hospitality Theresa situated herself and read. The lead article in the local pages announced dire troubles at Saguaro Canyon Estates. During the previous forty-eight hours an unpleasantly acrid odor had welled up from sources unknown, tormenting the nostrils of those suffering citizens. Public health personnel, called in to track the nuisance to its cause, expressed initial bafflement. The problem did not involve sewage or moldering garbage. One quote compared the smell to that of a "filthy slaughter house." A handful of tenants had departed, unable to stand the foul aroma. Investigation continued. The police, meanwhile, were called in for a different reason, to deal with a shocking case of assault. The previous evening a teenaged tenant, returning from a noisy bash with many like friends held at a favored partying nook on the edge of the desert, was attacked and injured by unknown assailants. Off the record informants of authority hinted at a brawl, but the statements of the victim served somewhat to counter that pedestrian hypothesis. Indeed, the young man seemed unable to clarify whether he had been attacked by persons or animals. A police spokesman noted that, while the poor fellow's wounds were "oddly atrocious," they were not the sort to have been inflicted by any creature known to dwell in that or any near locale.

"Is not that revealing?" crowed Vorchek. "Surely I am correct, that strangeness intrudes upon those precincts. I returned to the main petroglyph site in the wash this morning (inhaling that truly disgusting odor en route), found it soiled again with trash. Surely that was the site of this squalid orgy, or whatever proletarian rites our contemporary youths practice out there. They blew up a storm this time! Yet it may be they are not solely to blame. The stench arose shortly after our visit. Perhaps we, too, crossed an invisible line."

"It doesn't look good," Theresa broke in, eager to proffer her requested comment. "Something nasty plagues that place. I don't see from any of this what it is. The events point every which way."

"I can fill in the gaps," said Vorchek, "with a theory that incorporates our findings. I spent all day yesterday analyzing my photographs, then probing my collected documents on Indian lore and early settlers' tales. According to long standing oral tradition, only written down during the last century, there was a prehistoric temple situated on this side of the mountains, a structure that, my still living sources testify, was devoted to the worship of the god Xenophor, once known by his acolytes as the 'Creator and Destroyer of All Things,' the ultimate lord of the universe. I have heard something of this cult or religion, which largely died out before the white man came, though covert worshippers exist to this day. I was not aware of a temple site standing this close to modern civilization."

"You think the ruins and the petroglyphs mark the spot?"

"Indubitably! Since the development came in that holy site has been desecrated as never before. The pioneers and subsequent generations left it alone in the main, perhaps merely through indifference, but the new breed are infinitely more callous and destructive. That may be the unique factor I sought. What goes on here now can not be tolerated by the olden forces, which never really die, but are prone to lie quiet unless disturbed. Then they can awaken, to lash out vindictively. This is such a case, and I may be able to prove it."

"How on earth will you do that?" Theresa demanded.

"With your inestimable aid," replied Vorchek.

THE REVENGE OF THE PAST

He and his companion swung into action three nights later. At that time, just after evening fell, they drove in Vorchek's van to Saguaro Canyon Estates, stopping to open the gate at the end of Sedley Springs Road, then bouncing and rattling their way to the edge of the steep wash. They parked there, between the two of them managing to unload a cumbersome device, a hefty metallic box of instrumentation perched on ungainly tripod legs. This they conveyed by flashlight to the ruin site, a burdensome journey which drew scathing mutterings from Theresa, who was additionally put off by the ever-present stench.

Further developments had troubled the community since their previous visit. Weird sightings had greatly multiplied, with another case of unexplainable assault making the headlines. This time a gentle old lady had been clawed and scarred by something that leapt at her out of the bushes behind her house, something so manlike, save in its animalistic behavior, that the police began to speak of a psychopathic criminal on the loose. Vorchek ignored the official accounts, having already generated a firm theory of his own.

He and Theresa set up the machine on a broad granite ledge before the ruins, a spooky place, the girl opined, in its darkness and isolation. Said Vorchek, "Do not allow your nerves to fret you, child. You will need them later. My device is simple to operate and to understand. While of my own invention, anyone with the requisite mechanical skills could build one. It is left to me because so many otherwise intelligent men doubt the existence of arcane forces, or dispute their ability to reach into the natural world. I know better, of course, therefore can deduce the appropriate method of research.

"The machine acts as an intensifier, a means of amplifying the latent energies surviving within a proscribed location. Relics of the ancient living or cosmic energies remain here, but they have faded in strength, making them difficult to discern save at random, unplanned moments. That is ever the difficulty with hauntings."

"Not really," whispered Theresa. She could not bring herself to speak aloud in the creepy circumstances, and she wished that her companion would keep his voice down. She looked uneasily over her shoulder, her attention riveted by a crackling sound among the dry desert shrubs beyond the glare of the flash. In a low voice she said, "Surely the problem here is that the hauntings are so horribly plain."

"Definite enough to notice," replied Vorchek, "not sufficient for study. We act as scientists, my dear. We come for knowledge. Let us learn." He flipped a switch, activating the machine. It hummed,

147

tiny lights inside its glass-sealed meters glowing greenly. Vorchek said, "Seat yourself comfortably. I shall now draw out the forces of elder mystery, and we will behold."

They sat waiting, Vorchek with complacent ease, Theresa with disordered spirits. The professor had turned off his flashlight, so illumination came solely from his angular, spidery contraption. Theresa saw the needles of the machine's meters inching to the right, heard with furtive dread the escalating hum. Many minutes passed, perhaps an hour, before Vorchek sprang to his feet, pointing aloft, and cried, "Hark! Miss Delaney, do you see?"

She saw. With a gasp she spied the incredible pinwheels of blue electric arcs soaring up into the air and sailing across the starry sky. They seemed to emanate among the boulders and petroglyphs of the ruin. She saw, too, that several of the ancient images, those astronomical in nature, gleamed with a light of their own. Vorchek said triumphantly, "The forces intensify. The power builds! Now we may see with our own eyes what lurks here."

Shimmering pale shapes strode forth from behind the abandoned wreckage of once sacred walls. They resembled men, the men of another race, the men of another, half-forgotten time. They came dressed in loincloths and leather wrappings, with sandaled feet and ornate, beaded headdresses, with bracelets of ruddy copper banding their arms. They were there and not there, ghostly impressions, readily visible but transparent. A curiously harsh sing-song cant accompanied the visions. "The olden priests of Xenophor," said Vorchek, he too whispering now. "It is they who have awakened to repel the desecrators." Theresa shuddered and cried out as one grim-visaged shape walked determinedly toward her and passed through her. She felt a clammy chill as it did so. Only the professor's steadying hand on her shoulder prevented inadvisable motion.

"Oh, Professor," she almost screamed, "what is that?" She nodded at something more issuing from the dead temple, a series of slinking, crouching figures that ambled with horrid speed after the supposed priests. These were not men, could never be confused with such, yet they bore no relation to any sound creature of earth. In their misty ghastliness they looked moist, with gaping toothy mouths, slitted eyes and fearsome claws. Mostly they followed the human shapes, one pausing to stare and sniff at the rapt pair watching back. Vorchek hissed between clenched teeth, "Neither speak nor move, Miss Delaney. These beings are entities from other spheres of reality.

The priests have brought them with them into our world, I reckon without friendly intent. It is best that they not consider us enemies." In a moment the vile thing scampered on, loping away on an indeterminate number of multi-jointed, ropy legs.

A reddish glow began to burn within the rubble. It heightened, flared brightly, emitted dazzling sparks. "This I do not understand," said Vorchek. "What more can there be?" The glow became a glare, a painful brilliancy. Through aching eyes the two living witnesses watched a darkness emerge from out of the bloody light, a hole in visibility which swallowed the scene before them. They stared into black depths, as if peering down into a bottomless well. At the limits of vision something formless and unintelligible stirred within the absolute darkness.

Vorchek shouted, as a man on the edge of sanity might shout, "Run, Theresa, as your value your life and soul, run! Get out of here!" She did not hesitate, nor did he. They ran. As Theresa turned away from the swelling cavity of black beyond night she glimpsed that which terrified, but which only seared into consciousness later: a fleeting sense of compiling substance, a bulky grayness of immense size, with countless dull motes floating within like faltering stars... or cold, unwinking eyes, thousands of them, lurching suddenly closer. She squeaked in frenzied dismay. Amidst the confusion the professor's machine went over with a resounding crash. He would never subsequently admit to having knocked it over in his panic.

After a harrowing ordeal replete with stumbling and bruising they reached the dry ford where the dirt road crossed the wash, clambered up the bank and made for civilization. The glow of street lamps beckoned invitingly. Not so, however, the curious sounds they heard ahead, a muted roar and aural sensation of turmoil. Breathlessly they had slowed their gaits from run to walk, slowed further as they came to the van on the far side of the gate. "What is it now, Professor?" cried Theresa. "It sounds like the whole world is screaming." He opened the passenger door. "Get in," he commanded. "We're going straight through."

Seconds later he entered, cranked the engine ("Thank God," he said, "this old bus still serves me well."), spun round and trundled down the street. They drove through scenes reminiscent of a modern rendition of a painting by Hieronymus Bosch. Everywhere cruel shapes of strange men and stranger creatures rampaged, seeking, tracking down, slaying. The hazy forms preyed on the hapless, defenseless citizens of the community, striking them down and slaughtering them with fiendish glee. Many inhabitants must have rushed outside at the first advent of trouble, to be butchered where they stood in frozen amazement. Some were fleeing, waving their arms and shrieking, never getting far. Vorchek and Theresa continued from one lane to the next, one tableau of horror giving way to the next. The things ignored them ("Marvelously selective," he dryly observed), while the relative handful of unfortunates that made it into their cars and left their driveways were mobbed and dragged forth to the kill. Others floundered in the artificial pond amidst attackers and spreading red waves. It seemed that those who chose to huddle indoors fared no better. Flitting shapes could be seen gathering before doors and windows, silently chanting or threatening, while others simply infiltrated through the solid walls to get at those within. Quiet were those things, wholly silent now, the only noises detectable being the screams of the living and the dying, the various sounds of flesh in extremis, and the growl of automobile engines briefly heard above the grinding of Vorchek's van.

Then Saguaro Canyon Estates fell behind, and the van, picking up speed, hurtled down the solitary dark road leading to the city proper. Vorchek did not steer for his isolated home—Theresa cringed at the thought of such lonely surroundings this night—making instead for the girl's inviting apartment far across the bright, teeming valley.

Next day the papers presented initial accounts of some sort of disaster that struck the development overnight. The reports were hushed, fragmentary, tantalizingly inconclusive. The television stories were, if anything, less revealing. One talking head spoke of a riot, casualties undetermined, instigators unknown. Another alluded to an outbreak of random crimes, some deaths involved. Still another suggested as fact a number of disappearances from Saguaro Canyon Estates, in addition to signs of atrocities. More details were promised at the top of each hour. Maddeningly few were forthcoming.

Vorchek—still in his shabby, begrimed attire—and his assistant breakfasted in her apartment, he insisting that she feed them well, she morosely obeying. Neither had slept much if at all, yet the professor seemed fit and hail. Theresa lacked her customary perkiness. Pushing away from table in full satisfaction, Vorchek puffed on his pipe, saying, "It should be entertaining to see how they spin this one. What will the final verdict be: disease, madness, social pressures, contamination of the water supply? Prepare, my dear, to be heartily amused by this jumping through hoops to comprehend the incomprehensible."

Although Theresa had changed her clothing, and once more looked a class act (this she would do in the most tragic of circumstances), there was nothing in her demeanor or speech to indicate amusement. She said hotly, "It's a terrible thing, and nothing to laugh about. All those poor people were done away with. I'll never forget it."

"Nor should you, Miss Delaney. For them it was a catastrophe of finality. Death walked the earth last night, perhaps worse. I wonder about this reference to disappearances. Could it be true that certain victims were carried away bodily, to be forever lost in the unknown? I do not know yet how to approach that datum, if it be valid. It is, no doubt, a regrettable occurrence, all of it. On the basis of my calculations there can be no question that vengeful powers of the spirit world, angry, disembodied presences from long ago, have reached into the modern material world and struck with a cruel, heartless fist. From these stories it seems that the appetite for retribution has been appeased, for nothing untoward walks abroad now. I think the hauntings have concluded, a state of affairs which should continue so long as the area remains as depopulated as it is currently."

"What really hurts me," said Theresa, "is the possibility that we were responsible." Vorchek scoffed at this, reminding her that the mystery arose before their involvement. "Maybe," she replied, "but it got a lot worse all of a sudden. That machine of yours, that intensifier, operated to enhance the powers and draw them out. Didn't it cause the ultimate nightmare?"

Vorchek chortled sneeringly, but he grimaced as well, and his brow furrowed darkly. After a great pause he said, "Dismiss these suspicions. We were in no fashion responsible for the monstrous deeds. I will provide you with telling evidences at a later time. Quite the contrary, we may, inadvertently, have prevented much worse when you overturned my machine." The girl protested, but he continued, "I trust it is recoverable. Regardless, something more was coming through at the last, something vast and, I am certain, invincibly dangerous. We know to whom that ancient temple was devoted: Xenophor, creator and destroyer—especially the latter, I will bet you—whom the Indians termed 'He of the Thousand Eyes.' Actually they had no word for 'thousand;' perhaps 'many' or 'countless' would be a more appropriate translation. Nevertheless, the presumed destruction of my device may have halted an unintentional calling. Imagine the doomful tribulations if he came among us?

"Please, Miss Delaney, do not tax yourself with vain regrets. Be proud, rather, of the accumulation of knowledge which you have helped foster. We investigate, we learn, we incorporate data into our theories. The cause of science advances. That is the right way. That is the only way."

THE HOUSE ON ANDERSON MESA

"Call me Charley," I said.

"Mr. Robbins," Professor Vorchek said to me, "I offer you an interesting task, one worth credits to you, which should inspire a dedicated graduate student such as yourself. Far to the north, in the region of Flagstaff, is a remote area known as Anderson Mesa. Perched on the edge of this mesa is a house, a moldering edifice called the Tarrent House after its first and, apparently, sole owner. It has been abandoned for over a century. This weekend next I intend to lead a small party there (mainly student comrades of yours) for historical investigation. I expect much unusual material in my line. I want you, sir, as a kind of advance scout. I wish you to venture there ahead of the team—Monday morning, say—carrying in as many necessaries as you can for a stay of some days duration. You see, I have heard you speaking to others of your back-country hiking forays, and I observe that you sport a strong back, so a stout gentleman such as yourself is just what I need to lay the groundwork for the rest, who are not so accustomed to the rough edges of outdoor life. We may not count on the ancient facilities of the house (the whole structure being in, I understand, great disrepair), so think of this as an extended camping trip."

There was more, questions of detail, but I got the point fast enough, and I accepted, the offer of college credits and break from stale routine being more than sufficient. What I didn't really get, then, was Vorchek. I knew of Professor Anton Vorchek, I thought, from what I'd picked up took him for a physicist or researcher up that alley, a guy who spouted fancy, incomprehensible rubbish to other instructors, looked and sounded rather foreign, although he spoke better English than anybody I knew. From our little talk that day I wondered if I'd

153

missed the boat on the man. Vorchek came across much more as an historian, an archeologist, maybe a folklorist considering the way he kept alluding to "odd tales" and "curious claims" concerning the house and its occupants, his comments about "special studies." Certainly sitting there in his cramped campus office what I mainly noticed were shelves and stacks of dusty old books, yellowed papers, and mildewed diaries that properly belonged in a museum. So far from being space age, everything reeked of the old-fashioned as, in his own way, did Vorchek.

A folder of those papers he handed to me, explaining that they contained copies of his notes pertaining to the Tarrent House; dry stuff, he warned, but should I take him up on his offer I might use the reading matter to while away the long days until he showed up. Well, I agreed, we got everything straight, and come three-thirty Monday morning I was heading north from Phoenix on the Interstate, reaching the turn-off below Flagstaff shortly before dawn, and my parking spot twenty minutes later. Still just on the edge of civilization, I brought my van to a halt in the campground near Lake Mary. With explicit directions from the professor, and assurance that the campground host would watch out for my vehicle, without hesitation I locked up and set off on the still gloomy trail. I carried on my back my biggest pack, a heavy rig crammed with food and water, blankets, bedding, and outdoors kit to see me through until the others arrived on Friday. Vorchek had guaranteed that his bunch would haul in everything else required for our adventure, so I need not worry about that.

This was for me a stroll. The good path shot across a meadow, turned sharply left into the woods, then descended steeply into the volcanic southern end of Sandys Canyon. I needed a flashlight to pick my way down, but by the time I reached bottom a fair morning had broken. I sauntered north for a mile along the wide, grassy valley, until I reached the critical trail junction which diverted me from the popular, casual hiker's path. East I went, into the woods again, dense pines and stands of juniper, then up, up toward the high rim of the canyon, where lay Anderson Mesa. It was cool this time of year, downright chilly in the morning. I didn't break a sweat.

I didn't know what it was all about, either. Vorchek had referred to "intriguing aspects of the Tarrent chronicles" and such guff, but I scarcely paid attention. History wasn't my strong point, never had been. My degree was in software design, for God's sake. I didn't know the Tarrent House existed until the professor told me. I knew of Anderson Mesa, but had avoided it, thinking it too near civilization to stimulate my out-backing tastes. I was wrong about that. I had a stiff climb out of the canyon, found myself in forest on the verge of a grassy plain which afforded fine views of the distant San Francisco Peaks. The trail continued across the mesa, only my route didn't. As per instructions, I dived back into the pines and followed a rough course to the right along the canyon rim.

For a while that plunging drop was my sole guide. I picked a way through the trees, with the edge never far out of sight, for maybe an hour. Then I came to a terrain feature for which I had been prepared. This was the juicy part. The terrain to my left began to rise. The damp loam of the forest surrendered to bare rock, wide ledges of gray limestone alternating with orange sandstone. It was a lovely place. It was tricky, too. I was hiking below the rim now, on shelvings of the cliff, where the canyon grew narrow and murky, with a sheer plummet into the depths beneath my feet. In no time the path shrank until it was dizzying, scarcely wider than I was. I could take it. I wondered about Vorchek's other lackeys. He might have been playing it smart to send me on ahead to blaze the way, ensure that it was still possible for regular folks to attain the goal. I did my bit. There was no way I'd let this stop me. I'd dealt with much worse.

I made it through. Back on the mesa, I followed a shallow ridge with a moderate grade to the edge of a flower-speckled clearing. This I expected. Beyond I saw a wall of second growth trees. I trotted across the sunny expanse, spied a dim, angular bulk looming within those shadows on the other side. A few steps more, my eyes adjusting, and I saw the Tarrent House. I had arrived.

That wall of darkness under the trees developed into a tumble-down fence crawling with wild grape vines, and beyond that an awfully weathered house front. I climbed through a gap in a corner of the fence. The house had been a big structure in its day, two stories with several windows, those boarded up now, with slivers and fragments in the soil attesting to the broken panes. The door had been wired shut, but someone had clipped the rusty strands, leaving the entrance ajar. Brush grew thick along the walls. It was interesting, I guessed; kind of dispiriting, too. The history-minded might get a kick out of it.

A peek inside revealed fallen, rotten lumber and a weedy dirt floor. Within a couple of minutes I'd explored the place as best I could, got its measure. The Tarrent House was a dead loss. The first floor was a mess, empty of furnishings except for debris. The upper story was hopeless. I could see into it through holes in the lower ceiling, but the only stairs were a complete wreck. I wouldn't be going up there.

Frankly, I didn't see much point in staying inside the house. I intended to camp on clean ground beyond the ruined fence, but while I was figuring out my plan the rumble of thunder awakened me to the fresh situation. A quick check showed black clouds rolling in fast. I'd known of the possibility. The intensifying sprinkle that shortly commenced decided me. I'd pitch my tent within doors, make the most of the shelter provided by the remaining roof.

I leisurely made camp, fairly dry despite the vigorous shower that now roared against the walls, spraying through crevices in the windows and door, dripping here and there from above. I raised the tent in short order, not having to spike it down, got my gear inside. It was a small, flimsy tent for back-packing, rated for four people, which of course meant barely room for me and my stuff. It was now well on into the afternoon. What with the storm and the gloom and my early start, I felt good for a nap.

I didn't take one, although I wasn't sure of that at the time. I rested, fidgeted, maybe started to doze, was distracted by what sounded like voices. I wondered if other hikers had wandered off the trail, stumbled onto this spot. It was hard to tell. There were all the sounds of wind and rain and thunder, the noises associated with a creaky, dilapidated house, and I was tucked inside a cocoon of canvas as well, but for the life of me I overheard conversation. I couldn't pick out a single word, yet source and tone were clear enough. A harsh-voiced man was growling loudly to a meek-voiced woman. I strained to hear, finally got up, turned on my tiny electric lantern, unzipped the tent flap, poked my head out. These words came distinctly: "Another one to join us."

I wondered how many of them were out there. Armed with my folding umbrella I advanced to the door, pushed it open, hunched my way into the driving rain. There was no one. I walked around the house, shouting twice, without seeing or hearing anybody. They'd gone on, if they were ever there. I barely entertained the possibility of a lingering dream.

The rain died down to a drizzle by nightfall. I set up my collapsible butane stove, cooked a can of soup in my old Boy Scout kit, added a small can of cold beans, finished with a square of chocolate. Then I slept in earnest.

THE HOUSE ON ANDERSON MESA

That was Monday. When I awoke, just before dawn Tuesday, not feeling half as refreshed as I'd like, I found myself doubting the wisdom of Professor Vorchek's scheme. Why did I have to come out here so early? I had days to kill before he turned up with his gang, with precious little to keep myself occupied in the meantime. He'd told me to stick to the house and its environs (made quite a point of that, which didn't mean much to me then) and write down my observations as I saw fit, keep a record of interesting facts—"Enhance your research skills," as he put it—which I didn't get at all. Well, I could puzzle that out later. For the time being, I chose to explore the immediate countryside.

I spent the whole morning, a bright and sunny one, bush-whacking along the forested rim and the cliff ledges of the extreme southern end of the canyon. Once I spied a party of hikers on the far side, waved to them. They waved back. The afternoon clouds came rushing in just like the day before, so I beat a quick retreat back through the woods to the house, finding it again without a misstep. I also found the door to the house wide open, and my belongings disturbed. There were prints in the soft earth, but I couldn't make anything out of them. If anything, they looked like the tracks of bare feet.

Only mildly perturbed, I surveyed the damage, discovered there was none. Nothing was stolen, just fiddled with. I decided somebody had come by, thought my stuff abandoned, learned differently and took off. That made sense. I would have circled the area to see if I were alone, except that the rains came again. Once more I was stuck in the house. That was boring. Desperate for amusement, I plunked myself down in my folding canvas chair, munching chocolate and leafing through Professor Vorchek's notes.

They weren't at all what I expected. Dryly written they might be, but the subject matter was weirdly entertaining. It seemed that Vorchek had collected a series of tall tales relating to the Tarrents and their residence in the wild. The first page (all this being typed on a cranky machine, with plenty of mark-outs and penned corrections in the margins) consisted of names and dates, short entries like:

1894: Oswald Tarrent, wife Amy, build first house.

1895: Joshua born.

1897: Emily born.

1899: Tarrent arrested, released. Amy refuses to leave him.

1901: Tarrent arrested in Flagstaff. Newspaper account:

"crazy man." Released.

1902: Joshua dead; inconclusive hearing; Ebenson diary tells of "grave suspicions."

1904: Tarrent found alone in house, three graves in family plot. Has no explanation. Exhumations prove violent ends. Arraigned for murder. Escapes, tracked to house, trail lost. Never located.

1911: First report of hauntings.

Wow; here was thrilling literature to fill an afternoon. Just that much made me see my surroundings through different eyes. The Tarrent House boasted a grisly history of brutality, lunacy, and murder, maybe with spooks thrown in. That was more than I bargained for. I ate a tin of sardines and went on with my enlightening reading.

Putting all the hints together, I deduced that Oswald Tarrent was a creepy fellow from the start, engaging in casual wife-beating or something similar before he graduated to increasing nastiness. He must have gone off the deep end, killed his entire family, then run away or did himself in, anyway vanishing from history, leaving loose ends that created a legend. Inside of a few years folks were already seeing ghosts.

That was the focus of the professor's notes in the subsequent papers. Quite a number of people reported eerie occurrences during the next twenty years, not so many after civilization receded from the dwindling farms and ranches of the mesa. After that—hey, this was something—it was the infrequent tales of hikers that continued the morbid oral tradition.

Vorchek's notes contained references to presences, voices, shapes in the night, apparently causeless sensations of fear experienced at the site. He also wrote of three lone hikers who went missing in the area, one of them only a few years ago. In two of these never explained cases their camp sites were discovered in the vicinity of the Tarrent House.

These papers gave me sort of an answer to what Vorchek was all about. Otherwise, they generated more questions. Why did he send me up here alone? What was my enforced wait supposed to accomplish? What did he expect to happen? Why, why did he give me those notes to read?

One reference caught my attention, got me active in a form of research. The rain having sputtered out, with decent light despite the low black clouds, I went forth to investigate. In so doing I gathered data I'd overlooked before. See, I'd become vaguely aware that the raggedy fence didn't enclose the house. So what? Now I suspected it enclosed something else. Sure enough, its corroded remnants surrounded the site of the Tarrent family graveyard. The small plot was terribly overgrown, but I identified three amateurishly carved headstones, fashioned out of chunks of cliff rock, one of them bearing a portion of a legible inscription. I read the name "Joshua." There was more: near the three low humps of earth I found a broad slab of flat stone sunk into the soil, its surface barely awash. The stone was as long and broad as a man. I wondered what lay beneath it.

I wasn't a nervy guy. The close proximity of dead people disturbed me—of course it did—but I knew they were dead, had been for a lot longer than I'd been alive. It wouldn't surprise if they haunted my dreams, but that's all I was on the look-out for. I wrote down this discovery, thinking it the sort of thing that would tickle the professor.

Wednesday morning came full of sun, no sign of weather other than a brisk wind howling through the broken rafters of the house and the pressing pines. Over a breakfast of canned tuna and chocolate milk I scanned the professor's writings again, then cast them aside to go walking about. I admit that the close confines of the house got under my skin. I didn't recollect any dreams, preferred to concentrate on present nature rather than ancient history. A journey across the mesa might clear my mind of morbid thoughts. I set out for an easy walk. I didn't get too far. Within a few hundred yards I reached a substantial clearing, glimpsed the mountains to the north-west, spotted something else, too. In the shadows under the trees across the way I surely saw two human figures standing motionless, as if observing me. I called to them. They didn't respond. Unnecessarily irked, I strode slowly across the clearing, pausing to hail them. The breeze, perhaps, whisked away my words. When I got close I didn't see anyone. The taller bushes thrashed in the wind, shadows shifted and jumped. I couldn't testify that anyone had been there. I'd been sure for a moment, though; the doubt came after. I didn't uncover a clue there. I made to go on—had the impression that much open terrain lay beyond that mass of trees—only a nagging in the brain stopped me. I felt afraid. I retraced my steps across the clearing, turning back toward my rather unpleasant camp. The wind stalled of a sudden. All the sounds associated with air movement died. Unfortunately other noises intruded. Branches snapped a short distance to my rear, then to my sides. Once a gruff voice called—I was sure it did—and I

159

looked that way mighty startled, and a dark shape rose up, but no, there wasn't anything, maybe a toppled tree trunk, but that didn't exactly fit my initial impression. I scampered back to the house a bit faster, arrived, realized that wasn't where I wished to spend the day, went right back out to the canyon rim. This time I didn't connect with any hikers across the gorge, nor did I gain peace from this latest excursion. The scene appeared oddly dark, despite the sun, needlessly hazy, as if I viewed the landscape through thin smoke. In the dead air I felt a sensation of helpless airlessness, a constriction in the chest; fear again. The sound of a bulky object lumbering toward me sent me racing again for camp. Despite near panic—remarkably so—I staggered unerringly to base.

Up to that point Wednesday had been a bad day. I knew that I was shaken, more than I could explain. The day got a lot worse.

Following a skimpy lunch I went out of doors, just to escape from that ugly pile. The clouds hadn't come in this time. Round about it might have been a pretty day. There, under those trees, it was as if a weakened sun sent feeble yellow shafts cutting through chunks of lingering night. There was dim light, there was blackness, tangible like tar on shadowed surfaces. Everything felt wrong, the moment of hateful suspense before an unwelcome happening. It happened. When I peered over the fence I saw the oblong slab rising up, the soil trickling from its sides. The three grassy mounds were heaving. I could only think of forces pushing up from underneath, something coming out. I fled into the house. What a ghastly, pathetic fortress against peril! I darted my hand into my pack, pulled it out with my cell phone gripped tightly in fist, snapped it on, prepared to dial a friendly number. No signal. It should have worked there. It didn't, no matter how many times I tried it.

A trembling peek through a crevice in window boarding disclosed an agonizing sight. There were two definite human figures out there, curiously dark, no details, but harrowing silhouettes. No, there were four: two smaller ones crouched close to the others, obscured by shrubs. Their outlines struck me as peculiarly convoluted, unnaturally lacking in certain areas, an observation that insidiously gnawed at my mind. I backed away from the window, ran around to the door, barricaded it as I could with heavier debris. Make no mistake, I assumed immediately, without any cogitation, that these were not visitors I was prepared to meet.

Then the voices began calling to me. I couldn't understand them right off, but in time my ears seemed to tune themselves to a certain frequency, and I started picking up on the words. That harsh, assertive, demanding voice insisted that I come out to join them, "take what's coming to you." A whining, hesitant female voice supported him when he paused, tried to coax me. Childish tones chimed in, asking me out to play. I think I screamed wildly. Not for a moment could I convince myself that these were stray hikers dropping in by chance.

I don't know how long that went on. I know that in time darkness spread about and encompassed me, so night fell without change or release of tension. The voices spoke at intervals, from without a window, the door, from beyond a wall. I remained keyed up, my heart thudding madly, hammering at my ribs. I turned on my crummy electric lantern, good enough normally, now casting a sickening blue light that fostered hideous effects in that shabby room. I didn't dare turn it off, only I didn't want to see where I was. I scribbled down brief jottings of all my horrors for a spell, then threw aside the pad in disgust. I told myself that I'd dump everything, make tracks at first showing of dawn, get back to the proper world regardless of what Vorchek or anybody else had to say about it. It was his fault, I told myself fretfully, somehow, for some crazy reason, that I had the creeps so bad.

What happened then? I couldn't have intelligently narrated events at the time. It seemed to me then, impossible as it sounds, that I fell asleep. Of course that's nuts. I sat myself in my camp chair, huddled miserably, counted the seconds of night ticking away, horrified every time I dared check my watch, for the minutes and hours crept ever so slowly. I hadn't heard the voices for a while. That could have done it. Tired, mentally exhausted, I might have slipped into a kind of coma. That's an explanation I'm willing to hang onto. I say that I dreamed. Suddenly I jerked upright in the chair, in the feeble blue light of my lantern, that wretched room about me, to the shocking sound of battering at the door.

The man bellowed angrily, roaring, "If you won't take your punishment, boy, then I'll bring it to you." The door gave, cracked open. My extemporized barrier couldn't hold. The door fell in, just collapsed and in they came. I leaped up, shrieked. I could see them too well now as they clambered over the rubbish. I won't describe in detail those shapes of nightmare. They had been too long dead, all of them, just enough of them left to hang together, more bones than flesh, with shreds of filthy cloth in patches stretched over gruesomely thin arms and legs, wasted bodies. I wouldn't tell of their faces even if they had much there. Dream visions, after all, don't always jibe with waking logic.

They seized me with bony fingers, dragged me struggling and pleading from the house. I screamed until my cries grew shrill and I choked on my throat. They hauled me into the night, to the little cemetery, where I saw the pushed aside slab, the yawning graves. I saw this despite the darkness, vision without light. Oswald Tarrent laughed, if that gurgle was a laugh, said, "That's how I got away. I dug my own hole, carved my own stone, pulled it over me. The joke was on them. They never guessed I was still here." He added to his eager helpers, "Put him with our other guests." They took me around the old fence, into a thicket where I noticed three more slight mounds. These were undisturbed, but I had the loathsome impression that three more figures were lurking nearby among the trees, stolidly watching us. I couldn't concentrate on them, though, for I had eyes only for the fresh new grave, wide open there, waiting for me.

They pressed me down into it. I fought, sure, but not too hard, because even inside this apparent dream I didn't really believe it was happening. I didn't believe their laying me in the grave; didn't believe their scooping forest sod atop me; didn't believe the dirt in my mouth.

Then I woke up. That's how it happens in dreams. I came to in my tent, not remembering crawling into it, crawled out now to behold the interior of the house as I last saw it. Nothing looked out of place; well, everything did, but no more than before. The door was in a bad state, but hadn't it been already? Lethargically I made for the Tarrent graveyard, found the burials intact as they'd been for decades. I could have predicted that. In the end, a dream is nothing to worry about.

Actually I felt free of worry for the first time in days. It was another bright morning, the sun beamed, and I felt fine, an easy going, passive sort of fine. I couldn't put my finger on it, but I accepted that all my cares and fears were past. I didn't look forward to more trouble, reasoned to myself that I had at last mastered my imagination. If the dream were responsible, then I was grateful for it, horrid though it was to experience.

And that last full day on my own was one of invincible lassitude. I really didn't do anything, often lost track of time. I didn't feel like eating, lacked the get up and go to wander. I winked and nodded through the day. Oh, there were moments when that strange sense of presences returned, but nothing bothered me, not even when the thunderstorms returned and the night came like a thunderclap. Where had the time gone? And it was morning again, and I sat drowsy and contented in my chair, staring at rotten walls, and then Professor Vorchek showed up, staring at me dispassionately, and then he spoke.

Before he acknowledged me, however, I vaguely knew that he had arrived some minutes before, had consulted a notebook, read out some really goofy passages, singing them like a chant, and sprinkled a gray powder in the air with his free hand. Then he probed my belongings with a stick, peered inside the tent, before he turned to me, starting back momentarily as if only now noticing my presence in the chair. He stared, asked, "Mr. Robbins, is it you?"

Boy, was that old guy in a muddle. I shrugged, grinned, wearily replied, "Of course it is, Professor. Who were you expecting?"

"I hardly care to state at this juncture. Mr. Robbins, are you alone? Is there anyone with us? Have you been visited?"

That was too many questions. I tried to nod and shake my head at the same time, only smiled.

He asked if I had written a report as he requested. I pointed to the discarded pad, offered to get it, didn't. I felt too tired. He said, "Do not bother. I will fetch it." He read my few notes, "hmmed" and nodded to himself. He said, "Very good. This is more than I counted upon."

I muttered the query, "Where are the others?"

Vorchek answered, "They arrive this afternoon. I came ahead. It was critical to my analysis that I first investigate the situation on my own. You read my notes?"

"I surely did." Mention of those pained me. "Why bring those up now? It's pointless."

Vorchek continued, "You see, son, I wished to get to the bottom of this arcane mystery, the grotesque occult legends connected with the Tarrent House. I have studied methods, derived from scholars of past ages, that grant one the ability to tear aside the veil, to peer beyond life into esoteric realms. I proposed to come here, armed with the incantations of Jacob Bleek and the mystic powder of Azamodias, to see what I could see.

"All of this is purely experimental, of course. I, a sheer novice, doubted the efficacy of my program. It is rather outré, I admit, scarcely approved by my colleagues. Yet I had to know. Therefore, I conceived a plan. I sent you ahead, equipped with minimal information sufficient to enhance awareness, trusting that your preliminary sojourn here would stir the pot, so to speak, set the stew boiling. Considering how quickly the manifestations assailed you, it may be that those priming papers were superfluous. Still, they gave you a notion of what you faced."

"Nothing," I said. "Please, Professor, stop. I've been alone here. I faced nothing."

"You certainly did. I have these unadorned entries of yours, plus my current observations which prove that my technique works. You did not record all, did you, Mr. Robbins; particularly at the last."

"I wrote it all down, except for . . . except for that final dream."

"The dream you call it?" Vorchek glanced out the gaping door, turned back to me, said, "My technique is not yet strong enough to bring the dead past to my senses. It is perfectly effective, though, for illuminating the dead present. I am sorry, son. I confess to you that the cases of the missing hikers suggested you to me, but I did not thoroughly anticipate nor rely upon this stunning verification."

"You don't make sense, Professor," I cried weakly. "Drop it, will you? I'm tired. Once I've rested, I want to go home."

"Fascinating," he whispered. There was no sorrow in his face, only keen professional interest, when he spoke the words that caused the anguish to well up within me, vomiting from my soul. "A unique case of traumatic denial. Do you actually not realize the truth? My son, you are dead!"

THE HOUSE ON THE HILL OF STARS

"There is nothing intrinsically menacing," said Professor Anton Vorchek, "in the appearance of the Wilson House. It is not especially old, having been raised in the forties, nor is its structure alarmingly outré; no marble gargoyles, no hanging eaves, no tottering gables. Yet this former abode, this blandly styled Wilson House, bears the disquieting reputation for being haunted, and I dare say it does conceal remarkable secrets of a sort. These secrets, Miss Delaney, I mean to unlock, with your aid."

"I'm willing, I suppose," replied Theresa Delaney, "although I'm sure you haven't told all. For starters, what about him?" She cocked an extended thumb at the third one present, a young, shabbily dressed personage with a cynical smile, unshaven face, and backward baseball cap. She said wryly, "Introductions are in order."

"Ah, yes," said Vorchek. "Mr. Gale, thank you for joining us. This will mark your first exposure to the prime facts in the case, and I prefer to deliver one comprehensive presentation to all. That is why I called you both to my home, where, in the comfort of my parlor, we may speak frankly. Anyway, Miss Delaney: Mr. Ronald Gale, one of my faithful graduate students." The youth said, "Call me Ronny. Actually, I'm taking one of his classes as an elective, but it's great fun, if you're into that stuff." Theresa extended a limp hand. Ronny seized it, working it like a water pump. "Pleased to meet you," the girl said, with a certain reserve. Vorchek continued, "Mr. Gale: Miss Theresa Delaney, a special student of mine, of sorts, and my devoted assistant. I am sure she can be of great help to you. She knows something of my ways, and my proclivities."

"Suits me," replied Ronny, bobbing his head with a spastic motion and chuckling. "I'm game." Certainly he might well be. The invitation to Vorchek's solitary home could approximate an honor, for the professor was a powerful individual within his field, noted for the imaginative quality of his scientific views and an impressive figure of mature maleness to boot—ever tastefully dressed in a fine old-fashioned suit, his strong, hawk-like features, his black hair turning iron-gray at the temples, his short, well clipped goatee—but Theresa was something else again. Young, blonde, beautiful, in an age of aggressive proletarianism she, born into wealth and ease, chose to affect the most elegant and eye-catching of attire, being dressed at this time in a blouse and skirt ensemble of pink and maroon, with taupe hose and glossy black boots, and a little dark olive hat surmounting her full long hair. Ronny seemed amazed by her. Indeed, during the lecture that followed, an outside viewer might have suspected him of paying more attention to her than to the stirring narrative.

"All right, then," said Vorchek, in his pleasant, precisely modulated, slightly accented voice. "My dear, refresh my cup, if you would. More coffee, Mr. Gale? So, to business. We venture on Friday to the Wilson House. Its reputation, I think, is misplaced, for I expect to find the locale more intriguing than the structure. I begin the tale with the erection of the house, although that can not be the true beginning. The site, a low, broad hill far off the main highway, south of Sedona beyond Oak Creek, was purchased in 1941 by James Wilson, the great man himself, he of the Wilson Copper Mine, still a going concern, in those days a fabulously profitable enterprise. Mr. Wilson grew wealthy, developed a desire for the choicer frills of the good life. He wished to build for his wife and two children a fancy retreat, a haven from the noise and bustle of the big city. He selected the land, then semi-forested cattle country, hired the expertise of Rondeleur, the famous Southwestern architect, recruited laborers among the itinerant Yavapai Apaches of the region. The style of the house is rather interesting, being designed to mimic in its basic outlines the prehistoric Indian pueblos of the area. Its construction, carried out in the milder seasons, took four years. When it was done the remaining workmen were treated to a celebratory feast. Then the Wilson family moved in for the summer. June of 1945, that was. It was to be the last summer of their lives.

"I don't believe that the late Mr. Wilson had any inkling of difficulties in store. To be sure, there are reports that some of his Yavapai crew disliked his intentions, claiming that the site was sacred

166

ground. The new owner of the property heard some of their stories, may have heard more, but what of that? Can we blame him if, as I deduce, he ignored those fellows? There is scarcely a patch of ground within twenty miles of Sedona which is not held sacred by somebody. The house was built, the Wilsons did move in. That much is history.

"The Indian legends are not, but it is they that fascinate me. Old legends, recorded by scholars of yesteryear, and whispered accounts picked up and repeated by Mr. Wilson, identify the eminence upon which he erected his house as the Hill of Stars, the traditional sacred place of the Yotipai, the extinct tribe pre-dating the Yavapai. As Mr. Wilson told it, that was the hill where the olden ones gathered to watch the stars. The legends provide a very different picture, explain the name in a wholly different fashion. They describe the ancient function of the hill in unique terms.

"Forgive me, my friends, but I wander. I meant to tell you of the mystery surrounding the fate of the Wilson family. Mystery it is, and nothing more, you see. They settled into the house, that abode of luxury, and there they resided for the better part of two months, until they resided there no more. They then left the place, and so far as they were concerned, that was apparently that. It certainly was for the outside world, since the Wilsons vanished from the face of the earth, without trace, never to be seen nor heard from again. And there you have it all, the primary source of the haunted house claim."

Ronny said, "It's a silly story, Professor. Somebody's pulling your leg." Theresa said, "It is woefully incomplete. Come on, Professor, you can do better than that. What's supposed to have happened to them? What about the Indian stuff? How does that enter into it? Were the Wilsons murdered by their workers, or did ghosts eat them? You must have ideas." Ronny snickered, patted Theresa on the shoulder (which touch she shrugged off), said, "I go for the ghosts. The house was plunked down on top of an Apache cemetery. There's the answer."

Vorchek waited patiently until they had finished, then said by way of clarification, "I have told you the fundamental facts. Most of the rest is supposition, hearsay, second or third-hand rumor, possibly leavened with deliberate falsehood. I can not tell you now the truth, for I do not know it. We will learn it, when we undertake our expedition to the Wilson House. Be here, ready to go, six o'clock Friday morning."

Came the day. With the sun already creeping over the horizon, the last faint breath of chill dying on the breeze, the trio set out in Professor Vorchek's spacious van, a four-wheeled drive behemoth loaded with gear and supplies for a possibly lengthy sojourn at their destination. The vehicle trundled north, with Vorchek at the wheel, Theresa at his side, Ronny in the rear, from where he pestered the girl with relentless chatter intended to 'make an impression,' which it did, though not entirely as planned. The van struggled wearily but resolutely, climbing the many miles of interstate, then plunging sharply into the depths of the Verde Valley, where the travelers turned off onto local roads. Having breakfasted in the bustling town of Cottonwood they pushed on up the state highway to the rugged region south of Sedona, the famous vista of the Red Rock Country looming in the distance as they turned off again, this time onto a narrow back road replete with potholes. Their route led them across a lonely, unfrequented corner of Red Rock State Park, a wild and pretty area, and via graded dirt road to the green margins of placidly flowing Oak Creek.

Vorchek explained, "We have been granted permission to pass through the park, which had not been established in Mr. Wilson's day, so long as we do not disturb state property. The current owners of the house (absentee proprietors, no relation to the old family) have also graciously permitted access to the house for purposes of scientific research, on the condition that we deface nothing. I have the key. There will be no amenities, save for a roof over our heads, which will count for something during these cool nights. I need not inform you that we have arrived."

Quite so, for across the stream from where they had halted, emerging from a dense, sprawling thicket of scrub and scattered trees, rose the bulk of a broad hill, fairly low and gently sloped except where it approached the creek, at which point it shelved in cliffs of boulders and red earth. Atop the hill stood a house, the only such structure for a mile or more, which the professor's young companions immediately recognized from photographs as the Wilson House. It was, in its own way, an awesome sight. The architect Rondeleur had conceived a modernized version of the stark, angular, fortress-like structures built in that region during the Pre-Columbian Period, a massy pile in two stories that the workmen faced with smooth red sandstone, large slabs of rock wrapped around many large, rectangular windows. The house brooded darkly against the morning sun.

Theresa said, "I can believe its haunted. It looks hundreds of years old." Vorchek chuckled and responded, "The style is deliberately aged, of course, and, furthermore, it has not been regularly tenanted since the Wilsons left it. Nothing lasts long in these parts without maintenance." Ronny asked, "Does it have heating and air-conditioning?" Came the answer, "An electrical system was installed, but that is no more. I warned you that we must rough it."

The rapidly deteriorating dirt road dipped down the rocky bank, across the creek and up the far side. The van did likewise, and despite a tense moment in the middle of the stream clambered up the slippery opposite bank with ease, bouncing along the fading jeep trail that led to the flat top of the hill. In another minute they parked on the east side of the house, before the ornately carved oaken front door. Viewed closely, the house emitted a sad atmosphere of neglect or decay. Weather-gouged splits marred the stone walls, boarding concealed the remnants of several window panes. Rank weeds overwhelmed the surrounding level terrain, revealing mere hints of former lawn and gardens.

"All out!" Vorchek sang boisterously. He slapped a brown fedora on his head, said, "You two, unload the goods. I will try the key, find out if it still performs." A deal of stuff had been heaped into the back of the van. While Vorchek disappeared into the house his companions huffed and puffed in the quickly warming air, hauling onto the cracked, overgrown cement porch the food, bedding, and clothing, the necessary amenities, as well as the bulky scientific apparatus of their mentor. When they had finished Vorchek emerged, said, "Let us carry all inside, then take a break, that we may undertake the grand tour."

Presently they did so, with the professor in the lead. Once upon a time the Wilson House must have been a grand place. Its interior still imposed upon the senses. Furnishings there were none, and the fine appointments exhibited signs of disrepair, yet that which lingered gratified taste. The walls of what must have been the cavernous living room were paneled in rich mahogany, slightly worm-eaten or chewed by beetles, the floor laid with carpet, now soiled, that retained its brightness and beauty in patches. On these surfaces appeared exotic designs like those of the door, fraught with antique Southwestern symbolism: Kokopelli flute players, human stick figures, cartoonish renditions of deer, lizards, and other native animals. The massive fireplace stood empty, though still stained with ancient soot. A glorious electric chandelier hung overhead, dusty and cobwebbed. So it was in other rooms of the ground floor, except for the store rooms, the laundry, and the kitchen, which were marvelously utilitarian with their tools and formerly up to date appliances. The second floor, approached via a sweeping banistered staircase from the living room, contained the bedrooms, and a once quaint sitting area facing south into a hemispherical bay window, the glass shattered and mainly covered with two-by-four slats. These rooms were also finely appointed, and totally empty of all but dust and the scuttling intrusions of nature.

More heavy lifting conveyed most of the expedition's gear into a walk-in cupboard adjoining the kitchen. In the latter room Theresa made sandwiches for the crew among the dead machinery, while Vorchek organized between mouthfuls. "There is no reason," he mumbled, "why each of us can not have our own bedrooms. There is space for all, to put it mildly, and for many more. I lay claim to the big one overlooking the cliffs by the creek. It will hold me, and my materials, nicely. Foodstuffs we may leave here, sorting the necessities as soon as we get this room cleaned and disinfected. That might be wise for all of the enclosures we choose to inhabit. It is dirty here; furthermore, I detect the faint trace of unpleasant aroma. Miss Delaney, I packed folding aluminum chairs and a cheap folding table. Where would you recommend that we emplace them?"

"The living room," she replied. Though she had sought to restrain herself, Theresa was as ever dressed to the nines. "It's the best room in the house. We may as well treat ourselves." Ronny, still shabby in the modernist vein, piped up, mouthing around his second sandwich, "It's dark in here. Do we live by flashlight?" Said Vorchek, "What would you do without me? Provided I also kerosene lamps, and a reasonable quantity of fuel, in addition to a battery-powered desk lamp, which I retain for my writing." Ronny persisted, "There's no TV, no Internet, nothing. I didn't think to bring a radio. What are we going to do with ourselves, sing camp songs?" Said the professor, "Perhaps you should have brought a book. Reading, Mr. Gale, has long been a beneficial pastime. Nevertheless, what we will do is work. In the meantime, despite such atrocious lacks, we will manage to live decently during our stay." Then he detailed his companions to various tasks, in order to prepare one and all for their residency.

Theresa had occasion to observe with acerbity, Ronny with foul-mouthed vehemence, that the delegation of duties laid the majority of physical work on their shoulders—the really heavy stuff especially on his—while the professor indulged himself with what he called "vital ruminations." Nevertheless, the efforts of that long day rewarded the team with a livable habitat, one in which they could operate with the supplies on hand, if need be for many days. Late that afternoon Vorchek, having explained to Ronny the mechanics of water purification, set the young man to hauling multiple buckets up the hill from the creek, to be dumped into and treated in a big stainless steel canister. While the graduate student grumbled through the hot, tiring ordeal the other two took a break, relaxing seated on stones within a cluster of three tall boulders tightly arranged at a point on the hill's flat summit farthest from the house. There they sipped iced tea, Vorchek puffing on his pipe and fussing over his ever-present notes, Theresa smoking a cigarette and eyeing him dubiously.

She said, "So here we are, here we stay, I guess, until you learn what you want to know. You still haven't told what we're doing." "Because," replied Vorchek, "I do not yet know myself. We have entered a zone of strangeness, one wreathed in mystery. There is, I am convinced, knowledge to be acquired. What else can I tell you now?" Theresa cried, "How about, why we brought *him* along? This Gale person is a boob, I've figured out that much, having had to put up with his moaning and his not too subtle passes all day. He knows nothing, nor does he want to do so. Where did you dig him up?" Vorchek grinned, said, "Mr. Gale has his uses. He makes for a serviceable beast of burden, does not he? He is certainly making life easier for you at the moment. Before we are through he may repay my kind regard in other ways as well."

The topic of discussion appeared, glumly wiping grime from his clothing. "This is where I find you," he sneered. "Well, I've done it all. "Got any beer?"

"No," said Vorchek. "However, a glass of wine after dinner will refresh. Miss Delaney, let us commence that operation." As dusk closed in Theresa supervised by lamplight the preparation of canned roast beef hash on an electric skillet, powered by a battery system rigged by the professor. This entree, supplemented by fresh vegetables and milk from the van's ice chest, satisfied their stomachs if not their palates. Afterward they took it easy in the living room with their glasses of Burgundy. At Vorchek's urging Ronny had filled the fireplace with cut wood and sparked a crackling fire. It sputtered along, the little sounds breaking the otherwise oppressive silence.

"Sweet night," Ronny opined. "Except for slaving, I'm not doing much. Is this it? Is this why I'm here? I hope I'm earning extra credit."

"Tomorrow," said Vorchek, "we commence the delving into the mystery. While you youngsters have dealt with sundries, I have been analyzing pre-existing data in light of our surroundings. I have explored every inch of this house, seeking clues to the Wilson vanishment. I have examined the topography of our hill, the famed Hill of Stars, of which the Indians made so much. I have measured the angles of those three standing stones, where Miss Delaney and I enjoyed our tête-à-tête. This I have performed, attempting to relate observable facts to the many stories I have collected concerning this location."

"I knew you were holding back," said Theresa. "What have you got?"

"Hints, inferences, possibilities, theories; we begin with those, then advance by degrees." Vorchek paused to savor the dark red wine on his tongue, swallowed, went on. "My anecdotal data—all I have for the moment—consists of three elements: the legends of the Indians; a letter composed by Rhonda Wilson, wife of James, shortly before she went missing; and the more recent tales derived from statements made by subsequent tenants of this house.

"My students! Your lesson for the day: the wisdom of the red man. The Yavapai relate stories, descended to them from the long lost Yotipai, of the Hill of Stars. My primary informant is one Tonipah, a wizened old tribal elder whom I first met many years ago in connection with another peculiar case. In his day the man proved a gold mine of information. Listen to what he told me.

"When Tonipah speaks of the Hill of Stars, he has nothing to say about star-gazing, nor any conventional astronomical lore. Quite the contrary, for him the hill is a mystic place, where his forbears, or even earlier peoples, once congregated in order to commune with the gods. It is a key tenet of Southwestern aboriginal religions that certain narrowly circumscribed geographical locales constitute special zones of power, where the rules of nature alter, shift, transform. The kookery of the New Age movement has latched onto this belief, with its prattle about the 'vortex' or 'vortices' where the true believer may obtain 'oneness' with majestic cosmic forces. As those types practice it, the belief is a simple-minded corruption of genuine Indian theology. The Yotipai held that the vortices (we may as well term them thusly) mark intrusions into our space or dimension from spaces and dimensions beyond the material universe. It is within those mysterious, forbidden realms that the gods dwell—definite beings of some sort, known only through the effects of their power—awesome entities who are the actual controllers of the universe, the faces of the forces of nature, if you will. Tonipah has explained to me that these gods determine all eventualities, past and future, for good or ill, according to their own dictates, of which man may only postulate.

"Great and terrible beings they are, lofty, impossibly distant in a fashion superseding mere mileage or light-years, yet they may be approached, for they are wont, at times, to intervene directly in natural affairs, and they are prone to do so at these vortices, gateways from their realm to ours. The man who positions himself at the right time and place may greet them as they emerge. The Indians believed, furthermore, that one could call to them through a vortex, and if the gods deigned, they would come. That was not always, I gather, a happy experience for the supplicant. The gods, Tonipah assures me, are beholden to no man, nor do they always take kindly to being disturbed, or having their sacred places profaned.

"Tonipah emphasizes the danger, often extreme, of the vortices. He recounts cherished hero-myths of mighty warriors who dared gaze upon the gods, dared treat with them or demand of them, actually dared return with them to their celestial homes. One such fabulous story is set at this very Hill of Stars, which, by the way, is a crude translation of the Yavapai phrase 'Negozah-to-Vangah,' meaning 'Mound of the Burning Lights.' Oh yes, I derive from my sources the claim that the hill is an artificial structure, erected by the early pueblo builders to enable them to more readily reach a vortex that hovered somewhat above the natural terrain. That would have been a major engineering feat for barbaric tribesmen.

"But about this wonderful hero, this Vezimoox, who out of pride would seek the gods and wring from them his desire. He is a stock figure of legend, battling savage animals, crushing and enslaving tribal enemies, trekking to far lands in search of noble adventure; the standard catalogue of glorious enterprises, until he sought the gods, that is. Suddenly the tale turns morbid. We are told that he journeyed to the Hill of Stars, contrived to open the gate, passed through into strange outer spheres, came back—after many years, a long generation—changed in body and mind, broken, scarcely human, less or more so depending on the archetypal variation. Some of his tribe shunned him, fled screaming from him; others worshipped him as a demi-god; the elders, after long consultation in 'medicine' or magic council, ordered what he had become incinerated in a great bonfire. One variant claims that the gods destroyed him, that his soul would not find repose in proper burial. Whichever version we embrace, it is not a wholly edifying tale."

Vorchek rose from his seat to knock out his pipe into the dying fire. He turned and said, "As my last word this night, I inform you of my immediate conclusions derived from this day's observations, as they relate to these stories. I am absolutely convinced that this hill is of artificial construction. I examined the cliffs facing the creek. I discern no natural stratigraphy, rather a fairly homogeneous mass which, allowing for compression through centuries, exhibits the customary signs of fill dirt. Those three standing stones, also, have been emplaced by artifice, an obvious finding, since their mineral material resides not in this hill, but among the bluffs and formations over by Cathedral Rock, miles away. So far, then, my views are in accord with Indian legend. Tomorrow night, lady and gentleman, another lesson. Now I advise sleep."

Each to his room, each to his sleeping bag, they passed the night, an intensely quiet period, a stillness broken only by occasional stray cries of animals and the soughing of wind. Come the morn Vorchek and the girl were chipper enough, Ronny considerably less so, he not being accustomed to early hours, which he normally filled with sound and fury. "I felt weird without my earphones," he groused at breakfast; cold cereal and orange juice.

"Tomorrow I'll fry bacon and eggs," Theresa promised.

"Toward which," boomed the professor, "we will avidly look forward. A big day awaits. Mr. Gale, you will supply water for our washing and drinking, one item on a short list of chores, and later in the afternoon I will grace you with a perusal of my notes, thus stimulating your education. Miss Delaney, this morning I must activate my instruments, a task for which your aid will be invaluable."

Theresa smiled, glanced at the scowling Ronny. "Sounds great, Professor."

The machinery of Professor Vorchek requires description. On this expedition he employed three mechanisms of unusual make. The first, sized and shaped like a metal shoe box, resembled a conventional handheld Geiger counter, "Which in essence it is," he told his assistant, although it possessed too many dials and sprouted from its top surface something like a miniature Victrola horn. The second was a small cubic device with numerous mesh-covered orifices, tiny needles of antennae, and a single switch, all of which swiveled smoothly on a tall, spidery tripod, the superstructure being attached via tangled filaments of dangling wiring to a bulky battery box. The third device, from a remove, might be likened to a large, awkward keyboard, or an antique Moog synthesizer, but viewed closely one would see an array of meters, knobs, and buttons. The various dials, meters, and switches of these machines were annotated in a manner that guaranteed incomprehensibility to all but the initiated.

Taking them in order, Vorchek ponderously lectured Theresa, saying (in part, with much brain-stunning technicality omitted), "This device, a simple alteration of mine, picks up ethereal radiations of force not otherwise detectable by normal means. Its range is minuscule, so it must be portable, yet powerful enough to locate spot sources of uncanny influence. That justifies the cumbersome, wide-mouthed receiver. The next item detects similar emissions, but functions as a range-finder and directionality indicator, identifying, if it operates correctly, waves or beams of force coming at us. It may prove useful, if my hypotheses approximate accuracy. This final instrument, designed by me from scratch, is my magnum opus. If we detect curious energy frequencies emanating from this vicinity, the machine should allow me to boost and modulate the force, thus rendering it possible to capture or manipulate the unknown. More than anything, I wish to put this one to the test. It may reveal incredible mysteries!"

Some time later Ronny, drenched in sweat from the climbing temperature and his unwelcome labor, took a break and hailed Vorchek, who sat alone on the porch scribbling in a small black notebook. The youth collapsed heavily beside the older man, queried indifferently as to what he was doing, shrugged at the response. Then he broached another, apparently more interesting topic. Inclining his head to Vorchek's, Ronny said, "That Theresa's a real looker. I mean, she's all right. I could go a few rounds with her. You know, I think she's got the hots for me, too. What is she to you, anyway? Just another student, right?" The professor replied frostily, without looking up, "Miss Delaney's official position, I suppose, is my private secretary." "Oh, yeah?" Ronny said with a leer. "How private?" Vorchek now turned hard eyes to the boy, said crushingly, "Very private." Ronny shrugged again, shortly pulled himself wearily upright and grumpily pleaded the necessity of finishing his chores.

He stuck to those, and others laid upon him, throughout the day, accomplishing all, though increasingly interspersing his efforts with comments which Vorchek considered to border on the mutinous. For Theresa it was a day of mounting lassitude, verging on boredom once her minimal duties to her mentor were finished. Only the professor continued easily and happily, ever writing his notes about the nothing going on. This pattern held firm until after the evening dinner, packaged dried stuff which the girl boiled in the skillet.

Afterward the young people found Vorchek on the back porch, just outside the door, standing with his portable detector in hand at the edge of the cliff. The sluggish creek below glinted in the light of the gibbous moon. Somewhere in the darkling brush one quail called to another, anonymous insects chirped and buzzed. A different type of sound, a metallic hum, complemented the whispers of nature. Theresa, attempting to evade her eager admirer, struck up a conversation, idly asking the professor of his results.

Expecting nothing, she was surprised to hear him reply, "Yes, my dear, we advance, by the first infinitesimal degrees. I have achieved a reading. Listen." Vorchek swung the detector in an arc, generating a louder burst of clicking static. "Yesterday, at this same spot, I derived nothing. Now, the issuance of force, weakly so—very small scale, non-directional, scarcely present—yet unmistakable. It is there. Something develops. I think the pattern begins."

"What pattern is that?" Ronny asked dubiously.

"Come inside, both of you, and over our wine I will offer you, free of charge, another lesson."

When they were situated and refreshed with drink Vorchek said, "I present the second datum point, the letter of Mrs. Wilson to her sister, in which she outlines her observations on the strangeness of her household mere weeks before the world forever lost track of her. There had been previous occurrences of which we have no record, probably written down in correspondence now lost. What survives is surely indicative. I hold in my hand the letter, acquired from descendants. Before I analyze, I shall read the relevant portions. Attend, my friends, to the statement of Rhonda Wilson:

"'Something in this new home of ours continues to distress me. Yes, Josie, it's happened again. This time it wasn't in the house, thank goodness, but outside, by those three big rocks where the children play. Jimmy went out there after supper, when it had cooled off a bit, to get on with clearing away some of the smaller stones. We could make a mountain out of those! Well, the kids were there before him, inside the circle, and as he came near he overheard Bobby speaking, then Sally, only it didn't sound like they were talking to each other, but to someone else. Jimmy charged in among the rocks, wanting to see who was there, but it was only the kids. However, right when he arrived he thought he heard another voice, or some kind of sound anyway, which he first thought was speech, but wasn't certain after. Whatever he heard wasn't English, that he told me definite. It makes me think of the Indians, who might still hang around now and then, but Jimmy says it wasn't anyone. He asked the children what they were doing, they said, "Talking to the rocks." My husband picked on them for that, suggested they might find better things to do, Bobby sulked, but Sally said, "They talk to us." Jimmy said they didn't, threatened to swat her, Bobby blurted, "They do. They want us to go places with them," and Sally clapped her hands and said, "It sounds like fun. Can we?" Jimmy hustled them inside to listen to the radio. He doesn't know what to think. It's hard to keep children amused out here. Radio reception is terrible. I guess the Apaches put ideas in their heads. But remember what I wrote you last time. That happened to me, unless I dreamed it. Nobody put that idea in my head. I still haven't told Jimmy. Maybe I should, before something really odd happens.'

"There you have it," said Vorchek. "There is more, nothing of interest to us. I formulate ideas from this. What say you?"

"It's a joke," sniffed Ronny. "This old lady, this Rhonda, is pulling her sister's leg. She got the idea from living in a creepy old house, pretended it was haunted to liven up her dull life here. That's the answer."

"It's a stupid one," sneered Theresa. "You got everything wrong, bucko. Professor, you've already told us better than that. Rhonda wasn't old when she wrote that letter, neither was the house. It was brand spanking new."

"It looks old and creepy to me," Ronny muttered.

Said Vorchek, "Please, Mr. Gale, adhere to data. The Wilson House did not possess an evil reputation yet; indeed, it bore no tradition of character at all, with its mortar scarcely dry. One may, I suppose, speculate as to the information the Wilsons received from the Indian construction crew, and the extent to which they heeded those stories."

"Which should be," Theresa said decisively, "just about not at all.

177

As a matter of logic—right, Professor?—whatever legends about the hill the Wilsons picked up on, they laughed at. There's no way they took that stuff seriously."

"Wise of them," Ronny snapped. "It's nuts. I say it was a joke."

"I am inclined," said Vorchek, "to dismiss the mirth hypothesis. Mrs. Wilson has a tale to tell, more than one, apparently, and she reports on the situation as she understands it. Thus I see it. Peering back into that time, the question is: what really was happening?"

Theresa cried brightly, "Maybe it was an Indian trick. They knew the old stories. Maybe they were teasing the children, playing games with them."

"I'll buy that," said Ronny. "There you have it, all wrapped in ribbons, we can go home."

Vorchek politely demurred. To Ronny he said, "We have not yet begun. There is work to do. To you, Miss Delaney, I say, based on my information, that the Apaches returned to their homes, mostly quite some distance from here, once construction was complete, nor do they subsequently appear in the records of the house. They were not sneaking about firing arrows at passersby. This was the 1940s, not the Wild West. All evidence speaks to the extreme isolation of the locale at the time. There were no visitors, invited or otherwise; none human, at any rate.

"I desire from you both that you strive to, as it were, connect the dots. You now have two pieces of historical data. Also, forget not that my detector has begun to read something. I deduced that finding before it occurred. Fit together the pieces of the puzzle in your own minds."

A night of unquiet and disturbed rest followed. Professor Vorchek and Theresa bedded down early, Ronny attempting to maintain his normal schedule, a failed effort given the lack of his customary noisy pursuits. His light went out. Perhaps an hour later, or a little more—sometime before midnight, at least—something happened. The trio was individually awakened by sounds of unusual activity.

Probably Theresa's keen ears heard it first, then Ronny's, the professor's mature faculties requiring more stimuli. The girl awoke to the sound of heavy feet pounding downstairs. That someone was up and angry was her initial impression. When the loud steps mounted the stairs and passed into the hall she rose, felt her way to the door of her room in the dark, called out. No reply issued from beyond, but the steps approached, paused outside her door. She imagined she heard a peculiar, guttural voice speak her name. Theresa's impulse to throw open the door and complain died in her throat. Suddenly she knew that no one familiar to her stood without. She held her breath, listening intently.

The steps moved on. She heard the sound of a door hastily opened, observed faint light filtering from the hall, more steps, a frenzied rapping at her door. She drew back, until she heard a welcome voice whispering, "Miss Delaney, it is gone. Open, please."

Only Vorchek would have hesitated, under the circumstances, at a young woman's unlocked door. At her bidding he entered, carrying in one hand a lantern, in the other his compact detector. "The force mounts," he announced. "During the visitation it increased markedly. Now it fades to the earlier level. Did you see anything?"

"I certainly did not," Theresa hissed. "What was it?"

"Ask me that in a week."

Came more noise from down the hall. Ronny blundered in, drawn by the light. "Did you hear it?" he cried. "That was crazy. What's going on?" He looked ashen. Theresa sniped, "I guess it's a practical joke. Yours, mine, or the professor's?" Ronny snarled something not quite comprehensible, but obviously vulgar. Vorchek cut in, saying, "I find that sleep eludes me. I am going downstairs for a drink. I beg you both to join me. Given this event, I believe your third lesson comes due ahead of schedule.

"I can not properly explain," he said shortly, between puffs on his pipe and sips of wine, "what just transpired. I mean to do so in time. Suffice to say that it fits the pattern. In the years following the Wilson disappearance others briefly inhabited the house. None stayed long, a few told tales in order to justify their quick evacuations. This is piecemeal, fragmentary information, yet exhibiting a delightful sameness. The tenants disapproved of the dwelling, deplored the curious sound effects, the half-heard hints of strange voices, the sensation of brooding menace. Yes, the trappings associated with hauntings accumulated rapidly, long before the house acquired its current air of hoary seediness. There is more, although I can not confirm the report. According to one, very second hand source, there was a fellow, a squatter who moved in about fifteen years ago, who may have experienced more. This Mr. Olney, a counter-culture type, set up an impromptu household here, hoping to commune with the cosmos, attain oneness, the typical sort of thing that draws many to this region.

His intimates assure me that he dropped out of sight after a few weeks, never to present himself again before the world. No one has seen him since. His last known location: the Wilson House, atop the ancient Hill of Stars."

"Another disappearance," said Theresa. She stubbed out her cigarette on the floor. After this casual act of vandalism she continued, "This starts to seem a dangerous spot. I don't know that it's worth it."

Ronny, polishing off the wine bottle, said vehemently, "I say let's get the hell out of here. I can't sleep in this place."

Vorchek laughed, a fey sound redolent of forced ease. "My boy, such worries are needless. The majority of this house's occupants have come and gone unharmed, carrying away with them no more than charming tales of nondescript spookiness. They did not genuinely suffer. We come prepared, forewarned, forearmed. Do not fear. That, most likely, is your only bane. Miss Delaney, you know that I would never place at risk your health, your safety, or your sanity. I guarantee you, my dear, against all eventualities. I am here to learn, not to lend my name to another mysterious anecdote."

"But you'll push it to the limit," she chided. "I've seen you in action. It's clear that something mysterious lurks here. That's no tall tale. What can we learn here? What, that is, besides verification of the haunting?"

"'Haunting' is such an obscure word," replied Vorchek. "It means little, without a solid substratum of data. That I shall compile. When you and I leave here, Miss Delaney, we may know what happens here, how it happens, why it happens. That is far more, you must admit, than we currently glean from these odd items of history."

Theresa acquiesced, as always. Ronny argued the point, subsiding only when the girl proffered a cutting allusion to cowardice. The young man was forced to grant that nothing painful or overtly threatening had occurred. Why not ride out the situation, maybe come away with boasts of his involvement in a daring scientific enterprise? In one fashion or another his companions brought him into line.

With rest out of the question, the young people whiled away the hours until dawn, while Vorchek kept busy stalking the halls of the house with his portable device. In the morning they ate cold cereal with the last of the milk. "We'll need to make a run into town," said Theresa, "for more milk, or we eat this dry."

THE HOUSE ON THE HILL OF STARS

"I'll go," Ronny offered.

"Miss Delaney will do the honors," stated Vorchek. "Mr. Gale, you and I will be busy. My dear, here are the keys to my van. Forget not the wine. I appreciate that touch of civilizing influence more than I predicted. Purchase adequately, and attend to quality. Never should we slum through these doings. Take care crossing the creek."

Theresa had not thought of that obstacle, which she instantly dreaded. Regardless, she set out, did make her way across without incident, spun into Sedona for a refreshing two hours of shopping. She returned by midmorning laden with goods, bounced through the stream once more, found Ronny angrily chopping wood ("Your old pal thinks we need a fire every night"), the professor engaged in his favored activities. He reported cheerfully, detector in hand.

"The emanations continue," he said, "and they intensify. Apparently our presence acts as a catalyst. That makes sense, of a sort, for we deal not with natural radiation, but with directed force, an awareness which reacts to us. I would have thought so. The force rises and falls in spots, spiking in the terrain about the standing stones. Do you not recognize, dear girl, the establishment of that location as a focus, a vortex of energy? It must be. Add that to our knowledge of Mrs. Wilson's letter, deduce freely, and you will close with the truth, I say. It is near time to fire up the larger instrument, the direction finder, discern the topography of the powers surrounding us."

Theresa shrugged and "guessed so" aloud. Vorchek shortly became so rapt with his clicking and whining toys that he forgot about her, despite the fact that she produced from her purchased wares a block of imported Havarti cheese, his favorite. She eventually wandered to Ronny, eager to tease him for his perspiration-inducing contributions to the expedition. Surly described his mood. "I was stupid to come," he ranted, swinging the ax with venomous strokes, "stupid to stay. Your sweetheart has no use for me, except to step and fetch it. What am I doing here, besides carrying water and cleaning the portable toilet? He bent over backwards talking me into this, promised me the moon."

"Perhaps he desires to improve your mind," Theresa quipped; "a monumental task to be sure. Even the professor isn't that good." Ronny responded so nastily that she walked quickly away. She spent the period prior to lunch reorganizing the kitchen, hatching schemes for a nice meal. This she concocted, a goulash that brought all together with some show of civility.

EERIE ARIZONA

Vorchek lectured as he ate. "More patterns, more data, formless yet, but coalescing, I think. Wise it was to come fully equipped. The portable detector merely notes the effect. The directional unit, on the other hand, grants me delicious clarity. By the way, an excellent repast, my dear, one that I relish. My life and work would be so drab and Spartan without you. Well, the source of the emanations is definitely the standing stones. The field contaminates much else, including the physical structure of the house, saturates odd points of the hilltop, but it radiates like a bright beacon from within those stones. That is a great find. We know now where to focus our research. The Wilson House, in the main, is irrelevant. It was unfortunately located, no more than that. I find no mystery in its framework."

"What was that thing last night?" Ronny demanded.

Said Vorchek, "I can not reason to an answer at present. I must first explore the variables. Something manifested; that manifestation assuming a strong aural form, if nothing else. We saw nothing, must not assume physicality until the evidence requires. Give me time. This day will provide largesse. I feel it."

"I don't know what you're talking about," fumed Ronny. Theresa said quietly, "Ghosts, I bet." Vorchek grinned. "I will take that bet, Miss Delaney. Claims of ghosts—the basis of haunting tales—usually involve so much more or less than people realize. In this case, I believe we have grasped onto a lot more."

After lunch Professor Vorchek hauled out his third machine, which he designated the "modulator," dragging it on its wheeled metal carriage over the porch, where the range finder was set up, to a position halfway between the house and the three weird stones. He sat himself on a folding metal stool, attached cables to the boxed battery at his feet (one big enough for an automobile), connected more cords and wires, slung off his hat into the dust and clapped cabled earphones to his head. Then he began to play the instrument, appearing from a distance like a notable pianist in concert.

His companions observed him at whiles, chose not to interfere or be drawn in to his obscure labors. Round about three o'clock Theresa, studying him more intently, noted his lack of motion, his blank, staring expression, accosted him. Vorchek started as if from a dream, beheld her with puzzlement in his eyes.

Said he, "One never knows, until the testing, what results will be gained. I have spent these hours deciphering the frequencies of the stones. What did I expect? I operated on hunches. There were so many possibilities, all lacking probability. I have my result, or the initial one. I do not know what it means."

"What have you got?"

"An optical illusion, my dear, unless you verify it for me. I have boosted the radiation levels, concentrated them into a tighter beam, thinking to crack open an unseen door. I believe I have done that. Look straight ahead, Miss Delaney, at the stones, and observe with all of your attention. What do you see?" "Nothing." "That, of course, is a false statement. You see something, though perhaps not what I see. Decades of training have attuned my mind to such phenomena. It would be a pity if my current vision is constrained within the parameters of the psychological. Here: I turn up the modulator another notch; now, you take my place. The phones are unnecessary. Look there, clear your mind, and focus."

The girl obeyed wondering, wholly unsure of herself. What she saw were the tall red stones, upended and tapered like claws scraping at the blue sky, with the folds of rolling dull brown hills perceived beyond them. At first she peered this way and that, endeavoring to pick out the unique element that fascinated her mentor, but he cautioned her, repeating his strictures, so she banished thought and doubt, gazed upon the scene as upon a formless screen, stared unblinking, and—this was marvelous!—she indeed saw something other. The recognizable view wavered, a soft strobing effect, to be replaced by degrees with another scene. Her straining vision encompassed an alien landscape, a barren region of tumbled, broken gray boulders or blocks, with mighty stone spires and crags of jet black soaring beyond into a dim yellow sky. A fuzzy greenish orb lowered from between two jagged peaks, a form scarce brighter than that sky, yet difficult to look at long, painful to the eye. At last Theresa blinked, but the vision, though it flickered darkly, remained.

She exclaimed, "What is it, Professor? Where is it? How can I be seeing this?"

A heady laugh erupted from Vorchek. "You do perceive." He hugged her shoulders. "Theresa, child, you never let me down. I doubt that just anyone could surmount the perceptual barriers. I have opened the door. This vortex, to employ the common terminology, is a gate, normally opened only from the other side. I have broken the rules. Quite naughty of me, I dare say, yet undeniably thrilling.

"You are looking into another dimension, into a realm which does not correspond to our immediate geography. I consider it unlikely that it relates to any place on earth, question its connection to the known universe. I could toss you hypotheses concerning wormholes in space leading to odd planets in far galaxies, but a little birdie in my mind tells me that is much too conventional a conclusion. The vortex, I deduce, spans not distance, however incalculable, but entire planes of existence. You peer into another universe, or something higher than a universe, a domain of complete otherness."

Theresa dropped her eyes, shook her head. When she raised her eyes to Vorchek she stared strangely, glanced about in mild distress. "It's like looking into the sun," she said. "It's hard to see regular stuff." Said the professor, "You will snap back within seconds. That land possesses peculiar visual qualities, or the medium of transmission does so. One requires adjustment." Theresa said, "Okay, I'm all right now. Professor, it looks like a dead land, but things happen around here. We were visited last night. How do you put the pieces together?"

"Appearances deceive. Through that mystic tunnel there pass appurtenances of Mind. Remember, we see a tiny fraction of totality. Who knows what treasures of life and being thrive beyond the gate?" Vorchek turned at a sound. "Ronny, my lad, come over here and join us. You may finish fetching the water shortly. We perform an experiment that demands your studious input."

Ronny warily came, asking, "What is it now?" Vorchek directed him as he had directed the girl, only in this case, despite lengthy trials, without result. The professor chortled, "What did I say? Not all are vouchsafed that sublime experience." Ronny huffed, "I don't get it." Replied Vorchek, "You will, my boy, you will. I harbor enormously high hopes for you. Your presence may well prove the deciding factor in my success." The young man started to sputter a response, which Vorchek heeded not for a moment, instead shooing away his companions that he might dive into a furious round of note-writing. He tacitly left to Theresa the onerous task of explaining the meaning of what had transpired, a task for which, despite all her long training at the professor's feet, she was remarkably unqualified. Ronny, having half-heartedly attended to her account, proclaimed it all "hooey," in the process employing a more objectionable term.

Later Vorchek insisted on a fancy dinner, urging all to pitch into the effort of preparation. This Theresa appreciated, marveling that the staid professor should stoop to matters less than ethereal, but then Vorchek was in a gay mood of unbounded ebullience, almost frighteningly cheerful and eager to please and promote an air of festivity. "It has been a great day," he explained when pressed, "and I expect further greatness in the offing. We stand on the brink." He had brought the modulator back into the house, but he kept it running, breaking at times from culinary duties to check its settings and examine the meters.

During the meal of grilled pork chops, potatoes roasted in foil, green beans from a can and packaged dinner rolls, Vorchek, dropping all restraint, kept up a stream of shop-talk, discoursing on "channeled energy flows," "bodiless sense impressions," the possibilities of what he (even for him) murkily termed "intrusive reversal." He ate with gusto, gesturing between bites as he made points largely to himself. Theresa grinned at his antics, the more so when she failed to understand him, which was often. Ronny rolled his eyes and wryly grimaced at the girl, but she refused to rise to his bait.

Daylight dimmed, fading entirely away during this dinner. With the gathering gloom, defiantly held back by the lighting of lamps, a more somber tone invaded the bleak living room where they were sequestered. Conversation, even casual chatter, muted and died. Each occupant of the room seemed inwardly drawn, wreathed in his own brand of thought. Theresa appeared bored, Ronny frustrated, the professor—well, difficult to read he might be, but attentive would do—his posture, the hunch of his shoulders, the tilt of his large head, the mannered stroking of his manicured beard, suggested listening.

To the latter amazement of the others present, Ronny heard it first. "There's something outside," he said, "something whistling." Vorchek said, "Cicadas, as may be. Miss Delaney, is this the season?" "How should I know?" she snapped. "I don't hear . . . wait, there is something." Ronny pushed away from the table, muttering, "I said so, didn't I?"

"I hear it now," agreed Vorchek. "A thin whine, very low. Are the windows shut?" Theresa informed him that she had opened them for air. The professor rose, pulled closed the grating panes. "I still hear it," he said, "getting louder. Folks, brace yourselves for wild times. A visitor comes, and my modulator is blowing at full blast."

Ronny's frantic query was stifled by the roar of noise that suddenly ensued, a sound as of great force vigorously applied to the walls of the house. A disagreeable sensation of extreme pressure beat down upon the three, rendering them airless and gasping. Now it was as if sonic booms shook the earth, like the sounds of the previous

185

night, yet ferociously greater in magnitude. This was not an unseen entity stamping through a corridor, but rather a behemoth pounding on the house's shell of stone, thrusting itself against the stout door and the thin glass of the windows. In no direction could structural deterioration be seen, but it felt as if the house, and its tenants, were being crushed.

The background whine escalated to an ear-splitting shriek, mingling with Theresa's scream and Ronny's hapless bellow of fear. Professor Vorchek dashed to his modulator, set up in a corner of the room, twirled knobs and pressed buttons. Over the din he cried out once, "I am trying to understand. Our minds are too hardened with age. Speak plainly, to the impulses of our brains, or heed the machine, which I have readied for you." The agonizing sound mounted further, attained a devastating crescendo, then ceased in an instant. With that, no trace of the baleful effects remained.

Ronny waved his fingers in the air over his head, a spastic motion, cried, "I'm out of here." Vorchek strode forth, gripped him savagely, hissed, "Are you insane? That thing waits outside, in the dark, primed to pounce on anybody foolish enough to confront it. If that must be, let us choose the time and place." Ronny slumped into his chair, babbling, "This can't be for real. You two set this up for me, to make me out an idiot. You both look down on me, treat me like trash." So he said, but spoke no more of departing.

"It is over," said Vorchek. "The manifestation subsides, as they always do. We are hail and hearty, without cause for fear. I counsel deep sleep, and no dreams."

"That's a laugh," said Theresa. "Surely, Professor, this means trouble. That thing wants to eat us, or whatever. Did your machine draw it to us?"

Vorchek appeared nonplused. "Too many variables," he absently replied. "Answers will require months of analysis. The modulator may be a factor. Bear in mind, however, that strange things occurred here long before I activated the device."

"And what was that you were carrying on about," Ronny demanded, "while all that was happening? Who were you talking to?"

"I do not know," Vorchek said pensively, "that I spoke with anyone. I, too, am capable of guesses. I refuse to act on them, however, without appropriate evidence. No more. I tire. To bed I go. My friends, suit yourselves."

Eventually the young people, out of sheer ennui, went their

separate ways, but Theresa did not sleep. She sat brooding in her room for a lengthy passage, her mind working, until she could stand it no more, went forth to speak with Vorchek. Light gleamed under his door. She knocked, he admitted her, asserting that he was just that minute bedding down. He was still dressed, though, wearing his reading glasses, and he had a batch of notes and electrical gear laid out on the tiny table he used for a desk.

"More happened tonight," Theresa said, "than you let on. You weren't speaking to Ronny or myself there at the end. And what's all this? What are you up to now?"

Vorchek hesitated, shrugged, told her, "That's my old fashioned tape recorder. I am transferring digital recordings of those odd sounds to this, where I may control speed and pitch." "What's the point of that?" "To better understand what was being said."

Theresa caught her breath. "That's a mighty big deduction," said she. "It sounded like angry bees to me."

"It did not sound like that," the professor pointed out, "to the Wilson children. They heard speech, something that made sense to them. Their juvenile ears were tuned to extremely high frequencies. Mine are not, nor are yours and Ronny's. I believe you two barely miss the threshold. With my apparatus I can tinker with the frequencies, reduce them to a level my aging ears can grasp. I have been attempting to accomplish that."

"Why would anyone—" Theresa paused—"anyone on the other side, want to speak with us?"

"Do not ask me. I would gladly speak with them, because I wish to learn. That may justify their actions, or not. What could they learn from us? Perhaps they want something."

"What?"

"Us." Vorchek sighed, removed his glasses, rubbed his eyes. "The Wilsons are gone. We can not account for the whereabouts of other specimens of humanity who have ventured here. There are ancient legends. My imagination waxes richly. In the absence of hard data, I may conceive anything."

"How do you collect that data?"

Vorchek chuckled, an easy, disarming sound, patted her cheek, as a devoted uncle would his favorite niece. "I suppose I do not. How do I begin? Some mysteries, unfortunately, must remain forever beyond me. Now to bed, little girl, before I call in the riot squad."

If Theresa slept, she did so without enthusiasm. Sometime later still she jolted awake, her nerves tingling, springing to her feet in darkness before she asked herself the meaning of her actions. She listened, heard, wondered. There was movement in the house. Her first thought—an icy spike of fear!—was of another horrid visitation. Fervent attentiveness indicated another answer. The movement was next door, in the room to her right. A door opened over there, followed by furtive steps in the hall. Professor Vorchek was up and about. The steps creaked away along the hall, down the stairs. Shortly the girl barely discerned the groan of the front door.

Curiosity and dread assailed her. The former won. In her filmy nightie she slipped out of her room, pausing only to apply slippers to her tender feet, and crept across the chill hall into an unused room that faced the open expanse of the weedy front yard. Through the cool pane of the window she peered. Down there, by the light of the moon, Vorchek occupied himself with emplacing his modulator in its previous position. When that was done, and he had manipulated its many controls, he advanced slowly toward the three standing stones that loomed in the murk like giant, cowled Druid priests.

The professor stood before the stones. Slight motions indicated speech on his part, a desire to be noticed, although he stood entirely alone. After a minute he proceeded within the confines of the stones, partly vanishing into shadows the moon could not dispel.

Now Theresa saw something weird. She wondered if it were a trick of the eye. A second thought indicated to her the occurrence of another vision similar to that she and the professor had experienced, only with different effects. Peering into the space between the stones, where Vorchek had gone, she beheld a skyscape of stars, an awesome panorama of brilliant, densely crowded motes. Through a telescope such a sight might be realized, but here she received it unaided. Cosmic wonders flashed and twinkled where they should not be.

What the professor said she could not hear, but a rumbling noise responded, seeming to burst forth when he paused in speech. The sounds were wholly alien, yet there was that in their timbre and cadence which suggested intelligent communication. If that were a voice, it was no kind that she had ever heard or wished to hear. Indeed, it so pained her ears that she clapped her palms to them to shut out the dreadful impact on her ear drums, a defensive action of no consequence. Still the harsh aural bombardment rattled her brain.

Ultimately Theresa realized that the voice had stopped, that the strange tapestry of stars had vanished, revealing the dim hilly terrain beyond the stones, and that Professor Vorchek had returned to his instrument, which he was packing up. When he strode for the front door she left the window and dashed back into her room, shutting the door and waiting breathlessly. She heard him presently ascend the stairs, return to his own room. Occasional, trivial sounds were soon replaced by silence. The odd episode had concluded.

That morning Vorchek slept late. Theresa came down early, having fitfully slumbered, ate a dish of bacon and biscuits alone. Through the kitchen window overlooking the creekside cliffs she recognized another sunny, warming day, ever the norm for this season, in the offing. Ronny appeared, looking scruffier than ever, his hair tangled and backward cap askew. He said of a sudden, "I'm all for getting out of here today. I can't take this anymore. Whatever we're supposed to learn, it isn't worth it, not to me. I couldn't care less. None of this interests me, none of this matters to my life. I signed up for Vorchek's class because I needed three credits, not because I want to risk my neck chasing wacky mysteries. I thought it was nonsense, laughed with my buddies behind his back. Okay, I was wrong. This joint is dangerous. I'm going to insist that he take me out of here, get me back to the sane world. If he won't, I'll hike out. Five lousy miles will take me to safety. With luck I'll never even hear about the Wilson House or Hill of Stars again." Theresa replied somewhat, saw no point in arguing with him if he lacked enthusiasm to that degree. She had not wanted him there in the first place.

Ronny skipped breakfast, went back to his room, saying he intended to pack. While Theresa scoured her dishes she overheard a muffled but heated exchange overhead. Shortly steps descended the stairs, evolved into Vorchek briskly entering the kitchen. Fully attired and looking ready for action, he clapped his hands and with cheery countenance said, "Miss Delaney, I discover that our medical supplies run low. I snagged my finger, yet I have no bandage. We must supplement our stash." Theresa offered to attended to his wounded digit, but he waved her off, refusing even to show her the cut. "It is minor," he said, "but it reminds me we should be prepared. You must go into town again in order to stock up."

Theresa frowned, responding with puzzlement, "I packed a ton of that stuff, hydrogen peroxide, rubbing alcohol, and a big box of bandages and gauze. It's in the store room."

"A mistake on my part," said Vorchek, "led to a little accident; water damage, you see. The bandages are soggy. Take the van—you will have no trouble—get what we need, as well as anything else you can think of purchasing. Take care of it at once, and fear not. I have no activities planned for this morning."

She agreed. Vorchek nodded excitedly, stalked from the room. Within a few minutes Theresa had pulled herself together and was once more braving the tricky creek crossing and the long dusty drive back to firm pavement. Given all that had happened, all that she had heard, it did her good to get away, to be out and about with normal people in normal situations. That strange outpost in the wilderness felt so far away, so meaningless. After buying the requested wares at a grocery store she spent another couple of hours touring the marvelous shops of Sedona. She bought herself a wind chime, a hand-made trinket of burnished copper and prettily colored glass, as a memento. She did not see the Wilson House again until that afternoon. As it turned out, it would be her last sight of that disturbing locale.

With a distant glimpse of the state park's visitor center behind her, she and the van jostled along the forlorn dirt road toward the creek when she began to perceive something unusual happening. Bright sun, steady, relentless, vivid blue sky bereft of clouds or haze—every vista crisp, harshly defined—yet the scene before her appeared disconnected from all around it. Beyond the creek she strained with narrowed eyes to see the infamous hill with its lonely house atop, experiencing difficulties in this mundane task. A shadow, of the sort overlaid by a heavy, dense black cloud, hovered there upon the land, without any cloud as cause. She stopped in the rutted lane at the gravelly bank. Yet, the hill was over there, and the house, but she viewed them through a mirage of smoked glass, the scene resembling a still, bleakly painted landscape. Her nerves strummed discordantly. Fear? No, not yet at any rate; a humming, a virtually subliminal vibration, tugged at her psyche. What did it mean?

She crossed the muddy waters, the four-wheeled drive scampering up the far side, drove around and up the hill. The hideously artificial gloom intensified, as did the tormenting vibration. Like an angry hive of bees it sounded, bees trying to speak, to make themselves heard and understood, a senseless sound redolent with unwelcome significance. She pulled onto the little mesa at the summit, drew up before the front of the house. No living thing was in sight. The professor's modulator sat on the porch, squatting on its stand, red lights winking. From the three standing stones to her left, wreathed in deeper darkness, a stream of green stars shot like meteors into the

190

encompassing blackness.

Theresa forced herself out of the van, stood with her hand clenched to the driver's side door. She was scared now, terrified, knowing that something had gone horribly wrong, dreading the revelation, sick with horror at her own presence there. Emotion urged her to flee, mind counseled investigation. Her companions were thereabout, unseen.

A soul-chilling scream rent the air. She recognized in a flash Ronny's voice, agonizingly distorted though it was. She could not locate the source. It came from everywhere. It came again, more ghastly still. The cries came—the realization hit like a sledge hammer—from the unhallowed standing stones, from which the green lights gushed. Ronny was in there!

She stepped toward the red rocks with the jerking motions of an automaton, calling out, "Ronny, can you hear me? It's Theresa. What are you doing in there? For God's sake, get out!" Amidst the glare of hurtling orbs she saw faintly swirling hints of form, movement of shadowy shapes, writhing travesties of fleeting solidity. She did not relish what she saw of them. Theresa screamed.

Ronny shouted hoarsely, his voice emerging as from an echoing tunnel of impossible length, "He did this to me, he set it up. He planned it from the start, all of it. He knew, lured me in! Now they've got me. Oh God, I don't know where I am. Everything is upside down and crazy—a world of madness!—and I can't get out. They block the way. They're closing in, they're coming for me, and they've told me what they want—over here I understand them—they laugh without mouths, telling me what they'll do, what will become of me! Better to die a thousand times than that!"

Ronny's disembodied voice shrieked wildly, and then silence descended like reverberating thunder. The preternatural gloom and the awful vibrations cleared on the instant, leaving Theresa standing before the rock sentinels blinking against the sunny glare. She turned away, her knees faltering, spied Professor Vorchek on the porch, his index finger on the power button of the modulator. She endeavored to speak, could not frame the words. She would have fallen, but he came to her with gigantic strides, wrapped his big arms around her.

He said, "Mr. Gale is gone. It happened, I believe, as in former cases. It was reckless, magnificent foolishness on his part, a risk that went awry. There is nothing we can do. Now I must get you out of here. Our belongings will keep. I can return for them later. For the nonce, your safety only concerns me."

Vorchek proved as good as his word. Before another minute passed they were in the van, the professor at the wheel, crossing the creek and racing for healthy, conventional surroundings. Theresa was not fit for human company at that juncture. In Sedona Vorchek purchased refreshment at an upscale sandwich shop, drove his charge to a secluded overlook out on the highway that provided a lovely view of the majestic red formations dominating that countryside, and there he gently insisted that she eat and restore herself. His aplomb recovered considerably faster.

In time she began to speak, hesitantly blurting questions on an array of apparently interconnected subjects. When she had sufficiently broached her concerns Vorchek smiled grimly and launched his amazing tale of what occurred that day at the Wilson House on the Hill of Stars. He said:

"I was close, so close, to grasping the key that unlocks the ultimate gate. Communication through the vortex was at hand! Who knows what worlds or universes lie beyond, who knows who or what lurks there, what entities operate across the gulf for purposes of their own? I imagined myself unpeeling the film off of the first, modest mysteries. What I would have done, what I could have achieved, I can not say. The perils were so profound and so obvious to me, that I tarried, scarcely daring to proceed. Remember, little girl, that all those who have, unwittingly or otherwise, trafficked across that barrier have come to bad ends, suffering fates we can hardly fathom; nor would we wish to do so, if we could.

"It is partly my fault. I accept a modicum of blame! I communicated my concerns to Mr. Gale, explained why I held back from the critical step. To enter blindly into that hyper-cosmic region, I told him, to meet face to face its denizens, be they gods or devils: such was folly, I said. I opined that age and worry tamed my ardor, fettered my resolve.

"Mr. Gale laughed at my fears, which he openly deemed pusillanimity. Truly, Miss Delaney, we greatly underestimated that fine young man. I did not credit as I should his extreme dedication to this project, his hearty eagerness to further my project and the cause of science. His devotion to knowledge was such that he demanded immediate action, that we inaugurate contact across the spheres without delay. Against my better judgment, yet with similar eagerness, I activated my machine, opened again that invisible door.

THE HOUSE ON THE HILL OF STARS

"I desired speech with those others, those who dwell in that infernal realm beyond the ancient stones. No more did I ask. The front porch was close enough for me. Mr. Gale, however, could not resist the unholy temptation of that grand moment. So soon as I announced the opening, he sprang unbidden with a shout of youthful triumph—'Leave this to me, Professor!' he cried—lunging forward between the stones. That required incredible bravery on his part. The optical effects of the entrance . . . well, I believe you saw some of that. The titanic weirdness cast a spell over him, drove him on to new heights of devoted heroism. He entered that mystic land, where he was greeted by the inhabitants, and then followed the final horror.

"For our own sakes, we must concoct a tale to account for his disappearance, one that will turn the authorities from us. What may we convincingly report? It is pointless to inquire of his fate. We may never know. Perhaps in time he may return, although that may not be the happiest outcome. Perhaps in a hundred years those who come after us shall delve deeper into these secrets, reveal the unutterable truth. For us it is to push back ignorance by degrees, to collate what has been gained, to analyze at leisure so that other researchers may benefit if they will. Nothing more is open to us. We live, and in life we revere our lost comrade Mr. Gale."

The professor and Theresa sat close together in the front seat of the van, gazing out over the convoluted skyline of jagged sandstone spires and massive bluffs. The girl saw none of this. Turned within, she recalled jeering at Ronny for a coward, tried to pretend how that would have spurred him. She thought this, but it did not help. A different kind of horror seized her: the astounding realization that what the professor told her made no sense, was hopelessly unbelievable.

"He wasn't eager," she murmured, "he wasn't dedicated to anything, much less to your high-flown ideals. I talked to him this morning, heard the same old whining we always got from him. Ronny was an empty-headed, self-serving moron. He meant to cut and run at the first opportunity."

"We all descend to moments of weakness," Vorchek observed. "Think no more of that."

Theresa continued, in a tone approximating accusation, "You did make contact with those others. You figured it out, maybe from those tapes. You did it last night. I was there, at the upper window."

"You were present then?" Vorchek eyed her guiltily, a furtive, sidelong glance. He stroked his beard nervously. "Did you hear my words? Did you understand their response?"

"No. You were too far away. Their sounds were gibberish. What did they say to you, Professor?"

Vorchek relaxed visibly. "I have no idea. I did try to reach them last night, in a controlled setting, but my efforts failed. Hence, I felt no need to mention it; a slight conceit of mine."

Theresa blinked back tears. Still an ugly thought tormented her. She stuttered, "His last words—he tried to tell me—Ronny said 'he' planned it, 'he' trapped him. Oh, Professor, what did he mean, who was he talking about?"

Vorchek said soothingly, "We shall never know. 'He,' 'they,' 'it;' how does one refer to entities from beyond the pale? Our language groans under the load. Perhaps they did lure him to his doom in some fashion. That is compatible with the evil record of the Wilson House and the Hill of Stars. Terrible things happen there. It is our misfortune to have tasted the bitterness of a fresh occurrence as we strove to study the old. Spit out these useless doubts, my dear, leave be these questions until you have regained your composure. Tragedies happen, bidden or no. Let us get home. When you have collected yourself, all will seem right and proper as before."

Theresa fervently hoped so. She wanted to believe that more than anything in the world.

INTO THE VORTEX

To the town of Sedona they came, those three young people—Theresa Delaney, Aaron Rucobi, Josh Fentz—came as bidden in Josh's old sedan with its peeling decals and broken muffler, and as bidden squealed to a halt that morning in the parking lot of the run-down (but not inexpensive) motel just outside the mouth of Oak Creek Canyon. The driver drew alongside a familiar vehicle, a big boxy van with high, deep-tread tires. They got out, those three, a motley crew, hefting backpacks and duffel bags, dissimilar despite their fresh faces and their loud young voices, an odd assortment of traveling companions. Aaron, tall, dark, serious of demeanor, in his casually smart attire and light jacket whipping in the stiff cool breeze, looked the budding scholar, which he sought to be; Josh, with his beefy face and red complexion, his conventionally squalid duds and his backwards baseball cap, impressed rather differently; and then there was Theresa, who might have stepped as a model from a fancy designer's magazine, a lovely fair girl who seemed dressed for an old-fashioned safari in that matching tan blouse and skirt ensemble with those tall boots and that spreading floppy hat.

A minute only they tarried to chat, perhaps admiring the stark, shadowed vistas of red sandstone bluffs and weather-worn spires looming overhead in all directions, before the fourth appeared. He descended the creaking iron stairs from the upper floor, a lean, imposing figure wearing a fine suit and rakish hat, sporting a short, well-manicured beard beneath his striking hawk-like features. The trio knew him, for he it was who bade them come to this place, he—Professor Anton Vorchek—who would act as their leader and colleague during the days ahead.

Professor Vorchek hailed them as he reached the littered concrete. "My friends," said he, his voice pleasantly modulated and slightly accented, "so good to see you, and on time at that, which makes for a

195

favorable start. I desire to get underway as soon as possible. What you need not carry may be deposited in my room, which I have rented for the duration. Then we must breakfast at the restaurant down the street, which I have already scouted for us. A hearty meal will spur us to great exertions this day."

They ate a fulsome feast, most of them at least, for Vorchek, despite his sound advice, picked at his food. Conversation was restrained, an indulgence of small talk and aimless chatter. Little more need be said by them at this point, for only two weeks before, at a posh Phoenix seafood restaurant, the professor had hosted the same group, and there he had regaled them with an outline of his grand scheme.

"I called you here," he said on that evening, over a scarcely nibbled dish of fried oysters, "to tell you something of my recent adventures, and to invite you all to partake in the next stage of my work. Miss Delaney necessarily knows something of my doings, for while she took no part in my recent delvings, she and I go back a ways together, and I have ever considered her my faithful assistant. Mr. Rucobi, you were my best student last year, prior to my sabbatical, and I kept you in mind throughout. Mr. Fentz; well, you came to my attention—chose a course of mine as an elective, did not you?—had to drop out—financial difficulties, I presumed; nevertheless, I concluded that you possessed qualities of value to me.

"To the point: my researches into the arcane, unfathomed mysteries of our world and universe led me to focus attention upon the unusual characteristics of the Sedona region. You have all heard tall tales and bizarre claims made for the place by the woefully unscientific New Age crowd. Scarcely a tourist's guidebook fails to mention the furtive powers and astral influences said to emanate from the area, glorious cosmic forces into which especially open minds are keen to tap, so that they may achieve 'oneness,' or enlightenment, or inner peace, or some such rot. Most of that, I tell you, is rubbish, yet there remains, once one clears the wishful detritus, a substratum of potential actuality which intrigues the genuine scientific spirit. Something goes on out there. I took sabbatical that I might investigate.

"Armed with a sheaf of notes derived from many sources, a collection of maps, and a battery of scientific instruments, I set forth to discover the pristine truths underlying the accumulated heap of claims. During my labors I tramped across an area of 2500 square miles, probing, testing, observing, collating data. In the end, after many a trek to specific locales, some popularly known, others—several others—largely unknown, I believe I uncovered evidence of a real effect, some sort of emission or presence neither hitherto defined nor investigated by science. Through intense analysis I think I have located the focus of the disturbance, that which is styled in populist literature as the 'vortex.' My time ran out—conventional duties called—but I mean to go back during the forthcoming break, and this time plumb the very heart of the remarkable force which does, I assure you, cast its spell over that land."

This soliloquy proved meat indeed for his fellow diners. Questions and comments ensued. Vorchek produced a map of the wild area into which they would go, a document he passed among them. Whatever features it revealed, centers of human habitation were not among them. The mystery and romance of the proposed expedition intrigued Theresa, who lived for unorthodox excitement. "Might we really find wonders out there," she asked, "wonders of a sort one hopes for, but no one believes?" The professor said they just might, with luck. Aaron, the student of physics, pondered aloud the possibilities of vital discoveries. "May I expect," he asked, "to take part in ground-breaking research that will lead to fresh avenues of genuine knowledge?" The professor praised his spirit, averred that his expectations could be satisfied. Josh shrugged, said, "Whatever. It looks to be good hunting country. I might carry along my rifle." This idea the professor squashed, saying, "All that land, untraveled though it may be, is Federally protected wilderness, guns forbidden. However, Mr. Fentz, we shall be roughing it, so your outdoors leanings, if any, will be gratified."

Vorchek spoke at length of the trip's fundamental requirements and hazards—a journey of many days into the wilderness—and when he had done demanded decisions from the three. "Of course I'm coming," said Theresa. "Don't I always, when you ask?" Said Aaron, "I wouldn't miss it for the world. If you're right, this could mean something big." Said Josh, "Yeah, why not? I don't have anything better to do." So it was settled.

Now the morning of departure had come. Breakfast concluded, they returned to the motel, sorted gear, packed or re-packed the necessary, checked and re-checked supplies, Vorchek overseeing these labors. When no more could be done he announced, "The march begins," and he escorted his three charges from the room, locked the door behind, led them down to the street. "From here on we walk," he said. They trooped along the highway north into Oak Creek Canyon, covering an easy mile or so with the gigantic sandstone and limestone bluffs rising above them in the early light. They started dressed warmly against the morning chill and the sporadic breeze. Each carried a backpack or rucksack containing one complete change of clothing, space-conserving food, a thermos of fresh water, chlorine tablets for purifying more. Vorchek and Josh also packed the folded materials for two-man pup tents. These items any hikers would appreciate. There were others, however: a fairly large briefcase, possessed by the professor, containing scientific instruments; a smaller satchel in Theresa's hand, containing Vorchek's relevant papers and writing materials; the camera equipment, Vorchek's old Minolta SRT-102 in a bag with an assortment of lenses and film carried by Aaron, while Josh slung the massive wooden tripod of German make over his beefy shoulder.

In time the good road took them to the picturesque bridge where deep, narrow Wilson Canyon ran down to meet the grander gorge through which they had passed. They paused at the guard rail, peering down into the majestic depths. Vorchek turned to his companions, said, "A beautiful view, is not it? Admire, too, this ribbon of asphalt, and the bridge, for they are your last taste of modern civilization for a mighty spell." All present knew the route thus far. They turned left, toward the west, stepping onto a thin dirt and gravel path, set off into the recesses of Wilson Canyon, the first stage of their journey into the unknown.

An interesting foursome they were to see, attired in their unique styles, the professor still the splendid fellow though he had shed the snappy city finery and brightly polished shoes for a more rugged suit and boots. The hike into the side canyon was reasonably effortless, the trail well marked, the scenery—especially the looming heights of monumental Wilson Mountain—breath-taking. The group chatted, joked, took in the sights. They had a good time.

Much could be said of that first day's uneventful, if delightful, advance through the coniferous forests of the canyon bottom-land, with its jumbled rocks and pools of standing water left over from recent rains, the flourishing green foliage, the towering massifs and unique formations to all sides, the scampering of wildlife, the singing of birds, the infrequent hails of a few hikers. More could be said of the increasingly difficult climb out of the canyon onto the wide open grassy saddle beneath the high flat peak of Wilson Mountain, a vantage that, in the late afternoon, afforded a stunning overlook of the vast Oak Creek Canyon twisting to the north. These subjects came up, naturally, yet this was no mere hike, nor were these mere vacationers. They came with purpose, and that purpose whispered to the minds of the three youths. Just what were they about, anyway?

The party made first camp on the saddle. The two tents were raised, a fire carefully ignited within a blackened stone ring left by previous campers. "This is about as far," Vorchek noted, "as even dedicated tourists are wont to go, save for the handful who follow the formal trail to the peak. Here we cross their path. Tomorrow we deviate irrevocably." They ate their bland but filling meal of dried, compactly packaged stuff by the light of the fire, under the twinklings of a thousand stars which sprang into brilliance when the landscape turned darkly invisible. The group sat on strategically placed stone seats around the flaring ring, Theresa at the professor's side, the two young men across from them.

Said the girl, "I'm still hazy as to our goal. You've been here, Professor, took your readings, wrote your notes. What else is there to do, under these circumstances?"

"Who cares?" said Josh. "It's a great excuse for a holiday."

"I want to know," said Aaron. "Professor Vorchek, I second Theresa's question. There needn't be any mystery in all this. I accepted your invitation as an honor, but I want more. What do you hope to accomplish, and how can we contribute?"

Vorchek grinned, paused an infernally long time to light his pipe. At his example Theresa lit a cigarette, Josh, with a smug chuckle, a long, fat, smelly cigar. Only Aaron refrained. The professor said, "I have told you. I seek the source. There is a power out here, an unknown force to be investigated. It possesses certain properties, may bring to bear certain effects upon the countryside and its inhabitants. There are tales of unusual occurrences in these parts, strange events and odd happenings which may correlate with this force. I wish to track it to its lair, stand on the spot from which it emanates, study it properly. We must cross much wild country, employ the instruments I have provided for this outing. I could not carry all that by myself. My primary excursion was by way of reconnaissance. This is the real thing."

"I knew it," cried Josh. "We're just beasts of burden. The prof wouldn't go for renting mules, so he dragged us out here." He slapped his knee and laughed.

"That I could almost believe," Theresa said cheerily. "Professor, you're a great man, but you always act for your own ends. Still, there's more to it than that."

"Entirely correct, my dear," replied Vorchek. He puffed on his pipe, exhaled, went on, "You three embody characteristics, incorporated within your psyches, which may serve me well, further my schemes of exploration and analysis. Miss Delaney here craves wonder and weirdness; oh, do not make a face, you know you do. Why else would you so charmingly tolerate my companionship these recent years? Our association has allowed you access to many curious cases. I tell you this investigation may constitute the culmination of our efforts together, the ultimate achievement of your dreams. Is not that enough, my dear, for a start?

"You, Mr. Rucobi, possess the perfect scientist's mind. You wish to know, despising mystery as an enemy to be defeated by whatever means. Normally you could go far as you are, delving into conventional questions of matter and being. I offer you more: amazing discoveries, life-changing knowledge, the shattering of barriers between thought and actuality. Does that suffice to tantalize you?" Vorchek gave attention again to his pipe.

"What about me?" shouted Josh, pointing with his cigar like a swollen, threatening finger. "Where do I fit into this rigmarole?"

Vorchek said, "A big, strong gentleman of your type, Mr. Fentz, may come in handy. There are different kinds of human fuel. If all goes well, you will play your part." Josh pressed, but the professor had nothing more to say.

Vorchek and the girl shared one tent, the boys another. This arrangement excited the curiosity of Josh, who delivered a muttered string of crude, insinuating comments to his exhausted tent-mate. "Does she see something in that old coot I don't?" Eventually, just to shut him up, Aaron deigned to comment. "I wouldn't put anything past Vorchek," he conceded. "He's famous for living by his own rules. That's true of his work as well. The professor dabbles in subjects shunned by most of his colleagues. Depending on who you talk to, he's either a genius or a kook, or both. Anyway, don't be surprised by anything he does. And Theresa's pretty wild, from what I hear. She's got tons of money—family money—can do whatever she likes, and she likes hanging around Vorchek. That's the way it is. You piece together the puzzle as it suits you." Josh said, "It's not fair. He ought to give us a crack at her."

Annoyed, he produced from his bag a surprisingly large portable radio—"My small unit"—on which he played a raucous station identified by a nasty voiced announcer. This was not an item on the professor's list of requirements. Aaron put up with that for a wearing while, then demanded silence. Josh shrugged. "Only trying to liven up our holiday."

Come the dawn, a minimal breakfast of granola bars, and the march resumed over the saddle into the diminishing chill. To the left hung the barren cliffs of Wilson Mountain, to the right a scrubby, nameless bluff. All semblance of a trail vanished at this point. The party bushwhacked, a slow, tiring process through the exposed, stiff scrub, especially when the heat of day intensified. By late morning the heights had receded behind, exposing to view a seemingly endless, undulating plain of grasslands and scattered pine copses. Considerably to the south distorted sentinels of the famous Red Rock Country of Sedona poked above the far horizon, dark orange fingers of primordial stone, carved from the solidified ooze of an ancient sea bottom. To the north, faintly glimpsed in the shimmering distance, brooded the massive bulk of the San Francisco Peaks, still snow-capped at this season. Vorchek led his folk west, into the void.

Shortly after lunch they reached the house. Vorchek greeted it casually, saying, "We arrive in good time. I was sure that we were on the right track., though in the absence of close landmarks I must rely on the compass. My first time out I circled for hours before I found it." His companions took it with less aplomb, for he had told them nothing of any house, nor made mention of anything like scheduled stops. Indeed, that a house should exist out there, however dilapidated its condition, astonished them exceedingly, for the region seemed a place untouched by mankind. Theresa said as much.

Vorchek responded, "On the contrary, my dear, there are few places on earth that have not felt the tread of man's heavy foot. A hundred years ago this was farming and cattle country. There were never many settlers, nor did they remain long. This land proved unsuitable for long-term habitation. Treat that as a datum. While we do not tarry long, here we do camp, at the Mathers homestead."

The house did not invite its guests. It was old, a broken down relic of a two-story structure that appeared ten centuries old rather than one, the sort of ruin an archeologist might happily sift for clues to foreign and forgotten life-ways. The door, the windows, the roof gaped, the bare, sun-baked planks of the walls sagged and tottered. A crumbling granite chimney stood out against the ravages of time. A stand of flanking elms had hidden the site until they were upon it. Aaron asked, "How did it come to be here? Did Mathers hike in like we did, build himself a house?"

"Nothing like that," said Vorchek. "Look there," he added, indicating with a wave of his briefcase. "Very faintly you may discern the trace of the old dirt road which once ran up from Sedona. A difficult ride in the best of times, but horses and wagons made it through. No one has come up that way, I suppose, for ninety years or thereabouts."

"Why didn't we?" cried Josh, who had collapsed with his load on the ominously uneven porch. "We could have come this far in your van, saved us a hell of a lot of trouble."

"I entertained that very idea," Vorchek said with a nod. "That makes sense, does not it? Unfortunately, my research, and personal exploration before you arrived on the scene, ruled out such a convenient option. The last of the pioneers abandoned the road in that former age. It has never been used, much less maintained, since. Back during the '30s a rock fall in Dry Creek Canyon (a long ways from here) forever sealed the lane. To open the road again, even to foot traffic, would require a major construction effort, one not in the offing. Therefore, we made do with our scenic shortcut."

"We needn't stop here," Theresa said. "There's plenty of daylight left."

"This locale is important to me," explained the professor. "We have entered the zone. Today we commence scientific investigation."

They camped in the front yard, if that patch of terrain indistinguishable from its surroundings could be deemed a yard. A placid spring behind the house provided plentiful water for purifying, a worthy reason in itself for halting. While his wards saw to necessities, Vorchek applied himself to setting up his instruments. He took many pictures, of what appeared nothing in particular, using his antique Minolta rig, the old camera and a succession of lenses atop the stout, heavy wooden tripod, deriving long, steady exposures via a remote shutter cable. As to his motives for photographing the site the others received no enlightenment, though they understood the principle he espoused of recording everything. Another machine he produced from his case when the picture-taking was done, and mounted on that same tripod, drew more interest and generated more puzzlement. It was a small, oblong contraption, with many dials and buttons spread across a metal panel, with a tangle of wires feeding in and out of the sides. One cord connected to a largish lithium battery. He fielded few questions. "Readings, my friends," he said shortly. "I postulate an influence. I must detect it anew, discern its elements and features."

Gloom crept about the shaded house by degrees. Amongst the shadows the Mathers homestead looked more somber and desolate still. Josh opined, "This trip is getting old fast. If we don't stir up some excitement soon I'm going to bolt." Theresa replied, "Good luck to you, sweetie. I trust your sense of direction is better than mine." Aaron said, "I can't wait to hear more about the professor's machine."

Josh fired up again his machine, the radio, derived from it only ear-grating, squawking static. "That's not right," he said, turning it off and pushing it away in disgust after fruitless fiddling.

While the girl cooked up over the campfire an impromptu goulash from dried beef and equally dry biscuits, Vorchek condescended to illuminate his activities. "I spoke of the zone," he said. "We have entered the radius of the reach of the vortex, the extent of its measurable power. I refer to the emission of unknown energy. It is neither light, nor heat, nor hard radiation, but something wholly other, something outside the ken of man. Its primary effects are currently elusive. Conventional radio receivers," he said with a courteous nod to Josh, "will not function here, which I am sure we all consider an extreme pity. For that matter, conventional systems will not detect it. This device is my own creation. With it I may control for normal emissions, screen them out, then sample the residue. Like so." Vorchek twisted a plastic knob. A needle swung weakly on a meter. An erratic, sluggish clicking chirped from the machine.

"It sounds like a Geiger counter," Aaron observed.

"The principle is the same. Watch and listen." Vorchek turned the machine about the tripod head. The noise waxed and waned.

Aaron grinned. "Directionality. It's coming from somewhere out there." He pointed across the darkening plain.

"Yes, from a specific location, well defined."

"I wonder that you couldn't reach it before."

Josh quipped, "So, are we going to lay claim to a uranium mine and get rich? I'll put up with a lot for that."

Theresa called, "Whatever we find will be, I'll bet, a lot less lucrative, and a bunch more exciting."

Josh sneered, "More exciting than weeds and rocks?

Impossible."

With her musical voice Theresa rang the bell for dinner. The young folk chowed down with gusto, relishing the calories more than the taste. Vorchek, withdrawn and preoccupied, ate sparingly.

"We shouldn't have any difficulty," Aaron said at one point, "getting to where we're going and learning what we can. Your detector, Professor, is the best compass we've got."

"Think you that?" said Vorchek. "That is welcome news, for the standard compass may prove irksome in this land. The influence of the vortex overrides all outside forces to varying degrees. Whatever the difficulties, keep peril in mind. I tell you, son, we have left behind the world as we know it. This is a realm unlike any you have ever conceived."

"I've seen plenty like it," Josh scoffed.

"Tell us about peril, Professor," Theresa pointedly suggested.

"Old man Mathers, I believe, would explain more than I," replied Vorchek, "if he were here to grace us with his practical wisdom. Sadly he is no longer with us, having died long ago, and before his time at that."

"Sounds ominous," Theresa said.

"His tale is a curious one. Contemporary reports strain credulity. Later claims verge on the legendary. Taken together they indicate a great deal."

"Tell us about him, Professor," said Aaron.

"Should I? Is this relevant?" Vorchek chuckled. "I think it is; I do believe the late Gerrold Mathers constitutes a classic victim of the power of the vortex.

"Mr. Mathers, a man of middle age, arrived here with his wife and three children, two of them grown, in 1901, heralding the new century with a fresh start in life as part of the final wave of pioneers to settle what was then the largely empty Arizona Territory. He sought flat, tillable land and a reliable source of water. Here he found that much. He staked his claim, built his house with the help of the elder sons, laid out his fields, purchased some livestock from the ranches around Flagstaff. The Mathers' came up the old southern route, where the road subsequently went through for a while, they and a handful of other homesteaders. Perhaps Mr. Mathers pushed farther out into the wild than the rest. That seems likely; and likely, also, that it was his undoing.

"I have in my files a private letter from Mrs. Mathers to her sister

204

in Omaha, dated 1903, complaining about the 'godless country' they had chosen to inhabit. What does that mean? I possess a sprinkling of clues. There are from those times references to 'dark influences,' occasional disturbing sounds, odd behavior of animals, glimpses of unfamiliar wildlife, recurrences of nagging, inexplicable sickness. There was something, they came to believe, not healthy about the place.

"In 1905 Mr. Mathers set out on a hunting trip to the west with his oldest son, Theodore. They expected to be gone two days. The father returned five days later, came back alone, told of an accident—Theodore was no more—spoke of an *in situ* burial. That was the first incident, calamitous though unremarkable on its own, yet the harbinger of much more.

"Mrs. Mathers (Jeannie was her name), in conversation with a few regional friends from miles away, averred that her husband was not the same man after that. Could one blame him, having lost a beloved son? He grew moody, unnecessarily secretive, prone to unexplained ramblings by night. At whiles he let slip that he visited neighbors on his wanderings, but no one knew to whom he referred, nor could or would he clarify. Apparently he spouted considerable nonsense during that period. So did, it seemed, his young daughter Annie, who claimed to have seen from her window, early one morning, her father returning with no less than her dear brother Theodore. Mr. Mathers entered the house alone, needless to say, nor could he in any way justify the child's mistake save to posit a dream. In fact he punished her severely, warning her never to spread such stories again. I gather that it was a troubling scene. The wife said later it was the first time she had ever detected cruelty in the nature of her man.

"Come the following week and, while Mr. Mathers was about by night, Annie slipped out or was otherwise made away with; whichever, she was never seen again alive, or in any fashion under clear-cut circumstances. What do I mean by that? Another month passed, and the surviving son, Thomas, awakened near midnight to the sounds of activity in the pigpen. He collected his shotgun, went out to investigate, observed in the darkness two men making off with the animals. He tried a long shot at them. By the brief glare of the blast he thought he recognized his father, and for a horrified instant the other. Mortified, he rushed forward, terrified by what he might have done, only he did not approach too near. Suddenly, for reasons I can not fathom from the accounts, he convinced himself that it was not his father, nor—mark this!—any human being at all. Thomas would not afterward explain, but mention of those intruders caused him to shudder in later years. Well, Mr. Mathers returned in the morning, claimed ignorance, announced that the horses were missing as well. Except for an enclosure of a couple dozen chickens, that fairly cleaned them out.

"It was the next year—1907 this was—that Mrs. Mathers and Thomas vacated the residence and abandoned Mr. Mathers to his own devices. Now, I must admit that something is left out of this part of the story. You must conjecture, based on what happened before and after. The lady justified her decision, with her son's full support, by pleading fear for her life at the hands of her husband. She advanced no specific cause or overt acts, instead alluding vaguely to the gentleman's 'crazy talk' and subtle hints of incipient frightfulness. She came to believe in the end that Mr. Mathers was—or that he believed himself to be—possessed by evil spirits lurking in that still wild country. Indeed, the expected flood of settlers never materialized, and several had left by then, an intriguing development. Mr. Mathers, apparently, had concluded that older, furtive denizens haunted that land; that they had initiated contact with him; that he cooperated with them, or was directed by them, toward the furtherance of unknown designs. From out of the west they came, or called him to the west, as they saw fit, delegating mysterious tasks.

"On what those might be the records keep silence. Mr. Mathers wished the members of his family to join him in his duties—one, he said obscurely, *had already done* so—and via subjection to the powers of the land they would realize a strange fulfillment of 'ultimate possibilities.' For the lady of the house this was quite enough. She would not, then or ever, accuse him of insanity. On the contrary, she earnestly averred that he was no longer himself, mentally or physically, that he was another entity masquerading as her husband. An odd conceit, that."

Dinner over, the stars winking, Vorchek knocked out the ashes from his pipe against a stone before refilling. He said, "There is little more to tell, though what remains savors even more of the grotesque. Mr. Mathers, left alone among the dead dreams of his house, lost contact with the outside world. He became a hermit, a recluse, for the short remaining span of his days. You see, during that final year here disappearances occurred among the folk who lived somewhat closer to Sedona, a new settlement then. People vanished by night, lone travelers mainly, with one case of a male child being removed from his bedroom. The people demanded action. The sheriff intervened. Questions were raised about that dreadful man who kept to himself, primarily by choice, partly because his wild discourse disconcerted all who met him.

"In May of 1908 a delegation called on him. The sheriff led it, and they went armed, so call it a posse. Struck by the declining state of the farm, the utter absence of livestock (even the chickens were now gone), and the abysmally unkempt aspect of the owner, they demanded an interview, plied him with questions, sought answers. Mr. Mathers seemed amused by their attention, admitted that he knew a thing or two of what brought them, courteously requested a moment to make himself presentable before submitting to their demands. Then he went inside and killed himself with his shotgun.

"A search of the house and the surrounding land revealed all, at least all that interested those men. They found bodies in various stages of decomposition, fragmentation, or completeness, the corpses of the missing locals, and that of Annie, too. Each was fearsomely mutilated, and certain items discovered within the kitchen established what Mr. Mathers had done to the remains. Have you guessed this? He butchered and ate of them.

"Just another lurid tale, you may say, of the vanished frontier. I ask you to ponder these elements: the spirits or beings from the west, the mental changes or aberrations, Annie's supposed dream. I can fit these data into a coherent account, one that opens the way to unimaginable vistas. Before long, all of you may gaze upon that view. What will you see, how will you react? That is a matter of no trifling importance."

Thus concluded the evening. In the morning the young people searched the house for a lark, finding nothing but rot and desiccation. "What did you expect?" asked Vorchek. "Time cleanses the most indelible stains. We must progress before we discover. Seek the now, where ever it be, that you may learn."

Utilizing his detector, the professor drew a bead on the subtle energy disturbance, marshaled his team and set out across the undulating plain, leaving behind, to the furtive amusement of some, the discarded, useless radio. They tramped through sear tall grass, they rested under clumps of trees, they picked their way over stones that protruded from the crumbly soil like tottering grave markers. Vorchek strode apart from the others, leaving them to their thoughts and ruminations. They spoke among themselves in halting fits, striving to intellectualize that nasty lecture concerning the remote past.

Theresa said, "A low mind, a stupid mind like that of this Mathers guy, breaks down under the stress of wonder. Facing the unknown, he sees in it only his own corruption, a mirror held to his crude self. If I absorbed a power, or if something came through it to greet me, I wouldn't fly off the handle and eat someone. That which is vast, even if incomprehensible, must be elevating. I would rise to the occasion, not sink. I crave the chance to enter a world where I may touch the stars."

Aaron said, "Very poetic, I'm sure, but hardly to the point. Cut out the obvious lunacy and tale-spinning, and what's left, if anything, is a mysterious elemental force, something to be broken down into its components, sorted, rendered comprehensible. Any power may be understood, even employed, if sufficient knowledge exists. Let's get that."

Josh said with a laugh, "You're both as nutty as Professor Fruitcake. We're kicking around in the tail end of nowhere, looking for nothing. I'll bet old Vorchek cooked up that story to bug us."

"Why would *Professor* Vorchek do that?" Theresa snapped. "He's preparing us for something, by degrees. I wish I knew what it was. He's naturally secretive, but not usually with me. It's never easy to guess what's on his mind, harder than ever lately. He's not himself, hasn't really been since he returned from sabbatical. There's more reserve, a coldness that he normally directs at the world. I can sense it. I'm getting some of that now. Of course, he has plenty on his mind, if there's anything to this stuff."

"Maybe," said Josh, "he's Mathers come back to eat us." The comment broke the tension, drew cheery scorn. They laughed a lot, for a while.

They camped in the middle of the plain, by a creek bed dry except for a number of standing pools, which drew the hot hikers at a run. The water, as they merrily splashed, was cool in the shade. A small herd of animals darted away at their approach. "We can drink that if we must," said Vorchek, after snapping a few pictures. "The creatures do. I will stick to my canteen of spring water until then."

"Were those deer?" Theresa asked. "I didn't catch a good look, but I thought—" Aaron cut in, "They looked a little off to me. I saw big teeth." Josh added, "And claws instead of hooves. Those weren't deer."

The professor shrugged. "I would not style them common deer, certainly. Have not you noticed the strangeness of the wildlife in this region?"

The question truly raised an intriguing subject. Throughout the expedition thus far the vicinity of their march teemed, at times, with the familiar natural denizens of Arizona. They had spied, chiefly down in Wilson Canyon, deer and coyotes, birds and insects, chipmunks and even minnows where the waters lingered. Since leaving the Mathers house they had spied few animals, those being unaccountably quiet and shy, their habits (come to think of it) peculiar.

"Mutations," Aaron declared. "This force of yours, Professor, insidiously affects them."

"Force of mine!" Vorchek cried. "Mr. Rucobi, what a way with words you have. Nevertheless, you are surely correct. That which exists out here too long, changes. The beasts can not participate in their change. Only man can do that. Only he can choose."

"What are we supposed to choose?" Josh asked plaintively. No one replied.

With the encroachment of evening, the four grouped about the camp fire, Vorchek mused, "I, for one, chose well my party of eager colleagues. Friends, I confess to covertly eavesdropping on your stimulating discussion of this afternoon. I enjoyed what I heard. Such differing reactions to the same stimuli! Miss Delaney, the shallow might accuse you of verging on New Age hokum, yet I appreciate your desire to embrace that which is the totality of being, to find greatness beyond yourself and the limitations of this world. That constitutes a natural avenue of personal exploration. Mr. Rucobi, your skeptical, inquiring mind demands an underlying logic and order to all things, something which, I dare say, you rarely attain in your daily affairs. It is appropriate that you question, that you demand answers. Mr. Fentz—"

"Doesn't care to have his leg pulled," interrupted that one, "especially pulled right off."

"I intended to say, young man, that you are earthy, basic; meat and bone and fundamental in life. You do not pester your brain with these clever, rarefied notions which do not fill your belly or gratify your senses. Quite a threesome you all are, running the gamut of thought and emotion, covering the human spectrum in its entirety. Oh, I could not have picked better."

"We thank you for the compliments, Professor," said Theresa, "if

209

that's what they are. It sounds more like you're praising your own wisdom."

"If you do not pat me on the back, then I must."

In the morning, just as a tinge of crimson illumined the east, they awoke to the most amazing development. Afterward Aaron and the girl argued as to who heard it first. It was a noise, a weird, whining buzzing or vibrant humming, that rose, mounted, exploded into a choking pall of stunning sound. It came from everywhere and nowhere, from within and without, blasting, shrieking remorselessly beyond the ears into the mind. Theresa crawled from her tent, leaped up and gasped, "What is it? What's happening, Professor?" He emerged behind her, stood silently scanning the murky horizon. Aaron came running, screaming, "I'm losing my mind! What is that God awful noise? What's causing it?"

It came on, great roaring waves of sound, and Theresa and Aaron thrashed and circled oddly, as if drowning in an unseen sea. Vorchek spoke not, but moved quickly to his instrument, activated it, toyed with dials and buttons. Now Josh sluggishly joined the trio, coming without haste or sign of distress, save that his sleepy countenance exhibited sure signs of annoyance and aggrieved curiosity. "What are you all carrying on about?" he shouted. What's the big deal?"

"Can't you hear it?" moaned Theresa. He replied simply, with no show of concern whatsoever, "Hear what? Your song and dance routine woke me up." Aaron growled harshly, as with enormous effort, "Scrape the wax out of your ears, punk, and listen."

The noise shut off like a thunderclap. The two suffering youths dropped as if exhausted. Theresa lit a cigarette, Aaron quite improperly ordered Josh to fetch his canteen. The professor jumped about with maniacal rhythm, fussing with his machine, observing his fellows, dashing up the slope from the creek bank into the sparse trees at the top of the rise. Josh sullenly returned with the water, tossed it down by his companion. "Will someone tell me what's going on?"

"Not much point," said Theresa dryly, "since you're obviously hard of hearing."

"Deaf as a post," Aaron said hotly, around a gulp from his canteen.

"Be not hard on the lad," cautioned Vorchek, emerging into their midst. He beamed a sunny smile, stroked his beard with a satisfied air. "All is well, everybody in one piece, I take it? Before I say anything, tell me, each of you, what you experienced."

They did. Vorchek nodded knowingly, announced, "The pieces begin to fit as ordained. The pattern holds. Come with me up the mound, while I speak."

From the little rise he gestured through the trees at the western horizon, where a low line of dark hills could be seen, one triangular peak rising slightly above the rest. "The emanation," he said, "came straight from that notable hill. We should reach it this afternoon. We are so far within the zone that we have been spotted. It calls to us."

"I don't get any of this," Josh grumbled.

The other two young people asked, "What emanation? What's calling?"

Said the professor, "We received an enormously strong, directional transmission of energy flow, one initiated for our benefit. The vortex activates, if you will, to a greater extent than we must deem, in lieu of a better term, normal. Those beyond the gate reach out to us. We shall proceed, that we may introduce ourselves."

"That's the first I've heard of a gate," Aaron said, "or of anyone on its other side. The data don't support your inference, Professor."

"Somebody makes these things happen," said Theresa. Aaron would have bickered over the issue, started to do so, until Vorchek weighed in:

"I derive my views from the testimony associated with the Mathers case and others from the historic period—there are others, though none quite so dramatic—as well as the remarkably coherent tales drawn from Indian legend. Do not treat such as proof, Mr. Rucobi, yet keep them in mind as we near our goal. According to the Yavapai, who recount myths descended from prehistoric tribes who came before them, the vortex represents an opening in our world, a passageway through the firmament from heaven or—depending on the mood of the particular myth—a tunnel driven through the underworld from hell. They claim that the gods, variously celestial beings or demonic entities, dwell on the other side, encroaching into our sphere of existence when they wish to communicate with men. Contact is chancy, avenues of discourse open to some, closed to others, with consequent difficulties of interpretation. You and Miss Delaney heard, as did I; Mr. Fentz felt nothing. Mr. Mathers, it is plain, also heard. Among the aborigines the wisest elders, the medicine men, conversed with their immaterial masters. That they say, and as a matter of formal logic I am willing to allow the possibility. There is, of course, only one way to advance from supposition to knowing. We go on, we face what beckons at the end of the journey."

As they marched over the plain Theresa's eagerness grew. Breathlessly she said, "I'd like to meet God on a lonely hilltop, learn from Him what everything's really about." Aaron politely chided her for her illogical leap of faith. "If there's anything at all to this, we'll find beings a lot like us, intelligence rather than deity. Call them aliens." Josh's concerns were more immediate and practical. "All I get out of this is sore feet. I hate these boots." Indeed, he limped, as his disposition soured.

"What puzzles me for the moment," Aaron wondered aloud, "is why Professor Vorchek didn't go all the way his first time out. He possessed the means, the knowledge, the desire. The only thing different this time is that he's got us in tow, and we haven't really contributed yet."

Theresa said, "Take it from me, he's got a secret. I know him that much. There's something he isn't telling."

The miles passed swiftly. Over the wild but still fairly level landscape the hikers progressed easily, with the sun at their backs, the clumped peaks of the snowy San Franciscos standing far to the north like a sentinel of that outer world from which they felt wholly disconnected. Once a jet soared high and far away to the south, a curious sight in that isolated realm, fleeting and unique.

By the time the sun approached the zenith the hill loomed before them, densely forested with pines mixed with firs and junipers. The party lunched at the edge of the silent prairie. Then Vorchek led his wards without hesitation onto a trail of sorts, no more than an animal path. Some living things had worn it, and shadowy bulks were spied dashing off into the close underbrush, perhaps—judging from their sounds—pausing to watch from deeper concealment.

So they came to the clearing in the woods. It was not much of one, a little space still cloaked in the gloom of the overhanging branches of large cottonwoods and sycamores and the rough, loamy embankment of the hillside that rose to the west, but that flat expanse of sparse grass cut by a trickling brook enticed the travelers to rest with its shade and coolness. "This is the end of the trail," said Vorchek. Someone else had thought so too, for a blackened stone fire ring lay in a spot by the thin stream which lacked any vegetation. "Here we make our final camp," he said.

"This fire doesn't date to pioneer days," said Theresa. "It looks quite recent."

INTO THE VORTEX

"Somebody has been here before us," observed Aaron.

"The professor's been here," Josh said. His young companions made to sneer, until Vorchek made an amazing admission.

"Yes, it is true. I did reach this point in my previous venture. That fire was mine, for three days." The statement brought on a storm of questions. "Why didn't you say so? Why keep that secret? Why make mystery, when we have enough already?"

Vorchek replied, in general, "Ever do I operate according to method. I attained my goal, achieved my opening, in those earlier days. I already know most of what I can know. In a real sense this is your adventure, not mine. Now you shall be opened to the truth. First, the tedious preliminaries: set up camp, take in nourishment."

This his colleagues did, laboring mechanically under the dim sunlight filtered through the rustling leaves of the stream-side trees, lost in dreamy reverie, or furiously calculating, or glumly brooding. Theresa purified water from the brook. They ate silently, nervously, no one very hungry, least of all Vorchek, who toyed with his bland meal, saying nothing, yet surveying at whiles the faces of his fellows, as if striving to read their inner thoughts from subtle indications of expression. Then he slung the old Minolta camera around his neck, hefted the tripod and said, "Come, it is your time. I grant you the first taste of the true unknown, the source of the vortex. It is not far."

He turned, strode under the embankment pierced by the stream, circled to a more level slope, went up. The youths followed, in wonder and concern, still intrigued by his assured progress into the forested murk. They did not climb far. Once they crossed the stream, an easy hop, and the trees pressed close like a retarding barrier, and they pressed through onto a surface of stony dirt. There the sound returned, akin to that which had assailed them from afar, only this time modulated and pitched to a lower frequency, less damaging to the brain, more a soothing call, a noise that beckoned weirdly. Vorchek glanced back with a grin but did not slow nor pause in his step. One thing remained the same: Josh again heard nothing, could only shake his head at the curious antics and statements of his companions.

The sound died down, without wholly dwindling away, keeping with those who heard as a beguiling whisper. They emerged onto another, smaller flat space, came abruptly to an earthen cliff studded with boulders, framed by tall, ancient conifers. From this gaped the large, cylindrical mouth of an inky black cave. Not a single photon of lighted penetrated its interior, into which a tall man could have walked upright. It looked a round door of darkness.

"This is the source," Vorchek declared. He quickly set up his Minolta apparatus. "Think not to explain the vortex in geological or otherwise material terms. It lies within the cave because it was placed there, in a pre-human era, by the cunning of cosmic wisdom. This I tell you is true, for I know. Gaze within, and absorb truth."

The professor stood aside that his people might see. Spooked and fascinated, they gazed, Theresa and Aaron lulled by the faint sound that reached their minds now as a kind of music. They could not see anything in there but the ebony darkness. No, there was something to see, for all of them, suggestions of light, alternating patterns arising from the fathomless void. A ghostly radiance formed, began to swirl about itself in languid spiraling form. The hazy shape turned slowly, hypnotically, brightened.

The radiance gleamed, flashed for the fraction of a second, a dazzling instant. The dark entrance seemed to expand, or the surrounding trappings of nature to recede or draw back; regardless, all vision was encompassed by that swelling circle of night and its luminous vista. Then the luminosity faded, diminished to pure darkness once more . . . and very definite shapes stepped forth from the blackness.

Josh screamed like an animal caught in the slicing jaws of a steel trap, screamed unintelligibly and fled precipitately into the engulfing forest. Theresa gasped in shock, Aaron choked out a feeble "My God," and they stumbled backwards, scrambled frantically and rushed away, retaining sufficient presence of mind to hold to their previous route and make for camp. What had been seen creeping towards them from the cave certainly shook them, though they would have experienced grave difficulties in describing the cause of their mental anguish. Those forms had appeared, three of them—one for each of the youths, it could be said—forms entirely unrelated to anything in the familiar world, or in the realm of nightmare. Something in their basic features and outlines might suggest the human: one could speak of arms and legs, of indeterminate number; a trunk, however disjointed and hatefully sculpted; some semblance of a head, with eyes, if one chose to call such those bulbous black globes, and jaws, that worked and twitched in insane directions. One could go that far by way of description, but no farther, for the totality transcended the limited comprehension of parts.

INTO THE VORTEX

Theresa and Aaron had recovered, adequately, their strength of fiber to wonder and worry, once they reached the clearing camp, about the professor's fate. They feared for his safety, dreaded the results of his questing mind under such stimuli, discussed with monumental reservations going back for him. They need not have plagued themselves. Vorchek presently reappeared, carrying his gear, sauntering down the slope and out of the trees with a disturbing air of weariness. A shaft of late afternoon sun caught his impassive face. Come to think of it, he looked more disappointed than tired. Indeed, he said to them, coming up close, "Your reactions sadden me. I offer you the ultimate secrets, and you respond with panic, fleeing like stupid children. Have I brought you here in vain?"

The girl, his devoted companion of years, tried to reason with him. "Nothing had prepared us for that, Professor," she said. She faltered miserably. "It was instinct in action. I didn't think. I felt the presence of deadly danger."

"That is nonsense. While you cowered here, I continued my never ending studies."

Aaron stepped up, cried, "I should've known better. It was the mad act of a moment. I shamed myself."

Vorchek said, "You can surmount weakness, so long as there is more to learn. I continue to gain insights. There is no limit to this knowledge."

"What of Josh?" Theresa demanded. "Good riddance to that bum, but shouldn't we hunt for him before he gets in a jam?"

Vorchek, uncharacteristically, snickered. "His jam, as you put it, can not be worse than it already is. Forget him. I brought Mr. Fentz for a limited purpose, and he has served the majority of that. I now know, through my own observation, the constricted ability of the power of the vortex to touch lesser minds, those nearer to the beast. That finding does not involve the two of you. Your minds are of genuine quality and open to the influences. It is time to indulge your full scope as entities of awareness."

The professor smiled through his beard, that boyish, charming grin that had pulled Theresa into many a grand adventure. "Miss Delaney, this is your time. Take my hand, and come with me. No, Mr. Rucobi, remain where you are. I will be back for you soon."

Theresa, almost fighting herself, gave her dainty hand into his big grasp, felt comforted at the touch, allowed herself to be led onto the close woodland path that ran upward to the cave of the vortex. As they walked Vorchek gently spoke, saying, "You come to this place armed with unassailable belief and a boundless craving to immerse yourself in the mysteries that lie behind the tawdry surfaces of things. Complete personal realization I offer you this day. Dismiss the fears of weak flesh, of phony corporeality. Stride like a true discoverer into the light beyond the darkness, and you shall stand like a goddess over infinity and eternity. Here we are, my dear."

They stood before the cave. Vorchek's words petted her ears, the celestial music stroked her mind. Theresa gazed into the revolving lights, sensed (rather than saw this time) others mysteriously beckoning to her. Vorchek drew his hand from hers. Theresa stood for a long moment, staring into the expanding sphere, seeing more than brain could immediately grasp . . . and she stepped lightly and vanished into the cave.

Aaron fretted woefully, squatting by the fire, debating furiously the proper course of action, in effect doing nothing but pile thought on clashing thought. As evening fell Vorchek reappeared. The youth came to his feet, adopted a guarded stance, framed the other in a circle of light. "We must make haste," advised the older man. "It would not do to carry that flashlight with us."

Aaron asked warily, "Where is Theresa?"

"She has crossed over, of course. Did you doubt she would? I never did. I know her."

"I won't go," Aaron cried. "It's crazy, too risky. Remember Mathers, his family, the monstrous deeds. I can't let myself succumb to that."

Said the professor, "Walk with me, son, as far as you wish, that I may speak to you."

The boy sighed helplessly, reluctantly went. Vorchek said, "You are not Mr. Mathers, you are not capable of being him. His was an admittedly strong mind, capable of full reception, but ignorant, tragically so. What he could not understand, he corrupted. Remember that. Our world is being strangled by those who, having glimpsed a minute fragment of reality, act only on that meaningless sliver. Your position in the grand scheme is wholly other. Your brain is designed to imbibe the absolute, to factor every step of the ladder leading from blinding darkness to heightened awareness. The knowledge is there for you to seize as your own. It belongs to you by right. Think, son, reason your way into knowledge beyond the mere trappings of time and space. It is all waiting for you, in there."

INTO THE VORTEX

They stood before the cave. Aaron stopped as if he had met a wall, but he peered into that orb of maddening strangeness, attended the musical calling in his brain, endeavored to reason to a conclusion . . . and then he grinned, nodded to the professor, and strode with set jaw past the darkness into the spiraling glow.

For Josh, this had been a bad day that only got worse. Smothered by terror he had abandoned his comrades, bulled his way by main strength into the pine forest, only later thinking to set a course that would get him off the increasingly gloomy hillside and out onto the plain where he might, unaided by others, chart a direct and swift journey homeward. He did not fare well. The wood lore upon which he counted availed nought, and sense of direction seemed impossibly broken in that awful, confining landscape. He ran, he thrashed, he climbed and crawled, without ever escaping the darkening canopy of conifers that cloaked the morbid hill. Many miles he desperately traversed, but the intense night still found him hopelessly flailing.

A glimmer of far off light caught his eye, drew him like a moth to flame. What was this? Where was he? A long way, evidently, from that foul cave and its sickening occupants, which was a good thing, evidently far enough to have stumbled upon other people—real people, he said to himself—campers out on a decent hike. It had to be, for that was surely a camp fire ahead. He bashed toward it through clutching branches and clinging undergrowth.

His stomach lurched.

Josh coughed back the bile, telling himself that it was impossible. There was no way he could have run so long and far, regardless of confusion, only to return to the detestable site of that last camp. Yet by the flickering flames of the ringed fire he recognized the clearing, the stands of cottonwoods, the glittering stream, the accouterments spread about by him and his fellow campers. All this he saw and knew, and something more.

The knots in his belly further constricted.

Vorchek was there, alone, seated casually by the fire, flares of yellow light clearly illuminating his unwelcome countenance. Josh did not want to see him, did not want to speak with him. That man, he felt, was the author of all his troubles, that high-faluting egghead with his crazy ideas and his slippery talk. Josh had never taken the professor seriously until that last shocking moment, when he suddenly experienced, before the cave, the horrid assurance of certain death confronting him. Josh knew that situation was no good, quite rightly took off. Old Vorchek was just the kind of clever fool to happily drag others into a mess, thinking nothing of it.

All that he felt, had done for hours, now felt more: a definite, if unreasoned, horror of the man himself.

Vorchek rose languidly, stood darkly, silhouetted by the fire, a large black outline. "I have been waiting for you, Mr. Fentz," he called. "Though you can not hear or feel them, the cosmic forces swirl about us. I was told they would draw you back. Come, join me by the fire. We will talk."

"There's nothing to talk about," cried the boy. "Look, Professor, I just want out of here. I don't want anything from you, you don't—don't want from me—I mean—"

"I have ideas on the subject," said Vorchek.

"Where are they?" Josh hollered. "Theresa, and Aaron; what did you do with them?"

"They are gone. They will return at the appropriate time. You need not concern yourself with them. They are, by now, joyously fulfilled."

"And I'm next? Over my dead body."

Vorchek laughed, a bubbling of genuine mirth. "Splendid, sir, those well-chosen words. You possess the knack, at odd whiles. Come to me, son."

And this was the most incredible thing: he, Josh, obeyed, and did come!

Said Vorchek, "The human race consists of an amalgamation of disparate units, the high and low, the evolved and the retarded. The most advanced, the objectively special members of our species, are fit to treat with those who dwell beyond the gate, to become one with them. That I did, months ago, as our colleagues have today. Others, perhaps, possess enough awareness to sense the powers, without ever really grasping their immensity. Therein lies frustration or tragedy. Then, Mr. Fentz, there are the rest, maybe the great mass, whom evolution has discarded, those who will not see because they can not. At the intellectual level they lack volitional purpose. Sometimes, like now, it is necessary to assign purpose to them."

Josh listened when he wished to run, but his feet were lead, his legs stiff posts. He wailed, "Please, I haven't done anything wrong."

"You have not," admitted Vorchek, stepping nearer, "a fact, unfortunately, of sheer irrelevance. You may not cross over, nor could you rationally obey. The ethereal entities of the vortex will not tolerate your presence nor, under the circumstances, your continued existence."

"For God's sake, Professor—"

"For this moment," Vorchek said, looming a head above the quivering youth, "I speak of my sake, and for the others who await over the strange passage." Josh screamed as Vorchek changed before his frozen eyes. Another image superimposed itself upon that human form; something not human, something that mocked the human frame with its hideous additions and alterations. The thing that passed for Vorchek, that reached through him, said in a dreadfully different hissing voice, one emitted by alien jaws, said as it stooped to its shrieking victim, "You may not join us, but you may still provide . . . sustenance."

Notable facts concerning the author:

A degreed anthropologist, wilderness enthusiast, and photographer who makes his home in Arizona, Jeffery Scott Sims is a writer of fantastic and weird fiction. He is the creator of popular characters such as Professor Anton Vorchek, investigator of strange mysteries; Sterk Fontaine, self-serving dabbler in the supernatural; Jacob Bleek, the obsessively questing medieval wizard; and the combative and colorful heroes of ancient Dyrezan.

His publications include the dark fantasy novel, *The Journey of Jacob Bleek*; the previous collections *Science and Sorcery* and *Science and Sorcery II*; plus many dozen short stories of the bizarre and the macabre. A number of these tales, like those in this volume, are set in the exotic and mysterious wilds of Arizona, or in imaginary lands of far times and places, ranging from forgotten eras to the distant future.

The author maintains a literary web site, *The Weird Writings of Jeffery Scott Sims*, which in addition to providing useful information on his works also offers an ever growing collection of entertaining essays devoted to unique or unusual topics related to the weird tale. This material may be freely accessed at http://jefferyscottsims.webs.com/index.html

www.ingramcontent.com/pod-product-compliance
Lightning Source LLC
Chambersburg PA
CBHW031324170626
46807CB00002B/555